DESTINY

Book Two
of the
HOPE SERIES

REIGN ATKINS

Dedication

To all those that have encouraged me to keep battling through this crazy little thing called life, and to all those who have inspired the characters, worlds, and elements that have shaped my very nature of storytelling. Always have *hope* that things will get better.

PROLOGUE

Despite the fierce pounding to her head and blinding ray of the lights above, Astrid Sutherland sat up and looked around. She was in a patient bed in what must've been an abandoned hospital, draped in a pale blue hospital gown.

There was an IV to her wrist and judging by the silence, she was alone. Astrid needed to know just who had been working on her and for how long she had been unconscious.

With careful precision, she disconnected the IV, then shuffled to the side of the bed until her bare feet met the cold marble floor.

With one big heave, Astrid pushed herself to stand. Immediately, she hit the ground hard, smacking her head against the metal wheeled trolley beside her. But Astrid had never been one to give up when life got hard.

She crawled to the nearby chair, in a second attempt to get to her feet. Using the soft blue chair for support, she climbed onto the seat. It was her first success since waking up. However, the answers she sought, lay beyond the door. Glancing back at the trolley, Astrid knew she didn't have enough strength to stand, let alone, walk by herself. So, pulling the trolley close to her, she pushed herself to stand.

Despite the atrophy of her legs, she was upright. As she pulled the patient gown tightly to her body, she pressed her weight onto the metal frame and made her way across the floor.

Once she had reached the door, she wedged the trolley against the wall and brought her right hand to the handle. The fear of being kept against her will quickly subsided when the door opened with ease.

Astrid pushed her makeshift mobility aide into the dimly lit corridor, where distant though strangely familiar voices could be heard. With every painful step, the metal trolley delivered an ear-piercing squeak, but her determination to make it to the other end of the corridor did not waver.

Her mission was simple. Find out who those voices belonged to, and if needed, take them out. No matter how vulnerable she was, she would not go down without a fight.

Then, at least ten feet away, she saw them at the nurse's station. Six faces. All of which tugged at her memories in unique ways. There were three women, two men, and a small child. The masculine voice of authority forced her attention as he barked at the man holding the child. "We have no choice, Cruz. The beasts are surrounding us, and this hospital isn't exactly the fortified base it once was."

"So, your decision is to shift us all in hopes of finding something better? That's just stupid. Not to mention, suicide! We shouldn't be risking Astrid's or my daughter's safety just to venture out there."

Astrid gazed down at the child in Cruz's arms and instinctively brought her hand to her abdomen… to the incision that had long since healed.

"Do you really think I want to? If we stay here, we're nothing more than sitting ducks. And it's just a matter of time before we're chased by another Cyclops. Or hell knows, maybe even Medusa!"

The thought of being forced to leave in the condition she was in, terrified Astrid. Her body ached. And judging by the fact that she couldn't remember a thing prior to falling asleep, she was certain that she was suffering from post-traumatic amnesia.

As she tried to muster enough willpower to speak up, the metal trolley slipped from her grasp, forcing her to fall to the floor with a hard crash and a loud "Owww!" A loud silence pierced the air as the others turned to her, astonished. But then Hannah immediately sprang into action.

"Tash, get the chair. You guys, help me get her up. Now!" Without hesitation, the others obeyed, and within minutes, Astrid was sitting on the soft desk chair with Hannah fussing over her. While Samuel seemed hesitant to go anywhere near her, Cruz looked as if he had just witnessed a miracle.

Stacey and Tash, on the other hand, fussed over Astrid as if she might smash into pieces at any given moment.

Which for Tash's usual seemingly insensitive nature, was highly unusual.

But while they all fussed over her, Astrid's attention remained on the child in Cruz's arms. A daughter who looked to be about a year old.

Despite her headache, Astrid forced herself to remember. Forced herself to relive those final moments before she fell asleep. And then, as if at will, realization struck her like a lightning bolt to a tree.

She remembered the ruins, the cultists and... DR Reynolds. She remembered not falling asleep... But DYING. Astrid's mouth went dry. Her words were involuntary, but not without purpose. "Hannah, what the hell happened to me?"

CHAPTER ONE

Since the day Astrid and Cruz had been taken captive in the ruins of Olympia, the world began to change. After Astrid's death, Samuel Davids and Mario Cruz led Joey Prescott, Hannah Jacobson, Natasha Martinez, and Stacey Raymond back to the United States to report their progress to the President, only to find that he too had gone missing.

Gradually, giants stormed cities and centaur tribes raided towns. Both events ended in the death of many mortals.

There were reports on old radios that humanity was falling into an extinction. Samuel was surprised to find that the words of DR Reynolds back in Olympia proved to be true, even if they did sound like nothing more than works of fiction.

Almost a year had passed since the team had left Olympia and exactly eight months had gone by since the fall of Washington, which had been crushed to rubble by three drunk giants.

As expected, Samuel took charge of the group and they travelled from town to town seeking shelter in hospitals run by back-up generators, working together to maintain their own survival.

Cruz took on the role as sole parent to Hope, whom he knew within his gut was a very special child. For one thing, she seemed to be growing at a faster rate than most children.

With the assistance of Joey, Hannah attended to the health and wellbeing of Astrid's unconscious body, which was a miracle within itself. It was as if her body continued to slip in and out of the voids of life and death, while remaining in an unexplainable state of stasis.

Stacey and Tash did their own parts in protecting Hope and assisting Hannah in her attempts to keep Astrid in good health. In their gut, they all knew that she would eventually come back to them in just a matter of time.

***

After escorting Astrid back to her room and assisting her into some comfortable clothes, Hannah, Stacey, and Tash delivered a full-detailed explanation of the past year.

"That just doesn't make any sense," Astrid said. "Mythological creatures. Really? Hey Hannah? Would you mind giving me something for this sudden headache?"

As Hannah gave Astrid some pain meds, which she eagerly swallowed down, Stacey replied with, "Sorry, Astrid. But it's the truth."

"So, a Cyclops?"

"With one eye...?" Tash chimed in. "Yep. Oh, and it gets worse... Cruz and Buzzkill haven't stopped fighting, since the day you… well… since the day your baby was born."

There was an uncomfortable silence which Astrid immediately picked up on. They were reliving that dreadful moment in the ruins. Knowing that she needed to break the tension, Astrid said, "You guys. I'm alive... it's okay, you don't have to tiptoe. Just say it... I died."

The others exchanged unreadable stares before embracing her in a big teary hug. But as they did, Astrid felt suffocated. And it wasn't because of her friends, but because of some strange insecurity within herself.

She ruled it down to Post Traumatic Stress Disorder. But for some reason, it felt like more than that. Astrid felt as if she had come back from the dead different, somehow.

She shook her friends away and forced a superficially optimistic façade. "Which reminds me, you never told me how I'm alive. I'm not a zombie, am I?"

Tash laughed. "God, I hope not... And I kinda wouldn't rule it out after what we've seen. Just let us know if you get a craving for brains. Alright, Sutherland?"

After sanitizing her hands, Hannah sat beside Astrid to try her best at delivering a medical explanation. "We don't actually know the answer to why you're alive. Joey and I spent long hours trying to theorize just why your pulse would return and disappear, sometimes without any medical intervention whatsoever. However, the day you died, Cruz mentioned something about hearing voices right before your pulse returned. He refused to leave your side even for a minute. It was like… Like he made a deal with whoever or whatever higher being it was to bring you back."

"Higher being? Like a god or something?"

Astrid thought back to those last few moments in the ruins. She could remember Cruz telling her that he was the descendant of Zeus. The thought of that being true seemed even more unlikely than her being the descendant of Pandora.

Hannah shrugged. "Yeah. It sounds impossible. But after what we've seen, I don't think we should rule it out."

"Hmm. Well, maybe I should ask him."

Tash stood from her chair and pointed to the closed door. "Looks like you'll get that chance. He and Buzzkill are right outside... with your beautiful daughter."

Following Tash's gaze, Astrid stared through the glass door at the two men on the opposite side. Again, her eyes fell to the baby that Cruz was holding.

"Do we let them in?" Stacey asked.

"Maybe they should take in turns visiting her," Hannah added. "What would you prefer, Astrid?"

Astrid shrugged. "It's fine, let them both in."

"In that case, maybe we should leave you guys in peace," Hannah replied, heading to the door. "I'll let Joey in on the news. He's been keeping perimeter watch."

Before following Hannah out, Stacey and Tash hugged Astrid. "Don't say we didn't warn you," Stacey added. "Those two are like dogs fighting over a bone."

Upon leaving the room, Tash motioned towards Cruz and Samuel a sign that could only mean, 'I'll be watching you,' as the men entered the room.

Taking the place beside her on the bed, Cruz positioned Hope in his arms for Astrid to see. The child had dark hair, dark eyes, and a very dimpled grin.

Cruz on the other hand, hadn't shaved in a while. His untidy hair was pulled back, his eyes appeared darker than usual, and he looked as if he hadn't slept in a very long time.

But surprisingly he appeared optimistic. He smiled down at the child in his arms. "This is our daughter, Hope."

"Hope?"

"Yeah, your middle name. It also sounded kinda right after everything we've been through. Hey *hija*, I want you to meet your mama. You know, that awesome lady I was telling you about?"

As Astrid allowed Hope to grip her finger, she giggled at the word. "Lady, Cruz?"

Cruz shrugged, forcing a light scarlet to fill his cheeks. "Okay, lady might be going a little too far. But, using the term heroine would've meant I'd need to teach our child the difference between the drug heroin and the female version of hero, and I just don't feel Hope is ready for the drug talk yet."

Astrid giggled, forcing Cruz to go on. "I mean, I'm sure I could come up with something a little more brilliant to describe you. Ass-kicking *Reina*, perhaps? Leaderette? Hey, I like that one… Leaderette."

Taking in the moment, Astrid felt that same feeling she had always felt around Cruz. Nervous, but at the same time, happy.

There she was, with Cruz and her daughter. The family she had always wanted. A gripping sensation that nothing else in the world mattered besides them.

Astrid had always thought that when a person died, that it was lights out and that the mind just stopped. Yet, staring into Cruz's dark eyes brought back a wish… No, not a wish, the very promise of a happy ending that she had clung to in her death.

A feeling within her surged, telling her that she had returned to the living for Cruz.

In that moment, she desperately wanted to cling to that feeling. She wanted to forget that he had left her before she had died. The very temptation to kiss him was the highest it had ever been before.

As if he could read her mind, Cruz bit down on his lip and turned to Samuel who had taken the seat across from the bed. She followed his gaze to the soldier who simply offered his reserved smile.

That smile had always hidden more than he wished to be brought to the surface. Whether it was pain, fear, or even happiness, his crystal blue eyes were the only windows to his soul.

"It's good to see you up and moving, Sutherland. I've missed your cover fire and your blatant disregard for the rules."

Her temptation to say something as equally witty, quickly diminished thanks to her need for an explanation.

She turned back to Cruz, hoping he might have the answers. "Help me understand. How am I alive? Hannah said something about there being whispers?"

Cruz's optimistic demeanour altered. He stared down at the ground and muffled his response. "I'm not sure. I still haven't figured it out yet. But at least you're awake... The Deadly Sins curse is over."

"How can you even think that?" Samuel scoffed. "The curse isn't over! We have a mission for self-preservation, and you know that!"

"Stop being a General Buzzkill. Astrid's awake, we should be using this moment to celebrate. Counting our blessings before we venture back into hell and lose somebody else."

Turning back to Samuel, Astrid intervened. "That's enough, the both of you. Why are you so eager to leave?"

The former sergeant pulled the chair over and sat, leaning forward. "It's chaos out there. We thought it was just the Deadly Sins that Cruz released, but we were very wrong. We've seen everything from centaurs to Cyclopes and, what's worse, is that they're hunting down humankind. We're going extinct."

Astrid rubbed at her temples. Sure, Hannah had told her the same thing. But the explanation of humanity dying out was impossible to believe.

"You can't be serious," she gasped. "Centaurs?"

"Yes and they're not exactly easy to kill with our conventional weaponry, either. We've had to resort to training with swords."

Barely altering her position, Astrid glanced up at him. "Wait, swords? That's… I must be dreaming."

In a bid to comfort her, Cruz brought his hand to her back and spoke up in a softer tone than Samuel had used. "Astrid, if the buildings didn't still stand, you'd think we'd taken a trip back at least five thousand years through history."

"Was the curse actually broken? Do people still suffer from the deadly sins? Are you guys still affected?"

"No, we're not," Samuel broke in. "Which is a relief. I believe the birth of your daughter ended the first phase of the curse."

"First phase of the curse?"

Before Samuel could respond to Astrid's question, Cruz broke in. "According to Buzzkill, DR Reynolds told him our daughter was going to lead these beasts. But that's not going to happen. Besides, we're safe here and we're not gonna let those creatures come after you or Hope. I promise!"

"Is that like your promise to put your own life before hers?" Samuel asked bitterly. "Because we all saw how well that went."

"Seriously, Samuel?!" Astrid snapped. "If you're going to fight, just leave, alright?"

From her peripheral view, Astrid could see a glimmer of a smile on Cruz's face, as if he was relieved to have her on his side. Samuel, on the other hand, sighed. " I'm sorry, but we need to at least consider..." Before he could finish his sentence, Tash and Stacey stormed into the room.

"Quick, the hospital's swarming with ants!" Tash exclaimed.

"Ants, Tash? Really?" Astrid laughed.

Samuel rushed to his feet. "Shit! Sutherland, Stacey, stay here, keep an eye on Hope. Cruz, Tash, let's go!"

"On it." Cruz obeyed as he gave Hope to Astrid and followed Samuel and Tash out the room, securing the door shut behind him.

In stunned surprise, Astrid turned to Stacey. "What's going on? They're just ants."

As if she had just asked the world's most ridiculous question, Stacey took the child from Astrid and led her to the door. "Look through the glass and tell me that those are just ants."

Astrid peered through the glass and was filled with astonishment, catching sight of Samuel, Cruz, Joey, Hannah and Tash fighting at least three bear-sized ants in the hallway.

After the initial surprise had subsided, Astrid's fight response kicked into gear. She hurried to the bedside table and rummaged through the drawers, pushing through her atrophy. "Stay here, Stace… Keep Hope safe."

"What are you doing? You just came back from the dead. What are you looking for?"

"My sidearm! Where is it?"

"Are you crazy? You can't go out there... it's too dangerous!"

"Where is it, Stacey?"

Defeated, Stacey shook her blond head and pointed to the large cupboard in the corner. "Please, don't do this. You're my best friend. I can't lose you again."

Ignoring her plead, Astrid raced over to the cupboard, pulled out her old semi-automatic, cocked it ready, and ran over to the door. "Lock the door after me!"

Aiming her gun at the large ant, which was advancing on Samuel, Astrid ran out of the room. She pulled the trigger once. Missing the first shot she gained the soldier's attention. "Sutherland! What the hell do you think you're doing?"

"You said you missed my cover fire, so what does it look like?" She shot at the large ant again, but the bullets merely ricocheted off its body. The ant shook its head and backed off, giving Samuel the chance to swing his blade perfectly, decapitating the insect's head from the body.

As the ant fell to the floor, Samuel turned his anger onto Astrid. "I gave you a direct order to stay in that room. You're in no shape to fight."

"At least it worked. Now stop complaining." Astrid shifted her aim to offer Joey, who had fallen onto his back in the middle of the battle, a little cover fire. Cruz charged past him and sunk his own blade into the ant before it could eat him.

There was a loud SQUELCH as Cruz's blade exited the other side of the ant's head, which forced Astrid to groan.

But at least the creature had been defeated. Hannah and Tash were fighting the third and final ant. They took it down perfectly.

Once the creatures had been defeated, Cruz, Samuel, Joey, Tash, and Hannah stopped to surround Astrid. It was Cruz who spoke first. "I totally get the whole freaky adrenalin thing, but maybe you should second guess using it while we're battling the Myrmekes."

"The what?"

"Myrmekes," Samuel replied. "That's what those things are called. But now they've found us, we won't be able to stop them from coming."

"They're clearly looking for those chocolate wrappers I left last week," Tash chuckled.

Before she could react to her joke, Joey pulled Astrid into an overly tight hug. "Welcome back to the land of the living. It's damn good to see you. Did Hannah tell you how many late nights we spent working on you?"

Locked in Joey's tight hug, a strange flicker flashed through Astrid's mind. She was in a dark wasteland. The dim lighting consisted of blood-red and black. And in this wasteland, Joey stood only a few feet away from her. Reaching out to her. And while she tried to reach for him, something… or someone kept holding her back. But as quick as the vision had come, it was gone again.

Joey released her and asked, "So how are you feeling? Do you remember anything?"

"What? Like, if I went to a Heaven or hell?"

"Anything at all?"

How could she even begin to answer his question? All that stood out for her was the feeling of dread that accompanied the very experience of being in that place. It was like waking from a nightmare that she still needed to piece together.

Astrid shook her head. "No, not that I can recall. But, don't we have more pressing matters to deal with? How did those ants get in, anyway?"

"One of the side entrances," he replied. "Someone must have left it open. But it's okay. I closed it and there didn't seem to be any more out there."

"You're the expert on Greek Mythology," Samuel said looking to Cruz. "What do you think they want?"

Surprised by Samuel's compliment, Cruz thought for a moment before responding. "Myrmekes generally protect precious items, while regular ants go in search for food. My guess is they've sought out Hope. She's the descendant of Zeus and Pandora so it only makes sense. The question is, why now?"

"Maybe they know that Astrid's awake?" Hannah suggested.

"The question to that one is, how?" Tash said, adding light to Cruz's earlier remark.

An eerie silence plagued the room before Samuel broke it. "There's no point in us standing around thinking up conspiracy theories. Our mission is to survive and now that Sutherland is awake, we should get moving, this hospital was only ever a temporary hideout."

"So, where do we go?" Stacey asked, joining them with Hope still in her arms. "We were lucky to find this place. The last town we went to was taken over by centaurs, the town before that..."

"...Giants," Samuel interrupted. "Yes, I know. I'm guessing we should head out to a smaller, quieter town, after what happened in Washington. Those beasts all seem to migrate to the cities. My family owned a farm before I joined with the military, it's about a day and a half's drive from here and if we're lucky, it could sustain us for a while."

Astrid took Hope from Stacey and turned back to Samuel with a half-assed smile. "Farm boy, Buzzkill? It's a good idea, but how do we know the smaller towns haven't been overrun?"

"We can't know for sure. But right now, it's all we have left. "

His final statement was a crippling thought. Humans had battled nuclear wars and had survived global environmental disasters and pandemics. The prospect of humanity dying sounded like something from a dystopian novel or a video game. But despite their odds, Astrid had faith that they could prevail.

"Why run?" she asked, garnering all their attention. "All we're doing is letting them cause our extinction.

We've survived so much more than this, and we've always rebuilt. How is this any different?"

Her speech brought about hesitant smiles from her friends. "I agree," Samuel replied. "But I don't see how. The odds are quite literally stacked against us."

"And how would we do that?" Cruz asked.

"Simple," Astrid said. "We do what my father did. We find a base, take in survivors, and build an army to fight these things. Many are mighty."

"Astrid, your dad's base was infiltrated from the inside," Tash replied. "How do we know it won't happen again?"

"Because we're fighting for humanity's survival. Something we can all agree upon."

A mixture of doubt and belief flooded the group. Just by the looks on their faces alone, Astrid knew she had the support of Stacey, Samuel, and Hannah. But Tash was plagued by fear.

Fear had always been her sin. Joey seemed to be on the fence. And Cruz, well… for the first time ever, seemed to have his doubts.

Samuel rubbed his hands together, more than willing to carry out the plan. "I like your way of thinking. We're best leaving tonight. I'll venture out to see if I can find us a mode of transportation. The rest of you, pack your things."

Without another word, the group dispersed, and Samuel made his way towards the exit.

Cruz, however, brought his hands to the back of his head, in frustration. "Astrid, you know I would walk to the ends of the earth with you… But this… this plan of going against the centaurs, giants, and the likes… It's reckless. We should be considering our safety."

"Well, what do you suggest we do, Cruz? I'm not ready to say goodbye to humanity."

"These creatures are Zeus's own creations. Do you really think raging a war on them is the best option? Do we really want to make him angry? Zeus is one powerful god and one hell of a vengeful *pendejo*."

"Well, we don't exactly have any other options," she said, placing her hand on his shoulder and adopting a softer tone.

Cruz took her hand from his shoulder and brushed his thumb against her fingers, studying her as if to be considering their options. After a moment, he sighed in defeat.

"Alright, fine. We'll do it your way. I just have a really bad feeling about all this."

Astrid gave him a slight smile of gratitude, before turning to leave. But before she could, Cruz turned her back to face him. "Can we talk for a moment?"

It was the first time they had been given the opportunity to speak alone in a long time.

It gave her the chance to take in his features. The slight glimmer of optimism in his dark eyes. The under confident, though honest, smile that radiated in his left cheek.

At that point she wanted nothing more than to kiss him, but she resisted to let him speak.

"I get there was something going on between you and Samuel before we lost you. But I need you to know the only reason I left when I did, was because I had no other choice. Deep down, I knew you were pregnant, and I didn't want either of you to have to suffer for my mistakes."

"Cruz…"

"Please, let me finish… in case I don't get the chance. I once thought we were only together because of the curse… That the way I felt for you was, because of some silly love spell… But that was never it at all. It extended beyond that, and it still does now. But you've just woken up from the dead and while I would love to just pretend that none of it happened, I can't. I screwed up, I hurt you and then because of that, you suffered. So, I think I'm best giving you a little time and space to think about what you really want."

Those words crippled her. Sure, Cruz was doing what he felt was best. But once again, he was treading lightly out of his fear of hurting her, despite how he really felt inside.

"You can't be serious, Cruz." Her knee-jerk of a reaction startled him.

"What?"

"I've been dead for a year and the moment I wake up, you tell me…"

"…No, I'm not trying to hurt you, I…"

"…I get that you're not trying to hurt me. You're trying to play it safe without even giving me the chance to tell you how I feel. For just once, I wish you'd stop self-sabotaging."

"I'm not self-sabotaging. Astrid, you died, and it almost killed me. Yet, right now, I can't be selfish with you. You should be focusing on yourself and being a mother to our child not on..."

The shrill cry of Hope in her arms forced them both to stop arguing and become fully aware of the reality of the situation.

Astrid rocked Hope on her hip and wiped the tears from her eyes. "Let's not do this now. I need to speak with Hannah." Without giving him time to respond, Astrid left with Hope in her arms.

***

Upon entering his room, Cruz closed the door and flicked on the light before turning his attention to the empty chair by the door. "Not yet!" he snapped. "But I will… soon."

A soft knock from out in the hall startled him. He opened the door to see Joey standing on the other side. In his usual light-hearted fashion, Joey strolled in and spread out on the bed, bringing his dirty shoes onto the white sheets.

"Hey, man. Who were you talking to?"

"Just myself," Cruz said, as he shot a sidewards glance at the chair. "Don't worry about it."

Joey glanced at the chair, then back to Cruz. "They say that's the first sign of madness."

"First sign of madness? Pfft. I lost my marbles a long time ago."

"It's called falling in love... and Astrid got you big time."

Crossing the room to the couch by the portable crib, Cruz sat down eyeing Joey suspiciously. "Joe, why are you even in here? Something tells me it's not to talk about my love life."

Joey sat upright. "I might've overheard your conversation."

"Which conversation?"

"The conversation you had with your girl out there. Or do you think I should be listening into the ones you're having with yourself, too?"

"Okay, out with it."

Shuffling to the edge of the bed to give Cruz his undivided attention, Joey leaned forward. "Look, we both know the main reason you're not willing to pick up where the two of you left off is because of those voices."

Cruz avoided Joey's eye. "I don't know what you're talking about."

A strangely serious tone took over Joey's entire persona. "Oh, yes, you do. I'm talking about the voices in the ruins the moment Astrid's pulse returned. Whoever the hell you prayed to brought her back and you're terrified what that might mean for you in the future."

It was as if Joey's words had stolen Cruz's soul entirely. His skin grew cold as a terrifying sensation crept up his spine. But Cruz remained silent. Instead, Joey continued. "We both know that you heard exactly what those voices said that day. But my question is, is this a secret really worth keeping from your best friend and the woman you claim to love? Relationships are based on trust. I trust you. Astrid trusts you and you need to trust us too."

Thrown off guard by those words, Cruz glanced towards the seat by the door, then lowered his voice to Joey. His voice was strained in panic. "You really don't understand, Joey. I don't have a choice in this. I wish I did. I tell you everything… Hell, I trust you and her more than I trust anybody. But, if I speak about this to anybody, the ones I love will all get hurt and I can't watch her go through that again."

"If somebody is threatening you, you can tell me. No matter who or what that someone might be."

Frustrated by his own predicament and not being able to tell a soul, Cruz got to his feet. "Man, this isn't just some schoolyard bully. This is much bigger than me being crammed into a locker."

For a moment, Cruz was more than willing to divulge everything. Instead, he sunk his hands into his pockets and headed to the door. "If I need your help, I'll ask for it. We should get ready to leave. Buzzkill was adamant that we be ready when he arrives."

Joining him, Joey got to his feet. "Are you sure?"

"Positive." Without another word, Joey left.

***

Sitting on the bed, Astrid held Hope close to her chest and slowly sifted through her memories of the blood-red wasteland. She only wished that she could at least tell her friends, but she knew that they wouldn't understand. Astrid barely understood the visions at all. Perhaps her coma had affected her sanity levels and this place was a false memory or even a hallucination.

In a bid to get a deeper insight, she pressed her back into the pillows, held Hope tight and closed her eyes.

In her mind, she saw the darkened skies and fiery wastelands vividly. She could hear the screams of torment as if they were all around her. Breathing through the devastation, she reminded herself that they were nothing more than figments of her imagination. They couldn't be real.

Her mind ventured even further. To the murky swamps and the blackened trees lining the banks. It was a place of death.

From over her shoulder, she could hear the voice of a woman, but she couldn't quite determine just who the stranger was or what they were saying. It was as if the woman was crying out in some foreign language.

Suddenly, another woman's voice broke into her thoughts. "Astrid?" Somebody was in the room with her.

Upon opening her eyes, Astrid saw Hannah approach from the doorway. "Oh good, you're awake. It's such a relief coming in here and finding you conscious and holding Hope. It's all any of us have wanted for so long."

As Astrid sat upright and positioned the sleeping baby on the bed, Hannah went over her vitals with the bedside manner which so few doctors were able to adopt.

Astrid had worked with many doctors and nurses in the past, and it had always surprised her just how many didn't suit the occupation despite working in the field for a very long time. Hannah was the opposite of that.

Using a pen torch, Hannah checked Astrid's pupils and became transfixed by something in her eyes. Something wasn't right. "Hannah, are you okay?"

Rubbing her eyes, Hannah took the seat beside the bed. "There's something off about you."

"Well, I did just wake up from a coma."

"I suppose so. But... Never mind. Admittedly, I've never had a patient come back from the dead, so I don't understand what I should be looking for. Possibly some signs of brain injury, yet your senses seem to be intact. Your combat skills are perfect. You passed that urine test earlier... Speaking of urine, your body didn't pass any while you were unconscious. Which is weird because when a person dies, their body normally expels gas and fluids. But it was like your body was in a state of stasis, yet rapidly recovering. That's why there was no catheter in place."

Stunned, Astrid's eyes grew wide. She knew that Hannah was merely asking her for the answers, opposed to offering them. "I'm sorry, I just don't know what to tell you."

"Still, if you need to talk to somebody, I'm right here."

"I know. And thanks. I guess I'm debating whether I've gone insane. I was a psychologist once... But now, I might have to admit myself into an asylum and get the doctors to throw away the key."

"You were pronounced dead for a year, Astrid. We should be dealing with decomposing tissue and brain damage, but we're not. So, maybe just go easy on yourself, okay?"

Taking in her words, Astrid nodded and smiled. "It's all way too unbelievable, isn't it?"

"Just wait until you see a centaur. All that doubt goes right out the window. They're so majestic yet so fierce. Samuel fought one and was almost killed... but somehow, they both walked away with a truce. It was pretty remarkable." Pausing, Hannah checked the watch on her wrist. "I should probably get back to packing. But I'll see you out there, okay?" Without another word, Hannah left.

Peering down at her daughter, Astrid prayed that whoever was calling out in her memories, would not be able to harm her child.

The fact that the wastelands felt far too real to be just some twisted hallucination sent a chill down her spine.

But if they were real, and the world had been taken over by the creatures of Greek mythology, then what did that mean for the future of their survival?

CHAPTER TWO

A few hours later, the group met Samuel inside the main foyer of the hospital where they could barely see the clear night through the cracks in the boarded-up windows. After unlocking the door with her sword drawn, Tash welcomed Samuel inside and refastened the locks on the door.

Garnering everybody's attention, Samuel addressed them all. "I must've won the lottery! I found us a motorhome big enough for all of us. It's not exactly bulletproof, but at least, we don't need to take multiple cars. It even has a big enough drawer for the mini ass-kicker to sleep in."

"A drawer?" Astrid asked, looking from Hope in her arms to Samuel, who approached her.

"A crib wouldn't fit. So, this was the next best thing."

"Is it fuelled up this time, Buzzkill?" Tash asked. "After last time, we don't..."

"...Yes, Tash, it's fuelled up. I had to siphon from a few other tanks, but, at least it's done. I noticed movement out there so we really should get moving. Sutherland, are you ready to see what's become of the world you once knew? It's gotten pretty dicey out there."

With a half-assed smirk, Astrid replied, "you guys won me over with centaurs. So, I guess, I'm as ready as I'll ever be."

"Good. Because it's going to get dangerous."

"Dangerous? I've literally saved your ass so many times, even I've lost count. I'm sure I'll be fine."

Samuel shot her a devilish grin and lowered his voice just loud enough for her to hear. "The thought of you even thinking about my ass is good enough for me."

Involuntarily, Astrid's voice hitched in her throat. Her cheeks blushed and she prayed for the very earth to swallow her whole. Or maybe she'd get lucky and go down in a fight against a Cyclops. As her mind frantically searched for a line to derail him, Cruz approached, adding to the tension.

"Just stop flirting and let's get everybody loaded on that thing, shall we?" He picked up the backpack by her feet, slung it over his shoulder and gestured to carry Hope. Astrid handed Hope to Cruz and followed him outside, doing her best to conceal the smile at the corner of her mouth.

They all stepped outside where Astrid marveled at their surroundings. The bright moon lit up the night, illuminating the buildings which looked as if they had quite literally been crushed by a strong force from above. Other buildings had been burned down, cars had been smashed up and all around them, litter and decayed bodies lined the streets.

But amongst the destruction, stood the diamond in the ruff. The white luxury motorhome that Samuel had acquired. It was huge, complete with windows and clearly enough room for them all. Grey and black streaks lined the sides of the vehicle and at the front was a very spacious cabin, large enough for three people.

"Wow! Whose girlfriend did you need to kiss for that, Buzzkill?" Joey joked at the proud soldier.

Despite Joey's remark being purely out of humour, Samuel seemed slightly offended. Hannah rolled her eyes and Cruz broke into a refreshing fit of laughter as he patted Samuel on the back, playfully.

"You kinda had that one coming. Hannah and Astrid? Who's next?" As Cruz turned his gaze to Tash and Stacey, they broke into a fit of laughter.

"Not gonna happen," Stacey replied. "Unless of course you happen to have a sex change. But even then… Nope, I'm a one-woman woman."

"That makes two of us," Tash replied, sweeping Stacey into a long, passionate kiss in front of them all to prove her point, before pulling away again. "See?"

"Very funny, Tash." Samuel said. He opened the doors to the back of the vehicle, allowing for Tash and Stacey to climb in first.

Amused, Joey shook his head, "You do know that they're going to christen the motorhome before we can get in there, right?"

Samuel sighed. "I do. Now, the rest of you, get into the Argo. She's all stocked up ready to go."

Astrid couldn't help but chuckle at the banter of her friends. Of how they had truly found their rhythm since her passing. It was the perfect alternative to the wastelands that plagued her mind. Feeling a hand on her back, she looked to Hannah standing on her right. "Are you alright?"

Astrid smiled. "Better than ever."

"Good. Just let me know if that changes."

"I will."

They looked back to Samuel, Cruz, and Joey making jokes. "So, this must make us your Argonauts," Joey chimed in. "Speaking of, I get that you're supposed to be the captain, but can I do the honors of..." Before he could even finish his sentence, Samuel threw him the keys. "All yours, Joe!"

***

After roughly ten minutes, they were on their way. Astrid lounged in the back with Tash and Stacey, while Samuel sharpened the swords at the fold-out table to the left. To the right of him, Cruz sat with Hope in his arms, staring out the window.

The Argo was much more spacious on the inside than they had first anticipated, housing four fold-out double beds which turned into seats, one single bed, a separate bathroom with a shower and a cooking area. Samuel's choice of portable home would be perfect for their journey to his family's old farm.

Tash was equally as quick as she was confident with her much-awaited interrogation, which surprised both Astrid and Stacey. "So, Sutherland, how does it feel being awake and seeing everything for the first time?"

"A little overwhelming? No, make that very overwhelming. We just fought giant ants and my baby is almost a year old... I just don't know how to deal with that... But I'm not freaking out if that's what you mean."

Astrid glanced over at Cruz and their child. She could hear him humming under his breath, seemingly deep in thought.

"Yeah, that would be hard," Stacey spoke up. "But at least she has a great dad, who has been taking the role of fatherhood very seriously... speaking of... who are you going to pick?"

Astrid did a double take. "Wait, what?"

Tash grinned. "The question on everybody's lips."

"What do you mean, who am I going to pick?"

Astrid looked to Tash and then back to Stacey, completely dumbfounded. Taking it upon herself to explain the scenario, Tash used a tone that mimicked an old game show host.

"Well, for the past year, you've had two men pining over you. In the far corner we have Cruz - the descendant of Zeus... the amazing father of your child and who, yes, did leave you but it was to save you from having to die... In the opposite corner, we have the ruggedly handsome soldier, descendant of Jason... that guy who led the Argonauts... and the man who has led our group through everything over the past year... and we all know that the two of you shared one hell of a night before you left the realms of the living... So, who will it be?"

"You make it sound like a game show, Tash. How the hell do we go from the conversation of me waking up from the dead one minute, to whom I'm going to end up with, the next? What did I miss here?"

Running her hand through her long black hair, Tash smiled a wide grin. "Sorry, but we've had a year to deal with this. While we all knew you would wake up, it was just a matter of when... And in the meantime, Cruz and Buzzkill have had this major macho contest going on. It's like they were trying to compete with who loves you more. So, it had the rest of us all wondering just who you will choose. Hannah and Stacey have also been shipping!"

"Shipping?"

"Yeah... You see, Hannah is betting you'll end up with Cruz. Stacey on the other hand..."

"...I'm betting Buzzkill. No wait, I'm changing my ship. It's Cruz."

"You can't change your ship, Stacey. You betted Joey..."

"...What can I say? He was right. Have you seen the way she's been staring at Cruz?"

Amused by their antics, Astrid laughed. "You're betting on my love life? Are you sure you're not the descendants of Aphrodite with all this matchmaking? So, Tash... who are you shipping?"

"I'm undecided. They're both like brothers to me. They're both willing to lay down their lives for you and they've both won your heart. It's a tough decision which I don't envy you having to make."

"How much is my love life sitting at?"

Stacey smirked. "A hundred and fifty bucks so far."

Dumbfounded, Astrid shook her head. "Maybe we should just drop it for now. Because I'm picking my baby and myself for now, besides... I'm pretty sure they can hear us."

They glanced over at Samuel who was still sharpening the swords. He gave them a side smile without looking up. Cruz on the other hand was entirely lost in a world of his own.

"If you're picking yourself," Tash said. "I vote you pick both... None of that cliché love triangle Ross and Rachel, Edward and Bella bullshit. It's the end of the world so let them both treat you like a goddess. Put an end to their war and start the world's apocalypse with one hell of a bang."

Choking on absolutely nothing at all, Astrid's head snapped back to Tash. "Well, that's greedy."

"Think about it. It would solve all your problems. That's why they're so angry at each other... it's one hell of a competition. Love is love, provided all parties agree, so what's the problem?"

Astrid shook her head and got to her feet. "Can you guys give me a moment?"

Tash and Stacey shrugged as Astrid made her way over to Cruz, doing her best to keep balance thanks to the motion of the motorhome. Just as she reached him, the vehicle hit a bump forcing her to fall into the seat beside him. "Are you alright?" he asked, with a slight raise of the eyebrows.

"I'm good... I think. What were you humming before?"

Cruz planted a kiss on the sleeping child's forehead before looking back at Astrid. "You heard that?"

"I did."

Cruz's smile met his cheek as he brushed the hair from his face. "Do you remember that first song you were humming when we first started travelling together just outside New York? The one that was playing just before we met that cop?"

"Yeah, I think it was Bon Jovi or something."

Cruz's smile grew wider but vanished just as soon as it had appeared. "Bed of roses. That'd be the one."

Astrid was at a loss for words. Of course, he'd remember a minor detail like that about her. She wanted to keep him talking but wasn't sure what to say. She wanted to tell him that he had made a mistake by asking her to take the time to focus on herself. That they were destined to be together, even though she didn't believe in destiny.

"You sure you're good?" he asked, clearly fuelled by her silence. "Was that all you came here to ask?"

"No, it wasn't."

"It wasn't?"

"I wanted to talk about what you said before. About…" Before she could finish her sentence, she was distracted by the concern in Stacey's tone. "Hey, you guys? We've stopped."

Sure enough, the motorhome had come to a halt. Turning their heads, Astrid and Cruz turned to see Samuel heading to the cabin. "What's happened? Why've we stopped?"

Joey gestured his head toward the windscreen. "That... that's what's happened."

Following his gaze, Samuel looked past the windscreen. There was a beautiful pale-skinned woman with long dark hair, and from what they could see, she was naked from the waist up, standing in the light of the high beams, right in front of the motorhome. It was a miracle that Joey hadn't run her down.

Upon noticing Joey and Samuel equally staring with such fascination at the woman, Hannah looked to the others.

The moment Cruz saw the woman, he too was mesmerized by her beauty. Subconsciously, he handed Hope over to Astrid, then, he, Samuel and Joey left the vehicle, blankets in hand to offer the lady some assistance.

"Seriously?" Tash scoffed. "We're stopping for a naked woman?"

"Well, she is really pretty," Stacey replied.

Picking up a large blade from the table, Astrid handed Hope to Stacey. "Something just doesn't feel right. Stacey,

I need you to watch my daughter and lock the door after us. Tash, Hannah, grab a sword."

As asked, the women followed Astrid out of the motorhome, while Stacey locked the door behind them.

Swords in hand, Astrid, Hannah, and Tash approached the men who were staring up at the strange woman, as if entranced. "Am I the only one who sees that tail?" Hannah asked, tightening her grip to the hilt of her sword.

"Nope," Tash said, staring down at the large, black serpent-like body protruding from the woman's torso. "Because I sure as hell see it too."

The tail was easily thicker and longer than that of an anaconda. And the creature's once beautiful face was now fiercely pale and distorted.

But Samuel, Cruz, and Joey were entirely oblivious. They only saw a beautiful woman in need of help.

All of a sudden, a familiar female voice, which didn't belong to neither Tash nor Hannah, told Astrid exactly what the creature was and how to kill it.

Astrid gripped her sword with all the determination within her and commanded Hannah and Tash with the sheer authority of a battle maiden. "That's a Lamia, girls! Remove the head, now!"

"Sutherland?" Tash stammered. "Are you sure?"

"Yes. Now, do it before it kills them."

On her order, they charged for the beast only to be met by an eerily sweet and utterly hypnotic voice, further captivating the men. "Please, you must help me, these women wish to kill me." As per her request, Samuel, Cruz, and Joey turned to face them.

"What are you doing?" Samuel demanded. "Have you all gone insane? She's just a woman who needs help!"

"I think you're the one who's gone insane, Buzzkill," Astrid argued. "That's a Lamia! Look! She has the tail of a snake!"

"Astrid, I think that death might've affected your thinking abilities," Cruz added. "She's just a woman."

Angered by their behavior, Astrid ran for the beast, slipping right through the middle of both men. "Screw this! Do it, girls! Go for the head!"

Astrid made it to the Lamia's torso and swung up her sword. But before she could strike, Samuel knocked her to the ground.

***

Only a few feet away, Hannah struggled against Joey, who had his arms wrapped tightly around her waist from behind. "Hannah! I can't let you do this. You'll get yourself killed!"

But Hannah continued to fight against his strength, holding her sword out in front of her, out of his reach.

"We know what Lamias do, Joe! Don't let her manipulate you! She's a vampire!"

"Hannah, you can't kill her, she's too strong!"

Digging her nails into his arm, Hannah scratched her way out of his grasp. Joey groaned in pain but instantly caught up to her again, only this time, holding her even tighter than before. "Hannah, please… drop the sword, don't do this."

***

As Tash approached the serpent, she brought up her blade ready to take a swing. "Get ready to die mother-fu…"

The Lamia wrapped its thick long tail around her petite frame, knocking her off guard but Tash drove her sword right into the serpent's tail. The Lamia unleashed a high-pitched shriek and released Tash from its grip.

Tash staggered to her feet and went to strike again, just as Cruz ran over and restrained her from behind with his left arm. With his right hand, he grabbed for her sword.

"Don't be so thick headed, Cruz. That's not a woman, she's a snake thing. She wants to eat you and your baby!"

"Tash... now's not the time for jokes."

With one more heave, Cruz managed to remove her sword from her hand and held it out in front of them.

With each member of the group distracted, the Lamia began to slither towards the motorhome. Seeing this, Tash struggled to break free, retorting, "Don't be so stupid! This is no joke. Look, she's going after Hope. Would you really let her eat your baby, Cruz? Because that's what Lamias do!"

Despite how hard he tried, Cruz struggled to look up at the Lamia. Her compulsion was just so strong. "I...I can't... Tash... My... My head..."

***

"Stand down, Buzzkill!" Astrid demanded. "Don't make me sink this blade into you just to kill that thing.

Lamias devour men and children. I'm just trying to protect you and my child!"

Eyeing her, Samuel attempted to call her bluff. "Would you really kill me, Astrid?"

Refusing to back down, Astrid considered his question. She glanced over at Joey, who had a hold of Hannah and then at Cruz who was protecting the Lamia from Tash.

The Lamia, who was making its way toward the motorhome freely.

Astrid turned back to Samuel. "To protect my child, I'd do whatever it takes. That thing has us fighting one another, can't you see it?"

Keeping his eyes fixated on her, Samuel silently waited for her to make the first move.

"Seriously, Samuel? This isn't a sparring match! You need to focus!"

Dismissing her, he shook his head and chuckled. "I'm not going to let you hurt that woman. She's an innocent. Besides, I think Cruz might be right, you're acting unstable."

Furious to see that the Lamia had reached the door to the motorhome and was struggling with the door, Astrid could barely control the scream of words that poured from her mouth. "She's going for my baby. She wants Hope. I won't let her do this!"

Dodging past Samuel, Astrid charged for the beast. She made it only a few feet away before Samuel took a hold of her waist from behind and brought her back to the ground, instantly, forcing her to drop the sword.

Thanks to the injuries of her death, her entire body hurt.

"Get off me, Samuel! She's screwing with your head!"

Pinned to the ground, Astrid reached to the right of her, where her sword had fallen. But just as she stretched out her arm, Samuel removed the sword from her grasp. With her tears streaming down her face, she pleaded against the soldier.

"Samuel, no! You need to focus. Please, just look. Turn your head and see that she's at the door!"

It was evident by the pressure of his weight that he would not give in. She needed to think strategically. With a quick twist of her shoulder, she knocked the soldier in the face with her elbow, forcing him to hesitate just enough for her to wiggle free from underneath. But just as she had made it to her feet, he pulled her down again. This time she landed on her back.

"Sutherland, your own instability is getting the better of you. We can't let that happen!"

"So, what? You're going to kill me, to stop me?"

"No. Don't be silly. I would never hurt you. I love you."

Samuel's words stunned her. No, how could he even say that, let alone think that?

In that instant, time stood still as she attempted to process them. But instead of returning them, she used those words to her advantage. "So, give me my sword. If you love me, trust me. That woman is not a real woman. She has a snake body, and she wants to hurt my baby. Please, Samuel. You need to trust me."

For a moment, he looked as if he was trying to fight a battle within his own head. But he was taking too long.

Astrid had a second plan. "Kiss me!" she demanded. Samuel raised his eyebrows for a moment, but to her relief, he brought his hand to her jawline. His mouth travelled down to meet hers. But to his stunned surprise, she met his kiss with a fierce head-butt to the face, distracting him.

Next, she locked his legs in place with her own, rolled her hips, forced him off her and got to her feet. She was free, again.

Though, before Astrid could make her final strike on the Lamia, she stared down at the beastly woman's decapitated head which rolled around on the floor.

"What the…?" she stammered.

Her eyes fell to Joey, who was standing over the Lamia's deceased body, with Hannah's sword in his hand. He had broken free from the compulsion. In fact, so had Cruz and Samuel too.

Tears of relief welled up in Astrid's eyes and she breathed out her response. "Oh, thank God, Joey."

"How did you break free?" Tash puffed, exhausted from her fight with Cruz.

Joey looked over at Hannah and back to the others. "I'm not sure. I guess my love for Hannah conquered the compulsion."

Hannah stared at him, hard, and then at the rest of the group. There was something about her expression that told an entirely separate story altogether. There had to be more going on, than the story that Joey had just told.

Astrid glanced over at Samuel, then at Cruz and then finally back to Joey. "Well, at least one of you were smart enough to come to your senses."

With that, she stormed towards the motorhome, kicked the body of the Lamia out the way and knocked loudly on the door. "Hey, Stacey? It's okay, it's safe! You can open the door, now." But Stacey didn't answer. "Stacey? It's me, Astrid... open up!"

There was a shuffling from inside the motorhome and then the door finally opened to reveal a horrifying sight.

Stacey was heavily wounded with scratch marks to her face, arms, and body. Her blonde hair was mattered in blood, and clearly, she had just battled something else entirely from inside the vehicle.

Falling to her feet, Stacey sobbed loudly as she spoke. "Harpies... they came in through the windows and the roof and they took her... they took Hope. I'm so sorry... I tried to fight them. But I just couldn't... There were so many of them."

Cruz stormed toward the door in a furious frenzy. "Stacey, what do you mean they took her? Where did they take her?"

Astrid couldn't speak. She barely felt the weight of her knees give out as she collapsed to the ground in horror.

"I don't know," Stacey sobbed. "I'm so sorry. Astrid, Cruz... I'm so sorry. I didn't stand a chance."

In one automatic movement, Cruz's own dizziness brought him to his knees beside Astrid. He stared at her in disbelief, struggling to find the right words. Though instead of speaking, he cradled Astrid in his arms as the two cried.

CHAPTER THREE

While Samuel saw to the repairs of the motorhome windows with duct tape and old clothes, he watched Astrid and Cruz conversing on a rock outside by the river's edge.

Samuel felt entirely useless to them. He had once seen Cruz as a soldier, and then as competition for Astrid's affections, but besides all that, he saw Cruz as a friend.

He thought back to when he had told Astrid that he loved her. It had been a mere slip of the tongue.

When she had been in her coma, he had whispered it to her a million times over and had grown quite used to not hearing her say it back.

But earlier, those words had not only startled her they had proven to be the weakness that she had used against him. With the fate of Hope's life at stake, Samuel had understood entirely.

The problem was that his weakness had cost him greatly. His mind had been too weak to battle against the compulsion of the beast. Not only had he instructed the others to get out of the vehicle to help the woman, but he had also fought Astrid long enough to give the harpies time to take Hope.

Rattled by his thoughts, Samuel slammed his fist down on the bench. How would he ever be able to live that guilt down?

***

While watching Hannah tend to Stacey's wounds, Joey tidied up the mess that the girl's battle with the harpies had inflicted inside the motorhome. The harpies had only inflicted minor injuries on the poor girl, but they hadn't gone easy on her either.

Clearly, Stacey had put up one hell of a fight. She could be very tough when she needed to be. He had seen that back when they had been taken and tortured by the military. He had also seen it when she had shot DR Reynolds back in Greece.

Throughout time, the tales of harpies would always change. But, the one thing that always remained true, was that they were known as Zeus's hound dogs, and they would always carry out his bidding. Knowing what he knew about Zeus, and Cruz for that matter, Joey wondered just what the god had planned for the child.

For history had always proven to be quite barbaric especially when it came to the most vulnerable.

***

As Hannah finished bandaging up the last of Stacey's wounds, she did her best to offer as much reassurance of Hope's safety as she could. However, she struggled with her own faith to believe the words she spoke.

As if she was mirroring her thoughts, Stacey retorted, "Han, I just wish I could believe you. But Greek mythology has always been so dark. Even when it came to babies. He sent a Lamia to distract us, right before he sent those harpies. I should've done something more. Astrid and Cruz are going to hate me after this. I wouldn't be surprised if they never spoke to me again."

Hannah pursed her lips together, unsure how to respond. Instead, she handed Stacey some pain medication.

"You did everything you could," Tash said, rubbing Stacey's back. "Your injuries prove that you held up a fight. It wouldn't have been easy. They'll see that, and they won't blame you. I promise."

"Tash is right," Samuel said, joining them. "That attack was planned. None of us could've known what would happen. I get, that things are tough right now, but we'll find a way to get her back. I know we will."

***

While Astrid stared blankly at the reflection of the moon in the river, Cruz wiped his tears away with the palms of his hands and breathed out deeply. "I knew that taking up this war on Zeus's beasts was a bad idea. I shouldn't have listened to either of you. I just knew he would want his vengeance for us even thinking it. And now, we've lost our baby. *Nuestra hija!* You both should've just listened to me. The harpies work for him, Astrid. They were doing his bidding!"

"I'm... I'm sorry, Cruz." Astrid stammered, turning her tear-stained face to meet his.

Cruz softened his tone. "No, I'm sorry. But what do we do, now? Zeus is a very powerful and very vengeful *pendejo*! I just don't know how we're going to get her back."

Astrid tried to devise a plan, but she just couldn't. She was completely out of ideas. They were quite literally dealing with the gods. It wasn't like the old days where they could just get the authorities involved to track down their child. But at that moment, something that Cruz had said caught her attention. "How do you know what Zeus would want?" she asked.

As if caught in a lie, Cruz pursed his lips together and looked away for the briefest of moments, before shaking his head.

Astrid had seen that same look countless times. He was holding something back. Something big.

"She's just a little girl," Astrid persisted. "What would he want with her?"

"I don't know. I wish I did... but..." Cruz's voice trailed off as he stared back up at her wanting to open up... wanting desperately to reveal the secret he was hiding.

Feeling within the same torment, Astrid took his hand in hers. "But what, Cruz? Talk to me. What are you hiding? I believed you back when no one else did. I just need you to confide in me now."

Cruz smiled as he stared down at their hands intertwined. But that smile disappeared fast as he held tighter to her hand, needing her strength. "Astrid, it was Zeus that brought you back. Those whispers that I heard back when I opened the pithos... and then, when your pulse returned... they were the gods. I didn't want to tell anybody because it sounded crazy... And because they wanted me to keep it a secret."

"The gods?"

Cruz nodded. "*Mi amor*, I can hear them in my head. I know it sounds *loco*... This is a whole new level of crazy. But it's like... It's like my head has been opened to this whole new channel of voices. At first, I was really freaked out because I could hear them talking to one another...

but then, they started talking to me too. I should've been locked away a long time ago."

Astrid held tighter to Cruz's hand trying to come to terms with what he was saying. Before the pithos, a patient coming to her claiming to be hearing voices would require treatment, medication and sometimes even hospitalization. But it was Cruz, the one man she loved above all else. The one person she trusted more than anybody. The man who had opened Pandora's Box.

Not to mention the very distant voices within her own mind had her feeling the exact same way. She tried to tell herself it was nothing more than her conscience. But maybe once again, Cruz was telling the truth.

"You're not crazy," she said. "You're absolutely right. It sounds absolutely insane, but… I really do believe you."

"You do?"

"I always have, and I always will… Besides, it only makes sense."

There was a silent pause as Cruz studied Astrid's facial expression and caught a glimpse of something he recognized only too well. "Okay, so what is it that you're hiding, Astrid?"

"What do you mean?"

"There's something different about you. I've felt it since you woke up... Like there's an aura surrounding you or something. It's a different shade to the others."

Astrid shrugged. "An aura? What do you mean?"

"Maybe I'm just being corny... Or maybe it's just the reflection of the moon on your skin or something, I don't know. Like..." As he went to divulge deeper, something crossed his mind. Something far more important that he needed to get off his chest. "Hey, Astrid? There was something else about the voices. Something that Zeus wants me to do."

"Whatever it is, Cruz, he's playing us. You know better than any of us just how vengeful he is. Whatever he wants you to do, it can't be good."

"I know, trust me... That's why I didn't want us to fight his creatures and piss him off, especially after he saved you. But, if I..." Before he could continue, Astrid got to her feet lost in her own trail of thought.

"Maybe, our daughter was our sacrifice for bringing me back. Maybe... maybe I never should've come back." Her own declaration forced her anger to return. "Cruz... Hope was taken because of me..."

"No, don't say that... "

"What am I supposed to say? This isn't the Labyrinth. David Bowie won't be there at the end of this. This is reality and clearly the Greek Gods have quite literally sent in their flying monkeys to take away our baby."

"No, Astrid. We're not going to give in to defeat. I won't let us give in. I'm going to take him up on his offer."

"What offer?"

The moment was fuelled with serious tension. Cruz pursed his lips together. His eyes were filled with sincere desperation, but he remained silent until Astrid probed, "Cruz, what offer are you talking about? What did he ask you to do?"

But Cruz was adamant. Not even Astrid would be able to change his mind. "Please, Astrid... this is where I need you to trust me. I need you to trust that I would do whatever I could, for our child... and for you."

"Yes, I do trust you... But what are you planning? Do you need my help?"

With a smile of gratitude, Cruz cupped her cheek in his hand and kissed her on the forehead, before pulling away. "If I'm not back in an hour, tell the others to go without me, okay? Please, don't wait for me."

"What do you mean don't wait for you? Why wouldn't we wait for you?"

When it was certain that he would not inform her of his plans, she sighed in defeat. "Okay, fine. I'll tell them... just make sure you're back in time. Because we can't leave you behind."

"Gracias! I'll get her back, Astrid. I promise." As he flicked a lock of her hair behind her ear, he offered a smile which looked too much like goodbye, then disappeared into the nearby bushes.

"Where are you going?" Astrid called out after him. But he was simply gone. The last time she had seen him disappear in such a way, was that night in Washington, when he had broken her heart. That god-awful feeling of having her heart ripped out of her chest was exactly what she was feeling now. But this time it was for an entirely different reason. Her heart was breaking for her child who had been taken.

Wiping away the tears that had formed in her eyes, Astrid saw a shadow reflecting from the light of the motorhome. She turned to see Samuel standing behind her.

"I'm sorry if I scared you. Where's Cruz?"

"I'm not sure, but I think he has something planned. He kept talking about an offer and he told me about the voices. It was Zeus who brought me back. Cruz is convinced that he will be able to get Hope back too."

Clearly accustomed to this new world of gods and mythological creatures more so than Astrid was, Samuel barely battered an eyelash. "Is there anything I can do?" he asked, holding out his arms to hold her. Astrid shook her head and turned toward the motorhome.

"Yeah. Cruz said if he isn't back in an hour, to leave without him. I need you to wait here with the others. If either of us aren't back by then. Don't wait another minute more. We can't lose anybody else."

"Wait, what? You can't just go after him by yourself."

"Samuel, don't argue with me here, I need to go after him."

"I'm not arguing. I'm going with you. We'll get our swords."

Astrid led Samuel back into the motorhome, where her eyes instantly fell onto a very disheveled Stacey who was covered from head to toe in bandages.

Seeing her best friend in such a predicament, forced Astrid's reality to sink in. And before Stacey could even begin to get a word in, Astrid hugged her tighter than she ever had before. Involuntarily, the two sobbed uncontrollably.

They sobbed over the fear that they might not get Hope back. They sobbed over the fact their lives had gone from just simply going to work, shopping and gossiping, to living on the run from curses, mythological creatures and fearing for their own lives. They even cried for Astrid being in her coma.

They longed for the normalcy that they had before the curse had been unleashed.

"I'm so sorry," Stacey mumbled through sniffles. "When we get her back, you'll probably never trust me with her again."

"Hey, you have nothing to be sorry for! Okay? Nothing at all!"

"Okay," Stacey nodded.

"Thank you for fighting for her. You've been my best friend since high school, through college, hell for the past fifteen years of my life. Knowing that you just risked your life for my daughter, well, I trust you more than anybody else, okay?"

Stacey nodded again. "Alright."

After a short bout of silence, Joey's concern broke the moment. "Where's Cruz?"

His question forced Astrid to get back to the matter at hand. She retrieved her sword from Samuel as she answered Joey.

"Cruz went to get Hope back from Zeus, so Samuel and I are going after him. He mentioned something about an offer."

Rubbing his face in his hands, Joey swore in frustration. "Son of a bitch! I knew it. I knew he was hearing the voices again. He should've told me. Did he happen to let slip just what that offer might've been?"

"No, but he believes that Zeus was the one who brought me back."

Joey shook his head. "...and knowing Cruz, he's probably going to barter his own life away."

"Is that even possible?" Tash wondered. "I mean, what's he going to do? Pray? Cruz doesn't strike me as the type of guy who would get down on his knees in the prayer position. Unless it's for Astrid... Sorry, wrong time for a joke."

But nobody was listening to Tash. Hannah was in a serious state of shock. "He's going in search of Zeus? Actual Zeus? He'll get himself killed."

"That's why Astrid and I are going after him," Samuel replied. "Joey, we need..."

"No way," Joey snapped grabbing his sword and heading straight for the door. "There's no way I'm staying here while Cruz and the two of you run this little suicide mission. Are you coming?"

"Oh, hell yeah!" Tash said reaching for her sword, only to have Samuel stop her.

"No, we need you and Hannah to wait with Stacey. She's in no shape to fight."

"I agree," Astrid replied. "Stay here, arm yourselves, turn out the lights, and wait for us. If we're not back in an hour…"

"We'll wait as long as we need to," Stacey said sternly. "Ride or die, right, Astrid?" Astrid smirked as she remembered the inside joke that had stemmed from the movies of their youth. At least some things hadn't changed.

"Right, Stace." After Samuel handed Hannah, Tash, and Stacey their swords, he gestured for Astrid to proceed out the motorhome door before him. "After you, Leaderette. Let's go get him back."

Astrid led Samuel and Joey along the dirt path through the trees, scanning for not only Cruz but also any creatures that might pose a threat.

Samuel continued scanning with his eyes and the torch for any trace of Cruz's footsteps, while Joey monitored their surroundings. Once they had been walking briskly for at least twenty minutes, Samuel was certain that they were headed in the wrong direction. He gestured toward the ground where Cruz's footsteps had simply vanished. "It doesn't make any sense. His footprints have just disappeared."

"What do you think happened?" Astrid asked. "Cruz wouldn't just…"

"…Hey, shh!" Joey broke in, shining his torch into the darkness. "I saw something."

On his concern, Astrid and Samuel looked to where he was focusing his flashlight. The trees were still. Silent.

Astrid readied her sidearm and continued to stand perfectly still. Suddenly, movement happened within the darkness.

"It could be him," Astrid hoped, preparing to step forward, but Samuel brought his hand up in front of her, forcing her to change her mind.

He stepped in front of she and Joey then took a cautious step towards the large, moving silhouette amongst the trees, with his sword drawn.

There was the loud crumbling of many twigs underfoot and before any of them knew what was happening, they found themselves at the mercy of a large herd of men. No, not men. Fierce, mighty, and very bloodthirsty CENTAURS. There were at least five of them, all with long flowing hair, battle-scarred bodies, large weapons, and expressions that clearly meant business.

CHAPTER FOUR

"Best kidnapping ever!" Joey declared as he and Astrid sat at a table in an out-of-control bar, surrounded by drunk, masculine centaurs. They had been forced to drink bourbon and ale under the constant watch of their kidnappers.

Samuel, however, sat at the bar, forced to consume excessive amounts of alcohol as fast as he could by what looked to be the leaders of the herd.

"What are you talking about?" Astrid grumbled to Joey. "We need to find Cruz and Hope and then get back to the others."

"I know, but are you sure they're going to let us?" Joey motioned his head towards the two dark-haired centaurs standing at the end of their table.

One had the body of a white horse, Kumoth, while the lower body of his friend was brown, Systral. "Drink!" they demanded in unison. Joey shrugged and raised his glass.

"Bottoms up!" He shotted his bourbon, easily. Frustrated, Astrid drank hers up too. It was horribly bitter.

"More! Bring more!" Systral bellowed at the centaurs from the bar.

"No, no, no! We're fine, thank you!" Astrid stammered as they were brought another tray with even more shots than before. Having had counted all her drinks from the very first glass, Astrid was amazed that she still felt just as sober as she had from the moment they had first entered the bar. Surprised by the notion, she wondered if it had something to do with being brought back from the dead.

***

Samuel sat at the bar with three of the centaurs, a grey bodied one with a dark torso and grey hair, a brown bodied one with fiery red hair, and a black bodied centaur with a tanned torso and long black hair, exchanging battle stories.

These beasts had surely seen their fair share of war, and not only with humans. When Samuel had asked the centaurs where they had originated from before the curse, they merely looked at him as if he was drunk. It was as if the centaurs had no recollection of any events other than living on earth with the humans throughout the centuries.

However, they still remained very unsure of the evolution of technology and historical events that had plagued humanity. Waiting for the perfect moment to escape, Samuel kept track of his drink count and he was still relatively sober. It was evident that the creatures had a plan to get their hostages drunk and Samuel feared it might've had something to do with Astrid.

As the centaurs attempted to feed more beers down him, Samuel took the glass, brought it to his lips and poured it down himself, messily, making himself look so drunk that he couldn't even drink properly.

To his delight, it seemed to be working. They laughed raucously. "Is that woman your wife?" The centaur with thick black hair, and tanned torso, by the name of Strofan, asked him. Strofan had been sitting beside him and he reminded Samuel of a very merry veteran he had known when he first joined the military. Highly intimidating but very empathetic.

Samuel turned his head to the direction that Strofan had gestured, where Astrid was deep in conversation with Joey. Being in a bar filled with drunk men, sure, they weren't exactly human men, Samuel knew that Astrid was in danger.

Optimistic that he hadn't mentioned the location of the motorhome and put the others at risk, Samuel improvised in defense of Astrid. "Yes, that woman is my wife." Astrid could punch him later for that lie… when they survived. "So, where's your wife?" he asked the strong dark centaur.

"Clearly, she is tending to the herd back home. War is no place for a woman. I only asked because Kumoth and Systral have their eyes on your wife." Samuel looked over at the two centaurs that were keeping a close watch over his companions. "So maybe you should go over and join her. Show them that she is your property."

"You'd let me join her?" Samuel asked, having had assumed he was the captee of the large brutes.

Strofan nodded. "I've never approved of the barbaric acts my brother condones." He sent a look at the red-haired and grey-haired centaurs. They nodded in agreement. It was subtle, but enough to inform Samuel that something big was about to happen.

Instead of waiting around, Samuel got to his feet, and continuing his drunken charade, hobbled over to 'his wife' and Joey. "Hey, my beautiful wife! Stop being a Buzzkill. It's not every day you get to take a break... unless you count that coma you were in... then that was every day... for almost a year."

He ended his sentence with a hiccup. Just as he had been expecting, his statement caused Astrid and Joey to send him strange looks, but their centaur captors merely mumbled incoherently between one another, clearly believing Samuel's charade.

"Wife, Samuel?" Astrid asked in disbelief. "Oh, god, you're drunk!"

"And you're my beautiful wife," Samuel said loudly enough to garner attention. On her deathly stare, he leaned in to kiss her on the cheek and whispered 'play along' as quietly as he could.

Taking the empty seat beside her, he wrapped his arm around her shoulder and sent a side-eyed glance at the nearby centaurs. Shaking her head, Astrid looked back to Joey. They had been deep in conversation before Samuel had interrupted them.

"How is it that we can even understand these creatures?" she asked. "Shouldn't they be speaking in ancient Greek or something?"

Joey shrugged. "My guess is that it has something to do with Pandora's Box."

"Agreed," Samuel added. "They have no clue they were even in the pithos to begin with."

Joey focused his attention past Astrid and onto Samuel. "Sounds about right. My theory is that when they were released, false memories were implanted into their minds, making up for all the lost time."

Astrid looked around at the chaos unfolding in the bar, clearly analyzing the situation. She turned back to Joey. "It's still so hard to believe they even existed at all... I mean, there's evidence of dinosaur bones... but centaurs? There's nothing."

Joey nodded. "Yeah, but that just means that the curse of the gods was covered up perfectly."

"Who do you think covered it up?" Samuel wondered. "The military? The government? I doubt it." To Samuel's honest question, Joey chuckled and took another mouthful of his ale before leaning in closer and lowering his tone.

"The government likes to cover up aliens and tales of big foot… But no, it was the gods themselves that covered up the facts of Greek mythology… Think about it, if we'd known the truth, Pandora's Box would've been found by some random archaeologist or thief a long time ago. The gods are the ones to blame… the less you believe in the truth behind Greek mythology, the better they did to cover it up."

Astrid smirked a single word into her drink before taking a mouthful. "Hermes."

"Hermes?" Samuel asked her, raising an eyebrow. But as quickly as she had said it, the entire concept that she had done so escaped her entirely. She blinked quickly, as if puzzled by Samuel's question. "Hmm?"

"You just said Hermes."

Astrid stared at Samuel. "I did?"

***

Astrid stared long and hard at Samuel. She didn't remember saying 'Hermes' but he was adamant that she had. But as her attention was on what she did or didn't say, Samuel's attention was now elsewhere. He was looking over at one of the tables. "Hey, check out that bowl over there."

"What bowl?" Astrid asked turning to look. And sure enough, there was a golden helmet with two wings attached to either side of it being used as a fruit bowl. "Doesn't that remind you of that old superhero's helmet? You know, the one from the comic books? He wore a red suit."

Astrid took another sip of her drink to conceal a smile, she knew exactly what he was talking about.

"It's a helmet and it belonged to Hermes," Joey explained. "He was a messenger of the Gods and one of Zeus's sons."

"Well, why would it be here?" Astrid asked.

"Beats me! But it wasn't in the ruins with the other artifacts, that's for sure. We would have seen it when we hid the rest. Wait here, I'm going to see if I can..."

"...If you can steal it, Joe?" Astrid smirked. "In front of a whole bar full of centaurs?"

"They're drunk... They won't notice. Besides, it's not theirs, they must have stolen it first."

"Yeah, well... Good luck with that!"

As Joey got to his feet and headed in the direction of the fruit bowl helmet, he was immediately swarmed by a large group of centaurs. "I told him so," Astrid said, turning back to Samuel. "Now, they're going to get him just as drunk as they got you."

Shaking his head, Samuel leaned in close to Astrid's ear. "I'm not drunk."

"You're not?"

"No. But, right now, improv is all we've got."

"Drink, woman!" Kumoth bellowed at Astrid, forcing her to snap her head back in the centaur's direction, irritated.

"Fine!" she drank the rest of her drink in front of the centaur to appease him, so he sent for another one, leaving she and Samuel temporarily alone at the table for the moment. Having seen her take the shot, Samuel asked, "How many of them have you had?"

"That was my eighth shot. I've also had four glasses of ale."

On his surprised expression, she added. "Before you ask, I can't seem to get drunk. It's like dying did something to me and now it doesn't matter how much I drink, I still remain stone cold sober."

"Or maybe it was less so dying, and more so coming back. Maybe Zeus did something to you?" he suggested.

Astrid held onto that thought. She only wished that she could've asked Cruz the full details of that bargain, but that was impossible right now. She sighed and changed the subject. "So, why are we playing along again?"

"Well, right now we need to make them think that the whole getting us drunk thing is working. These guys will drink us under the table until we become submissive... and the two that have been watching you all night? Well... it will be as if they were both dealing with lust from the seven deadly sins."

"But they're centaurs, they're already far more powerful than we are. They don't need to get us drunk to kill us. "

Samuel nodded. "Yeah, but after speaking to three at the bar, I managed to get a little information out of them. Their king likes to play with their prey before putting it out of their misery. We're a game to them. Strofan was the one who told him to let us drink to allay our deaths. But that, might also give us the advantage of our escape."

On his words, Astrid grimaced and glanced over at Kumoth and Systral standing at the next table. "I really wish I didn't ask."

"Do you forgive the whole drunk husband act now?"

"I'll forgive it when it gets us out of here." Her mind was on Cruz and Hope and this entire kidnapping ordeal was nothing more than an inconvenience.

She drank the last drop from her shot glass, wishing that she could start feeling the effects at any moment. Improvising, she leaned in a little closer to Samuel. Her nose practically touching his own.

From her peripheral view, she could see that she was being watched. Forcing a lovesick smile, she spoke in a low tone so that only Samuel could hear. Anyone would think that they were in a long-term relationship, which is what she needed them to believe.

"Alright, Samuel, I'll play along. Because if a little false PDA on our casual stroll out of here is what you had in mind, this better work."

Cupping her cheek, Samuel mirrored her soft tone. "These guys aren't just going to let us walk out of here. Unless you haven't noticed, we were kidnapped by thirty-seven centaur soldiers."

"They're not?"

"I very much doubt it."

Astrid smiled lazily before breaking contact with him and stumbling to her feet. "I might have a plan, play along."

Throughout history, Astrid had heard countless stories about centaurs. Both good and bad. But unfortunately, it was the bad stories that had always stuck with her.

She knew that they were in the lion's den. That one wrong move could be their end. She turned to Joey, who was slowly staggering his way back to them. The centaurs had clearly succeeded in getting him drunk. Making herself look as if she could barely stand, Astrid pushed her weight onto Joey.

"I think I'm going to be sick! Samuel, Joey... can you guys escort me outside?"

"Absolutely," Samuel said, pulling on his best drunken charade. He got to his feet and joined them as they made their way towards the entrance.

For a few moments, Astrid's plan was working. Joey pulled his coat over his arm to conceal the round object he was carrying underneath, as the three of them staggered toward the door.

"Not so fast, two-legs!" the booming voice of one of the centaurs said, making them turn to look. "You're our hostages, we say when you leave." The centaur who had spoken had long blonde hair and a white lower body.

"Oh, we're not leaving... but I think I'm going to hurl," Astrid declared, bringing one hand to her stomach.

"We're all friends here. That's what the floor is for!" the blonde centaur said.

"Oh, no... please, I'd rather not. I just need a little fresh air. I'll be real quick, I promise!"

"Her vomiting isn't something you want to see," Samuel said.

"No, it isn't..." Joey added. "All this talk of vomiting... I think I'm going to..." he held back his own, "oh... false alarm."

"You're not leaving!" the blonde centaur demanded.

They were merely five feet from the exit and by now every eye was on them. The tension was hostile. Astrid kept eye contact with the blonde centaur, almost daring him to make a move. The familiar female inside her mind told her that no matter what happened, they would survive the bloodshed of the upcoming battle.

Samuel glanced quickly over at the weapons by the bar. Their own weapons were among them, and he was clearly strategizing. The entire bar was overly crowded, just as it was silent. The blonde centaur narrowed his eyes at Astrid menacingly.

But then, the still silence was broken by a drunkenly merry tone of voice. Samuel's dark-haired companion from the bar earlier. "Just let them go, Alafan!" Strofan stepped into the clearing in the middle.

On his request, Alafan turned his calculating demeanour to him. "Brother? Do you dare defy me?"

Astrid was met with a sense of amusement as she watched the two convene. "These humans are mere travelers. They pose no threat. Let them leave unharmed."

Astrid looked to Samuel silently questioning whether this elevated dispute would be the best time to make their getaway. They both turned their gaze toward the door behind them, just as Kumoth blocked their pathway. Their escape would need to wait out the brotherly dispute.

Astrid and Samuel turned back to Alafan who was zeroing in on his brother. "You're right, brother. We have wiped out so many of their kind. But even you can admit that it has been fun doing so. Their women have been just so... accommodating." Alafan's tone, blended with the way he squared his eyes back to Astrid so quickly, sent shivers up her spine.

But Strofan would not back down. "Brother, we are not barbarians. Look at what we have become. You use power and your brute strength to torture those weaker than us, as if they are nothing more than trophies."

"THEY ARE TROPHIES!" Alafan yelled, summoning forth the fear of all who were present, before he continued. "The two-legs are nothing more than animals. They have no souls, *brother*. Your pity for these creatures will be the death of you! We are the future... not these... these... apes! Now, if you continue to defy me... you know what the penalty for your actions will be..." Alafan paused.

His nostrils flared. His face was merely inches from Strofan's. "Now, brother... I will ask you again... Do you dare defy your king?" Seemingly defeated, Strofan sighed and stared down at Astrid, Samuel and then at Joey. He bore no loyalties to them, so why was he defying his own brother... his king? Strofan looked around at the other centaurs.

The tension was painstakingly silent. Was this lone centaur turning his back on his people? On his own king for them? As if by chance, Astrid spotted a golden bow resting against a bar stool, just as she felt the warmth of Samuel's hand covering her own.

It was a fight that they would not flee. Astrid felt the blood rush to her fingers. She was aching for another fight. Furthermore, the voice inside her mind was anticipating the bloodshed to come.

The silence was broken by Strofan's red-haired companion. He was aged with faded scars to his face and torso. "Strofan is right. The centaurs used to be a proud civilization. Under your reign, we've grown ruthless. We've become monsters. Do you really wish for us to be that way? I stand with Strofan and these travelers."

Astrid, Samuel, and Joey continued to watch on. Every eye was on the king. There were muffles, which resulted in a division of the herd. Kumoth and Systral sided with Alafan, along with many other centaurs. But there were still quite a number, who, from that moment on, had silently sworn a fealty to Strofan.

Samuel stared down at Astrid and offered her a look that she remembered far too well. "Let's do this, Sutherland."

***

After Stacey had finally fallen asleep in Tash's arms, Tash and Hannah were left sitting in the darkness in the middle of the motorhome chatting. "It's been three hours,"

Tash said, glancing down at her watch. "Do you think they found Cruz, yet?"

Hannah glanced over at Tash and then back down at the flashlight, in her hands. "I hope so."

Tash nodded. "I really hope they find them. It just doesn't feel right, you know? Knowing that baby Hope is out there all alone with harpies, lamias… and god-knows whatever else. It's like Cruz and Sutherland are cursed or something."

Hannah slightly raised the corner of her mouth. She understood exactly where Tash was coming from. She and Joey had been there the day that Cruz had opened the pithos. In fact, she had even warned Cruz that some things just weren't meant to be opened.

But Cruz, being a man fuelled by his own curiosity, just needed to know what was inside. Hannah remembered the first time she had met him on their excavation. Joey had been flirting with some random girl while Cruz had been poring over his notes in excitement.

Research had been his first love and that was what the two of them had in common, and because of that love, they had become fast friends. Strictly platonic, simply because Hannah had always seen him as a nerdy little brother with a childlike optimism. It had stunned her when he had been the one to rescue them from the military prisons.

A year of dealing with the burden of cursing the world had weighed heavily on his shoulders. But remarkably, Astrid had brought out a new side of him, something admirable.

Thinking back to the words that Tash had just used, about Cruz and Astrid being cursed, Hannah could only agree. They had fallen in love in the middle of something that defeated all logic... Something that was fuelled by magic and Greek mythology. They had conceived a child... a child who had been delivered by the means of a gruesome ritual, the aftermath which still haunted Hannah's memories.

She was a doctor. She didn't believe in magic, fairy tales and curses but she certainly understood their purpose. That purpose of knowing that true love could break any curse... And from what she had seen, the curse that plagued Cruz and Astrid might just be the only answer of standing a chance. Hannah smiled at Tash who was stroking Stacey's hair out of her face.

She could tell that Tash's mind was reeling over the possibilities of where Hope might be, but Hannah's mind had been on an entirely separate subject. "Hey Tash, can I ask you something?"

"Sure... anything to take my mind off this bullshit."

"Have you noticed anything odd about Joey?"

"Joey? What do you mean? He's just as 'Joey' as ever."

"That's not what I mean... I mean, that... well... I don't think that the Lamia was actually able to compel him." Even as Hannah spoke up, she had been predicting Tash's response.

"Han, we both saw him. He was doing everything in his power to stop you from fighting that thing."

"Yes, he was. But, at the same time... it was different… Joey was a little more concerned about me being hurt than me actually hurting the Lamia."

Tash's large dark eyes stared in confusion. "What do you mean?"

"Well, if you think back to both Cruz and Samuel. They reacted in defense of the Lamia because they saw her as nothing more than a helpless woman. But Joey was much more interested in protecting me from her... and after I gave in and said I wouldn't hurt her... sure, I was bluffing... he took my sword and took the kill."

Tash sat in silence, furrowing her dark eyebrows as she mentally began piecing Hannah's observations together. "But he loves you and he said..."

"I know what he said. That his love for me beat the compulsion. But the timing was pretty perfect. He made the decision when he saw that both you and Astrid couldn't. Samuel had Astrid pinned, and Cruz had you at sword point. That wasn't compulsion, Tash."

"Are you thinking there's something wrong with him? That, maybe he is a special descendant? If that were the case, he shouldn't have been affected by the curse in the first place. He was pretty raged out back when the deadly sin curse had a hold of us."

Hannah paused to reflect on the fact before continuing. "Honestly? I don't know." She was still trying to make sense of it all. Then again, there were times when they had been tortured during their interrogations, that she felt that Joey could control his anger.

Which was funny because no one could control themselves. Yet, no matter how angry Joey got when his sin took over, he never took out his anger on Hannah... Even when she had given into lust and had kissed Samuel.

As much as Hannah knew and loved Joey, it was almost as if he was hiding something from her. And no matter how hard she tried, she just couldn't let go of that doubt. There was something purely off about the man she loved, and she was determined to find out just what it was.

With a light shrug, Tash changed the subject to a topic that had clearly stolen her own attention. "While we're on the topic of what's up with our friends, Han... can I talk to you about Sutherland?"

This question easily piqued Hannah's attention as Astrid coming back from the dead was just as much as an enigma as the secret that Joey could possibly be hiding.

"Why? Have you noticed something?"

"Just that... I mean, I've seen a lot of movies in the past... back when we had movies, that is... but, for someone who has just woken up from a coma to suddenly throw herself into combat like that... well, it just doesn't seem normal. I'm not a doctor, so that's why I'm asking you, but..."

"...Thank god, I'm not the only one who's noticed! Her stats were just so perfect. She didn't pass urine or experience bowel movement when she was unconscious..."

"...Eww..."

"But, she was awake for a little over an hour before she was helping us with those ants... and then with the lamia... it's like she knew exactly what to do in the situation she had never been in... Astrid was in a coma for a year, maybe Cruz's right... maybe it is Zeus. Because... Well, I've just never seen anything like it before."

"Huh. So, what do you think it is?"

Once again, Hannah was in the dark. "I really have no idea."

Tash sighed. "So where do you think they all are?"

"Knowing them, wherever they are... I'm guessing I'll be needing to have the first aid kit handy."

"Yeah... they get all the fun!" Tash laughed.

***

Back at the centaur bar, a large fight had broken out between the creatures. To Samuel's delight, they fought with swords, shields, bows, and arrows.

Strofan had ordered for Samuel to take 'his wife' and Joey and leave. But after having seen the centaur fight his own brethren on his behalf, Samuel could not simply turn his back and flea.

He had found a stash of weapons in one of the corners of the bar and although knowing that Astrid would only disobey his orders, he still asked her to hide.

"Seriously, Buzzkill! Have you met me?" she snapped. Defeated, Samuel had handed Joey a sword, and Astrid the golden bow which had stolen her attention, along with some arrows. "Until I teach you to train with a sword, get behind the bar and use this. Joey, keep watch over her."

Disappointed, Astrid had scoffed but did as he asked just the same. She hid behind the bar with the bow and although she had never used one before, it didn't take her long to realize just what she was doing. She was taking out foes in an instant.

Joey stood right in front of the bar ensuring that no one got past him, as Samuel brought himself into the very thick of the battle, fighting alongside Strofan.

"I told you to leave, two-legs!" Strofan demanded.

"Well, one custom I've learned to live by is that you never leave your friends to die alone in a battle," Samuel said as he stabbed one of the centaurs in the side.

"Oh, don't count this as friendship... I just don't like seeing my kind carry out cruelty to other species."

"Good to know." But he kept fighting, nonetheless.

***

Astrid took down multiple centaurs from her location, but as she saw Joey battling with both Kumoth and Systral, she could see that he was in over his head. Currently facing Systral, Joey didn't see Kumoth go to attack him from behind with an axe.

But before Kumoth could do so, Astrid aimed the bow for Kumoth's humanly torso. Just as he took a swing at Joey, she released it, praying for the best.

To her amazement, the arrow lifted slightly in the air, getting Kumoth in the head... A direct kill. A miraculously impossible shot. Kumoth fell to the floor behind Joey, who had just taken down Systral at the same time.

As Joey looked down and saw Kumoth on the floor in a heap, he looked back at Astrid and smiled very pleased by her attack. "Well done, Sister! Something's never change."

"Sister? Where'd that one come from?" Astrid asked, puzzled.

"Well, I can't exactly call you my brother in arms, can I?"

"Right. Let's get back to it." Astrid readied her bow once more.

In the thick of the battle, Alafan had already taken down his brother Strofan, who was bleeding profusely to his side. Alafan was now backing Samuel into a corner.

"Joey, you take out the others," Astrid ordered. "I'll go for Alafan!"

"Got it!"

Aiming her bow straight for the centaur king, Astrid focused, breathed out softly, and then released. But the arrow didn't go far enough. She had one more arrow left. She needed to make it work.

Alafan readied his large golden axe above Samuel's head, he was so much taller than the human soldier. Furthermore, Samuel's dominant forearm bore a neat gash which was bleeding heavily at the hemline of his navy-blue shirt.

The fury in Samuel's eyes was mixed with something Astrid had only ever seen in him once before… the time they had been travelling together on the road and he had given into lust. It was fear.

As hard as Samuel was trying to hide his fear now, Astrid could see it clearly. She couldn't lose him now. He meant far too much to her for that to happen. She needed her shot to count.

Once again, she focused her arrow, just as Alafan brought down the blade of his axe toward Samuel. Then she released it, praying with every ounce of her being that it would make contact in time.

Both the action of the axe and the arrow appeared to happen in slow motion. Samuel slowly rose to his feet, bringing his gaze to Astrid, as the axe came down toward him.

Then as if by magic, the wind picked up speed. The arrow travelled even faster than the axe and it pierced the centaur king in the middle of his human torso. Alafan dropped his axe to the floor and time sped up again.

As Astrid and Samuel's gazes both turned to see the golden arrowhead protruding from the chest of king Alafan, the centaur collapsed to the ground right by Samuel's feet.

After realizing what had just happened, Samuel smirked at Astrid. "Seriously, Sutherland? You just had to take my kill! You're such a Buzzkill!"

Equally relieved that she had just saved Samuel, and astounded by the miracle of her shot, Astrid giggled. "Just saving your ass yet again... Next time don't send a man to do a woman's job."

Shaking his head with a smile that radiated up into his crystal blue eyes, Samuel brought his focus to his wounded arm.

Reaching for a bottle of vodka and a cleaning rag from the bar, Astrid tended to his bleeding forearm. The moment was filled with sizzling tension, fuelled by adrenaline thanks to the battle.

Still, Astrid avoided the smiling gaze of the handsome soldier. As her hand pulled up the hemline of his sleeve, his words altered her concentration level.

"I almost forgot the softness of your touch." An involuntary smile crept into the side of her cheek as she chose to ignore his words. But still, he persisted. "Not to mention, just how hot it is to see you save my life."

In response to his flirtation which was seriously getting under her skin, Astrid doused his arm in enough alcohol to make him flinch and smiled, before handing him the cloth.

"I think you can take it from here," she said casually. She made her way towards the few centaurs who had survived the battled and were now gathered around Joey and Strofan.

As Astrid and Samuel joined the wounded centaur, Joey turned to them. "His wounds aren't fatal. He's going to be fine."

There was a brief look of surprise in the centaur's face, as if he had been expecting to die from the large gash, which could now be likened to a very minor one.

Still, he brushed Joey away and got to his hooves, gathering his soldier pride to address them. "Of course," he huffed, brushing Joey away. "I've fought in many wars… It would take a lot to kill me."

At seeing that Strofan was still alive, the remaining centaurs began kneeling before him. Astrid, Joey, and Samuel lowered their heads too, in respect to the tribe's new king.

CHAPTER FIVE

Astrid glanced down at the arrow protruding from Alafan's body, then back to the golden bow slung over her arm. She couldn't help but wonder what magic might've assisted her to take the shot. There was no way in hell that she could've made that kill without godly intervention.

"Thank you, Astrid," the tribe's new king bellowed, pulling her from her thoughts. "You must be seen as a real warrior amongst your people. You took down a great king."

Samuel brought his left hand to Astrid's back, supportively and smiled.

"She certainly is," he replied. "I really hate to cut these pleasantries short, but we should be leaving."

"It has been an honor, Samuel. You and your kin have proven yourselves as friends among my people. If you should ever find yourself in the land of the 'fire human', we bid you welcome."

Ripped into the reality of the situation, Astrid gasped. "That's New York."

"New York?" Strofan asked her.

She nodded. She had lived in New York her whole life. That was until the curse had been unleashed.

To think that it was now nothing more than ruins overrun by centaurs filled her with the dread that her life might never be the same again. To her relief, Joey broke into their conversation, stealing Strofan's attention, entirely.

"Sorry to break up this goodbye. But we best be going. We're looking for a man... friend of ours, dark hair to here... brown eyes... and two legs. You haven't seen him by any chance, have you?"

Strofan shook his head. "No, but I wish you luck in finding him."

"Thank you, your majesty." Samuel bowed and led Astrid and Joey out of the bar.

The smack of the fresh night air hit them the moment they were outside, bringing a sheer sense of relief. Using the moon to guide them, Samuel led them back through the trees.

"It's so good to be out of that bar," Joey exclaimed. "Did anyone else see the humor of all those centaurs fighting drunk? We're all so lucky that we were all sober. They would have been so much tougher on us, otherwise."

His words forced Astrid to stop, abruptly. "Wait, you're not drunk?"

"Of course, not. The two of you aren't the only ones who can feign drunken antics." He shuffled his coat and revealed the golden helmet which he had taken from the bar.

"You stole the helmet, Joey?" Samuel snapped. "They just extended us an olive branch and you stole a golden helmet from them?"

"We should head back to San Francisco when we get the chance and hide it with the rest of the relics we found in Greece. Same as your bow, Astrid."

"What?" Astrid exclaimed, holding tight to her new weapon which she had become quite fond of. "Why?"

"Well, they clearly belong to the gods. Let's not anger them any more than we have. It's our only chance in a peace offering to getting back Cruz and Hope."

Removing the bow from her shoulder and handing it to him, Astrid agreed, disappointed. "Sure. Let's just go."

They walked for what seemed like an eternity through the trees, with no sign, whatsoever, of Cruz or Hope, until they finally reached the clearing.

"You guys," Samuel exclaimed. "It's the Argo!" The moment he spoke those words, Astrid ran excitedly to the door, calling out for Cruz, only to have Tash open the door, holding up her torch. "Did you find them?" she asked.

Astrid's excitement quickly drained. "No. I was hoping he'd be back, by now." Astrid turned back, just as Samuel and Joey reached her. "We need to go back for them!" Astrid demanded.

The men exchanged glances. "Astrid, we can't," Samuel said. "You know that Cruz would be back by now, if..."

"Well, then we can't leave. Not yet. What if he comes back? What if they both come back and we're not here?"

Heart-broken, Astrid immediately fell into Samuel's outstretched arms, relishing his warmth in that moment.

"Alright," Samuel said softly, giving into her. "We'll stay for the night. But we need to leave first thing in the morning. Is that clear?" Astrid nodded her tearstained face into Samuel's chest wishing in that moment that he wasn't as right as he was. They would need to leave first thing in the morning. But to where, was the real mystery.

***

After crying herself to sleep in the bunk above the cabin of the motorhome, Astrid managed to dream. But they were not peaceful dreams. She dreamed of her time before her coma, of her memories with Cruz, of Samuel and of when she had been pregnant with her daughter.

And then, as if on cue, her dreams changed. Once again, she was in those darkened deserted wastelands. But as she looked out to the murky swamps, she could hear a voice behind her.

The voice of the same woman that she had remembered hearing back at the hospital. That same voice that had told her how to kill the Lamia and that they would survive the centaur fight.

But this time, the woman's voice was filled with gut-wrenching dread. "I can't be here. I can't be here. Please, I beg of you to help me, help me, Astrid!" The echo of the voice grew louder and louder until it sounded as if it were screaming right in her ear.

"HELP ME!" Astrid awoke, sitting abruptly and smacking her head on the roof of the motorhome as she did. "Oww." The nightmare she had experienced, and her current fears of Cruz and Hope were a simple guarantee that she wouldn't be sleeping the rest of the night. But then, who needed sleep? She had just spent a year in a state of unconsciousness.

Climbing out of the bed, Astrid wrapped the blanket around her body, made her way down the ladder and headed outside, not noticing that Samuel was still awake as she passed him.

Stepping into the darkness outside, where the cold of winter had frosted the ground all around her, she found the same rock where she had sat earlier with Cruz. The cool winds brushed against her face, but ironically, she did not feel the cold. However, within the breeze, she heard the same whisper calling out to her.

"Who are you?" she asked, out loud. "How can I help you?" Unsure as to whether the whisper was in her mind or in the air around her, she heard the same woman's voice answer her question as clear as day. *'You are already doing all you can, and for that, I thank you.'*

In a sheer gasp, Astrid looked around her. But there was nobody else with her. Maybe she was going insane, but there was just something about the voice that somewhat soothed her.

Desperate to hear it again, she pleaded out loud. "Do you know where my baby is? Is she safe?"

But this time, there was a different voice. Still female, though somewhat wiser. *'Your daughter is safe, she is with me, just as mine is with you.'* A shrill deep seed of happiness forced tears to emerge in Astrid's eyes. She brushed them away. Eager to communicate with the voices more.

"So, Hope is safe? What about her father? Where is Cruz?"

'Yes, Hope is safe.'

But the voice didn't answer her the way she wanted. Astrid demanded a response. "What about Cruz? Is he alright?" Astrid clung onto hope that the voice would tell her, but to her desperate dismay, it didn't.

Instead, a voice that she knew far too well, forced her to startle from her seat on the rock.

"You couldn't sleep, either?" Samuel asked, approaching her from behind. Him following her outside had been the last thing she had expected, nonetheless, she welcomed him to sit to the right of her.

"I heard you tossing and turning in your sleep," he said, sitting beside her. "Did you want to talk about it?" As Samuel brought his arm around her, Astrid tilted her head up to face him and shuffled in closer.

"I would... but, I don't know where to start. I just don't understand any of it." Breaking eye contact, Samuel turned his gaze to the moonlit river, forcing Astrid to do the same.

"Maybe you will over time. Just remember, I'm here if you need me."

"I know. Thank you. So, how's your arm?"

Samuel shrugged his right arm freely. "Surprisingly, pretty good. Healing quite rapidly. In fact, it doesn't seem natural for it to be healing this fast... but then, none of what the world has become is natural. Just look at you, Sutherland. You're a living miracle."

Pulling the blanket tighter to her body, Astrid chuckled. "A living miracle, Buzzkill?"

"Astrid, you were… you were dead. The sight of you in that way… Well, it's haunted every single one of us. What those butchers did to you… I've seen so much in my lifetime… but that… You…" Samuel turned his gaze back to the river, doing his best to conceal his pain. Sympathetically, Astrid took his hand in hers.

"I'm fine, Samuel. I'm right here."

Turning his eyes back to her with a delighted smile, he nodded. "Yes, you are, Sutherland, and that's why you're a miracle."

Remembering that night in the ruins, brought a chill to Astrid's core. The cultists had drugged her, putting her to sleep, so fighting them off as they had tied her to the marble table had been impossible. But then the sedative had worn off and she had woken up to the sounds of Cruz yelling hysterically and to those 'butchers' holding her down as they cut into her.

There was no pain, just the sheer terror of her reality as they took her baby away from her. Astrid wanted desperately, to fight them off, but she had been too weak and too dizzy to do a thing but mumble incoherently, "No… don't… my… my baby…" From her position, she could see Cruz chained to his post calling out to them to leave her alone. "Cruz," she had mumbled. "…our baby."

Cruz's expression had changed to that of a helpless cry as he was unable to save her. "*Mi amor…* You need to rest… I won't leave your side, no matter what… Listen to the voices."

As the scene faded from Astrid's mind, Samuel's hand brushing the tear from her cheek pulled her back into the moment. But Cruz's final words, 'listen to the voices' continued to resound in her head. Looking up at Samuel, she asked, "do you believe Cruz about the voices?"

As if he was considering his words carefully, Samuel hesitated before he answered. "At first, I didn't. But, after seeing everything we have faced. From you coming back from the dead and after all the beasts we've faced, it has certainly opened my eyes to the impossible. So, yes, I do believe him. Why do you ask?"

"Well, I've been hearing things. Normally it's just the voice of one woman pleading to me for help. But just before you joined me, I heard the voice of another telling me that Hope is safe. Now, I guess, I just don't know what to believe."

Astrid's posture straightened as she waited to hear what he would make of that information.

"Regardless of how that sounds," he replied. "How does it make you feel? Do you believe them? Do you believe that Hope is safe?"

"Yeah. I think I do. I feel I have no reason to doubt this woman, but it's strange as I'm not sure if I've ever even met her before."

"Then. I guess you have your answer. If you feel that Hope is safe and that you can trust the woman's voice, then go with your instincts. If it feels right to you, trust in that."

With a simple nod, Astrid stared back to the river before them. Knowing that Samuel was still watching her, she changed the conversation. "I remember what you said to me tonight."

"What I said?"

A slight smile tilted up into her cheek as she faced him again. "You know, during the encounter with the Lamia, when you told me, you loved me."

Samuel's entire body stiffened up as he evaded her eye, but Astrid continued. "Is that really how you feel?"

Swallowing down the saliva that had made its way to his mouth, Samuel turned back to her. His words were soft and quiet, but they were still loud enough for her to hear.

"Yes, it is. We were together so briefly before you were taken, but I've felt this way for a long time. The stories your father would tell me before I had even met you inspired me to stay alive for the very chance to meet you. Then, when we finally met, you captivated me entirely."

"Samuel, those were just stories. Parents are biased when it comes to their children. You can't fall in love with someone you barely know. It's just so… cliché."

"Like you and Cruz?" His answer, while defensive, certainly left her in a verbal checkmate, leading him to go on. "How soon did you know Cruz before the two of you fell for each other? And it can't just be because of the curse because that virus ended when your daughter was born." Astrid pursed her lips together.

Whatever she felt for Cruz defeated all logic. It was something she couldn't quite put her finger on. But this wasn't about she and Cruz, this was about her feelings toward Samuel and his feelings for her.

She sighed, knowing that she needed to be honest with him. "Samuel, I remember that night back in Greece, the night before I died. It was… well, it was amazing… and yes, I still feel the same way as I did then."

Samuel's expression shifted only slightly, as he studied her closely. "You still feel the same way?"

"I do. But, right now, I'm just torn. There's a whole lot going on with me and with Hope... and with Cruz..."

"...Astrid, I get it. I do. I mean the fact that you do feel something, that's... well, that's big. But, let's face it, I don't want to push you into anything that you're not ready for and I'm not going anywhere. I'll be right here. I'll be your shoulder to cry on and your sparring partner, in more ways than one if you want me to be," he smirked.

"In more ways than one, huh?"

His eyebrows raised in unison with the devilish grin on his face. "You know, if you need to get those endorphins pumping."

Filled with blush, Astrid lightly elbowed him in the rib. "So, if I ever need a midnight sparring match, I can depend on you?"

"On the battlefield or between the sheets, I've got you covered."

Succumbing to a fit of laughter, Astrid allowed for Samuel to hold her even closer, and rested her head against his chest. The guy was strong, handsome, and sweet. There was no wonder why Cruz always felt inferior to him.

Unfortunately for Astrid, as much as she wanted to fight it, she loved Samuel just as much as she loved Cruz. And that kind of love was highly likely to end in heartbreak for all three of them. Listening to the raised rhythm of his heartbeat, Astrid let herself feel at peace with Samuel.

"Why do you have to be so perfect?" she accidentally thought out loud. She could feel his breath hitch before he spoke.

"I'm only perfect because you make me want to be." Feeling him land a kiss against her forehead, captivated her. And in their bliss, they watched the river until the night turned into day, in silence.

***

"Hey, Sutherland. You might want to wake up and see this." Samuel's voice entered Astrid's dreams, forcing her to open her eyes. She had fallen asleep and as she came to, she glanced around them.

They were still sitting on the large rock by the river. But the sun was high in the sky shining over the very beautiful flowerbed that now surrounded them. Astrid was certain there had been no flowers the night before, and what made the fact even stranger was that they had only grown in the location that Astrid and Samuel had been sitting.

"This is amazing!" Samuel exclaimed. "I swear I only rested my eyes for a minute. It wasn't like this last night." Picking a purple daisy that had grown right in front of them, he handed it to her, forcing her to smile sheepishly as she smelled it.

Deep down, Astrid felt that maybe these flowers had something to do with the voices of the women that she had been hearing. She took the flowers as a sign that she could trust them when they told her that Hope was safe.

"Holy...!" Tash's voice carried from the doorway of the motorhome behind them, forcing their attention.

As Samuel got to his feet, he pulled Astrid to stand as they both turned to face Natasha. "You guys!" Tash called out to the others, "Come and check this out!"

As the others followed her out of the vehicle, Tash approached Astrid and Samuel. "You two didn't get married overnight, and not invite us, did you?" she asked them.

"No? Not that I'm aware of," Astrid replied.

"But Buzzkill was calling her his wife at that centaur bar, last night," Joey chimed in.

"That was only to establish a sense of dominance over the centaurs," Samuel replied.

"By the looks of those flowers... you two must have pleased the gods in some way," Stacey smirked.

"No, Stacey. Don't be silly," Astrid replied. "But I need to speak with all of you. Last night, I was hearing these voices..."

"Like Cruz was hearing Zeus?" Hannah probed.

"No, these were women. One of them assured me that Hope is okay." Joey stared at her silently with an expression on his face that informed them all that he knew more than he was letting on. "What is it Joey?" Astrid asked.

"Nothing, why?"

"You know something. What are you hiding?"

By now, all the attention was on Joey. He sighed in defeat. "Well, the only beings that come to mind are Demeter and Persephone. You know, the whole mother daughter connection?"

"But it's only winter," Hannah started. "Persephone only comes up from the underworld for..."

"Yeah... Summer and Spring, I know. Astrid, I don't think you're alone," Joey said, studying her.

"What do you mean, I'm not alone?" Astrid asked, defensive.

"I think you might have brought someone back with you. But if they are telling you that Hope is safe. I believe you can trust them because, from everything I've ever studied in the past, they must mean well. Just let me know if they tell you anything. It's exciting, don't you think? Now, we just need to find Hope and Cruz, so let's get going."

Joey's sudden subject brush off frustrated all of them. As he picked up his pace and headed back towards the motorhome, Astrid stopped him, furious.

"You mean that I'm being used as a tool for the gods again? Seriously?!"

To diffuse the situation, Joey patted her on the shoulder. "Hey. Calm down. If you knew her story you'd understand. Persephone would do anything to get out of the underworld. She was forced there against her own will."

"So, is everybody else who dies! Besides, didn't she fall in love with Hades? I've seen cases like that before. Stockholm syndrome. After an eternity with Hades, I can't see Persephone desperately scrounging to get out." But her response was met by Joey's cold-stone serious expression. His usually calm persona reflected something else entirely.

"Well then, maybe, I should refresh all of you with the story over breakfast." As Joey stormed into the motorhome, Astrid exchanged concerned glances with the others. Even Hannah seemed astonished by the fury in Joey's eyes.

***

The group sat around the crackling fire eating breakfast, which consisted of cereal and cooked fish, as Joey sat cross-legged on the rock and begun his story. "So, Persephone was the beautiful daughter of Zeus and Demeter. But when Zeus's brother, Hades, saw her, he became so infatuated that he concocted a plan to kidnap her. One day, when Persephone was in the garden with her friends, the nymphs, the grounds opened below, and she fell through. This gave Hades the chance to swoop in and take her."

There was a real energy as Joey told the story. He told it with emphasis and gestured with his hands to illustrate. But what caught Astrid's attention was the far-off look he adopted as he told it.

She had seen that same look with patients retelling their own personal experiences with trauma. Clearly, Joey was seeing everything within his mind in vivid detail. "When Demeter found out that her daughter had been taken, of course, she threw a fit. She went to Zeus, who I believe was in on Hades' plan. In turn, he sent good ol' Hermes down to try and bring Persephone back. But Persephone had eaten four seeds of a pomegranate, and back in those times if your captor gave you food and you ate it, then you had no choice but to return to them. So, while Persephone was able to return to her mother back on the earth, she still had to go back to the Underworld, later... this whole coming and going business is how the Greeks believe we get our seasons."

As Joey finished his story, he looked as if he was trying to shake off a sadness. Taking a sip of his water bottle, he swallowed his mouthful without locking eye contact with anybody.

"It's no wonder that Persephone would use Astrid to get out of there," Stacey said. "The thought of being kidnapped and forced to marry someone against their will. She would have been desperate."

Astrid considered all that her friend had gone through when she had been kidnapped by the military. Stacey had been raped repeatedly for interrogation purposes.

Wrapping her arm around Stacey's shoulders Tash addressed Joey. "But isn't Astrid right? Didn't Persephone fall in love with Hades afterward? That's what the stories said."

Joey gave Tash an iced cold look. "Do you really believe that, Tash? Because I sure as hell, don't! I believe that she just became submissive over time. What was that term? Stockholm Syndrome? Persephone lost her will to fight. But Astrid, you were never kidnapped. Maybe Persephone knew you were being brought back and it was her final bid to escape that hell."

"So, if her spirit is in me, then how do we release it?" Astrid asked.

"I'm not sure. Maybe, she'll tell you?" he shrugged.

Staring down at her hands in her lap, Cruz's words, 'listen to the voices,' echoed through Astrid's mind, once again. Maybe that was her only option.

Samuel who had been sitting beside her in silence, finally spoke up. "Wouldn't Hades be mad that

Persephone left?" As he directed his gaze to her, Astrid knew exactly what he was thinking before he even said it. "He might come after us."

"Great," Tash exclaimed. "Look at us just pissing off the gods, today."

"I wish we knew where Cruz was right now," Hannah replied. "He could be..."

"Don't you dare say it!" Joey said, cutting her off. "If Zeus has been speaking to him, maybe he was favored by him. Cruz could be fine, just as Astrid has clearly been favored by Persephone and her mother."

Getting to his feet, Samuel turned his focus to the motorhome. "Well, we should get moving."

"You guys. Look around us," Hannah said, grasping their attention. Looking around, they saw for miles, the beautiful, brightly colored flower arrangements, the green grass and leaves on the trees that had only just appeared over the last half hour. It was as if Spring had come early, and they were standing in the most beautiful garden paradise they had ever seen.

"Wow!" Stacey exclaimed as she ran to smell some of the flowers.

"Sutherland... I think you did that," Samuel said. "This is amazing!"

Getting to her own feet and looking around, Astrid considered that maybe the goddess she had brought back with her was working through her. And for the first time in a while, she was hopeful.

CHAPTER SIX

After breakfast, the group packed their things and climbed into the motorhome, with Samuel driving and Joey accompanying him. They had been driving for the entire morning and were now in the middle of nowhere.

Astrid sat beside Tash at the table to the left of the motorhome. Whereas Hannah and Stacey sprawled out on the couches to their right. They had been in full discussion about the river's events since they had hit the road. "Hey Sutherland, do you think you could do it again, by will?" Tash asked.

"I'm not sure," Astrid replied. "It all happened without me realizing. But at least we know that Hope is safe. I just don't know where she is or when we'll get her back."

"Not to mention where to even start looking for Cruz," Hannah added. An unwelcomed silence washed over them as they feared for Cruz's whereabouts, until Tash broke it again with a lighter conversation.

"So, those centaurs. You guys actually befriended them, right? Well, I guess that screws with our plans on bringing down Zeus's creatures. Because we can't exactly go killing our friends. Well, we could... but that would make us the bad guys."

In agreement, Astrid chuckled. "Maybe we can find a way to live side by side?"

"That's a brilliant sentiment," Hannah replied. "It sounds good... in theory. I mean humanity has never been good at working towards peace. Even before we unleashed the curse. Do you think we could learn it now?"

"Alafan prided himself on wiping out so many of our kind... I think we have no choice in the matter. We're no longer the top of the food chain."

As if to emphasize her point, there was a sudden low rumble and a loud clap of thunder, as the sky turned dark. The motorhome's lights flickered, and they peered out the window to see the upcoming storm. "What the hell?" Astrid asked, "Where'd that come from?"

"Uh oh!" Tash gasped, just in time for dark clouds to produce the instant heavy rainfall, which seemed to have come from out of nowhere. Bolts of lightning lit up the sky, offering a marvelous light display. "It looks like we succeeded in angering Zeus."

"Maybe Cruz found what he sought," Stacey suggested.

"Maybe Cruz is the reason for Zeus's sudden outburst," Astrid said. "Because that storm just doesn't feel natural."

***

The storm grew heavy, and the rain bucketed onto the roof of the motorhome. Flicking on the windscreen wipers, Samuel slowed the motorhome down as he struggled to see past the hood.

"We need to stop," Joey exclaimed. "We won't be able to make it through the storm." But Samuel was determined to make it to the next town before stopping again.

Raising his voice over the rain, he said, "There's nowhere to rest, Joe. We need to keep going."

But Joey was adamant. "If we do, then we'll all be killed. This storm isn't normal."

Fiercely glancing at him through the corner of his eye, Samuel gave in. "Alright, we'll stop," he grumbled, pulling to the side of the road, and turning off the engine.

Joey was right. The storm was like nothing they had seen in quite some time. The ground outside flooded quickly, as Samuel and Joey joined the others in the back.

"Did anyone pray for rain?" Joey asked, waiting for Samuel to take his seat across from Astrid.

"Not this time," Tash replied. "A few weeks ago, maybe. But this time it was to win the lottery."

"You know it isn't possible to win the lottery, these days," Stacey said.

"I do," Tash chuckled. "That's why I prayed."

As a bolt of lightning shot forth from the sky in the distance, it drew Astrid's attention. There was something so chaotic about it. "I don't think this storm is going to let up for a while," she said to the others.

Thanks to the storm, the moment had grown somewhat sombre. Even though they were going on faith that Hope was indeed okay, they still couldn't be sure about Cruz's wellbeing.

Knowing that Zeus had the power to control storms and that Cruz had been conversing with him was chilling to say the least.

Feeling uncomfortable over the awkward moment of silence, Tash held up a deck of cards. "Well, I guess we're all going to be waiting here for a while. Anyone up for a round of poker?"

"What are we betting this time, Martinez?" Samuel asked, "and no, we're not playing strip poker."

"Damn, that's why you're such a Buzzkill," Tash said with a smile as she stood to deal the cards on the table and gestured for everybody to play. Hannah and Stacey pulled a couple of chairs across and joined them at the end. As Stacey sat beside Tash, she sighed at her girlfriend, "You're only disappointed because I always lose."

"Dammit, she saw past my façade. Now, everybody, we're playing for mints. Because I found a whole pack in one of the cupboards. Joey? Buzzkill? You guys in?"

"Sure, I'm up for a game!" Joey said, examining the cards Tash had dealt him with a confident smirk to his face.

"Do those mints have an expiration date?" Hannah asked, taking her own cards, while gesturing to the bag of mints that Tash had placed on the table.

Having noticed that neither Astrid nor Samuel had taken their own cards, Stacey asked, "Are you guys playing?"

"What do you say, Sutherland?" Samuel smiled. "It could be fun." On his smile, Astrid couldn't help but mirror the flirtation in his voice.

"Alright, I'm in… as long as we keep it a clean game… clothes stay on… unless of course Samuel has the losing cards."

"Well, in that case, I don't mind losing to you." His immediate response forced the others to groan, but Astrid to grow a deep shade of scarlet.

***

Standing in the middle of the road amongst the chaotic storm, Cruz stood with his palms facing the sky as the winds around him blew with the strength of a thousand tornados.

His long hair hung in soaked dreads down his face and his clothes were drenched. But there was a smile to his face and delight which danced in his eyes for the freedom he felt.

He felt rejuvenated, refreshed and for the first time ever, he felt alive. Within his mind he heard the sheer voices of the gods, but most of all, he heard the voice of Zeus as clear as day.

After he had left Astrid, the night before, he had gone in search of Zeus, on his mission to find his daughter and he had in fact, spoken with Zeus. But, while the king of the gods had sent for Hope, the child had not arrived to him. The harpies had been stopped and she had gone elsewhere.

At first Cruz had felt that Zeus had lied to him about the whereabouts of his daughter. But now, Cruz knew otherwise.

There were about a thousand different voices in his mind, but it was the voice of a wise woman, in particular, that told him that Hope was safe.

Alas, Cruz had already accepted the first part of Zeus's deal, and in doing so, Zeus had unlocked a part of him that had remained dormant his whole life.

This storm that Cruz was standing in was of his own doing. He was not only a descendant of Zeus, but also a demigod and with Zeus's voice in his head, Cruz was currently learning how to use his new powers. To be able to channel every one of his emotions into a wild storm of his own creation felt euphoric.

As Cruz released another bolt of lightning with just the flick of his wrist, his smile shun even brighter. Amidst the rumbling thunder and the heavy pour of rain, Zeus called out to him. *'Now, Mario Cruz, I have done my part. You must assure me that you will carry out yours. When you are strong enough, I will seek you out again. Do you understand?'*

But Cruz was lost within his own creation. With this level of power, he finally felt strong enough to take on the world.

***

"No fair! You're cheating, Sutherland!" Tash whined as Astrid managed to play the girl out of mints, along with the rest of their friends once again. "How am I cheating?" Astrid laughed.

"You have divine intervention going on all up in there," Tash said, pointing a finger at Astrid's forehead for emphasis.

Stacey giggled. "Sure, Tash... divine intervention. I doubt they even had poker back in the Underworld. Did they, Astrid?"

Astrid shrugged, "Not that I know."

"Well, maybe Persephone was a psychic," Tash argued.

"Sorry, Tash. I don't think she was," Joey replied. "So, just face it, Astrid kicked your ass fair and square."

"Alright. Fine," Tash sighed. "Another round?" Upon getting to his feet, Samuel opened the overhead cupboard and said, "I would say 'yes'. But it looks like the storm has passed. You guys can play another round, I'm heading back to the cabin." Pulling a chocolate bar from the cupboard, Samuel made his way towards the front of the cabin as he continued speaking, "Remind me on our next supply run, to add chocolates to the list."

"Will do, Buzzkill," Tash said, while stealing the last chocolate before dealing another round of cards to those who were left sitting at the table.

Without looking up, Tash interrogated Astrid very swiftly. "So, now that he's gone... what were you and Sergeant Buzzkill doing up all night? I mean the ground was quite literally filled with flowers surrounding you both."

"I was wondering when this would come up," Astrid sighed.

Staring at her cards with an intriguing smile, Hannah added, "Well, you both were out there for hours in the blistering cold and neither of you froze. I think Tash might be onto something. You would've needed to be doing 'something' to keep your bodies warm."

Bursting into laughter at Hannah's observation, Stacey squealed in amusement. "Han! Do we really need to know the details?"

Tapping the table for Tash to hand her another card, Astrid shook her head. "No, we were honestly just talking. Samuel and I... well, it's complicated."

"Just as complicated as you and Cruz?" Tash asked as she handed over Astrid's next card, and then one to Joey too. Stacey and Hannah both placed their cards face down onto the table, but Astrid, Tash, and Joey continued playing.

"You could say that," Astrid replied.

Tash turned over the remaining cards on the table as Stacey insisted on keeping up the conversation.

"Do you love them? Both of them?"

Placing his cards face up on the table, Joey stood and made his way towards the front of the cabin. He had lost another round. "Okay, I don't need to be present for this female bonding session. I'm out!"

Because Astrid had managed to evade Stacey's question, Tash took it on board to ask again. "So, do you love them?"

Astrid placed her cards face up on the table, as did Tash. Astrid had won another round, but she was growing tired of the interrogation. "Can I just not answer that question?"

While Tash was annoyed that she had lost yet again, her smile grew even wider than before. She was thoroughly enjoying the conversation. "It's a simple question. You and Cruz have this intense, destined by the gods romance, while the chemistry between you and Samuel… Well, damn girl! That shit radiates the room."

"Tash, leave it alone," Hannah said, steering the reigns of the conversation. "Besides, have you thought about what we discussed last night?"

Looking from Tash to Hannah, that question piqued Stacey's attention. "What did you discuss, last night?"

Gathering the cards together and shuffling, Astrid asked without looking up, "It wasn't about me and my love life again, was it?"

Handing over the remaining cards to Astrid, Tash replied "No, not your love life this time, Sutherland. But considering we don't have television to binge on anymore, your love life is the closest thing we have to a telenovela. Just so you know, we were talking about how weird Joey is."

"Correction, how weird he has been acting," Hannah said. "...and about how he didn't really seem compelled by that Lamia, last night."

Astrid stopped shuffling and stared directly at Hannah, in concern. "What are you thinking? Is everything okay?"

Glancing over to ensure that Joey couldn't hear them, Hannah lowered her tone. "I hope so. But I just want to keep an eye on him. Maybe with you having a goddess hiding inside your mind, we might be able to find out if there is something wrong with him… and if so how to help him."

"Something wrong, like what? Like, maybe he's possessed or something?"

"Something like that."

Nodding, Astrid continued shuffling again. Hannah was her friend, there was no way that she could turn down her request for help. Furthermore, if there was something wrong with Joey, he was still one of them. She would help him any way she could.

"We can certainly try." Turning her gaze back to Joey she tried to piece together any clues. However, the voice inside her mind silently offered to reveal all in due time.

But Hannah couldn't hear the voice in Astrid's head. "Thanks," she said. Astrid dealt the next round of poker and they played for a few more hours until they had reached the next town. By then, the sky had cleared up to a cloudless blue.

The temperature was relatively warm, and they were all more than ready to soak in the fresh air. After parking the motorhome, Samuel stood in the doorway and addressed them all. "Alright guys, it's time to stretch our legs and look for supplies. We should also fuel up too, so we don't end up stranded before the next town. I would also like to give Sutherland an intro into training with swords. Last thing we need is her going into a battle unprepared."

"Sure thing Buzzkill," Tash sniggered. "That's exactly what you have planned."

"Martinez, you need to keep that mind of yours out of the gutter. If Astrid wants to stay alive, she needs to learn to train with a sword like the rest of us."

As Samuel led Astrid, Stacey, and Tash to a grassy patch just outside the vehicle, Joey and Hannah lingered just inside the doorway to talk quietly.

The abandoned town was filled with smashed up cars and rundown buildings. Graffiti lined the walls and they only prayed that they would find enough supplies to keep them going until the next supply run.

"It never gets any easier seeing the towns so... dead... like this." Stacey remarked as she looked around at the crumbled buildings. But then she noticed a street that had been completely left alone. And to her delight, there was a store with some dresses in the window.

Stacey's dismay turned into a glimmer of excitement. "Maybe we should split up and cover more ground," she said. "I can go in search for food... and maybe clothes."

With a laugh, Tash placed her arm around Stacey's shoulders and started leading her away. "I'll accompany my girlfriend and make sure she doesn't go overboard… or fall into a shopping trap, for that matter."

Chuckling to himself, Joey handed two blades to Samuel. "Then, I guess Hannah and I will refuel the Argo and go in search for medical supplies. We'll leave you two love birds to start your sparring match."

With a roll of his eyes, Samuel took the swords and handed one to Astrid, before leading her to the other side of the road, to a playground with a large patch of grass.

They walked in silence until he finally found an area which he deemed the perfect location.

Surprisingly, Samuel seemed nervous to be alone with Astrid again. In fact, his entire demeanour reminded her of a lovesick teenager going on a date. "We should perform a quick warm up, maybe, run a few laps first," he suggested, which forced Astrid to give into a fit of laughter. "What's so funny, Sutherland?"

Shaking off the humour of the situation, Astrid shook her head and loosened her shoulders.

"Nothing. Don't worry about it... and I'm feeling pretty warmed up anyway."

"You are?"

"Yeah. It must be Persephone."

Biting down on his lower lip, Samuel loosened his own shoulders to prepare himself. Breaking the silent tension between them, Astrid spoke up again.

"Where did you learn to use a sword? I never saw you using one under my father."

"I took a fencing class back in high school. I used to be a big fan of the medieval times and that was the closest thing I had to actually being a knight."

"A knight in shining armour, huh? So, that's why you joined the military. To be a heroic knight. I can actually picture you in all that armour."

"You can?" His question was accompanied by a flirtatious smile which made him look even more handsome.

Astrid nodded and gestured for him to go on, which he did. "So, then when all these creatures started to surface, I got to practicing again... It wasn't long until I was teaching the others."

Astrid looked around at the park, which once upon a time, would've been filled with children playing ballgames on the grass. It surprised her how much the soldier had evolved in the time she had known him. He never used to speak of his past, but now this was twice in two days.

Samuel glanced down at the sword in his hands, before turning his gaze back to Astrid. "It's ironic that the fair maiden happened to be my general's daughter. A strong woman capable enough to take down a centaur king. The furthest thing from a damsel in distress."

Caught in a blush, thanks to his words, Astrid was about to say something equally as witty until something caught her eye in the tree. Something that must have been there the whole time, yet she had only just noticed. There were birds. "What's caught your eye, Sutherland?" Samuel asked, staring in the same direction.

"The birds... It's a simple sense of normalcy."

"The birds and animals never disappeared. It was only ever the people."

"I know... don't mind me, it must be a 'Persephone thing'. Why don't we just get to training?" Loosening her shoulders again, Astrid stood with her weight evenly distributed on both feet. "Is this the best stance?" She asked, noticing the moment he pulled on his mentor persona.

"Yes. Now bring your sword up like this." He stood with his sword held steadily in front of him.

She mirrored him. "Like this?"

"Perfect. Now, I want you to come at me, I want to see your moves... Come on, attack me."

She did as he commanded, quickly bringing up her sword and swinging it in his direction, as he held his left arm behind his back and moved his own sword to block her move. There was a 'ching' as their blades met in the middle. She tried again, and he did the same thing, only altering his position just a little.

"Wow, you're good!" she smirked.

"It's kind of like dancing. Don't you think?"

"Dancing? Trust you to come up with that one. But then, I didn't think you could dance."

She continued to lunge at him, as he persisted to deflect every one of her attacks. "Well, it is. And I'm always up for a good dance if you're interested. But, anyway, you're not swinging your arm properly. It's supposed to be an art, not...whatever the hell you're doing there."

"What do you mean? How am I not doing it properly?" Astrid stopped maneuvering immediately.

"Watch this," he said, taking a few steps away from her and envisioning an invisible foe standing before him. He moved skilfully and swung his sword gracefully, but effectively.

"What do you know, Sergeant Buzzkill can dance!" Astrid grinned.

"I'm a man of many talents. I could surprise you. But now, you try... Come at me, again!"

Astrid did her best to mirror his performance, but once again he deflected every one of her attacks and shook his head.

"You're so ruthless, aren't you?" Stabbing his sword into the ground, he stood behind her and guided her hips with his hands into the right position before taking control of her right hand. "You need to calm yourself down, take it easy... but be fierce!"

He directed her to slice her sword through the air rhythmically, while keeping his hold on her left hip with his other hand. Astrid could barely focus on what she was doing.

With him standing so close to her, holding her the way he was, she could feel her emotions surge.

"We should stop, Samuel." She said, knowing full well that he too was feeling the tension.

"Just ignore the chemistry," Samuel said in a low gruff, as if he needed to clear his throat. "Don't let your emotions distract you, as that will be your undoing. Just focus."

Losing control of her own breath, Astrid brought her fingers to his left hand, on her hip. "How am I supposed to focus, Buzzkill? Especially when being this close to you after what you told me last night makes it so damn hard."

Astrid lowered her right arm, and dropped her sword to the ground, just as Samuel removed his grasp to her hand. She turned her body around to face him and peered right into his eyes.

"Ignore the tension, Sutherland," he stammered. "We should be training." But his words were empty. Neither one of them were able to focus on anything else but each other. As Samuel's hands moved to her lower back, Astrid brought her right hand to his jaw, losing herself in his blue eyes.

Samuel tilted his lips toward her, and Astrid stepped up on her tiptoes to close their gap. Instantly, his warm lips crashed against hers as he held her.

The intense rush which accompanied the need to have Samuel's fingerprints against her skin, forced her to hold him tighter than she even thought possible. With her heart threatening to pound right out of her chest, Astrid trailed her hands under his shirt, tickling the skin of his firm back.

Samuel's kiss passed from her lips and dotted along her jaw, teasingly, making its way towards her neck.

"Oh god," she moaned, like putty in his hand. But before they could escalate the moment further, Samuel pulled his lips away with a mere weakened whisper.

"We should... we should probably get back to training." Pulled back into the moment, Astrid opened her eyes. The want in his eyes mirrored her own. There were both battling against the power of their thirst for one another.

With a sheer smile, Astrid used that power to her advantage. She dotted his lips with small kisses between words.

"You're right," she said, lightly dragging her nails across his back. "We should stop doing this." On to her scheme, Samuel ran his own hand up the back of her shirt.

"You're trying to distract me, Sutherland... it's not going to work. Besides, two can play at that game." Once again, he was derailing her. To break the connection, Astrid stepped backward, bringing her hands up in defeat. "I feel so wounded that you would think that way."

"You feel wounded, do you? Well, let me apologize," Samuel replied, stepping forward to again break the distance. Caressing her chin, he gave his apology, stopping frequently to kiss her.

"I'm so… sorry… what was I… thinking?" Smiling up against his kiss, Astrid brought up her arm between them and in doing so, she brought up the blade of her sword so that the cold metal pressed against his chest.

Barely surprised, Samuel raised up his hands, defeated. "Nice trick. You got me… I never saw it coming." Darting in the opposite direction, he turned away for merely a second to retrieve his sword.

In unison, Astrid swung her sword in his direction, just as he lifted his own and swung it up, deflecting her attack. Astrid countered his attack with another, which once again, he deflected. They continued sparring until she felt that she was getting used to the rhythm.

After a while, Samuel brought up his sword and disarmed Astrid of her own. Holding his sword to her chest and her sword behind his back, Samuel positioned himself merely a breath away from Astrid.

"Okay, you win," she puffed. "I still have a lot to learn."

"Yes, you do. But for now, we need to head back, the others will be waiting for us." They jogged, in stride, toward the motorhome which Joey had parked on the side of the road. Neither of them, speaking about the kiss they had shared in the park. The complexity of the situation would need to wait for the time being.

***

Only a few hours later, they were all packed up and driving along the road again. The sun was setting over the horizon and rays of orange illuminated the dark sky.

Astrid had taken over the driving with Stacey sitting up alongside her. They had seen some old signs which had certainly seen better days. But now they had come to a crossroad with two signs. Astrid had pulled the vehicle to park on the side of the road. The crossroad forced Persephone to speak up within Astrid's mind.

'I promised you answers. You will find them if you take the road to the left... Just as you will find your daughter.' This time Astrid thought back to the goddess within her mind,

ensuring that only Persephone could hear her and not her friends.

'My daughter is there? Are you sure?'

'Yes, you need to trust me. Take the road to the left and all your questions will be answered.' Astrid knew that taking the road to the left was something that Samuel would not approve of, but this was bigger than all of them.

She turned to Stacey to inform her of the change of plans. "Hey Stace? Do you remember that time we took that road trip to Vegas?"

"Oh, that was fun! Remember that Elvis impersonator? And oh my god... those dancers! Of course, I remember. Why do you ask?"

"Well, I know we're supposed to be going to Samuel's old farm, but Vegas is only a few miles away... just a small detour..."

"But, there won't be anything fun or anyone there to tend to us... We passed through months ago and it had been brought to ruins. What's the sudden desire?"

"Well something tells me, that that's all changed and that we're about to receive all the answers we've been searching for."

"Does this have something to do with your extra passenger?" Stacey asked.

"Maybe."

Stacey nodded, "Well, I know better than to argue with you... But you do realize that Buzzkill will freak, don't you?"

"Yeah, and I'm okay with that. He's expecting me to disobey his orders... so, why should I disappoint him?"

Stacey's smile lit up her entire face. "Vegas, baby!"

Astrid grinned and repeated Stacey's words, "Vegas, Baby!" And without another word, she turned left at the crossroad and drove the motorhome all the way to Las Vegas.

CHAPTER SEVEN

As Astrid drove the motorhome to the outskirts of Las Vegas, there was no mistaking the lights in the distance that were visible against the darkness of the night. And judging by the flurry of high beams on the road, there was quite a commotion in the shimmering city. After having parked the motorhome to the side of the road to get a good view of what they were getting themselves into, Astrid marveled at the sight.

"I don't get it," Stacey gasped, "How are there so many people?"

"Where?" Samuel asked, approaching them from behind. "Why have we stopped?" Glancing out the windscreen, then back to Astrid, Samuel's frustration was very evident. "You took us to Vegas, Sutherland?"

"It was less me taking us, and more Vegas pulling us in."

A sudden rumble shook not only the motorhome, but also the earth around them, forcing their attention. Before Astrid could ask if it was an earthquake, a huge sandaled foot came crashing down directly in front of them, followed by another.

"Oh my god. That's a giant!" Astrid exclaimed, both equally terrified and excited. The giant passed them by, leaving them unharmed. But it only angered Samuel more.

"That's the reason we were staying as far from the cities as possible! I just wish you could follow my orders... just one damn order is all I'm asking for, Sutherland!"

"Well, I have an order!" Tash said, appearing beside Samuel. "Let's party in Vegas, baby!"

Ignoring Samuel, Astrid grinned and drove them into the beautiful sparkling city as fast as she could, until they reached a street filled with clothing stores, casinos, restaurants, and bright lights at every angle.

"Wait, Astrid! Stop here!" Stacey said abruptly.

"What, why?"

Stacey directed her to a shop that had mannequins draped in beautiful gowns displaying in the window. "We need to be dressed for the occasion," she said excitedly.

"Agreed!" Tash added. Astrid parked the motorhome on the side of the road, and the women all climbed out of the vehicle, eager to stare up at the store before them. Inside, there were women bustling around serving customers. "Well, it looks like they're in business," Tash exclaimed. She, Astrid, Stacey, and Hannah all bolted inside, as fast as they could, while Samuel and Joey remained outside shaking their heads.

"None of this feels right!" Samuel said. "There's just something wrong here. None of this seems at all logical. Why here and why now? Do you think it might have something to do with Persephone?"

Refusing to remove his eyes from Hannah in the window, Joey responded to Samuel. "What makes you think that?"

"Well, look at it this way. Las Vegas was one of the many cities that had fallen into chaos. It was destroyed.

But now, there are people everywhere. It's as if... as if it's all magical. It feels like a trap."

Glancing around them, Joey considered his words. "I think you might be right... look... there are mythological creatures here too." He pointed to a centaur that was walking side by side with a human. "...and over there." Next, he pointed to a group of beautiful women walking down the street. They had wings attached to their backs. "Despite the creatures, consider the fact that nobody here seems hell-bent on destruction. Like there's a sense of peace throughout this place. I think we should explore what the new Vegas has to offer, stock up and take the load off. Just for a little while at least."

For a long moment, Samuel seemed to be considering his words until finally he spoke. "Alright. I see your point."

"But on that note, maybe we should avoid the beautiful, winged women. I'd rather not be eaten alive."

"You're thinking sirens, aren't you? Okay, well that store looks like they have suits in there as well. Let's party in Vegas."

As they stepped into the store, where beautiful young women were catering to the girl's every need and adorning them with fine clothes and fancy jewelry, Samuel took note of the sales staff themselves.

"Something tells me that those aren't regular women either," he whispered to Joey, upon noticing the pointed ears that were hidden under their beautifully styled hair.

Biting down on his lip, Joey whispered back under his breath, "They're nymphs." But Samuel had already caught sight of a black suit on the far end of the room. One of the nymphs, a petite woman with dark skin, deep dark eyes and an innocent smile approached Joey and gasped. "You're here? Whatever you need, your majesty… I never thought I'd…"

Nervously, Joey spoke in a hushed tone. "…er, I think you have me mistaken for somebody else, miss." He pulled the woman behind a rack of dresses to speak privately. From behind the clothing rack, the woman gushed over Joey.

"No, I could never forget you. The way you would play the lyre, so beautifully. And that voice. You're making me feel all excited just hearing it. You might be wearing another's skin... but your aura is... Well, it's unmistakable." Annoyed, Joey whispered in a very hushed tone to the woman and thought that he had gone unnoticed.

Unfortunately, Hannah had been standing on the other side of the dress rack and she had heard them. Heartbroken, Hannah placed the dress that she had been holding, back onto the rack and stormed out the door. Joey, who had seen her leave, chased after her immediately. "Hannah! Hannah! Please, wait! Let me explain!" He managed to catch up to her just outside the window of the store and turned her to face him.

"What, Joey? Do you think I'm stupid? Those women in there... they weren't just ordinary women! How do they know you?"

Shaking his head, Joey agreed with her. "No, I know it doesn't make sense. I need you to trust me. I never wanted to hurt you."

"Trust you? I don't even know you! The Joey that I fell in love with. The man who watched everything that those monsters did to me... That's not you. So please, help me understand."

"I'm still me. I'm still... I'm still that man... Please, trust me. Because the only thing that needs to make sense is how we feel about each other. And how much I love you."

Cautious, Hannah held his gaze trying to determine just where he was going with his words. When he didn't speak up again, she asked. "What are you talking about? What's love got to do with this? Because I can't love somebody that I can't trust."

Taking her hands in his, Joey pleaded with her with tears in his eyes. "You can trust me. I would give up my life for you and that's saying something."

"So, tell me what it is you're hiding, Joey. What is it that you're keeping from all of us? Does Cruz even know?"

Joey shook his head. "No, Cruz doesn't know... and if he did, it could change everything entirely."

"Change everything? What does that even mean? I know that you weren't affected by the Lamia. And sometimes I wonder if you were ever really affected by rage when the curse first broke out, please just tell me, Joe. Let me try to understand."

Joey knew just how much he loved Hannah. But his secret could change everything. Not only could it change the way she felt about him, but it could change the very future of mankind. But, no matter what, it would not change his love for her. Joey trusted Hannah more than anybody. She was perfect, innocent in the grand scheme of things, and he loved her with his every breath.

"Okay, Hannah. I'll tell you... but, you need to swear... You need to promise me, that you'll keep my secret, no matter what happens."

Hannah studied him. "Of course! I promise. I'll keep it. Whatever it is, please just tell me. How big is this secret?"

"It's big... but even if you can't forgive me for keeping it from you and you choose not to stay with me any longer, you need to promise that you will still keep it. Please."

"Yeah, I promise." Joey stared deep into Hannah's brown eyes and brought his hand to her auburn hair, pulling her close, and whispered into her ear the secret he had been keeping from everybody since the dawn of time.

***

While Astrid allowed herself to be pampered by the three sales assistants, she noticed one brush her hair behind her ear, revealing it to be very pointy, and not at all humanlike. Before Astrid had the chance to question the young woman, Persephone spoke within her mind again. *'They are friends, Astrid. Nymphs. Do not be alarmed as they will not harm you.'*

'But I thought nymphs lived out with nature.' Astrid thought back.

'Normally, they do. But tonight is a special occasion and so, every creature of importance has been summoned. I feel that it will be the start of a new and peaceful era.'

'Does this have to do with my daughter?' Astrid asked. But Persephone did not respond. Instead, Astrid's thoughts were cut off by a blonde nymph holding up a beautiful royal blue gown and some elegant black heels. "Wow, it's beautiful," Astrid said. "But I really can't take it. We can't afford it."

"Nonsense, Astrid," the nymph replied. "These are gifts, this one was handpicked especially for you... It even has your name on it."

Glancing at the price tag, Astrid took the dress from the woman to study it much closer. Instead of a price, it did, indeed have her name on it. There was also a folded note pinned to the tag. Curious, Astrid unpinned the note from the dress and read. 'I knew you wouldn't be able to get comfortable without a change of clothes or a shower, *querida*. I even found one beautiful enough in your color.'

Reminded of the time that she and Cruz had first gone on the road together and were forced to spend the night in an old motel, Astrid smiled to herself. But then the thought, that Cruz had been to that store before them and was currently expecting them brought forth a shrill of glee. But how was that even possible? How could he have known that they were even there? Her instincts told her that it all had something to do with Zeus.

"Miss, would you like to try on the dress?" the nymph's bittersweet voice pulled her from her thoughts.

"Yes, I'd love to, thank you." Taking the dress, Astrid headed in the direction of the change rooms to try it on. With its low cut at the back, figure hugging style and perfect shade of blue, it made her look and feel like a princess. The best part was that it fit her perfectly. Astrid flickered her hair out past her shoulders, put on the heels and stepped out of the change room where Tash and Stacey were waiting in their own gowns. Stacey was dressed elegantly in a short white strapless dress, while Tash looked perfect in the long red one that she was in.

"Can you believe it, Astrid?" Stacey marveled. "These dresses had our names on them. They've even been paid for! They're so perfect!"

"I know, but where's Hannah?" Astrid asked.

"Um… I'm not sure," Tash replied, focusing her fixed gaze on Stacey. Gathering up the front of her dress, Astrid went in search for Hannah, whom she could see standing outside with Joey. They looked to be involved in a very serious conversation, so she thought it best to not disturb them. At least, Hannah would be safe with Joey.

Changing her mind, Astrid whirled back around in a bid to head back to the change rooms, only to come face to face with Samuel, who was dressed handsomely in a neat black suit and a white shirt. There were two buttons at the top of his collared shirt which he had left unbuttoned, revealing a hint of his bare, muscular chest. "Sutherland? Wow, you look..."

"Finish your sentence, wisely, Buzzkill."

"You look incredible. That dress is really... it's really you. But how are we going to pay for all this? According to those nymphs, these clothes had our names on them."

"It's already sorted, apparently." Slightly disappointed that he would ruin the moment by bringing up the issue of money, Astrid forced herself to remember that he was only being logical.

"Sorted, by whom? The nymphs?" While Astrid wasn't entirely sure how the clothes had been paid for, she thought that Cruz must've done something big to arrange all this. The thought that he could already be there, covering all their expenses intrigued her. She needed to find out more before she spoke of her assumptions to anybody.

"I'm not sure. But you told me to trust my instincts and right now, being here... it feels kind of right. It feels safe. So, let's just go with it."

"Alright. I'll follow your lead. But please stay vigilant. Okay? The last thing we need is an entire city of monsters out for our blood." Offering him the hint of a smile, Astrid attempted to pass him, but he placed his hand on her arm to stop her. "You really do look beautiful, Sutherland. Maybe we should go out dancing tonight or something."

"Maybe." Without another word, she made her way back toward the change rooms to join Stacey and Tash.

***

With the gowns, suits, shoes, and accessories in hands, the group made their way to an elegant hotel, which just like the rest of Vegas, was filled with not only humans but also many different mythological creatures. It was as if they had all just stepped out of a history book. The group was also provided with beautiful suites, which once again had already been paid for in advance.

"I could grow to love this," Tash commented, as she, Stacey and Astrid led Samuel, Hannah and Joey through the hotel.

"They're treating us like queens," Stacey replied. "Next thing you know they'll be feeding us grapes on beds of silk. Let's not ask too many questions in case they change their minds and make us pay for everything... or we wake up and this is all just a dream." With a smirk at Stacey's comment, Astrid turned her head back to see Hannah trailing behind, by herself.

She stopped and shifted to the side, allowing Samuel and Joey to pass her as she waited for Hannah to catch up, only to realize that the woman had been crying. "Hey, Han. Is everything okay?" Before Hannah could respond, Joey turned to face them, giving Hannah a concerned look.

Hannah shook her head at Astrid and shrugged. "Everything is fine. I don't know what you're talking about."

Having seen Joey's concerned look, Astrid stared at Hannah and wished that she had only possessed some sort of telepathic ability to read their minds, but unfortunately, she didn't. "Alright, Han. But, if you need anything, I'm in the room across from you." Hannah nodded, but followed Joey into their own room, where they both disappeared, closing the door behind them.

"What's wrong with those two?" Samuel asked.

"I'm not sure. I think they might have had an argument."

"Well, this is our room," Tash said standing outside the door next to Hannah and Joey's suite. "Let's go check out the spa, Stacey. We'll meet you guys downstairs later. I saw a sign earlier, that there's meant to be some big show on tonight... maybe that's what the dresses are for."

After a moment's awkward hesitation, they escaped into their room, leaving Samuel and Astrid out in the hallway, entirely alone. "Well, they were in a rush," Samuel joked.

"Yeah. They were. I just can't get over how..."

"...how much this all feels like some big dream? I'm right there with you. Which reminds me, we should get back to training tomorrow morning. We don't know what else might be coming our way."

"Agreed. Every important creature has been summoned here."

"How do you know that?"

"It was just something that Persephone said earlier."

"And you didn't care to tell me sooner? Why didn't you mention this to me at the store?"

Astrid thought back to her earlier reasons as to why. Her main reason was because she felt that Cruz was behind it all. But she just couldn't determine how. Evading eye contact with Samuel, she apologized. "I'm sorry. But I've just been trying to figure it all out by myself."

"Let me guess, it's something you would have told Cruz, right away."

"Where's this hostility coming from?"

"I'm sorry. I guess I'm just exhausted," Shaking his head, Samuel attempted to flee into his room, but Astrid held him back. "No... What's going on, Samuel?"

"I said don't worry about it. Can we just let it go?"

But she wasn't convinced. His usually strong demeanour had certainly been shaken by something. It was as if he was bursting to say more. "This isn't just about me disobeying orders, is it?" she asked. "Please, just talk to me."

Then suddenly, Samuel's entire facade change. A weakness in him he had been hiding for so long became unveiled. "Do you really want to know, Astrid?"

"Yeah, I do."

Unleashing a low sigh, Samuel finally broke. "Alright fine, I'm just over all of this. Our kiss today was amazing... that night we spent back in Greece... I would give anything to relive it over... and not just that night, but also the next day. I would've stopped you from looking for Cruz. But let's face it. He is the only reason that you and I aren't together. When he's around, it's almost like you both have your own little world and the fact that you have a kid, well it solidifies that. But still, it doesn't stop me from wanting you. But unfortunately, try as we might, you and I will never have a normal relationship. Will we?"

"Samuel, that's not very fair, I..." her voice trailed off.

"See? You can't even finish your sentence... You love Cruz, I get that, but sometimes I just wish things were different. You and I could be amazing together, Sutherland. I just wish you could see..." Before Samuel could finish his sentence, they were interrupted by the click of a door and Stacey's sudden announcement.

"We're getting married!"

"I'm sorry, what?" Astrid stammered.

"This hotel has a chapel," Tash said, joining her. "So, we're tying the knot, tonight."

"Are you sure?" Samuel asked, irritated by their interruption. "This place is swarming with..."

"Yeah, yeah, yeah... swarming with mythological creatures... the end of the world... blah, blah, blah... Don't Buzzkill the moment... We're doing it, regardless. You should be happy for us!"

"I am happy for you," Samuel said, adopting a softer approach. "It's just... Well, it's a surprise, that's all. Are you sure you really want to do this? Tonight, of all nights?"

"Hmm... Am I sure I want to marry the woman I love? Of course, I am! Don't tell me that if you had the chance to marry As..." Tash instantly held her tongue mid-sentence as she looked over at Astrid.

Knowing exactly what Tash had been about to say, Astrid decided to intervene. "If you girls want to do this, we'll be there. You can count on it." Stacey let slip a high-pitched squeal as she grabbed hold of Astrid's arms and began jumping on the spot, as Astrid joined in on her excitement.

"Congratulations, Stacey!"

Stacey pulled away from her and grinned. "Thanks... Oh, and Astrid, you have no choice but to be my maid of honor! So, go and get ready... I'm wearing my new dress!"

"I'd be honored, Stace. Alright, just let me go and shower and I'll be right out."

Astrid entered her suite and shut the door behind her. The room was huge, complete with a king-sized bed draped in golden linen, a black-tiled bathroom to the left, a balcony, and even a bar. Slightly relieved to have been rescued from her conversation with Samuel, she pressed her back against the wall and sighed, taking sight of a flier sitting on the bed. Curious, Astrid made her way over and picked it up to read. 'Tonight, will be a night to remember. The dawn of a new era. Let there be peace.'

On the back, there was a time and a location. It must've been the event that Persephone had told her about. But as she went to place the flier back onto the bed, she noticed a hand scribbled message at the very bottom of the page. '*Mi amor*, meet me tonight before the ceremony. Come alone!' There was no doubt in her mind, that she would finally receive all the answers she sought later that night.

CHAPTER EIGHT

Having been tasked with purchasing the rings, Samuel and Joey found that the streets were ever bustling with activity. Crowds of people and creatures all in a rush to get somewhere, which astonished Samuel at just how many people had actually survived the deadly sin curse. But what really pulled Samuel's attention was the fact that there didn't appear to be any danger, whatsoever, in Las Vegas. It was as if some sort of protection spell had been placed on the entire city.

"Shouldn't Tash and Stacey be doing this?" Joey asked, breaking Samuel from his thoughts. "It's their wedding."

"You can't expect tradition when it comes to Tash," Samuel replied, hoping that would be a good enough answer for Joey.

"I suppose so." Samuel was about to continue speaking, when he was shouldered by a passer-by that he felt he recognized. He stopped and scanned the crowd, but the person had disappeared entirely.

"Are you alright, soldier boy?" Joey asked, stopping two feet ahead.

"That was Cruz," Samuel said, scanning the crowd.

"Cruz? Are you sure?" Joey asked, looking around. "Why would he be here?"

"I'm not sure. Perhaps the same reason we were brought here?" Confused as to whether he had actually seen Cruz, or his mind was playing tricks on him, Samuel brushed it off.

"I heard your argument with Astrid, earlier," Joey said. "It's no wonder you thought you saw him. He has you paranoid."

Joey's comment was enough to send Samuel's frustrations on fire. "And we know all about the argument you had with Hannah. So, why don't we just leave it be, alright Joey?"

"Fair point." Joey led Samuel inside the brightly lit store filled with jewelry in white and gold glass cabinets.

After having taken a few moments to scan cabinets filled with fancy engagement and wedding rings, Samuel spotted a set he knew would be perfect for the occasion. They were both golden, but while one was a simple yet elegant band, the other had a perfect diamond heart built into the band, and two diamonds on either side. "These will do."

"You're sure?" Joey asked.

"Positive. I know Tash and Stacey loves the finer things."

Standing on the other side of the counter, was a very pretty, dark-skinned woman with long dark braids and hypnotically grey eyes. She barely looked much older than them. "May I help you?" she asked, with an accent that was somewhat hard to place.

Samuel pointed down at the rings and glanced back up at the woman. "Can we just get these two right here?"

The woman stared hard at Joey as he stared right back. A large wall of tension sat between them, which was highly unmissable. "They're for some friends of ours," Joey stammered. Clearly, he had wronged this woman at some point in time. Samuel and the woman both gave

Joey an awkward glance, but he shrugged it off. The woman packaged up the rings, but her eyes did not break contact with Joey.

"Do you two know each other?" Samuel asked, slightly amused by the display. Avoiding his eye, Joey stared down at the counter.

"No, Samuel, I've never met her before in my life." With a scoff, the woman ignored Joey entirely and addressed Samuel. "So, what are the ladies' names?"

"Names?"

"Yes. What are the names of the ladies getting married?"

Stumped, Samuel tried to determine the woman's agenda. Sure, Joey had mentioned the rings were for their friends, but neither of them had said that it was Tash or Stacey. Samuel glanced at Joey, who now had his back to the counter and the woman.

"Is that for engraving purposes?" Samuel asked, his eyes narrowing, "Or, something else?"

"Engraving purposes, of course."

Before Samuel could persist, Joey turned back to the woman to take the reign of the conversation. "If you must know, their names are Stacey Raymond and Natasha Martinez. But, whatever you do, don't write Natasha on the ring. We all know her as Tash. Okay?"

Samuel witnessed the entire shift in the woman's demeanour at Joey's tone of voice. Or maybe it was what he had said. Regardless, there was a sincere solemn expression that had come over her. "Seriously, Joey?" Samuel snapped at his friend. "Where the hell did that come from? I don't care what went down between the two of…"

But the woman held up her to stop Samuel. "It's okay. I take it the decision for these two ladies to get married was a very sudden decision. Of course, it would be. Why else would they be doing it here in Vegas on this special night of all nights?"

"What special night are you referring to?" Samuel asked. She curled her smile up at Joey. "What? You never told him, Herm... er, Joey?"

Joey glared at the woman. His fists were clenched down by his sides and voice strained through gritted teeth. "How could I, when I have no idea what the hell you're talking about?" But the woman ignored his anger. In fact, she seemed delighted to be angering him.

"Because as far as I've heard a new god will be crowned... or so the rumors go... This new god will bring about a new era. Those creatures out there and humankind will all walk hand in hand. It will be a new beginning for the earth."

At that moment, Samuel remembered the very words that DR Reynolds had spoken back in the ruins. "There has to be some kind of mistake," Samuel said becoming very aware of his own rising frustration. "How is that even possible? Humanity is dying out. Have you been hiding under a rock for the past year?"

"Oh, that's all according to rumour. The designated heroes will change all of that... But we're safe here in the city. I won't charge you for the rings. Love should always be free."

"Yeah, that sounds like something from out of a fairy-tale," Joey grumbled. "Samuel, let's go. If we don't hurry up the girls will be getting married without these things." On his final words, Joey led Samuel out the store, without even thanking the woman for the rings. Once they had made it back into the street, Samuel couldn't hold his curiosity in anymore. "What the hell was that all about, Joey? And don't tell me you don't know her. Because she sure as hell knew you!"

"Okay, yes... I do know her, she's an old ex. And as you can tell, we didn't end things on the best of terms. It was a long time ago. Long before I met Hannah."

"An ex? Well, what was she talking about? What's this about a new god? DR Reynolds said something along those lines after... after..."

"Before Stacey killed him? Yeah... but, it's probably just some gimmick to celebrate the mythological creatures... its Vegas after all. Anything's bound to happen." As Joey took off in the direction of the hotel, Samuel was left doubting that Joey was telling the full truth. There had to be more to Joey's story than he was letting on.

***

In Tash's hotel room, Hannah had been helping Tash with her hair and makeup in preparation for the wedding. While Tash sat in front of her mirror in her red gown, Hannah neatly pinned her hair out of her face. Even though it had been Tash that had popped the question to Stacey, she was now far more nervous than that time she delivered her valedictorian speech in high school. Normally, she would deflect her nervous tension with jokes, but right now she couldn't even think of a simple 'knock-knock' joke.

"So, don't keep me in suspense, Han... What's the deal with you and Joey?" Smiling at their reflections, Hannah secured the last pin into Tash's hair.

"There's nothing to tell. We just had a minor argument. I thought he was checking out that pointy-eared woman earlier and got a little jealous. That's all."

Tash laughed. But it wasn't her usually confident laugh. "Are you sure that's it? It's so hard to picture you as the jealous type."

"Positive, now stop deflecting your anxieties just because you're nervous."

"Me? Nervous? I don't know what you're talking about."

"You're about to marry the woman you love and declare it to the rest of the world and you're not nervous?"

"Not helping, Hannah. Besides, while we're on the topic of weddings… you and Joey have been together for quite a while, when do you think you'll get married?"

With a far off look in her eyes, Hannah sprayed more than enough hairspray in Tash's hair to freeze it permanently before setting the can down beside them. "Not, right now. Let's just take things one day at a time, shall we? It's your wedding and if my knowledge serves me correctly, you have the chapel for eight-fifteen. We have twenty minutes to get down there." Hannah stared at her watch and added, "I'll pop my head into the hallway and make sure that Astrid and your lovely bride aren't in there, okay?"

While Tash had a tendency to overstep many boundaries, she felt that she had certainly done so in Hannah's case. For a woman who always seemed to be so caring and conservative, the anger in Hannah's tone had certainly been unmissable. Hannah peered her head into the hallway, then grinned back at Tash. "Okay, we're good to go! Now take one last look in the mirror and come with me."

Hannah led Tash down to the hotel's chapel, where they met with Joey and Samuel outside the waiting area. The minute Tash laid her eyes on Samuel, she pulled him aside to ask him a very important favor in private. "Hey, Buzzkill?"

"Are you okay? What's wrong?"

Taking a very deep and nervous breath, Tash chose her words carefully. "Do you remember the moment that we first met?"

"Yeah. We found you in that closet. Why?"

"Well, that was a big moment for me. I had lost my family, and you were the one who found me. You made me feel safe and you became like a brother to me... you and Cruz both... and I know, this isn't the time to bring him up... because, we have no clue where he is, and because of the drama with him and Astrid... but, man. This is just so hard." She wiped the inconvenient tears away from her eyes, trying to not mess up her mascara, as Samuel put his arm around her shoulder.

"Hey, what's going on, Tash? You're getting married in less than ten minutes. You need to pull yourself together."

Tash took a deep breath, "Okay. Pulling myself together. Alright, so… Will you be my… hmm… I'm not exactly a groom, but you're the closest person I'd ask to be a bridesmaid… Actually, Sutherland is… but, she's taken..."

As if he was blessed with mind-reading capabilities, Samuel smiled and said, "I'd be honored, Tash. Now, they're opening the doors. You're up next."

Linking his arm through hers, Samuel led Tash toward the doors just as they opened, while Hannah handed her the fake bouquet from the vase beside the door. The moment they saw the woman standing in the open doors of the chapel, Samuel and Joey's eyes instantly stared in stunned surprise.

"Joey, it's your ex," Samuel said.

On his words, Hannah's eyes gaped in bewilderment as she stared at the beautiful, dark-skinned, pale-eyed woman in the elegant black gown. "Joey's ex?"

Tash giggled in amusement. "Really? Joey dated our Aphrodite impersonator celebrant. Damn! This show is getting good."

"You're going with a Greek mythological theme?" Samuel asked her quietly. "You never mentioned that."

"It seemed kinda fitting. Don't you think? What, with the Greek Mythology Apocalypse and all. It's just too bad we couldn't get the actual Aphrodite goddess, know what I mean?"

Drawing all their attention, the Aphrodite 'Impersonator' looked up and smiled. Her voice came across as bittersweet, though somewhat impatient. "Welcome to Aphrodite's chapel of love. Is everybody here?"

Mentally preparing herself, Tash replied, "My bride to be and her maid of honor will be down shortly. Do we need to pay for the services now, or later?"

"Oh, this one's on the house, my dear. Now, why don't you all come in, so we can get set up. Tash, was it?"

"Yes, that's right," Tash replied, amazed that the woman already knew her name. Nonetheless, the group followed Aphrodite into the chapel as they prepared for the arrival of Stacey and Astrid.

***

Astrid could sense Stacey's nervousness from the moment they had left her suite. They were headed towards the chapel, but before they could even reach the doors, Stacey came to an abrupt stop, forcing Astrid to do the same. "Stacey, what's wrong? Are you okay?"

Stacey's hair was long and straight, and she was wearing a delicate tiara neatly positioned on the very top of her head. But this time, her eyes were bloodshot. Fearful. And she was trying desperately to wipe the tears away without smudging her makeup. "I don't know if I can do this. Get married in the middle of an apocalypse. Am I doing the right thing?"

Astrid's concerns turned to relief as she wiped Stacey's tears away carefully with her thumbs. "Do you remember that time in high school when Brent asked me to prom?"

Stacey nodded. "You really had it bad for him. Somebody needed to knock some sense into you."

"He was handsome, yes. But do you remember how you knocked that sense into me?"

As the memory flashed through Stacey's mind, she was met with a confused expression. "I don't know. I know I told you that I didn't trust him. That there was something about him that didn't feel right."

"That's exactly what you said. While all I saw was the unbelievably hot school's quarterback asking nerdy old me to prom, you saw him for who he really was. Despite being really annoyed by what you said, I listened to your intuition and turned him down. But do you know what happened to Sara Laurence when she accepted his offer?"

Stacey's expression grew cold. She certainly did remember. "Yeah, I do. That poor girl."

"Thing is, that could've been me. By listening to your intuition, I saved myself from that hell. My point is, when you said yes to Tash it was your intuition and your love for her that said yes. You love Tash everybody knows that. Whether we're living in an apocalypse or not, you owe it to yourself to listen to your intuition and to be happy. Do you understand?" Stacey's happiness finally emerged from her sorrow, forcing her to hug Astrid tightly before backing away again.

"Sometimes I hate that psychology skill of yours, Astrid."

Happy to have helped, Astrid grabbed Stacey's hand. "Come on, the others are waiting for us." Astrid led Stacey to the doors, then looked back at her beautiful friend, wishing her luck.

It was time for the happiest moment of Stacey's life. Astrid entered the chapel, but before she could even take in any of her scenery, Persephone's voice rang through her mind once again. *'There is one thing you need to know. That woman is really the goddess, Aphrodite.'* She almost tripped over her own heels as she looked to the celebrant performing the ceremony. It was almost as if there was a bright blue aura surrounding the woman, which was what caught Astrid's attention immediately. After retaking her balance. Astrid made her way toward Tash at the end of the altar, basking in Tash's smiling face as she hugged her before taking her place in the maid of honor position, beside the goddess in the black gown. As Aphrodite smiled at Astrid, she felt as if she was in the presence of royalty, which technically, she was.

"Hello Astrid," Aphrodite spoke under her breath, forcing her to nod towards Tash.

Astrid's eyes glanced over at Samuel who mouthed an apology for their earlier conversation, but she evaded his eye and turned to watch as Stacey elegantly walked down the aisle, like a supermodel on a catwalk.

There was a beautiful song that had only been released a few years before the pithos had been opened. It was all very typical Stacey. As Stacey reached the altar, she hugged Astrid and took her place beside Tash.

"Good evening, ladies and gentlemen... I am Aphrodite! We are gathered here to celebrate the beautiful union of these two souls. Natasha Martinez and Stacey Raymond. Now, I believe that everybody deserves to love and be loved by the person that they so choose..." As Aphrodite continued with her speech, Astrid could feel the sadness inside of herself. But it wasn't coming from her own emotions, it was coming from Persephone.

She remembered the tale that Joey had told them, and she understood perfectly just why Persephone had clung to her in a bid to escape the Underworld. Astrid thought back to what Samuel had been trying to tell her, earlier. It didn't take a mind reader to know what his next words would have been. But Samuel was right. No matter how much she loved Samuel, they would never be able to experience a normal relationship. And not only because they were in the midst of an apocalypse, but because of just how much she loved Cruz.

'It can't be easy for either one of us,' Persephone said, as if on cue. *'You are torn between the soldier and the descendant of Zeus who snuck into the ceremony earlier and has been watching your every move.'*

On her words, Astrid looked towards the doors, where Cruz was standing, dressed in a neat black suit and a white shirt. There was a red rose in his jacket pocket and his long hair was pulled back into a ponytail. He had certainly dressed up for the occasion, and it made Astrid's heart melt seeing him looking so handsome. He had clearly heard the news that Tash and Stacey were getting married, but the question of how, was what intrigued her. But what was more, it was as if there was something different about him. Just as she had seen the blue aura surrounding Aphrodite, there seemed to be one surrounding him too. *'Persephone, what's going on with Cruz?'*

'I have merely unlocked some of your true abilities, Astrid. You are seeing the aura that surrounds his very soul. It is the same with Aphrodite and the man you have come to know as Joey.' Before Astrid's eyes could snap to Joey, Aphrodite's voice pulled her from her thoughts.

"Now, who has the rings?" Startled, Astrid reached into her clutch purse and pulled out the ring that Joey had slipped to her before the ceremony. She handed it to Stacey, who started speaking her own vowels that she had spent the whole half hour working on.

"Natasha Martinez, I never thought it would be possible to find someone that I would love more than my best friend... sorry, Astrid..." Stacey paused for a moment but continued on. "But I have. I met you. After Cruz saved us from that prison cell, I got back to the camp, and we met. I felt that my life was over, but you granted me with the hope and courage to believe that there was a light even in the darkest of times..."

Astrid continued to focus on the wedding with a sense of excitement, every so often, smiling over at Tash whose eyes were entirely on Stacey. It was sweet knowing that her two best friends had found each other in the middle of an apocalypse.

Tash was clearly nervous, but she spoke confidently, regardless. "When Buzzkill first found me, I was scared and alone and I thought that that was how I would die. The world was quite literally going to shit... Pardon my French... but, I would never have expected to find the woman that I was meant to be with, out in the very midst of it all. A flower in the middle of a weed garden... and that's what you are to me, Stacey. So, whatever this world is going to bring us... we've quite literally seen curses, harpies, Cyclopes, lamias, centaurs... shit, we're even dealing with gods... but, whatever comes along our way, I'll be happy knowing that I found you among it all."

Astrid wiped away a few tears that had formed in her eyes, while refusing to look up. She could feel the pull of both Cruz and Samuel's gazes on her. Instead, she looked to Aphrodite, to conclude the ceremony. By the time the wedding had finished, Cruz had made his way towards them, immediately pulling Stacey and Tash into warm hugs.

***

Upon noticing his presence, Joey immediately led Cruz to the back of the chapel to interrogate him in private, but Cruz really wasn't in the mood. "What the hell, Cruz? We've been worried sick about you!"

"Oh, cut the crap, Joe! I know your big secret. I can't believe you lied to me after all these years. We've been friends since... well, I thought it was our whole lives... But it's nice to know that that's not actually the case. Is that even your real face?"

Gob smacked by Cruz's words, Joey groaned. "You know? Of course, you know... You're hosting the big celebration tonight, aren't you?"

"Actually, no... That's not my doing. But at least we know that Hope is safe. Does Astrid know?"

"About you or the ceremony?"

Glancing over at Astrid in the distance, Cruz mumbled under his breath so that only Joey could hear. "Man, this is going to destroy her. How do we tell her?" Before either of them could come up with a worthwhile strategy, to break the news to Astrid, they were interrupted by Samuel. "What's going to destroy her?"

"Such a Buzzkill, as always," Cruz mumbled.

But Samuel was unaffected by Cruz's ignorance.

"What's going to destroy her, Cruz? Where the hell were you? Don't you know how worried sick Astrid has been?"

"For your information, I met up with some centaurs and they led me here. And to answer your earlier question, I'm leaving, that's what will upset Astrid, but I'm guessing it'll keep you happy."

But the look on Samuel's face gave Cruz the impression that he was anything but happy for the news. "Is it to find Hope? Or are you leaving for good? Whatever, it doesn't matter. You can't leave. We're a team, remember? Or have you forgotten that?"

"Why, Samuel? It sounds like you're worried about me."

Samuel's blue eyes narrowed at Cruz. His patience was growing thin incredibly fast. "Look, this isn't my business. Just go and talk to Astrid." They turned to see Astrid, Stacey, Tash, and Hannah all in pleasant conversation with Aphrodite. Disrupting her current state of happiness was the last thing any of them wanted to do.

***

Astrid had just spent the last few moments congratulating Tash and Stacey on their wedding along, with Hannah and Aphrodite, right before Aphrodite had stunned Tash and Stacey with the news that she was in fact, the actual goddess of legend.

Astrid noticed, however, that Hannah did not seem surprised in the slightest. As Stacey and Tash gushed to Hannah about how an actual goddess had performed their ceremony, Aphrodite pulled Astrid away to speak in private.

"I know that you carry the spirit of Persephone within you," she began. "But do either of you understand just how much danger you are in?"

"Oh, I can imagine," Astrid smirked. "I'm doubting Hades will just let her go so easily."

"Well, Demeter is also here. She has some information on behalf of your daughter, from one mother to another. You already know that she's here, don't you?"

"I do, I just heard."

"Well, then you and Mario Cruz should seek them both out before you miss your opportunity. Oh, and Astrid?

Take it from me, you have two men equally pining for your favour. A powerful woman such as yourself, should not limit herself to just one."

Embarrassed by the woman's forward nature, Astrid's cheeks flashed a crimson shade. "I'll… err… I'll bare that in…"

But before she could finish, Aphrodite continued on with an almost vindictive tone. "Humanity wouldn't have needed the intervention of the gods if they had only understood that love need not be caged like an animal but shared willingly."

Eager to break away from the conversation, Astrid excused herself to speak with Cruz. She was fortunate, that Aphrodite was determined to speak with Stacey in private, just the same. Unsure where to begin, Astrid approached Cruz, who immediately pulled her into a tight embrace.

Although it had only been a day or so since they had last seen one another, it felt like it had been forever. And as Astrid breathed the captivating musk of his cologne, she wished that he might never let her go. Furthermore, the thought that both he and Hope were okay made her entire body jitter with excitement. "How did you get here?" she asked, finally pulling away. "I thought you weren't going to meet me until later."

But his delight to see her immediately turned into an uncertainty of where to start his explanation.

"Well, that was the original plan, but then I overheard Samuel and Joey talking on their way to pick up the rings and I couldn't miss Tash and Stacey's wedding. Could I?"

"I suppose not. Did you know Hope is here?"

"Yeah, I did. Have you seen her? She's gotten so big."

"No, I haven't seen her. What do you mean 'big'? It's only been a day."

Taking her by the hands, Cruz started towards the doorway, struggling to articulate his thoughts into words.

"Maybe we should leave for the ceremony now. There's so much you don't know. I'm just glad you're wearing the dress I picked. It was all paid for because of our daughter."

But Astrid was determined for him to provide her with an answer. "What do you mean, Cruz? What the hell is going on?"

"Okay, you guys," Stacey said with major irritation in her tone. "We have this big celebration thing to get to... Let's just... let's just go." As Stacey led the others out of the chapel, Astrid forced Cruz to stay behind.

"Cruz, please just tell me what's going on!"

Breathing out a low and controlled breath, Cruz looked as if he was preparing himself for a battle he might not walk away from. "Okay, so Hope has been with Demeter. But you need to remember that she was born during a curse, with me as her father and you as her mother. So, she was always going to be special... but, we didn't anticipate just how special she would be..."

"Just spit it out. What's wrong with her?"

Cruz nodded. "The gods have been feeding Hope ambrosia and other stuff that is a little too grueling for my liking."

"What?!"

Cruz offered Astrid a sympathetic smile. He had never been great with words or expressing himself in general, that was Astrid's strength. But now he needed to explain the most important news in a way that she could understand. In a way that didn't make any sense to him either. "That's just the thing, Astrid. She already was immortal. When I opened the pithos, mine and your powers were unlocked. We just didn't know. But then, Zeus taught me how to channel them. I was able to create a storm and..."

Astrid shook her head. "I'm sorry, I'm having a hard time understanding."

"Astrid, you and I... We're demigods and our baby... well, she is too. I only just found out all of this before I came to the wedding. This celebration is to celebrate our daughter. She will bring peace to this earth and..."

"What the actual fuck?" Astrid was stunned speechless. "I'm not a demigod, Cruz. I don't have powers. Neither do you. Okay? If that was the case, we would've been able to stop the curse last year."

"I wish that was the case. Especially after everything I put everybody through. But the only reason we weren't able to do anything was because we didn't know how to channel our abilities."

Astrid's eyelids closed long enough to soak in the tears that had emerged. She had no idea what to say. Everything that Cruz was saying sounded absolutely insane. But what made matters worse, was that he was the only person in the world who could say such things and she would never doubt him. He was her weakness. Astrid allowed for Cruz to pull her into his arms. "Come with me," he said softly, "Let me show you."

CHAPTER NINE

With Cruz's hand pressed supportively against Astrid's back, the two followed Aphrodite to a very large and elegant Greek church adorned in gold and white stone, where their child was being kept. The stage was lined with an array of beautifully colored-flowers of every different kind, and in the middle of it all, stood three thrones of solid gold. In front of the stage a young girl of about three years of age with long dark hair, dark eyes and lightly tanned skin, playfully ran about the seats chasing an older woman with long strawberry blonde hair. They were both draped in white gowns. Upon seeing them, Astrid stopped stunned, instantly knowing who both those people were. The woman was Demeter. The goddess mother of Persephone and the child was in fact, Hope.

"I will leave you," Aphrodite said, heading towards the exit.

"Mama! Papa!" the young child ran towards them, forcing Astrid to crumble to her knees as her daughter ran right into her arms. Seeing her daughter having grown up so fast in such a short amount of time, forced Astrid to experience a serious combination of mixed emotions. Hope was technically barely a year old, yet there she was, in the body of what looked like a three-year-old girl. Astrid hugged the child, picking her up as she stood again to greet Demeter. The goddess saw right past Astrid's face and immediately spoke to Persephone with tears of happiness glistening down her pale face. "As pleased as I am that you are here, Persephone. You are only putting this woman in danger." Controlling Astrid's voice to address her mother, Persephone responded with such sheer excitement.

"I didn't have a choice, mother. But I am willing to keep Astrid safe at all costs, provided she allows me to stay with her."

"Are you sure about this, Persephone?"

"Yes, mother. Just until we can find a way to change the will of Hades."

"And what of you, Astrid?" Demeter asked, shifting her gaze only slightly. "How do you feel about this offer? You are very blessed to have the spirits of two goddesses working through you. But you still have a say in the matter."

Feeling Persephone's compulsion subside, Astrid felt the sheer weight of shock from not only Persephone's ability to control her, but also due in part to Demeter's words. "I'm sorry, did you just say two goddesses? What do you mean?"

But Demeter merely shook her head. "All in due time, child. But what do you say? Will you allow my daughter to walk within you, if only for a short time?"

Completely baffled, Astrid gave into defeat. "I suppose so. Yes, I agree." Just maybe she could at least get the answers she sought from Persephone later.

Demeter nodded. "Well then, so be it. Now, I believe you have questions in relation to your child. So, let me answer all your questions at once. Since the day the pithos was opened, it caused the return of many beasts and some of the lesser favourable gods and because of that, there is now a war brewing. But those of us who have congregated here, want a peaceful world, and your child represents all of that. Thanks to you and Mario Cruz, she is the one who will seek to lead the mortals into this new era. Hope was brought here for her protection because we could not risk the alternative."

"The alternative?" Cruz asked, from beside Astrid.

Demeter studied him closely. "As the champion of Zeus, I am surprised he has not told you."

From Astrid's perspective, Cruz looked to be harbouring a silent war within himself. "No, he didn't. But is Hope safe here?"

A slight glimmer of a smile reflected in Demeter's cheek "For now, she is not in any danger. As are you and your friends. You see, Las Vegas is lined with a protective barrier that only the descendants of the gods and Greek heroes can cross, provided they mean no harm. That is why Hope must stay until she is strong enough to venture outside."

"When will that be?" Astrid asked.

"When all those who are after her either die or stop hunting her. I will not let her leave here under any alternative."

"How the hell can you say that?" Cruz demanded. "We're her parents, not you."

But Demeter continued to speak with her calm tone. "And as her parents, wouldn't you want the best for your child? Wouldn't you want her to remain safe? Your vehicle was stopped by a lamia and was then attacked by harpies. Hope is extremely lucky that we were able to intervene before the worst could come to pass."

Glancing back at Cruz, then back to Demeter, Astrid wanted nothing more than to argue with the goddess. But nonetheless, Demeter was right. Instead, she clasped Cruz's hand in her own and said, "We'll do whatever we need to do to make the world safe for her. As her parents, that's our sole responsibility."

"But, neither of you are ready." Demeter replied with a somewhat dismissive tone. "Even with your powers, the help of my daughter and your little team you stand no chance of success."

The patronization in the woman angered Astrid. But she was well aware that getting angry would not help her case. "So, help us," she said. "You're a goddess, you have the powers to do so."

"While that may be the case, my skills would be better suited in protecting your child. I would recommend you stay here and let yourselves grow familiar with your own abilities. Learn how to use them before you even think about leaving. I'm sure Athena would have no objection to your training for it will be the only chance any of us have in protecting your daughter. But just remember while you stay here in the safety of this city the world will continue to go into ruin. It will only be a matter of time before our enemies come for us. Which now includes Hades."

As Cruz ran his fingers through Hope's long hair, he addressed Demeter in a much lighter tone than he had used before. "While we're here, will we get to raise our daughter, as a family?"

"Yes, by all means. She is still your child, but I will protect her, just as my daughter will protect Astrid. Just remember that Hope will continue to grow into adulthood at a very rapid rate. Within a few months, she will be full grown, and her abilities will be at full strength, so use this time wisely. The ceremony will begin soon, and I recommend you choose to sit beside your daughter."

Astrid smiled at Hope, then hugged her tightly. "I'd like that very much."

As the church began to fill up with guests, Astrid and Cruz sat beside their child's throne on the stage. Humans, centaurs, nymphs and other creatures that were once nothing more than beasts of mythology filled the audience in a spectacular display.

The gods themselves, were made to stand at the very front of the stage before the throne. As the church's commotion died down, a dark-haired woman with pale grey eyes, the absence of a smile and a golden sword sheathed to her side, entered the stage and stood in front of Hope. Astrid needed no introductions to determine just who that woman was. She was the goddess, Athena and she was very beautiful, without a doubt. Astrid gave her a polite smile, but the woman did not smile back.

Instead, Athena addressed the audience confidently. "Immortals and mortals alike. Do not fear. Take courage that while you are amongst these walls, you are safe from the destruction and the chaos that lurks beyond them. Sitting before you, we have the prophesied child who will bring about a new beginning and a new hope to us all. The opening of Pandora's Box might have brought destruction, but it also brought about a new beginning amongst the old and the new. This earth will experience something that it has never seen before. There is so much that we can teach one another, provided we live in peace. This young child beside me will teach us that and to guide her on her journey, I grant her the gift of wisdom. May she always make wise decisions." Athena knelt in front of Hope and brought her hand to the child's forehead making her blink, before leaving the stage and joining the remainder of the gods.

The next goddess to approach was Aphrodite, she too addressed the audience. "I am Aphrodite, and this child is surrounded by love. The love of her parents, of their companions..." she looked directly at Stacey as she spoke, and then continued on, "...and by the mortals and immortals alike. I grant her the gifts of love and empathy. May she carry them and share them wherever she goes."

Aphrodite kissed her fingertips and placed her hand on Hope's chest, forcing the child to giggle. She then left to join the rest of the immortal gods, just as Athena had done before.

Next, a bare-chested muscular man, who looked to be in his fifties with dark hair, piercing blue eyes and a neat beard, approached the thrones. The trident in his hand, made his identity evidently clear to all who were present. The man was Poseidon, the god of the sea. When he spoke, his voice boomed amongst the chapel, drawing the attention of each and every one present. "Hope! It is what we're striving for on this earth. But it is not only what you are all seeking among the lands but what we crave amongst the seas. As Poseidon, the god of the sea, I give this child the influence over the creatures of the waters. May they obey her and help her with her destiny."

Poseidon took Hope's hand within his own and smiled down at her, forcing her to grin up at him, happily, before he joined the other gods again.

This time, a very handsome man, who looked to be barely twenty years of age, with short fair hair and blue eyes approached Hope with a golden bow and a sheathe filled with arrows. The young man rested his weapons beside the throne and turned to address the crowd. "I am Apollo. I grant Hope with two gifts. The first being music. May she always sing a song in her heart. I also grant her the gift of archery. If she can wield a bow like her mother... well, then that's just half the battle!"

As Apollo took a hold of Hope's hand, he glanced over at Astrid and smiled a charming smile in her direction, before turning and leaving to join the other gods in suit.

Astrid peered down at the golden bow that Apollo had left by the throne and immediately recognized it as the one she had wielded during the battle with the centaurs. She had handed it to Joey directly after the fight and had not seen it since.

Things were finally making sense. Hannah had been right to be concerned about Joey, for he had been deceiving them all the entire time.

As if on cue, Joey made his own way to the stage, forcing Astrid's very soul to grow cold. She looked to the surprised expressions on her friends' faces. Ironically, Hannah didn't look surprised like the rest of them. Instead, there was an expression of betrayal, which Astrid empathized with.

Astrid turned to Cruz, who had merely turned his head away to avoid eye contact with Joey. Clearly, he had found this truth out for himself. Joey had been the one person that Cruz had trusted more than anybody. That kind of betrayal would have been crippling.

Joey turned his gaze to Astrid and mouthed what looked to be a sincere apology. In return, she offered him a polite smile, knowing that she would receive a full explanation from him later.

Hunching his shoulders, in a very un-Joey like manner, the man turned to the audience, to deliver his speech. "I am... I am Hermes. I was sent to ensure that Zeus's descendant, Mario Cruz took the first step in building this new world. I manipulated Cruz to believe that we grew up together. I funded the excavation when his boss was going to give up on Cruz's hunch. I encouraged him to find the pithos and then I talked him into opening it. He was never supposed to find out any of this."

Joey turned to Cruz and then back to the rest of the crowd. Joey was hurting, just as much as Cruz was, but he needed to get through his speech.

"...But now Cruz knows the truth... Most of it, anyway. What he doesn't know, is that I was supposed to leave after he opened it. I was supposed to encourage him to open the box and then just walk away as if nothing had ever happened. But I allowed myself to be captured by the military and withstand everything that they put Hannah, Stacey and myself and the countless others through... I watched as everything unfolded and then when we were reunited again, I found that the rest of the gods had done their part in introducing him to Astrid. Astrid, the descendant of Pandora... But that's not all she is..."

Joey turned to Astrid, forcing her to raise her eyebrows completely baffled as to where his speech was going. There were muffles amongst the gods, and Joey was at the attention of angry glares from all around, both mortal and immortal alike. As Joey hesitated, wanting to say so much more than he had said, Astrid's hands grew iced cold.

She could see his aura perfectly. She could see the tears in his eyes. She could see the truth in the very messenger God who was known for deception. But instead, Joey shook his head and turned to Cruz. "To answer your question, you guys were destined to find each other. You were fated to fall in love. It wasn't some spell… It was your very souls calling out to one another… I know I should have told you a long time ago, but your spirits… your very destinies will always be intertwined. You were both born for greatness, and you'll always be stronger together."

Both Astrid and Joey's gaze turned to Samuel, whose expression mirrored incredible heartbreak. Shaking his head softly, a tear trickled down Joey's cheek as he continued his speech to the gathered audience.

"I'm probably breaking all the rules with this speech. But I was sent to lie to them and to pretend that I was somebody that I wasn't. I was told that it was for the good of mankind… That me, lying to my best friend, was for the sake of humanity. Yet, we have seen so much suffering, it is seriously, so damn hard to believe in hope. But hey, I know that things will get better. I know this because of what this child and her parents... and what our family means to me."

Joey looked back at Cruz and then to the rest of their friends. He was pleading with his eyes for forgiveness. "Right now, I'm not talking about my family of immortals or even the nymphs. I'm talking about the descendants. About Cruz, Astrid, Tash, Stacey, Buzzkill and especially Hannah. The woman I have fallen so madly in love with. I'm not sure if any of them will forgive me but, I really hope they do because I'm doing it for them... For their futures. And for the future of young Hope, who is such a beautiful child. And so, to Hope, I give the gift of luck... May she be as lucky as I have been, in knowing such amazing people. Yes, Buzzkill... it was my luck that got us the Argo too."

Surprisingly, the audience fell into a roar of applause as Joey turned back to Astrid and added, "Zeus wasn't the only one who helped bring you back from the Underworld... that was me too."

Astrid stared in stunned silence as Hermes knelt in front of the throne and kissed Hope on the forehead.

Her eyes drifted to Cruz, who was doing his best to force back the tears in his eyes and ignore his best friend. As Joey departed from the stage, solemnly, Astrid turned her gaze to Samuel standing in the crowd. His expression was unreadable, and he seemed to be staring into a void of nothing. The pain of actually hearing that she and Cruz were destined to be together must've been crushing.

But it was something that she could not deny within herself. Her soul ached for Cruz, but there was a side of her that loved Samuel more than she could explain. Astrid reminded herself of the words that Tash, and Aphrodite had both said. For her to pick both Cruz and Samuel. While theoretically, the answer seemed easy enough. The practice of doing so was a whole different story.

Demeter was the last to come up onto the stage. Her energy worked wonders in providing a harmonious atmosphere after the tension caused by Joey's speech. She approached Hope with a smile, her loose white gown flowing as she spun.

"I am Demeter," she said. "I grant this child with a one-time offer of rebirth so that if she or if anyone she ever loves dies... They can come back. But it will only be once and for the one person whom she so chooses only. Let's pray she never needs to use it." On those last words, Demeter glanced back at Astrid and Cruz and then ran her fingers under the child's chin, before taking her place amongst the gods again.

***

The ceremony concluded with food, wine, music, and a large celebration. Cruz and Hannah found themselves leaning against the stage, where Cruz had been venting to Hannah his frustrations in relation to Joey. Hannah, on the other hand, was trying to get Cruz to see reason. "Cruz, Joey means well. He just... He couldn't tell us because it was dangerous. I know you're mad, but..."

"Han, all those memories of him, were just planted there. I believed that he and I had met in our first year of high school. That guy changed my life. That's almost fifteen years of lies planted in my brain. At least your memories of Joey were real. Can we just drop it? It's my daughter's crowning ceremony and I really can't deal with this right now."

Looking as if she wanted to continue with the conversation, Hannah took a sip of her drink and nodded. If she could be entirely honest, she would say that she too was experiencing difficulties accepting Joey's true identity. But she loved him, so she needed to accept who he really was.

Upon noticing Astrid holding Hope and conversing with Stacey by one of the tables, Hannah changed the topic. "Okay, so how are you and Astrid? Joey's speech was a pretty big one. Kind of a little hard to get past."

Blushing a deep shade of red, Cruz took another sip of his drink. "Anything besides that topic," he said, glancing over his shoulder, where he managed to exchange subtle glances with Astrid before they both turned away again. Seeing this minor interaction, Hannah smiled.

"Come on, it's me. Hannah. You know you can tell me anything." Resigning his silence, Cruz smiled.

"Okay, I'll give you the truth. Because I know this whole love triangle thing is everybody's favorite topic. I love Astrid. But Buzzkill and I both agreed to give her some space when she awoke from her coma… and I think that space is exactly what she needs right now."

At those words, Hannah felt a pang of frustration for her friend. From where she was standing, Samuel was doing everything but giving Astrid space. She wondered if Astrid was even aware of this pact that Samuel was surely going back on his word from. She couldn't bear to leave Cruz pining over her thanks to a pact with the soldier.

"Ah, Cruz? I think there's something you should know."

***

Alone, by a large table filled with foods, some of which he had never seen before, Samuel proceeded to examine what looked like a small, raw crustacean. That was until a booming voice startled him enough to put the food back down and stand at attention.

"You're the descendant of Jason, are you not?" The moment Samuel laid his eyes on the bare-chested man who had spoken, he was driven to awe. He was in the presence of Poseidon.

"Yes, sir… your majesty… Sorry, what do I call you?"

"Poseidon is fine. I have some items for you, if I may."

"Sure."

Removing the blue-stoned amulet resting on the thick golden chain, from his neck, Poseidon handed it to Samuel. "This is my amulet. It will grant you protection should you ever sail my seas as Jason once did." Samuel examined the stone. Before the curse, this very artefact would've been priceless. He imagined that it still was. Humbled by the token, Samuel needed to be honest with the man.

"Thank you, Poseidon... but I don't sail... I mean, I can't sail." Believing that the god had mistaken him for somebody else, Samuel attempted to hand back the amulet. But Poseidon would not accept Samuel's refusal.

"You can lead men, can you not? I assure you that sailing will come quite naturally when you choose to do so. Should you change your mind, I also have another gift waiting."

Samuel had known many superior officers in the military with the same level of tenacity that Poseidon seemed to possess. And for that reason, Samuel knew that his only option was to agree. "Thank you, sir," he said, fastening the amulet to his neck and admiring it.

"You're welcome heir of Jason. We will meet again." As Poseidon took his leave, Tash purposely pushed into Samuel to garner his attention.

"So, Buzzkill… What the hell was that all about?"

Turning in the direction that Poseidon had left in, and then back to Tash, Samuel replied, "That... was Poseidon giving me a magical amulet... I think he wants me to take up sailing. But you're a married woman now, so let's go and celebrate."

"I thought you'd never ask. Last one to the drinks table is a rotten egg."

"You're on!"

***

As Stacey marveled at just how much Hope had grown, Astrid noticed that something seemed off about her friend. She shifted Hope to her left hip and voiced her concern in a softer tone. "Stacey, are you okay? You just got married, yet you seem, off."

Stacey shrugged, defeated. "I just found out that my own ancestor just officiated my wedding. I had no idea that I was a descendant of Aphrodite. It's just a lot to swallow. Like I have some big shoes to fill or something.

I guess it doesn't help that she is the actual goddess of love, now does it?"

"No, I guess not. She didn't tell you that you have some big destiny or anything, did she?"

"No. But think about it. This changes everything I ever knew about myself. It means I need to measure up to some weird expect…"

Stacey paused as she realized Astrid's intent behind her words. "Oh. Ha. I see where you went there miss-destined-by-the-gods. Can't you just let me complain for five minutes?"

Her feigned disappointment forced Astrid to break into laughter and shake her head. "Why don't we go over and speak to Buzzkill and your wife instead, huh?"

"Fine, but only if you let me hold Hope."

Astrid handed Hope over to Stacey as they joined Tash and Samuel at the drinks table. The moment Samuel saw Astrid, he handed her a glass of red wine, doing his best to maintain a formal composure.

"Hey, Sutherland. That ceremony was really something… not to mention, Joey's speech… I mean, wow!"

After relishing the sweet taste of wine on her tongue, Astrid addressed him. "I know. How are you feeling about what he said?"

"I'm not sure. I mean, yeah, he lied to us about who he was but..."

"...I was talking about him referring to Cruz and I being destined."

Stepping towards her, Samuel shook his head, surprisingly relieved. "We make our own destinies, Sutherland. I thought you knew that."

Pleased by his response, she smiled and took another sip of her wine. "Damn, Buzzkill, this wine is so good. I still can't believe we're surrounded by actual gods. I just feel like I need to watch my words and actions. Like I'm going to say something wrong. I'm surprised I haven't tripped in these heels yet."

"Hey, it could still happen... But if it helps, you've been carrying yourself very well. Your father would be proud."

His words made her blush. While the thought of her father almost brought a tear to her eye, Astrid knew that Samuel would be feeling the same way. Noticing the amulet sitting just above the neckline of his shirt, she needed to ask about it. "What's with the necklace?"

Smiling proudly, Samuel removed it from his neck and passed it to her. "Poseidon gave it to me. He said he wants me to take up sailing." Before Samuel could go into further detail, Joey joined them, looking very anxious.

After handing both the amulet and her wine glass to Samuel, Astrid gave Joey a tight warm hug. "Thanks for helping us. Your speech threw us all a little off guard... but at the end of the day, we're still family."

"Wow, you're very forgiving," Joey smiled.

"I get why you did it. Plus, you helped bring me back from the dead. How did you do that anyway?"

As Joey grinned, his green eyes twinkled. "Long story. I'll have to tell you over drinks sometime."

"Done deal, Joey... I mean, Hermes!" Astrid replied, taking back her drink from Samuel.

"Call me Joey. I've been going by this name... This face... for so long that Hermes, just doesn't feel right." Joey looked to Tash, Stacey, and Samuel. "Do you guys forgive me?" he asked. Stepping up on her toes, Tash ruffled his hair. "Of course, we do, dork!"

Stacey nodded. "Yeah. Just a question though… You and I aren't related, are we?"

Joey shook his head. "I take it you just learned that you're a distant child of Aphrodite?" Stacey nodded but said nothing further. "No, we're not related closely if that's what you mean. You're not one of my descendants. Unlike Samuel, that is."

As Joey turned to him, Samuel choked on his wine as he quickly processed the information, before brushing it off. "Wow, you're my ancestor? Huh… Anyway, you've given us nothing but luck so, of course, I forgive you. Though, I might need your help with a mission later. If you're able to, that is."

"I can try… I mean, now that I've been outed… it will change things a little, but… I guess I can still pull a few strings."

"Great!" Again, Astrid found herself at the attention of Samuel, as the others got lost in conversation. "Well, we found Cruz and Hope and we're safe here for the moment. How are you feeling?" Samuel asked.

"Surprisingly good despite everything that's happened. Why?"

"I want to apologize for earlier..."

But before he could go on, Astrid raised up her hand to stop him. "Samuel, you have nothing to apologize for. But Hope will be an adult in only a few months, so I'm planning to stick around for a little while longer. If you're still looking to go to the smaller towns, I won't stop you." But his reaction to her words surprised him. He was relieved.

"Astrid, if you're staying, I'm staying... It'll also give us some time to work on your sword training." As he spoke those words, the slight smile she recognized in him told her that it wasn't so much the training he was looking forward to, but the kissing.

Astrid felt her entire body blush all over. "Well, let's just make it through tonight's ceremony first, shall we?"

For the rest of the evening, they all enjoyed the night's festivities. It felt remarkable not having to be on the run and simply having the opportunity to relax. Deep down they all knew that those moments would not last long, so they needed to savor them while they could.

CHAPTER TEN

Over the next few days, Astrid and Cruz spent as much time as they could with Hope. When she wasn't training with the gods, that was. Just as Demeter had warned, their child was growing so fast before their very eyes.

In just three days, the toddler had grown to approximately five years of age, physically, which neither Cruz nor Astrid could get over.

Cruz spent a large percentage of his time either learning to channel his powers or contemplate his own theories behind the secrets of the gods. After having worked in archaeology for a long time and then being exposed to the reality of the gods, he bore no trust for any of them… And that included Joey.

After everything they had been through, Joey had hurt Cruz more than he could ever imagine. They had been friends for such a long time, or so he had thought. But at the same time, Cruz understood that Joey was no less a pawn to the gods, than he was. Furthermore, Cruz hadn't heard a word from Zeus since he had reached the Las Vegas barrier. Even after he had attempted numerous times to communicate with him.

The final matter that plagued him was the subject of Astrid when it came to Zeus and the other gods. It was no secret that she was special in more ways than one. But at the same time, she was still such an enigma. Not only a pawn of the gods, but a well-kept secret that nobody would answer. It was almost as if she was a celestial secret weapon which was yet to be wielded.

This theory kept Cruz obsessed with uncovering the answers. While he and Astrid had been given a place to share with their daughter, they had taken to sleeping in separate bedrooms. And honouring his decision to give Astrid the space she needed to clear her head, Cruz refused to enter her room or invade her privacy. Until the night he awoke to the deafening sound of Astrid screaming in her sleep.

After having ensured that Hope was indeed asleep in her own room, Cruz crept towards Astrid's room to witness her clawing at her royal blue sheets and crying out in agony. Whatever nightmare she was having certainly had her trembling in fear.

Aside from that traumatic time in the ruins, he had never seen her so afraid. Unable to watch her at the mercy of such torment, Cruz climbed onto the bed beside her, just as Astrid shrieked out in alarm, startling him.

Surprisingly, she was still asleep. Pulling her close, Cruz stroked her dark hair from her face and made the same soft hushing sounds he normally made to calm Hope.

"It's okay. I'm here."

"Cruz?" Astrid murmured lazily in her sleep. "I missed you."

Her voice forced Cruz's breath to hitch in his throat. It was killing him not to be with her. He should've left when he said he would, but he had stuck around for her. And for Hope. He continued to stroke her hair from her face and spoke in the same soft tone. "Who is hurting you, Astrid? Tell me and we'll stop them together. Okay?"

Though her eyes remained closed and her breathing soft, Astrid spoke ever so clearly, as if she was fully aware of his presence. "It's Hades. Please, Cruz. You need to run. You need to get out of here."

***

In her mind, Astrid was back in that desolate wasteland sitting by the bank in a tattered white gown with tears streaming down her face. To her surprise, Cruz was standing on the other side of the bank reaching out to her.

"You need to run, Cruz. Go. Get out of here!" she begged. But Cruz would not leave.

"I'm not going anywhere, Astrid. Take my hand." She wanted desperately to reach for him, but then, to her surprise, the grounds began to rumble, shift, and move, forcing the distance between them to diminish. On noticing, Astrid got to her feet and reached out her hand. But somebody was coming for her. "Astrid," Cruz called, now only a few feet away. "Take my hand."

"I can't,' she demanded. "Hades is coming. He's coming for me, and he'll get you too if you don't leave. Go now."

But Cruz refused to listen. Instead, he took a giant leap across the river. Now they were together on her side of the bank. He held her tight enough to make her very world spin. "Cruz…" she gasped, only to have her fears met by his kiss. But just as soon as she had him, he was ripped away by the very beast that she had been fleeing. Astrid watched as Cruz was swallowed up into the darkness. "NO, CRUZ!"

***

Astrid shot up from her sleep as if she had been struck by lightning. It was dark and her tears were still fresh on her face. But as she turned to see Cruz right beside her, she was met by a sheer sense of relief.

Before he could even begin to explain why he was there, she pulled him into a tight embrace and relished the contact of his skin. "I thought I lost you." She sniffled into his shoulder as Cruz ran his hand through her hair, holding her close.

"You could never lose me," he smiled. "We might have our differences, but I'll always be there for you."

His words were like music to her ears and at the same time, they altered the moment. They reminded her of just how much she wanted him. Of how much she needed him.

She was wide awake in the dead of the night, in Cruz's arms. And in that moment, the entire reality of their situation escaped her. She became ever aware of her heart pounding hard in her chest, and to his heart doing the exact same thing.

As his fingers scattered through her hair and his other hand skidded up her back, she ached for him. Tilting her face towards his, Cruz tilted his to her. As his dark eyes studied her, she wondered if he was feeling the same way.

Astrid brought her hand to his stubbled cheek. "Cruz, I..." But before she could stammer her sentence, he kissed her deeply and passionately, engulfing her senses and setting her very soul alight at the mere touch of his tongue.

Taking control, Cruz pulled Astrid onto him as he pressed his back into the pillows, where they gave into their desire for one another. Forgetting all about their duties to the gods and of the other cares in the world that waited beyond their door.

***

The next morning, Astrid awoke in Cruz's arms before the sun had even risen. Cruz on the other hand, was still lost in a deep sleep. Trailing her fingers through the dark hair that lined his muscular torso, Astrid tried to think back to the last time they had spent such an amazing night together. As she brought her hand up to trace his lips, he subconsciously rubbed at his face.

There was no surprise that he was her weakness. He could make her feel so alive, so in love and so complete all at once.

"Mmm," Cruz groaned, upon opening his eyes. "I was having an incredible dream. We ran away to a deserted island where there were no gods and absolutely nobody to stop us from running around naked and making love endlessly."

"That sounds amazing," Astrid grinned. "Maybe one day we should see if there are any deserted islands left and do just that."

"You really think so? Because I'm game."

"Definitely, but until then, we have a child in the next room who we'll need to get ready for her first training session of the day."

"Yeah, but that can wait. For now, we can just enjoy the moment of just us… Oh, while I have you alone, can I show you something?"

"You already showed me your new skill. Are you telling me you have something else up your sleeve?"

With a sheepish grin, Cruz sat up. "When don't I? But this isn't about my prowess between the sheets. More to do with my awesome new abilities to control the elements." The thought of Cruz having magical abilities equally astounded and left Astrid highly skeptical, even after everything they had encountered. "Alright," Astrid said, sitting up, "Show me."

"Okay, so do you remember when Demeter told you that you have two goddesses inside you?"

"Yeah, why? What's that got to do with your new abilities?"

"Well, I added that to the list of knowledge we gained from Joey's speech. Now, this is just a theory, so don't go quoting me or anything in case I'm wrong… But just maybe the history books weren't one-hundred percent accurate about Pandora."

Piecing his words together, Astrid thought back to the moment when he had told her that they were demigods, as Cruz continued to fully immerse himself into his theories.

"Well, I'm thinking that the first supposedly mortal woman who was built on Hephaestus's sacred anvil and gifted the abilities of the gods, wasn't in fact who the gods led us to believe."

"You think she was a goddess, don't you?"

"Don't you? It isn't really that far a stretch from everything else we've seen so far. My point is, I believe that the second goddess riding shotgun in your head is Pandora."

Shaking her head, Astrid struggled to believe him. If that had been the case, how long had Pandora been possessing her and why had she never known until now? The entire concept sounded way too farfetched for her liking. "Okay," Astrid replied. "Just say I believe you. Why haven't I heard her voice?"

"I don't know. Maybe that's a question for Persephone. And now for my magic trick. Hold out your hand."

Astrid did as he asked. Face down, Cruz held out his own hand over hers roughly leaving an inch of a gap between them. As he focused on their hands, Astrid focused on the seriousness in his eyes.

That passion had always been something that drew her to him in a way she couldn't comprehend. "I can sense you watching me," he said, not removing his eyes from their hands. "I need you to focus on the energy that's bustling between us. Do you feel that warmth?"

Astrid stared down at his hand and sure enough, she could feel it. A bustling burst of warmth like pins and needles radiating between them and with it, a golden glow of light. "Wow, this is amazing."

"It really is. It's not like creating your own lightning storm, but it's a start. The best part is when you channel every ounce of power within your entire body. It's seriously invigorating. It unleashes all those bad emotions and feels so damn good."

"Better than sex?" Her comment forced him to stare up at her with a delightful grin radiating into his eyes. "Now, there's an idea."

But before Astrid could get any ideas, Cruz stared back down at their hands, before pulling away. "And *voila*!"

The golden glow had disappeared. Instead, a small red rose with water droplets on the petals, as if it had just been freshly picked in the rain, was resting in the palm of her hand.

"How did you do that?" she asked, thumbing the flower and looking up at him.

"Not me, you. While I summoned it, your abilities created it. Like a 3D printer." Breathing in the scent of the rose, Astrid considered the storm that they had experienced in the motorhome, and it dawned on her.

"Wait, so that storm the day after you left us… that was you?"

Cruz pressed his back confidently into the pillows. "Sure was. I was blessed with similar abilities to Zeus. Everything from lightning storms to channeling the abilities of others… What's more is that he's been teaching me how to harness them."

"I thought you didn't like Zeus. You were always the first to call him a *'pendejo'*… did I say that right?"

"Almost. Keep practicing. Don't get me wrong, he's still a narcissistic dick. But he's the only narcissistic dick who has been willing to teach me how to use my gifts. The other gods just look at me like I'm a ticking time bomb. But anyway, let's stop ruining the moment, okay? You should let me teach you how to harness the powers within you. We'll need to if we want to defeat Hades and whatever other threats are out there. What do you say?" Resting her head on his shoulder, Astrid curled up beside him.

"Alright, do it. With you training me to harness my so-called powers and Buzzkill teaching me how to use a sword, hopefully I'll at least be able to stand a chance with whatever else lies beyond the barrier."

On her mention of the soldier, Astrid felt Cruz's entire body tense up. Clearing his throat, he asked. "How is he by the way?"

"Samuel?"

"Yeah. Hannah said she and Joey saw the two of you kissing after I left to find Zeus."

Her blood running cold, Astrid sat up to face him. "Yes, we did."

The moment she spoke the words, she saw the optimism drain from his eyes. "Look, Cruz. It's not like you and I were together."

"I get that. I'm not mad at you or anything. But I just…"

"Just…?"

Cruz's need to avoid her eye, ceased as he mustered the courage to speak up. "Astrid, I told you'd that I'd give you space. So, whatever happened or is happening between you and Samuel… that's got nothing to do with me. But I think you should know that Samuel and I made a pact."

Things were starting to sound as childish as high school.

"A pact?" Astrid probed. "So, who won?"

"No, I didn't mean it like that. Just… It was if you woke up from the dead, we'd give you the chance to get used to the state of the world and having a daughter before we pestered you with the whole 'who you should be with' dilemma."

Once again, Cruz was trying to spare her feelings. He meant well. But that didn't mean it didn't hurt any less.

"I don't think the others got the message," Astrid joked, trying to maintain her composure. "Tash was adamant I picked you both."

"As usual, Tash thinks she has all the answers," Cruz replied. "But I just thought that Samuel of all people would've made good on his word in giving you space."

While his words came as a surprise, Astrid bit down on her lip before addressing her own argument.

"You need to stop trying to protect my feelings all the time, Cruz. You should've..."

"...I'm sorry if I was protecting your feelings, but somebody needed to do it. You've been through trauma, Astrid. You died."

Before she could hold it back, her anger came out in a large burst as she got out of the bed and pulled on her robe. "I know what trauma is, Cruz. I was a fucking psychologist, remember? And what I needed, wasn't you giving me space, it was you. I wanted you. I needed you. Instead, you thought that breaking my heart for the second time, immediately after I had come back from the dead was a goddam good idea! You should've helped me figure out what had happened to me, and we should've searched for Hope together. But you just had to go off by your-fucking-self again."

Soaking up her words, Cruz got to his feet and pulled the sheet around his waist. "I'm sorry, Astrid, but…"

"…Quit apologizing, Cruz! Stop spearing my goddam feelings! Because here's the thing, while you weren't there for me, Samuel was. You've always been so concerned that he could just steal me away at the drop of a hat. But news flash, I have always put you first. Unfortunately for you, it's your self-sabotaging nature that pushes me to Samuel."

Her words hit him like a slap to the face. But Astrid would not take them back. There was a far off look in his eyes, which told her that he had just pieced together a puzzle within his mind. "Zeus was right," Cruz muttered as he started towards the door.

"What the hell does that mean?" Astrid demanded. "What has Zeus been saying about me?" After a strained silence, Cruz turned to her. His tone somewhat void of all emotion.

"Zeus told me when we first met, that as a side effect of the curse you would inhibit every single one of the sins and that you wouldn't be able to control them. From fear, lust to greed… all of them."

Astrid scoffed in sheer disbelief. "That's ridiculous, Cruz. You know damn well that I'm immune."

"That's not the point. It's a side effect of you being the vessel for the cure. I didn't believe him, back then, because you don't exactly have a bad temper thanks to all those anger management classes you used to take before all this. But the lust part? Well, no offence, but that's you, all over."

"Screw you!"

As quickly as he had said it, the remorse was evident in his eyes. "I didn't say it to hurt you, Astrid. I mean, there's no shame in women owning their sexuality, it's super sexy. But even you have to admit that you've always lusted over Samuel. Maybe you did it with me too. I don't know."

Astrid's stomach wrenched. Tears forced themselves down her cheeks. "You know damn well how much I love you. It sure as hell isn't lust. Why else would I believe you when nobody else would?"

Her words gave him pause. There was so much pain in his eyes, but despite him trying to hold it in, his words were drenched in sarcasm. "I'm sorry, but sometimes that message gets a little lost in translation when I see you smiling up to soldier boy like a love-sick schoolgirl every other minute."

He had her there. But still, he wasn't done. "Besides, if you are in love with the both of us, how do you know it's love and not lust?"

"Cruz, you need to shut up, right now before you say something we'll both regret. Clearly, Zeus has done something to your head."

"No, Astrid. This is one hundred percent me. The only way that that *cabron* had any hand in this is by creating Pandora to begin with. Because, let's face it, the poetry behind a beautiful woman cursing the world to embrace its own destruction is right on the…"

Astrid tried to slap him but Cruz caught her hand before it could make contact. What hurt her the most about his harsh insinuations was that she could see the bitter truth in them.

Oh, how she wished she could turn the hands of time back to when they were making love in her bed. But now, Cruz was staring at her in the same way he had done before he had broken her heart in the past.

Releasing her hand from his grip, Cruz added, "Astrid, I love you in a willing-to-give-up-my-soul-for-you kinda way. But you... You need to take the time to figure shit out for all of us. Because I can't let my heart get destroyed in the process. And as much as I can't stand the guy, I don't want to see you, or Buzzkill get hurt either." Before she could figure out a response, Cruz left, closing the door behind him.

***

Later that day, Tash and Stacey were enjoying the peace and quiet at their modern-styled apartment. As Stacey sat on the sofa watching a rerun of one of her favorite telenovelas and painting her toenails a vibrant pink, Tash had engulfed herself in a mystery novel which she had borrowed from Hannah. As Stacey stopped mid-toenail polishing waiting for the heroine to declare her love for the blonde waitress, Tash's voice carried in over her thoughts. "So, have you spoken to your ancestor since the wedding?"

"Jesus, Tash!" Stacey snapped, pausing the television. "Sophia is about to tell Anamaria that she loves her. You really know how to spoil the moment, don't you?"

"Sorry, but haven't you already seen this one? Sophia tells her she loves her. They have some steamy hot sex, then Anamaria tells Sophia that she still has to marry the old guy for his money so she can tend to her mother's medical bills."

Bitter, Stacey finished painting her toenails. "That's not the point. It's not like I can watch anything new, now, is it?"

"Alright, I'm sorry. Maybe if we're able to bring peace, they'll make brand new programs and you and I can binge them until your heart's content. How does that sound?"

That sounded very good to Stacey. But then, she was met by a crippling thought. "Wait, what if all the actors have already died... God, I never thought of that. What if...?"

Tash burst into laughter. "I'm sure they're all fine. And maybe there are some actors who are also descendants. Maybe they're here in Vegas already, who knows."

"I guess so. But that just made me wonder... If only descendants can pass through the magical void, who do you think you're related to? Athena, maybe?"

"I thought that at first... but, she never really had children. Just one, I think... Athena was a virgin goddess."

"Oh, but I thought..."

"That's all Hollywood, Stacey. So, enough about me... What's the scoop on Aphrodite?"

Having been hoping to avoid all talk on her ancestor, Stacey sighed. "You're not going to let this one go, are you?"

"Hello! Have you met me? It's the most exciting thing since the drama that is our best friend's love triangle, and Joey turning out to be Hermes. Seriously, who needs TV? Because you really can't make this shit up. In fact, they should just make a show based on our life... I wonder what sassy Latina would play me... I hope she's hot. I'd so do her."

At Tash's comment, Stacey burst into a fit of giggles. Despite the awkward tension Stacey got every time she was around Aphrodite, she was relatively happy with how her life was turning out. But Tash's interest in forcing a family bond with the goddess not only puzzled her it also infuriated her. That being said, she knew that Tash would not give up on the subject.

"Okay, for your information, I spoke to Aphrodite for a little bit yesterday and she seems lovely. I mean, I never had a mom who stuck around. So, having an older female role model who wants to look out for me is weird. Especially because she... she just looks so young. So, next topic, please? Do you think Joey... I mean, Hermes will stick around? Poor Hannah, I don't know how she's dealing with all of this."

On Stacey's concern, Tash changed her seating position to face her and placed her book faced down on the coffee table. "Joey said he wants to stick around. But I really don't know if that changes the rules. I don't think Cruz is taking it well either."

"Well, do you blame him?"

"Not really. But I understand why Joey did it."

Frankly, Stacey didn't know what to believe when it came to Joey. Sure, Joey was one of their closest friends. He had been there doing his best to protect her when they had been imprisoned. She had come to trust him immensely. But this Hermes character was a total stranger that made her doubt everything she had ever believed in. "You're still going to call him 'Joey' aren't you?" she asked Tash.

"Sure am. Hermes just doesn't feel right. So, do you think that you have any special powers like Aphrodite? Did you know that Cruz does? He has some pretty cool powers! Have you tried channeling your inner goddess? Damn, that sounds so sexy. Can I channel your inner goddess?"

Amused, Stacey tried to consider Tash's remark from a rational standpoint. "None I can think of. Aphrodite apparently had some irresistible spell over men... but, I don't think that's applicable to me... so, frankly, I wouldn't care if I did. I don't really want to have any powers... I like myself for who I am."

She couldn't tell if Tash was either disappointed or satisfied with her answer, but there was clearly something else she wished to discuss. "What is it, Tash?"

After taking a large breath of hesitation, Tash gave her response. "Alright, I have to confess... You're probably going to hate me, but there is a reason I keep bringing her up... You see, I invited her to dinner tonight... please, don't hate me. I'll even cook."

On her news, Stacey glared at Tash with an unimaginable fury. Her wife had just done something big without talking to her first. They were about to have their first argument as a married couple.

***

Since the night of Joey's speech, Hannah and Joey had barely spoken a word to one another. Sure, they were living together, and she was doing her best to mend the bridge that he had broken, but Joey was desperate for reassurance that things could just go back to normal.

That afternoon, he found her at the table reading a book on horse anatomy. "Hey, Han, what are you reading?"

"A veterinarian's guide to horses," she answered without looking up at him. In fact, she hadn't delivered full eye contact since the night he had confessed his identity. But Joey refused to give up. He sat beside her, taking her hand in his.

"That sounds fun. Do you want to go out for dinner tonight? This place has restaurants open for business... We could go to a casino... we could do anything. Just like before when..." Letting his voice trail off, he registered Hannah's look of fury as she finally stared up at him and pulled her hand from his reach.

"You weren't exactly human before all this, Joey, so why try now?"

There was the anger he was waiting for. "I thought you understood why I did it. I didn't exactly have a choice." For a moment, Hannah looked as if she was trying to keep her feelings in check.

"I do, Jo... sorry, Hermes. But it's not like you need to keep pretending with me. You're part god, part nymph and you're parading around trying to act human. I just wish you would stop pretending with me."

"Hannah, I'm not pretending. This is who I am. I might've spent over a millennium being Hermes, but I love being Joey because it's the man I am when I'm around you." But his words seemed to only anger her more.

Slamming her book shut, Hannah got to her feet and tucked the book under her arm. "But don't you get it? All you've been doing since day one is pretending. You really hurt Cruz and you really hurt me. You said that you have the power of luck... but right now... I don't know if you'll be lucky enough for everything to go back to the way it was." Storming towards the door of their apartment, Hannah retrieved her purse.

"Where are you going?" Joey asked, following after her.

"I really can't do this with you."

"Hannah, no. Don't go!" Joey pleaded. "Look, we can talk about this. Just let me try!"

But Hannah shook her head and pulled open the door, only to see Cruz standing in the hallway ready to knock. Seeing her in tears, Cruz peered into the apartment at

Joey then back to Hannah in concern. "Han, is everything okay?"

"It's fine, Cruz," she snapped back. "What do you want?"

"Umm… I… err… I just came to see Joey."

"Well, I can't speak for Joey, but Hermes is right there," Hannah spouted as she pushed right past Cruz and left as quickly as she could.

Miserable, Joey gestured for Cruz to enter, equally curious as to why he was even there in the first place.

As if unsure of himself, Cruz stepped into the apartment, staring awkwardly at Joey. "Joe, when a woman says its fine..."

"...It's actually not fine? Yeah, I was the one who taught you that, remember? So, why are you here?" Joey closed the door and took a seat beside Cruz on the white couch while mentally praying for his forgiveness.

"Look, Joe…" Cruz began. "I get what it's like to have no choice but to keep a big secret from the ones you love… and because of that, I want to hear what you have to say."

A mixture of emotions flooded through Joey's very immortal soul. He had witnessed the rise and falls of empires, raged riots to fight slavery, and had even fought in wars. But being given the opportunity to come completely clean about why he had lied about his identity was certainly a first.

"Where do you want me to start?" he asked.

"Okay, tell me this… How much of our friendship was a lie?"

"None of it," Joey said in a matter-of-fact kind of way. "The only lie was me not being who I said I was... oh, and everything to do with not knowing anything about the pithos... but, everything else was the truth."

Cruz sat in silence, pondering his words. "So, you're the reason the world blames me for bringing about an apocalypse?"

Guilty, Joey wasn't sure how to answer that one honestly, without digging himself in an even deeper grave. But Cruz didn't even give him the opportunity to start.

"Is that all? Because, put yourself in my shoes, Joey. What if I had lied to you about something so big that it twisted your entire perception of not only me, but also the entire world in which you lived, breathed and studied about in history."

The very thought of Cruz lying was almost amusing. Sure, he had taken the lead role in his high school play, and he could improvise when he needed to. But the guy was too honest. He had always worn his innocent heart on a sleeve in a way that made him absolutely vulnerable to others. "You? Lie?" Joey scoffed. But Cruz sighed, a physical indication that he wasn't kidding. Joey sunk even deeper into his seat. "Cruz, I don't know how many times I can apologize. To you. Or to Hannah. But I'm willing to apologize until the end of eternity if I have to. But honestly, at the end of the day, I am so truly glad that it was you and not somebody else that I was tasked to guide because you've been like a brother to me."

On his response, Cruz rubbed at his eyes as if he was trying hard to hold back emotion, before looking back at him. For a moment he looked as if he wanted to say something, but then changed his mind again. Then, finally after a large sigh, he turned to Joey and said. "You too, man. *Mi Hermano.*"

Smiling, Joey repeated his words. "*Mi hermano.*" Riddled with insurmountable emotion, they gave each other a quick hug before breaking apart again. "So, we're good?" Joey asked.

"Not by a long shot… But we'll get there… under one condition."

"Name it."

"Show me your powers, and I'll show you mine." Cruz smiled.

"Deal!" Joey vowed. "But, can I add something to that deal, though?"

As if to ask, 'what kind of something?' Cruz gave him a look.

"Help me win back Hannah?"

"Man, if I knew how to do that, I wouldn't have to compete with Buzzkill all the damn time. But I can certainly help you try."

Patting Cruz on the back, Joey shook his head in sympathy. "Well, aren't we a bunch of suckers to a couple of strong women?"

"Here, here!" Cruz agreed, getting to his feet. "Now, let's go find a bar and get blind drunk."

"Damn straight!" Joey agreed, standing. "I've had enough emotions to last me an immortal lifetime." Despite his grief with Hannah, Joey felt optimistic that while it would take a while, at least his friendship with Cruz was on the mend.

***

Astrid brought up her sword and went to drive it into Samuel's abdomen, only for it to be met by his counter and a step backward. They were in an empty gymnasium that they had turned into their own sparring grounds.

Their swordplay continued for another ten more minutes, with them both breathing heavily and Astrid focusing on everything but what they were supposed to be doing.

Finally, she swung up her sword again, just as Samuel stumbled back and fell to the floor, dropping his sword in the process. Lost in her fury, Astrid was seconds away from impaling him with her blade. Her mind had travelled back to the underworld wasteland to a memory that Persephone had brought up at the wrong time. But before her sword could come into contact with Samuel, she froze, lost in the void.

"Sutherland... Earth to Astrid, what are you doing?" As Samuel lay with his back to the floor, staring up at her with the tip of her blade to his throat, he attempted to pull her back to the present tense before she killed him. "Astrid, are you alright?"

Rattled from her thoughts, she begrudgingly withdrew her sword. "I'm fine," she said, holding out her hand to help him stand.

"I know when you're lying. We'll hold off on another round until you talk to me."

"Is that an order, Sergeant Buzzkill?"

"No, because I know you'll only disobey me. It's a recommendation. Now, come... sit."

Astrid allowed for him to lead her to the chairs and took a mouthful of her water bottle as they sat beside one another.

The early morning's argument with Cruz had left her beyond furious. Not to mention her situation with Persephone and ever-increasing visions of the underworld continued to plague her endlessly.

Still, she refused to let her problems with Cruz hinder whatever her relationship was with Samuel. But of where to even begin to tell the former soldier all about her problems was a mystery. "Do you realize what day it is," she asked, avoiding Samuel's eye. But instead of giving him the chance to respond, she continued. "Tomorrow Hope will be a year old. Which means that tomorrow will be a year since the day that I died."

"Yeah, I know. That day has been etched into my brain. How are you dealing with it?"

His question gave her pause. How was she dealing with it? She didn't want to admit that Cruz was right. She had gone through trauma. She needed to deal with it. But dealing with it was, by far, the last thing she wanted to do.

Before she could hold back anything, her problems poured from her mouth like a waterfall. "Honestly, ever since I woke up, I've been feeling like my head is about to explode. Cruz believes that Pandora is riding shotgun with Persephone and that she was a goddess, no less, which makes me a demi-goddess and he also believes that I should be dealing with all of that. Not to mention, I have Persephone feeding me memories like miscellaneous pieces to a puzzle that I'm really struggling to piece together… Then there's the fact that my own daughter who will technically only be a year-old tomorrow… Well, she'll be a full-grown goddess in only a few months. How's anybody supposed to deal with any of that? I really wish I had an instruction manual, Samuel."

As she gave her long-winded vent, Samuel sat in silence, clearly searching for a cure in his mind. "I take it that sparring isn't helping. It's always helped you in the past."

Such a typical response, but at least he was trying. "Yeah well, that was before the queen of the underworld was showing me memories of torment, murky swamps and people screaming."

"Well that explains you almost impaling me back there," he chuckled. But he didn't stop there. "Look, I don't envy you, Astrid. But, if there's anything I can do to help, all you need to do is ask."

With the sheer weight of her problems having been lifted just by talking to him, Astrid couldn't help but smile. But the subject of Persephone clearly had Samuel intrigued. "So, I'm curious. Just how much do the goddesses in your mind actually see? Do they constantly pilot you or do they… you know, respect your privacy?"

"For starters, I'm not sure if Pandora is actually in my head or not, but Persephone… Well, it's like she's only using me as a warm body to hide from Hades. I hear from her when she needs to communicate or when she's helping me remember what happened when I died. Other times, it's like she's not even there."

"Well, that's good, I guess. I mean, I'm sure she means well but I just don't trust the gods using you for their own agendas. What if Persephone decides to take you over completely? She has the power to read every single one of your thoughts and use them to fool us."

It was cute to see his concern. "If it helps ease your nerves, I don't think she's there right now. It's like I have to focus to open the channel of communication. Besides, I can feel her fear that Hades might come after her again if she makes any large movements. Not that I blame her. Hades, he…"

Astrid's voice faltered as she noticed just how close Samuel was leaning towards her. Their faces were merely inches apart and she was beginning to feel a little too relaxed with him.

Turning away, she tried desperately to break the moment. But Samuel was still watching her. Studying her. "I won't let Hades come after you, Sutherland. I won't let him take you back to the underworld. You have my word."

Leaning back in her chair, Astrid turned back to him, doubtful that Samuel was strong enough to even stand a chance against the figure of her torment. "As strong and as skilled as you are, Samuel, he is the god of the Underworld. I'm not sure how you'd be able to stop him. I don't even know how I can stop him... But thank you, just the same."

"Yeah, I know," he replied. "But it sure as hell won't stop me from trying. Look, maybe we should get back to sparring. You're getting good at your swordplay, and it won't be long until you'll soon surpass me."

Joining him, Astrid got to her feet and considered what Cruz had said about figuring out how she felt. And while she was equally torn between both men, one thing was for certain. That was that she could tell the difference between the way they made her feel. Both were willing to offer her different things, in the name of their love. But the problem was that what she needed and what she wanted were two entirely separate things. She loved the companionship she had with Cruz. She loved the romance and the way he made her heart melt when he was around. He was her ultimate weakness and her love for him was indescribable.

But the way Samuel cherished her and challenged her… The way he was the perfect temptation and the perfect distraction, was what she needed. Samuel could obsess her mind in a way that frustrated her very core.

Maybe Cruz was right. Maybe what she felt for Samuel was nothing more than unadulterated lust. But in that moment, that unadulterated lust was all that she required. Her temptation to kiss him was far too strong to resist.

Breaking her concentration, Samuel handed Astrid her sword, ready to spar again. She studied the hilt. It was silver in colour and an A had been crafted inside a blue-colored stone. Samuel had forged it himself. Just another amazing thing that he was capable of. Shaking her head, Astrid handed it back.

"I think that's enough training for today."

"Why?"

After all that had just gone through her mind, she really didn't want to explain her reasoning. In fact, she felt embarrassed for even thinking those thoughts, so she gave the only answer that fell from her lips easily. "Because right now, I just can't be around you."

And without another word, she turned to leave the sparring room. But instead of allowing her to go, Samuel dropped her sword to the floor and grabbed her hand in a bid to stop her. "What the hell did I do wrong, Astrid?"

"You didn't do anything. I just… I don't think we should be spending so much time alone." Staring down at her, Samuel brought his hands to her shoulders in a bid to look her squarely in the eyes. Astrid couldn't help but stare up at his lips, tempted to kiss them. But before she could give into her urges, she considered what Cruz had said and looked away.

"Why not?" he asked. "It's not like we're doing anything wrong."

"But we are doing something wrong. And I need to be totally honest with you. Last night, I slept with Cruz."

"You slept with…"

"Yes. And I'm not even sorry about it. But he also made me realize something." Samuel's hard to read expression took over his entire demeanour as he removed his hands from her.

"Okay? So, what…? He made you realize that we shouldn't spend time together?"

Astrid needed to be entirely honest with him. Just as she had been with Cruz. "No, Samuel. It's not that… It's just… Well, apparently, Zeus told him I'm cursed to exhibit every single one of the deadly sins and so Cruz believes that me being in love with you and him… well, that it's nothing more than lust."

Samuel furrowed his brows and surprisingly lowered his tone. "Lust?"

"Yes."

"Well, as somebody who has, in fact, dealt with lust firsthand, I think I can help with that."

"You can? How?" Samuel closed the distance between them, wrapping his hands around her waist.

"The best way to ride it out is to get it out of your system like an actual virus." Samuel's lips landed just under her ear as he planted a kiss. His whispered voice tickled the nape of her neck, sending her senses into overdrive as he spoke. "I'm not mad that you and Cruz hooked up. In fact, it actually makes me want you more. But I'm guessing, that if this lust side effect is like the lust virus, then it'll either be out of your system after a steamy afternoon of passion, or it'll develop into something much stronger. Either way, you'll have your answer."

His soft whispers evolved into dangerously intoxicating kisses that he trailed along her collarbone leaving her breathless.

"But..." Astrid stammered. "What if it turns out to only be nothing more than lust? I don't exactly want to hurt you."

"Shh..." he whispered back, running his fingers up the back of her shirt. "I'm man enough to take anything you throw at me. Besides, I know it's so much more than lust."

Closing her eyes, Astrid gave into him as his kiss travelled back up to her mouth. With his lips crashing against hers, and his fingers sending shivers up her spine, there was nowhere else she wanted to be. Feeling him smile against her kiss, she pulled away for the briefest of moments.

"Alright, Samuel, have it your way. But why don't we take it back to your apartment, instead?"

"That's exactly what I was thinking," Samuel replied. And with that, he lifted her up in his sheer determination to carry her back to his apartment.

CHAPTER ELEVEN

For the moment, Astrid's mind had gone back to its blissful state of peaceful serenity. Sure, there were about a million problems waiting to be handled, but her current state of bliss allowed her to surrender to the moment. After having spent the last hour enraptured in the heat of passion, Astrid and Samuel were sprawled out naked in his bed, with the white duvet draped loosely over them.

"You're actually happy right now, aren't you?" Samuel asked, twirling a lock of her hair between his fingers. "All that anger before it's simply gone. I told you a while back that sex releases endorphins and how right was I?" He ran his hand down the side of her arm then to her back, sending shivers throughout her body. Unfortunately, her peaceful state couldn't wipe the thought of Cruz's words from her mind. Pulling the blanket up to her chest, she leaned her head up against the headboard. "Alright, yes, you were right. But I don't exactly have an answer to…"

"Shh… Stop overthinking things. Right now, we owe it to ourselves to be happy. With the way the world is crumbling outside of Las Vegas, it's only a matter of time before we'll have to go back out there and fight again. We deserve to be happy, Astrid… even if it's just temporary."

A smile crinkled up in her right cheek as she took in his words. He was unbelievably handsome. She could get lost in his blue eyes alone. Not to mention, his dominant jawline and muscular body made him look like somebody who had just stepped out of Hollywood. What was more, was that everything that he was saying was correct. They were safe in the Vegas barrier for now and despite her feelings for Cruz, she owed it to herself to be happy. Astrid breathed out slowly and trailed his jawline with her fingertips. "Alright, you're right."

"I'm right? Are you feeling okay?"

"I'm feeling better than alright, Buzzkill. But do you know what will make me feel even better?"

"Do tell."

Astrid pulled his head in close, brought her lips to the nape of his neck and whispered, "You."

"Is that so? God, I love you, Sutherland."

High on the excitement that had taken over her entire body, she couldn't help but voice out her honest response. "I love you too, Sergeant Buzzkill."

***

That night, Aphrodite accompanied Stacey and Tash at their apartment for dinner. Tash had gone out of her way to cook a beautiful meal for the goddess and had even served up some wine. Tash couldn't help but remember the last time she had organized such an elaborate dinner.

Meals with her family, when they had been alive, had always started off perfect but would always explode spouting words of frustration and honest truths in the air as if they were candies at Christmas. Surprisingly, the meal with Stacey and Aphrodite was oddly reminiscent of those times. Stacey refused to even open up to the goddess. It was almost as if she was afraid to.

They were halfway through their meal when Aphrodite eventually addressed the tension in the air. "This was a beautiful meal, Natasha. But I must ask, why did you go through all the trouble when it is evident that Stacey wasn't in favor of the idea?"

Leaning back in her seat, Tash took an uncomfortable mouthful of her wine before speaking. "Well, I figured that you're the closest thing that Stacey has to family, and in our modern-day culture this is what we do. We invite our in-laws around for dinner."

"She isn't technically close family," Stacey argued quickly. "She's an ancestor, a goddess."

"She's still family, Stacey... She is where your bloodline originated from."

"Girls, girls... Please, don't fuss over me," Aphrodite broke in. "I just wish that I was at my full strength, and I could make you both see reason."

"Can you even do that?" Stacey asked, but Tash was more curious as to the 'not at full strength' part of the sentence.

"What do you mean you're not at full strength?"

"Oh? You didn't know? All the gods have had our powers siphoned since the beginning of the curse. Even Hermes is far weaker than he once was. Athena believes that it all has something to do with Hades."

"I'm still having a hard time understanding everything," Stacey said. "So, if Zeus started this curse to seek out his revenge on humanity... and all of you are trying to create peace... What is Hades doing? Why would he take your powers?"

"Hades wants to turn the earth into a mere wasteland, just like the Underworld. He seems to believe that limiting our powers will help him with that endeavor."

"But, why now? And why didn't Astrid say anything? Wouldn't she know? Surely, Persephone would've told her," Stacey said.

While Tash watched Aphrodite and Stacey conversing, she couldn't help but wonder what things would've been like if her own family had survived the deadly sins curse. They would've loved Stacey. Her very energy could light up any room more so than Tash could. The curse had taken so many things away from them, but at least it had given back in return.

As she swallowed down another mouthful of the sweet red wine, she mentally washed down the last memory she had of her family. The horrifying sound of their deaths being carried out in the living room, while she cowardly hid in the bedroom closet.

Tash brought her consciousness to the display being carried out at the dining table. It seemed like the typical family debate, with only two differences. Aphrodite was a goddess and the conversation being had was about Hades consuming their powers.

Aphrodite pulled her wine glass from her lips and set it down on the table, focusing on Stacey. "Well, maybe Persephone has not yet revealed this information. There could be a number of reasons as to why. One of which could simply be that she just doesn't know."

Tash thought back to Persephone's possession over Astrid. Astrid was a tough leader... No, a leaderette. And with a goddess in her head she could be unstoppable. "Wouldn't Persephone be our best shot in stopping him?" Tash asked.

"While that may be so, your friend is not yet ready to stand against him. But I feel she may be if we give her time. Now, enough about the gods, please, Stacey, tell me more about how the two of you met."

***

After one too many beers, Cruz and Joey spent the afternoon reminiscing about their excavations in Greece and their times in college, at a bar packed with gods, mortals and creatures alike. Thanks to Cruz's newfound abilities, it was impossible to get drunk from regular beer, which was why Joey had introduced him to an old recipe originally brewed by Dionysus himself.

To Cruz's relief, Joey had clarified that they had truly met at a college party, after Cruz had experienced another failed attempt at impressing a girl. Joey had witnessed him drowning his sorrows and in turn gave him some century-old pointers on impressing women. 'Flatter them just enough to get their attention, then let them chase you.' To Cruz's surprise, Joey's advice had worked.

"I was so clueless," Cruz smirked, reminiscent, as he took another mouthful of beer.

"You still are," Joey chuckled. "But at least your luck with women has improved since then."

Cruz shook his head. "I'm not so sure about that… So, what are you going to do about Han?" It was Cruz's desperate attempt to not think about Astrid. Judging by the look of puzzlement that Joey was wearing, the man was stumped about how to make it up to Hannah. Instead, he shrugged, forcing Cruz to change the subject. "Shouldn't you be able to fly?"

"Hmm?"

Cruz placed his now empty beer bottle on the bar. "You're Hermes. It was your job to escort all the souls to the underworld... Wait, shouldn't you be doing that now?"

"While that is true, Hekate has taken over the role of soul escort... also, thanks to all this business with Hades, my powers have been limited. I can fly, but not as fast as usual. Not to mention, my sandals have been sort of misplaced over time which slows down my speed."

"Sandals? Actual sandals?"

Joey did not register his sarcasm. "Yeah, I found my staff back in those ruins and my helmet just recently in fact. My sandals went missing a few centuries ago. I can still fast travel to the underworld though, but only when people die. That's because their soul opens up a portal instantly. I can even travel there through a person's dreams." Cruz remembered seeing Joey's staff back in the ruins of Greece, back when Astrid had been murdered.

His sudden anger got the better of him as he spat the next words at his friend. "That was the staff you handed me to save Astrid. That could've brought her back. You could have saved her!"

"Ah, calm down. No, it wouldn't have saved her. Unfortunately, I had to wait for Zeus to give me the go ahead."

Cruz took a sip of the freshly opened beer bottle that had been planted in front of him amidst their discussion. "Oh, sorry. Did you ever you know… visit Astrid when she was there?"

Joey took a sip of his own drink. "Every now and then. That's why I asked her if she had any memories of her life after death. I needed to know what she could remember."

"How was she?"

Joey's solemn nod hinted to dark memories, but he didn't elaborate. "Let's just say, I promised her that I'd bring her back. Why? Did she say something?"

Cruz thought back to Astrid screaming in terror in her sleep. As much as he wanted to help her, and as powerful as he was, he felt absolutely powerless to help her. "She's been having nightmares, Joey. Really bad ones. Whatever happened to her in the underworld, whatever they did to her… I think it's changed her. It's like she's broken… and the scariest part is that I don't think I can fix it."

In that moment, Joey adopted a haunting look. It was evident to Cruz that he had witnessed things that he didn't want to speak of. Instead, Joey drank the entire contents of his beer in one swift action before ordering another. "Whatever Astrid is going through, Cruz. And whatever she went through… I think this is where you need to just let her go through it herself. You can't save her."

Those words, 'You can't save her'. While they angered Cruz deeply, he knew that they were inexplicably true. The woman had two goddesses inside her head. She was battling with a hell of a lot of traumas, and she was tired of him tiptoeing around her feelings. Whatever the gods had planned for her, he merely prayed that she was strong enough to battle through it.

***

In Astrid's mind, she was back in the underworld, sitting by the swamps. Her head was buried in her knees, and she was crying but couldn't quite remember why.

She took a rock and threw it into the swamp and watched as it disappeared before her eyes. Then she heard him. Hades. His booming voice yelling out her name.

Startled, Astrid turned away from the swamp and up at Hades. His hair was as black as the night. His eyes, crystal blue. His dominant demeanor scared her to the core. "You're lucky I found you, Pandora. If you ever try…"

"Leave her alone!" the voice of Persephone called out over his fury. Astrid's eyes darted to the young woman with long, strawberry-blond hair and eyes as green as the springtime as she grabbed the back of Hades' cloak. "She will not be another concubine. You will not force her as you did me!"

With the sudden pound of his fist against her cheek, Persephone hit the ground, hard. Hades stared back at Astrid. "It's just a matter of time, Pandora! You are nothing but the curse that was released onto the mortals… and soon, the whole world will see that. You will be mine. Nobody can stop me from getting what I want!"

In an instant Hades was gone, leaving Persephone wounded on the floor. Despite her fears, Astrid pulled the girl into her arms to comfort her. "Are you okay?" Astrid asked, cupping Persephone's head in her hands, examining her bloodied face.

"Please," Persephone pleaded. "You must take me with you when you go... Please."

Holding the woman close to her, the same way that she had held Stacey numerous times before, Astrid vowed to protect her no matter the cost. "I'll help you, Persephone. We'll bring that bastard down. Just tell me what I need to do."

"Astrid?" A voice so familiar forced them both to look up. Joey was standing behind them. Concern filled his face. Had he seen everything that had just transpired? "Joey?" Astrid gasped. "What are you doing here? How did you..."

Joey shook his head. "No, I'm not Joey. I'm going to get you both out of here. I promise." His voice was filled with such conviction, that Astrid couldn't help but believe him.

***

Astrid awoke with a gasp. She had been dreaming. No, not dreaming. She had been remembering her time in the

Underworld. In the bed beside her, Hope lay sound asleep. Within the night, once again Hope had aged. She now looked about ten years old. The thought that time seemed to be escaping them, was almost gut-wrenching. But those memories of that man in that place filled Astrid with undeniable dread. *'Was that a memory?'* she asked Persephone.

'Yes, it was, Astrid. I'm sorry I didn't let you see sooner. But you weren't ready. You still aren't ready to see everything you suffered. Unfortunately, Hades is growing stronger, and he has surfaced. I can feel him. He'll come for us, and he'll come after Hope too. We need to be stronger and then we need to stop him… For good.'

CHAPTER TWELVE

Four months passed, and as predicted, Hope grew into a strong and powerful goddess. Astrid and Cruz found it strange to have a child who physically looked as if she was a late teenager when she was only a year old. Hope had long dark hair and piercing brown eyes, like her father, but her face resembled that of her mother.

Thanks to the gifts at her crowning ceremony, Hope had been blessed with wisdom, love, empathy, a love for music, archery skills and as Poseidon had granted, an influence over sea creatures. She had inherited her mother's determination and her father's passion, which meant that if she wanted something, she would stop at nothing to see it through.

Unfortunately, despite her training with the gods and her godly wisdom, both her parents and their friends saw her as a young child. Astrid and Cruz had taken up training, not only by the gods but also each other. After roughly two months, they had somehow managed to put aside their feelings for one another and focused solely on co-parenting and channeling their godly abilities.

Despite Cruz's patience, Astrid continued to struggle with her powers. She knew the basics but felt as if Persephone was holding back the full force of her abilities, along with an entire collection of memories.

Over time, Astrid and Samuel carried out their relationship in secret, doing their best to not let it intervene with their duties, friendships or Astrid's relationship with Hope and Cruz. Their relationship, to Astrid's surprise, proved to be passionate, challenging, and the only aspect of normalcy they had in a city surrounded by gods, magic, and mythological creatures.

Cruz's friendship with Joey certainly picked up. The two chose to get an apartment together in a bid to diffuse the tension of their own failed relationships with Astrid and Hannah. Having Joey close at hand, also proved especially useful when it came to Cruz mastering his powers, for who better to help than his best friend, Hermes.

Joey and Hannah's relationship remained strained, which was the sole reason behind Joey deciding to move out of her apartment in the first place. Knowing that he had Cruz to fall back on helped Joey through his break-up more than he could ever imagine… Along with the countless gambling casinos in Vegas, that is.

Stacey and Tash enjoyed married life, but with Tash aching for a sense of action, they both missed venturing out into the real world. While they were all able to enjoy their current blissful ignorance, it would only be a matter of time until they would all need to venture out of the magical realm, once more.

***

Finally, the day came when Athena delivered the highly anticipated news to Astrid. They had been sparring at exceptional pace with spears for the past four hours until Astrid finally fell to her knees and wiped the blood from the fresh wound to her cheek, defeated by the goddess. "I… I can't do it."

"Nonsense, Astrid. Stop acting like a mortal. When will you learn that you are beyond who you think you are?" Athena demanded, bringing the end of her spear to Astrid's chest.

Enraged by Athena's words, Astrid pushed the point of the spear away from her and got to her feet. "You want me to stop acting like a mortal? Well, I'll stop when you tell me what the hell I am. Cruz seems to think I'm a demi-god, yet the last I heard was that I was nothing more than a goddam vessel being expected to use the powers of the gods."

"You will know in due time, Astrid."

"Oh, don't give me that. Answer me this, why did Hades refer to me as Pandora when I was in the underworld? What is it that I'm missing? Is Pandora using me too? Why have I never heard her voice?"

Athena's pale eyes bore into Astrid as if she was strategizing the best answer to give. "Have you been recalling your memories?"

"Some of them. The ones that matter, that is. My point is, that Hades believed that I was Pandora. Cruz believes that Pandora is possessing me, and I get that I'm her descendant… But wasn't she just a mortal woman? How does that make me more powerful than a mortal?"

Silent, Athena led Astrid to the benches and set her spear against the wall, gesturing for Astrid to do the same.

"I am sorry, Astrid. I cannot give you the answers you seek. Nobody can. But I assure you, you will understand them all in due time."

Feeling her anger building, Astrid felt a shift in the air. In fact, a heavy breeze blew against her face. In her anger, she was channeling Persephone's powers. But before she could do anything with the winds, she was met by Athena's cold glare. "Control your temper, Astrid, for I have news that will be the perfect opportunity to unleash your anger."

Taking a few deep breaths to calm herself down, Astrid knew there was no point in angering the goddess. "Okay, so what's the news on the grapevine?"

Athena looked into the distance as if she was listening to somebody else, before turning back to Astrid. "It is time. Hades has made his presence known and is looking for you and Persephone. It will only be a matter of time before he comes here, you need to bring him down."

Surprised by the news, Astrid replied. "But I thought the barrier would keep everybody safe."

"This barrier was never meant to last."

"I just don't get why Zeus won't help. He wants peace just as much as everybody else does, doesn't he?"

"Zeus's relationship with Hades has always been... difficult to understand."

"Difficult to say the least. He helped Hades kidnap his own daughter."

"While that may be true... Wouldn't you want your daughter to see the world that she is set to lead? I know that you and Cruz volunteered to battle him when you first arrived, but your daughter also requested to go with you."

"No, absolutely not!"

"While I do believe her skills are adequate, this decision belongs to you and Cruz."

"I'll ask him, but I know that we're both going to agree that it's far too dangerous."

With one last hard-to-read nod, Athena left with her staff, leaving Astrid alone to collect her things and take an after-work out shower.

Soon after, Astrid met with Cruz at their favorite bar.

It was midday and he had started his day's mission of seeking happiness at the bottom of multiple glasses of bourbon designed to get an immortal drunk. Exhausted from her sparring session, Astrid took the seat beside him, ordered the same drink and informed him of Athena's news.

"Nope, it's not happening," Cruz demanded, knocking back another stiff drink and pushing back a lock of his hair from his face. Relieved they were on the same page, Astrid took a sip of her drink. "Thank the gods you agree."

"It's the obvious decision. She's almost eighteen months old."

"You know that's not true... she's just a goddess and they age quicker than the rest of us. But I'm glad you agree. It's too dangerous for her."

"Much too dangerous," he added, with a smirk in her direction. "Which is why I don't want you or the rest of the group going either. Joey and I have this one handled."

Astrid choked on her bourbon. "Excuse me?! You won't stand a chance by yourself. You're nowhere near as strong as Hades, you'll die, so I'm going with you."

A drunken grin flashed across Cruz's face, "Is that so? Who was it that taught you how to use Persephone's powers? That's right, I did. So, you can relax here in the barrier where it's safe, *mi amor*. Joey and I've got it covered."

His words were deliberately infuriating. Knowing that Cruz was purposely baiting her, Astrid concentrated on her next sip to ensure that she didn't choke again... or choke him instead. She swallowed down her mouthful and spoke as calmly as she could. "In case you had forgotten, Cruz I've also trained with Athena, so I think I know a trick or two... and if you call me *mi amor* again..."

Cruz grinned wider as he pushed her hair behind her ear, leaving his hand there for a little too long. "You'll what, *mi amor*?"

"I'll kick your drunk ass so hard in front of this bar, leaving you unconscious, and we'll all leave the barrier without you. I mean, somebody's gotta stay here with Hope, may as well be her papa."

As a clear hint of drunken embarrassment flushed through Cruz's cheeks, they both became increasingly aware of his hand which was still holding her lock of hair behind her ear.

Quickly, Cruz removed his hand and turned his eyes to Joey, who was playing poker with a centaur, a nymph and a mortal human, before turning back to Astrid. "Alright, fine," he finally said. "But do you really want to leave your boyfriend here, alone, and come on a suicidal trip with me and Joey?"

"What do you mean leave him here?"

"Don't take this the wrong way, but it's too dangerous to bring him… or any of them, really."

"Are you actually insinuating that Samuel isn't…"

"See? I knew you would get this way. For your information, I'm actually trying to look out for the guy. Hades is an immortal god. If Samuel, Tash or the others come with us, they could die, and you could never let that happen. Could you? So, your choice is to either stay here with him, keeping up your little…whatever the hell the two of you are… Or come with me. Either way, they stay here."

As usual, Cruz was right. There was no way that she could risk Samuel getting hurt. Sure, he was strong, and he could fight like the amazing soldier he was. It was in his blood. But he was still mortal. She sipped the last of her bourbon and nodded. "Alright, just meet me here tonight. We should say our goodbyes first."

Upon merely thinking Samuel's name, Astrid smiled over at the entrance to see him leaning against the doorway speaking with Stacey and Tash by the poker machines. That smile, however, didn't go unnoticed.

Cruz sighed. "Speaking of your perfect boyfriend… How are the two of you?"

Astrid considered his question. Cruz was generally interested in her happiness, despite the pain it caused him. "We're good," she replied.

"Good? Not great?" he asked with a half-assed smile. "Because you know, you and I… Well, we were always great. In fact, I kinda remember us being…"

"Cruz! Just stop right there. Samuel and I are good. Just leave it at that. Besides, I think Joey is gaining a few enemies over there."

On her word, Cruz followed her gaze. Joey was using his power of luck to cheat at his poker game and his opponents were growing furious very quickly. Concerned, Cruz stood from his seat. "Yeah, I should go and help before he actually gets himself killed this time."

As Cruz left to deal with Joey, Astrid made her way over to Samuel, Tash, and Stacey by the entranceway to find that frustration was written all over their faces. "Hey, what's happening?" she asked, as Samuel pulled her into his arms and planted a kiss on her forehead.

Stacey looked to the door leading out into the street and then back to Astrid. "Your daughter Hope is what's happening."

"Uh oh... Elaborate." Astrid said, pressing the back of her head into Samuel's chest. But Stacey and Tash were waiting for Samuel to fill her in on the news. Clearly, whatever it was, had to be serious. "Okay, what's Hope done now?" she asked the soldier.

"Apollo has his eye on her," Samuel said, hesitant.

"His eye on her?"

Samuel nodded.

"But she's only a child," Astrid argued. "That's practically… Well, no! She's too young!"

"Actually, while we all think that," Tash started. "Hope actually has the mindset and the body of an adult... she's a goddess. And no, I don't mean that in the way it sounds... I'm her aunt, for god's sake! Not to mention, Apollo looks roughly her age. Those two could pass as high school students."

"Well they're not high school students. Hope has never even set foot in a high school. Damn Apollo, Cruz is seriously going to flip."

"That's what I said," Samuel added. "That's what we were arguing about before you stepped over here. Apollo's a god, he should know better than to take advantage of her that way."

"You were arguing?"

"Buzzkill was going to kick Apollo's ass," Tash replied. "I was merely looking out for him."

Sighing, Astrid turned her gaze onto Cruz and Joey who were leaving the bar through a side exit. "Good thinking, Tash. Unfortunately, that leaves me to deliver the news to Cruz that our little girl needs to remain at least a hundred feet from the handsome young archery god. How the hell has this become my life?"

Tash shrugged. "It could be worse."

"How so?"

As Tash opened her mouth to respond, she looked up at Samuel, then back at Astrid with a grin. But then at the last moment, she shook her head with a change of heart. "Never mind."

Knowing that she was merely holding back a joke, Astrid looked to Samuel who merely nodded in the direction of the door that Cruz had left through. "Speaking of Cruz, what were the two of you talking about? It seemed intense."

On that note, Tash and Stacey excused themselves, as Astrid took Samuel's hand and led him outside into the sunny street.

"Is everything alright?" Samuel asked after a long and stifling bout of silence. "Don't tell me Cruz talked your ear off about those comic books again. I don't think I can handle another debriefing of your endless 'who would win' battles."

"Why not?"

"Because the two of you take that stuff way too seriously. You're not children."

Shocked, Astrid gasped. Who was he calling a child? "Excuse me, Samuel? There's nothing wrong with…"

But before she could finish her sentence, Samuel kissed her quickly on the mouth to silence her and grinned. "Besides Sutherland, we all know that Batman would win against Wonder Woman."

Before she could argue, Samuel took off along the footpath forcing Astrid to chase after him. "Such a typical answer for a Sergeant like you. But Wonder Woman would go all Amazonian on his ass and leave him for dead." After running only a few feet ahead, Samuel turned and raised his hands in defeat.

"Alright, fair point."

Pleased with her minor victory, Astrid pulled Samuel into her arms and adopted her serious tone. "You're only saying that because you're desperate to find out what Cruz and I were talking about."

"True," Samuel said planting a kiss on her forehead. "So, what's the news? I'm assuming it had something to do with Hades."

"Yeah, it does. And I'm sorry, Samuel, but you're really not going to like what I have to say."

As Samuel waited for her to elaborate an amused smile crossed his face. "Uh oh, Sutherland. Has anybody ever told you that you look like your father before you give bad news?"

"No, I don't think anybody has," Astrid replied, a little off guard. "Is that good or bad?"

"I'd say weird. That serious expression on him was always a cause for alarm… But on you, damn, it's sexy as hell." Samuel brought his hand to her cheek, as if to be studying every detail of her stern face. The smile to his lips while it made her blush, it told her more than his words ever could. For the first time in a very long time, Samuel was happy, and it was because of her. Still, he seemed to be missing the seriousness in her tone. "Samuel, this is important."

"Alright, I'm sorry, I'll stop." He planted another kiss on her mouth and pulled away again. "What's up? What won't I like?"

"The fact that Cruz and I... and quite possibly Joey... well, tonight we'll be leaving the barrier in search of Hades."

"Why just you three?"

"Samuel..."

The happiness in his eyes was quickly replaced by the disappointment that followed her words. "You know I'm really starting to miss all the action. I can handle my own, you know that."

"I'm sorry, I really am. But this is something that Cruz and I need to do alone. He's a god and I can't risk you getting hurt."

"What? No! What happened to us all being a team? Come on, I'm the one who trained you to use a sword, remember?"

"That's why I need you to watch over my daughter and the rest of the group. Hope is the most important person in all of this and if anything happens to her while I'm away… Well, I'm looking to you to make sure that she and the others are kept safe. Please, Samuel."

Samuel gave her an unwavering look as if to be weighing up his options. "I'm a soldier, not a damn babysitter."

"And right now, I need you to be that soldier. Please, this is an order I'm giving you because the fate of the world quite literally rests in her hands. Please."

Samuel hesitated, but reluctantly gave in, while bringing his arms back around her waist. "You do realize that you just tasked me with the same order your father did before he died. You're going up against Hades, so you have to understand my hesitation in all this."

"What can I say? I get my judge of character from my father. So do you accept my order or what, sergeant?"

"Of course, I do, Sutherland. But if something happens to you again, just know that I'll stop at nothing to bring you back. Hades won't know what hit him."

"And that's why you're staying here." Astrid stepped up on her tiptoes and met his lips with her own.

Every kiss, every embrace with the soldier overwhelmed her in a way that she couldn't quite shake.

She loved him. But as much as she wanted to give her heart fully to the soldier, there was an entirely separate identity that loved Cruz. Undeniably, Samuel was perfect, brave and capable, but Cruz was… well, he was Cruz.

This hurricane of emotion-filled thoughts obsessed her mind more than it should have. And while she wanted to blame it on Persephone being present in her mind, secretly, she knew that just wasn't the case. Nor was the case a lustful side effect from the curse. It was plain and simple. Astrid was head over in heels in love with both men. Unfortunately, that type of love was doomed to fail.

"Hi mom… Buzzkill. Have you seen dad?" Hope's voice broke in over her tender moment with Samuel, forcing them to startle and turn to Hope standing only a few feet away with Apollo. Astrid eyed Apollo suspiciously.

If she had met him on the street, she would've assumed he was no older than a high school student and not the immortal god that he was. "Yeah," Astrid managed to say. "He and Joey just left the bar a few moments ago. What were you two doing?"

The way Astrid eyed Apollo with such suspicion could only be likened to the same expression that Hope sent in Samuel's direction. She was certainly not a fan of the soldier. But she also had the wisdom of Athena, so she knew better than to let that frustration fester.

"You mean, Uncle Hermes. They've probably gone to go visit Aunt Hannah again." Hope went to brush past them, but Astrid stood in her way.

"Hope... Can I have a word?"

Frustrated, Hope allowed for Astrid to lead her a few feet away from Samuel and Apollo to speak in private.

"What's going on?" Hope asked, curiously.

"Your dad and I need to go away for a little while. Samuel is going to stay here with you."

"As, what? A babysitter? Look at me? I'm not a child! I wasn't born yesterday!"

"No, you were born just over a year ago, so yes, technically you are still a baby."

"No, mom! I'm not! I'm a demigod, raised by gods and humans, with wisdom far greater than you can comprehend."

"Don't pull that card, Hope. Hell, I was pregnant with you two years ago. You're staying here, and Samuel will look out for you and that's it." Astrid's anger had escaped from her unexpectedly, but it was enough to make Hope sink back with frustration.

"He's such a Buzzkill. Where are you and dad going, anyway?"

"I'd rather not say."

"You're going after Hades, aren't you?" But Astrid refused to respond. "You are, aren't you? Do either of you know how dangerous that is? Of course, you do, it's why you're leaving me here with your boyfriend, so he can play the role of stepdad. Well in that case, no! I'm coming with you. We'll make it a family vacation and maybe you and Dad can rekindle your romance, because come on, we all know there's still some serious chemistry between you… Even Buzzkill can see it."

Utterly annoyed, Astrid stared in disbelief at her child, "Seriously, Hope! Where do you get this attitude from?"

"I'd rather not say," Hope grinned, mocking her mother's earlier statement.

"You've been watching reruns with Tash and Stacey again, haven't you? I'm serious. You're staying here. And while we're at it, the other gods and nymphs have been having children, so why don't you find somebody your own age to spend time with... Apollo is, well..."

"Seriously? Now you're poking at my friendship with Apollo? For your information, we're just friends, mom."

"It doesn't look like it." While Astrid's voice raised, Hope's voice lowered in embarrassment.

"Well, that's exactly the case. For your information, he turned me down. Said I was too young. Do you have any idea how much that hurts?"

Astrid couldn't help but secretly smile. "I'm... I'm sorry, Hope."

"Yeah, sure you're sorry. You're just like dad." Without another word, Hope stormed off, grabbing Apollo by the arm.

"Apparently they're not together," Samuel said to Astrid when they were out of earshot.

"Yeah... I still don't trust them. Hope's been watching Stacey and Tash's rerun collection."

"Damn, all those 'will they-won't they' relationship drama, it's enough to make me want to rip off my ears and claw out my eyes. I'm going to have my hands full with her, aren't I?"

"You sure are. But you can handle it."

"So, when do you leave again?"

"Tonight. Wish us luck!"

"You want luck? If you guys are taking Joey, you'll both be fine! Just promise me you'll come back safe." Samuel planted another kiss on her forehead. Unfortunately, that was one promise Astrid couldn't make.

***

As Cruz knocked back two glasses of regular strength bourbon at the bar, he was joined by Astrid, who was more than ready to leave.

"Are you ready to hit the road, *mi amor*?" he asked, slinging his faded black backpack over his shoulder.

While he knew the words '*mi amor*' irritated her, in that moment, that need to annoy her was all he had to distract him from wanting to kiss her. With a roll of her eyes, Astrid ordered them both an immortal strength drink.

"A little liquid courage, Cruz. Because we're sure as hell going to need it." Their drinks came quickly.

"Here's to that," Cruz agreed. He clanked his glass against hers and grinned as she consumed her entire glass of bourbon in one mouthful before wiping her face with the sleeve of her dark leather coat. "Chill girl. You're getting a little ahead of yourself, aren't you?"

Astrid scanned the bar and shrugged her shoulders. "So, sue me. I've had a lot going on. I thought you were inviting Joey."

"You know, I was going to invite Joey... but then, I thought of how much fun it would be to spend some alone time with you. Brings us back to the old times, you and me on the road... alone... slipping into motel rooms, making out in that old clinic just a few hours outside of San Francisco..." Cruz allowed for his voice to trail off as he studied the expressions on her face. He knew every single one of Astrid's expressions as if they had been imprinted on his brain permanently.

It pleased him to know that her current expression was optimistically reminiscent of the seriously steamy memory they both shared. Her expression was followed by a sudden look of embarrassment and then her sheer sense of vulnerability. It was those expressions that told him all that he wished she would say out loud.

That she still loved him. It wasn't lust that she felt for him, but something that ran far deeper than anything either of them had ever felt before. As if caught off guard by her own emotions, Astrid turned away and ordered another drink. "One more for the road, please... I'm going to need it."

Cruz bit down on his lower lip, and got to his feet, just as Astrid finished her drink in the same quick mouthful as before.

"You're an insufferable prick," she said, knocking him with her backpack as she slung it over her shoulder. Her insult would've been easy to ignore had it not been lined with her infuriating smile. Instead, he leaned in close and whispered,

"I'm still the same insufferable prick that knows you better than anyone... in more ways than one... wouldn't you agree, *mi amor*?"

Once again, he had knowingly gone too far. He considered Samuel. Sure, they were rivals. Cruz was the nerdy underdog, Samuel was the popular jock. But no matter how much Cruz loved Astrid, he wouldn't make her betray her loyalty to the guy.

On Astrid's unwavering stare of death, Cruz sighed and walked on ahead. "Come on, Astrid. Let's get this over with. Let's take down Hades of the underworld." As they neared the exit, Athena stood in their pathway, cutting them off to address the mother of his child, and in doing so, forcing Cruz to stop too.

"Astrid, I know I can't go with you, but I wanted to give you this." Athena handed over her golden spear. It glistened in the lights and was elegantly crafted, revealing a very sharp pointed arrow at one end. Cruz looked from Athena to Astrid. A gift from the goddess, and not just any gift, but her actual weapon. Astrid, however, was highly hesitant to receive it.

"I'm sorry, Athena, but I just can't accept this."

"Why? Surely, you will need it to bring down Hades, it has the power to kill a god."

"Yes," Astrid started. "But this is your weapon. Anybody who knows anything about history…"

But Athena would not listen. "Astrid, my spear is simply just a tool to be wielded. Your real weapon is your mind. You carry with you the elements of Persephone and Pandora. But my spear carries my own essence. It will help against your battle with Hades and if you come into any danger along the road."

"Are you sure you're willing to just give it to me?"

"Take it and go. I have trained you well, so I know you will succeed. You and Mario Cruz." Astrid glanced at Cruz, then hesitantly accepted the spear.

"Thank you." Athena went to say something further, but instead chose to remain silent, allowing for Cruz to lead Astrid out of the bar.

Over their time being there, Cruz had done his best to keep out of the way of the gods, particularly Athena. She scared him extensively. And with Zeus being paranoid not knowing just whom had trapped him in the pithos in the first place, he had once asked Cruz to be his eyes and ears. But Cruz had always hated confrontation. Even so he had remained nothing more than a fly on the wall as the goddesses and even Poseidon busied themselves with the others of his group.

He and Astrid stepped outside to where the cool night air filled their lungs. The familiar sight of centaurs, nymphs and other creatures caught their attention, along with the variously expensive cars that lined the streets. Catching sight of the spear in Astrid's hands, Cruz tried to brighten the mood.

"That's some pretty cool spear. It suits you."

"You really think so?"

Approaching a bright red convertible, he pulled out the remote from his pocket and turned back to her. "I sure do, just as this baby suits me. Jump in."

"A convertible, Cruz? Driving in style, aren't we?"

"I always wanted one, but I could never afford one on my archaeologist wage. I picked it out this afternoon with Joe." They climbed into the car and Cruz started up the engine with delight. He couldn't help but grin excitedly as he looked over at Astrid as she fastened her seatbelt. "The night is young, and the road is long. But being with you on this journey feels far from wrong."

"You're so lame, Cruz. Just drive."

"As you wish."

***

Samuel knocked on the outside of Hope's locked bedroom door. Her music was blaring on the inside in an attempt to drown him out. "Hey, Hope? I fixed you some dinner." To his surprise, Hope opened the door and glared at him.

"What do you want, Buzzkill?"

"I made you some dinner." Catching sight of the backpack on her shoulders as she stormed passed, he followed after her. "Wait, where are you going?"

"I'm not staying here with my step-father."

The word 'step-father' threw him off guard. He wasn't sure how he felt about that elevation in status. Nonetheless, he had promised Astrid he would watch over her. "Look, your mother asked that I look out for you and that's what I'm trying to do. Why don't we arrange something with your aunts Tash and Stacey... or even Hannah? I'm sure they'll come right around and..."

"...No! There's no point because I'm not staying. I'm going out."

"With your backpack? I'm sorry, but I can't allow that."

"Get out of my way, Buzzkill. You're not my father!"

"I'm not trying to be. But I still care about you and I'm going to..."

"...Carry out their orders? Like the good little soldier boy, you are? Well, stand down sergeant, you've been dismissed."

"Excuse me?" Samuel refused to step out of her way. Hope might've been Cruz's daughter, but she sure had that same Sutherland determination, he had seen in Astrid and her father. It was nothing new to him. But just like Cruz, Hope could be very unpredictable.

Still, Samuel stood his ground, neither he nor Hope dared to move. "You're not leaving, Hope."

"Is this how you stole my mother from my dad? You ruined my family, Buzzkill." It was evident that Hope was an overgrown daddy's girl who wanted nothing more than her family to go back to normal. Still, he tried to reason with her. "Hope, that's not how it happened. I know you don't like me but..."

"I don't care how it happened. How long after my mother woke from the dead did you pursue her? You knew that she was vulnerable and unstable with Persephone in her head... but you barely even gave her a moment to catch her breath. The deadly sins curse is over, but you're clearly still suffering from your sin, sergeant. Now get out of my way!"

Hope pushed passed him with every ounce of her strength, which more than doubled for Samuel's strength, but he was quick to keep up. "Hope, don't do this! I know what you're intending, and I won't let you go through with it. Both your mom and dad will kill me."

By this point, Hope had reached the door to the apartment. Samuel held himself against the door, refusing to move. "You're not stepping foot out of this apartment. Now, why don't we pick a movie and…"

"I really don't have time for this." With a flick of her wrist, Hope sent Samuel flying through the air, across the room and into the glass coffee table. He landed with full force, smashing it on impact. As he quickly clambered to his feet to examine his bloodied back and arms, he found that Hope had left, slamming the door behind her.

CHAPTER THIRTEEN

As their car left the outskirts of Vegas, with the top pulled up and Astrid and Cruz singing along to classic music, Cruz was the first to mention just how much it reminded him of the old times. "I'm half expecting us to run into that town with Vince and his men… or even get lectured by that traitor Reynolds, may the man NOT rest in peace."

"In the end, he did what he thought was right for humanity," Astrid replied, remembering just how much he needed to end the virus.

"How can you defend him?" Cruz asked. "The man killed you. We trusted him and he… I… well, you know what he did, you were there." Focusing his attention on the darkness before them, Cruz stopped speaking.

On his silence, Astrid could see just how much those final moments plagued him. "Cruz, in the end, Reynolds did what he thought would end the curse. The guy had lost his entire family and was suffering from intense rage. He was broken. In the end he felt he had no choice but to give into those warped delusions of making the world better." Cruz sent Astrid a look which spoke in volumes about his own state of mind. Finally, he released a long sigh. "Hey, look. We've officially left the barrier. Wow these roads really are deserted, aren't they?"

"At least there are no creatures about... No giants to crush our car."

"I'll say." Suddenly, there was a bump, and the steering wheel began to jerk against his grip. "Looks like you spoke too soon," he said. "What the hell?"

"What do you..." before Astrid could finish her sentence, the car was lifted off the road and into a very strong gust of wind. "Cruz, what are you doing? Put us down."

"That's not me," he replied, while pushing the buttons in between them to open the windows. "Astrid, take the wheel!"

Astrid removed her seatbelt and leaned across him to take control of the steering wheel, while Cruz removed his own and reached one hand out his window and the other towards Astrid's now-opened window. He focused his energy and his powers to battle against the force which had completely enveloped the car.

"Who's doing this?" Astrid gasped. "Do you think it's Hades?"

Cruz continued to focus until he finally managed to take control. The car slowly travelled back down until it hit the road with a forceful thump. Cruz steered the vehicle to the side of the road and set it into park, just as they caught sight of the individual responsible.

Standing in front of their car was their very powerful daughter, Hope with her backpack filled with all her necessities.

"I thought you left her with Buzzkill!" Cruz grumbled, unfastening his seatbelt.

"This is your influence!" Astrid groaned, unfastening her own. They stormed out of the car and towards their child.

"What do you think you're doing, Hope? You could have gotten us killed?" Cruz snapped. "Do you even understand how dangerous that stunt was?"

"Relax, you guys were fine," Hope replied, with a smile that was almost identical to her father's. "I had it handled. Besides, you would never let mom get hurt. You love her too much... But, while I've got your attention, I'm coming with you."

"Does Samuel know where you are?" Astrid snapped. "Don't tell me you snuck out."

"Oh, he knows... I walked right out the front door. Wait, there he is now. Oh, crap!" Hope glanced over their shoulders to see the high beams of another car approaching. It neared and pulled over behind their own. As it stopped, Samuel climbed out of the driver's seat, with Joey and Tash not far behind him. "Thank god you guys found her!" Tash declared.

"We had no choice!" Cruz said. "She made our car fly up into a goddamn gust of wind!"

"Really?" Joey smirked. "I'm glad you guys made it out safely."

As Samuel approached, he was instantly apologetically. "I'm sorry, babe. I did try to stop her. She has your blatant disregard for the rules." On his note,

Hope grinned proudly, but instantly lowered her optimism at Astrid's glare.

"Hope, you're going back with Buzzkill," Cruz said. "It's too dangerous for you to be out here. Get in the car, now!"

"Dad, please, just let me go with you. Aunt Tash is always telling me how important family is... yet my family is just so... it's so dysfunctional. I'm getting older and we all know that this could be the only chance that I can experience an actual family vacation."

Astrid watched as her very words won Cruz over. It astounded her at how easily Hope could manipulate him. Unsurprisingly, Cruz looked back at Astrid. "A word?" Shrugging her shoulders, she followed him a few feet away from the others to discuss their verdict, as Samuel headed toward the trunk of his car.

"Why did you have to bring me into this argument?" Tash asked Hope. "They're going to kill me."

"But I really want to go. And they both think so highly of you, that..."

"Tash, get Hope in the car, now!" Samuel said, returning with two swords. "Astrid, Cruz, Joey. It's a chimera!"

"A chimera?" Tash gasped, immediately pulling Hope into the car as Cruz ran to retrieve their own weapons.

"I knew I sensed something," Astrid said looking towards the bushes that Samuel was focused on. Within minutes, Athena's spear was in her hands and she, Cruz, Samuel, and Joey stood prepared just as the monstrous beast with the head of a lioness, the body of a goat and a tail with the head of a serpent appeared out of the trees from the side of the road.

With the high beams of the cars illuminating the beast in pure detail, they could see that the beast stood at least ten feet high. Therefore, strategy was key. "We'll never out run it," Cruz mumbled. "Suggestions anybody?"

"I don't know, Cruz," Samuel retorted. "Can't Zeus do something to help? You are his chosen one, after all."

Cruz pulled a face but refused to break eye contact with the creature. "Shut up, Buzzkill. I can't hear him right now. Let's just focus on bringing this thing down before it tears us apart, alright?"

"Precisely what I was thinking... Now!" On Samuel's command, both Samuel and Cruz charged for the beast with their swords drawn, while Astrid and Joey stayed back.

Naturally, the chimera attacked in retaliation. "Samuel, Cruz!" Astrid called out, but the two were entirely focused on the beast, who fought back with its claws, teeth and serpent's headed tail. Frustrated, she stepped toward Joey.

"What do we do?" she asked him. "They're going to get themselves killed for being so stupid."

"What does Persephone say?"

"Persephone?"

"Yes, right now, she might be our answer."

But before Joey could give Astrid a chance to respond, he stepped toward the others careful not to step in range of the beast. "You guys, back up," he said. "These guys breathe fire!"

In the instant it took for Cruz to turn his attention onto Joey, the chimera launched itself onto him, giving him no chance to move out of the way. Cruz was knocked to the ground. The chimera breathed in his scent and flared its nostrils.

"Hey, you don't want to eat me... I'm too chewy," Cruz cried. "Eat Buzzkill, he'll make a much better meal... He's the taller one over there with the muscles."

"Not a time for jokes," Astrid called out, slowly stepping towards him and the chimera. As she did, Samuel reached for her hand, but she nudged him away.

"Not a time for jokes?" Cruz whined. "What do you mean? I'm about to be eaten alive! Maybe if I can make this thing laugh it'll keep me around a little longer."

The chimera growled low and focused on Astrid who was slowly approaching as Cruz continued to mumble. "...or maybe not. Get back, Astrid." Cruz said, beginning to focus on his powers.

The moment he did, the winds began to howl, violently. Thunder rumbled in the distance and the first few drops of rain began to fall from the sky, but the chimera still refused to back down. This time it focused its concentration on Cruz and licked its lips. A drop of saliva fell onto Cruz's face distracting him from his own focus. "Eww! Girl, you need to clean your teeth. That's just… that's nasty."

Now only a foot away, Astrid could hear her daughter's fearful cries from in the car. *'What do I do?'* she questioned the goddess within her mind.

The plan that Persephone suggested forced Astrid to doubt with every ounce of herself that it would work. But she could see Samuel readying his weapon, preparing for another attack. Astrid had no time to lose. She shook her head at Samuel, sending him a gesture to stand down, with the palm of her hand.

On her command, Samuel nodded and retreated as the chimera growled once more. "Hey girl," Astrid spoke softly to the beast.

"Babe, what are you doing?" Samuel called from under his breath as the beast looked her way.

"It's okay," Astrid said in the same soft tone. She showed her spear to the beast and lowered it to the ground right beside its large paw. From Astrid's position she could see the fear in Cruz's eyes. If Persephone's plan was to fail, she and Cruz could both be killed right in front of their daughter.

There was no way in hell that she would let that happen. Astrid raised her hands to show the chimera that it had nothing to fear from her and then gave her request. "Please, release him." The chimera gave another low growl, warning Astrid to back away.

"Astrid, are you crazy?" Joey snapped. "That thing is from the Underworld! If this is Persephone's plan, tell her, it's stupid." Ignoring him, Astrid continued to watch the chimera, pleadingly. It growled again, blowing smoke into Cruz's face, forcing him to cough, while Astrid brought the palm of her hand against the creature's fur. As the chimera eyed her curiously, Astrid whispered in her ear, "Persephone speaks through me. You can feel her, can't you? You need to leave us. Let us go free."

Joey and Samuel stood on guard, ready to pull her out of the way if necessary. "Samuel, Joey," Astrid instructed. "Put down your weapons. She won't harm us."

And sure enough, Astrid stroked the beast's soft fur as the chimera's cheek pressed softly into her hand like an oversized cat. Obeying her command, Samuel and Joey laid down their weapons, as Astrid continued to communicate with the creature.

"Their weapons are down. Please, release this man." The chimera looked down at Cruz and then back up at Astrid as if to ask if he was the man that she was referring to. "Mm-hmm," Astrid nodded in return.

Hunching its posture, the chimera stepped backward, freeing Cruz who quickly clambered to his feet as Astrid offered him her hand in support. Before Astrid could thank the chimera, it disappeared back into the trees, leaving them all unharmed bringing about an incredible silence.

"Well, that just happened," Cruz mumbled, turning to Astrid in a bid to break the ice. "Was that you or Persephone? I mean, that was… that was awesome. I don't think we covered that part in our magic training." Astrid wasn't sure just how to answer Cruz's question. She turned her gaze to Samuel, who remained silent. When they were sure it was safe, Tash and Hope climbed out of the car and joined them.

"I don't understand," Astrid said. "That was me in total control… the chimera must have felt the influence of Persephone... Because that was far too easy, for my liking."

"It's possible that it was Persephone's influence," Joey added. "Her aura is clearly visible within your skin… But it could also be a Pandora thing."

"A Pandora thing? But I thought you said…"

But Joey shook his head. "We'll talk about it later."

"See, Hope?" Cruz said addressing their daughter. "That's why you need to go back with Buzzkill. I get that you don't like him, I mean he really likes to kill the fun and all, but..."

Samuel glared hard at Cruz. "Seriously, Cruz?!"

"Hold on, let me finish," Cruz replied casually. "There's not really anybody else I'd trust with my daughter's life on the line."

"Thanks, Cruz."

Cruz smirked at Samuel. "Even if you did almost flea like a coward to let Astrid handle it."

Tash broke into a fit of laughter while Samuel and Astrid each gave him a sour look. "Let me deal with this one, okay?" Astrid suggested.

Cruz shrugged. "Okay, I'll meet you in the car."

***

As Astrid left to speak with Hope in private and Samuel and Tash headed towards their car, Joey whispered in close to Cruz. "Why didn't you tell me you were leaving tonight?"

"Because I knew you would want to come with us."

"Damn right, I do! You're planning on taking down Hades... You're going to need my help. Both of you will. But let me guess, you just didn't want me acting as the third wheel. Face it, Cruz. She's moved on. When will you learn that?"

"You want me to move on? Like what you're doing with Hannah, right now? You're the one who declared in front of everybody that Astrid and I were destined to be together. So, let's face it, the heart wants what it wants." Joey gave Cruz a stern look and glanced back over at Samuel ensuring he was out of earshot.

***

As Astrid hugged her daughter, she did her best to get Hope to understand that she needed to stay behind. "Look, I get that you want to come with us, Hope. But that chimera was just the beginning of what we're going to be facing. Please, just this once, I need you to go back with

Samuel and stay where it's safe. You don't even need to stay with him... stay with Stacey and Tash or even the gods... or even your aunt Hannah. If you do this for me, I promise that I'll make it up to you... and when the world is safe, your father and I will take you somewhere very special. I might even send you to a proper high school if the world ever goes back to normal."

"Do you promise?"

"Of course, I do, just stay here where they can keep you safe. Please. For me." Defeated, Hope nodded, hugged her mother and then went over and hugged Cruz goodbye too. Instead of heading to Samuel, Astrid made her way over to Tash, who was leaning against their vehicle, "Take her to your place if you need to. Maybe some time with you and Stacey might do her some good. While you're at it, look after Stacey for me." Tash nodded.

"Always. Just stay safe, okay?"

"We will."

As Tash led Hope into the car, Samuel pulled Astrid into his arms, pulling her in tight. "Are you sure you want to do this?" he asked. "I have to admit when you approached that thing, I was scared I might lose you again."

"I'll be fine, Buzzkill. Remember, you trained me."

"That doesn't bode well for my confidence."

"Okay then, Athena also trained me. Does that help?" she smiled up at him, doing her best to persuade him.

"A little bit. I love you. You know that, right?"

She stepped up on her tiptoes and kissed him. "I do, and I love you and stop worrying. I'll be fine, okay? Just be here when I get back." They kissed passionately, before he broke away again. "Stay safe, Sutherland!"

"Is that an order, Sergeant Buzzkill?" Samuel saluted her playfully, so she saluted him back before hopping into the passenger side of the red convertible.

As she fastened her seatbelt, Cruz turned on the ignition and said, "I really could have gone a century without having to see you and Buzzkill doing... that."

"Call us even. You could've told me we had a stowaway."

"Hey, Sutherland," Joey piped up. "Would you mind putting on some road trip music? Maybe something with a little bass?" Astrid shook her head in disbelief and glanced over at Cruz, who smiled back, and carried on driving up the road.

***

Once Samuel had dropped Tash and Hope at Stacey and Tash's apartment, he headed over to the group's usual bar where he found Hannah burying her sorrows in a glass of red wine.

"Hey, Han... Here again?" Over the past few months, Hannah had taken up a day job at the local clinic, but by night she would come and drink away her miseries.

"Of course, I am. What else would one do if they found out that the love of their life had been hiding a secret that they weren't even human?"

"They would get over it and be thankful that they were actually in a relationship with the person they love in the first place," Samuel replied.

"Maybe I shouldn't be coming to you for advice. The love of your life is also the one destined to be with my best friend... Or so, Hermes, the man I am in love with believes." Hannah shook her head and drank the last drop that was left in her glass, before pouring herself another. Samuel nodded.

"Yeah, it couldn't get more complicated than that. Oh wait, I just watched Astrid tame a chimera before it could make a meal out of Cruz… Not to mention I was supposed to be babysitting their daughter who flung me across the room with a flick of her wrist." Hannah grinned. And then her grin turned into a hysterical burst of laughter as she imagined the entire scene vividly.

"Your next drink is on me, Samuel. You've successfully managed to beat me when it comes to relationship complications and make me laugh at the same time." Hannah gave a signal to the waiter to bring two more drinks their way, before turning her attention back to Samuel. "I take it Cruz is fine, by the way."

"You'd be correct with that assumption. The very moment Astrid saw Cruz at the mercy of that thing… she froze. It doesn't take a genius to know that she still loves him. But the way she tamed that thing? It was absolutely majestic."

The waiter brought over their drinks and Hannah waited for him to leave before she addressed Samuel again.

"She loves you too, you know. And how could she not, you're one hell of a kisser… if I remember correctly." She was referring to the moment they had both given into lust before the deadly sins curse had ended.

Samuel raised his eyebrows. "And you're a little drunk, Han."

"Not drunk enough. I'm still in love with the man who turned out to be the son of Zeus and the messenger of the gods."

"Not to mention, part nymph. As well as my own ancestor… I don't actually think that's what Hermes really looks like. Shouldn't he have pointed ears or something?"

Hannah was about to reply, when they were joined by Poseidon. "Samuel, it is time," he said, without even saying 'hello'. "I have gathered an army, and you have a ship waiting on the coast of the angels."

"The angels?" Samuel asked. "Don't you mean on the coast of Los Angeles?"

"I need you to travel to my home of Atlantis. You will find that it has been corrupted by my brother, Hades. My people are not themselves and with my powers being as limited as they are, I need you to help me reclaim my home. The amulet you are wearing will provide you with safe passage."

Samuel brought his hand to the blue-stoned amulet at his neck and he and Hannah exchanged confused glances, trying to determine whether they had heard that correctly. "You want me to go to Atlantis?" Samuel finally asked.

"Yes, and you must leave tonight. Gather your team and meet the soldiers at the ship. We will meet again when you arrive."

Samuel sent another look at Hannah and then turned back to where Poseidon had been sitting. The god was gone.

"Did that just happen?" Samuel asked her.

"If you're asking if the god of the sea just sent you on a mission to Atlantis, then yeah. I think it did," Hannah said, pushing her glass away. "Maybe I am a little too drunk."

"But I'm supposed to be keeping an eye on Hope. I promised Astrid, and there's no way are we bringing her with us."

"Maybe we should discuss this with Stacey and Tash to see what they think of the situation," she suggested.

***

Merely ten minutes later, Samuel and Hannah found themselves sitting with Stacey and Tash in their living room to see what they made of the conversation with Poseidon.

An hour later, it had been decided that Tash and Hannah would accompany Samuel while Stacey would remain in Las Vegas with Hope.

"Could you let Sutherland know..." Samuel asked Stacey.

"That you'll be back as soon as you can and that you love her? Of course, I will. Just stay safe and bring my wife back safely too."

"Will do, Stacey. Same goes for you and Hope."

Samuel finished collecting the rest of their luggage and then he, Tash and Hannah drove out of the Las Vegas barrier headed for the Los Angeles coastline. As Samuel drove, he felt the warmth of Poseidon's amulet at his neck, as if it were guiding him on his journey.

When they reached their destination, it was evident by the large solid gold ship that stood marvelously on the water, they were in the right place.

"Whoa!" Tash exclaimed.

"I'll say," Hannah remarked. While the golden foundation reminded them of the vessel that Jason and the Argonauts had once sailed on their quest for the Golden Fleece, it looked as if it had certainly received some modern-day upgrades. There were at least nine decks and the ship itself used a built-in engine so it would not need to be paddled by oars. Adorning the bow of the ship was a golden statue depicting the head of a mighty dragon with fierce red eyes for navigation. At the stern was the golden end of the dragon's tail neatly curled inwards. The ship was absolutely beautiful.

As Samuel gazed up in wide-eyed wonder, he barely noticed the soldiers that were working tirelessly preparing the vessel for its voyage. One of the soldiers, an African American man dressed in a dark blue uniform and a cap, approached to greet Samuel. While Samuel saluted him, his eyes remained transfixed on the ship.

"She is beautiful, sir. I heard stories that Jason once felt the exact same way."

The man's words grasped Samuel's attention. "Wait, are you saying..."

"That she is the exact same vessel, saved, preserved and upgraded by Poseidon himself?" The soldier smiled as Samuel nodded, dumbstruck. "That is entirely what I am saying. The Argo is a real marvel... and she is yours. Sergeant Jenkins reporting for duty, sir." It took Samuel all his discipline to not allow his own rush of excitement to devour him. But he knew he needed to maintain his composure.

A hard elbow nudge to his waist brought his attention to the very giddy Tash, who was standing right beside him. She let out a loud an involuntary giggle.

"We sail on your command, sir!" the sailor told Samuel. "Who are your companions?"

"This is Sergeant Martinez my second in command, and this is Doctor Hannah Jacobson."

"A doctor? We have been blessed. Poseidon must be looking out for us, sir," the soldier said. "We leave on your command, General Davids."

As the man left, Tash asked, "Did Poseidon tell him your name? Because that was just so..."

"He must have. Let's go check out this thing, shall we?" Hannah and Tash followed Samuel as he boarded the ship, set sail for Atlantis.

CHAPTER FOURTEEN

In Astrid's mind, she was back in that desolate underworld, but this time, she was in an old, dark castle. Curled up in a ball, in a luxurious bed, Astrid stared down at the bruises to her arms and legs. Her white dress was torn beyond repair and there was no mistaking what had happened to her. Through tears, she looked up at the man, who was putting on his clothes, with disgust and loathing. Hades.

"Persephone will bring you food and you will eat. You need your energy." His voice was cold, and it chilled her to the bone. Astrid was disgusted with herself, disgusted at what had happened. She shook her head but said nothing, only feeling the hint of relief when he had left the room.

Astrid pulled the blanket around her tightly for the mere comfort that it provided. A sudden click of the door startled her and she jolted to see it reopen, but this time she was drenched in relief to see that it was Persephone. The woman had come with a bowl of fruit. She placed it onto the table by the door and approached Astrid empty-handed. As Persephone sat beside her, she pulled Astrid in close and held her tight.

"I've heard news," Persephone whispered. "The gods are trying to bring you back. If that happens, Hermes will come to collect us both and he will take us far from here. We must do it together, or I will never be able to leave again."

Astrid looked up at Persephone. "How can they do that? I've been down here for far too long. I'm just lucky my soul hasn't gone into the river with all the rest yet."

"Above ground, the time works differently, Astrid. You see, months down here is barely equal to a few hours up there. Just please, promise me that you will take me with you."

Nodding, Astrid wiped away a few stray tears. "I promise. I won't let him hurt either one of us again."

Unsure as to how much time had passed, they sat in silence, until the door was violently pushed open again. Hades was back. Astrid screamed out in terror as the tears ran down her face. "It's okay, it's going to be okay." Persephone's voice rang out in her ears in a bid to keep her calm. But then the voice changed.

"Astrid, it's okay." This new voice was masculine. She remembered it vividly in her thoughts. Calming, soothing, loving. It was Cruz's voice that entered her mind.

***

Astrid was still being held but she was no longer in the room with Persephone and Hades. Instead, she was being restrained in a seat by a strap. A seatbelt. And somebody else was holding her tight. It was a man holding her, but luckily, it wasn't Hades, this time.

The scent of the man was somewhat familiar and soothing. Astrid opened her eyes to see that she was in the front passenger seat of the car with Cruz, parked to the side of the road. Cruz's arms were wrapped around her, as if in a bid to comfort her.

As realization sunk in, she shook him off and yelled.

"Get the hell off me, Cruz!" The tears were still fresh on her face. Concern mixed with confusion weighed down on him as he looked to Joey, sitting in the back, for assistance.

"Hey, Astrid," Joey said as calmly as he could, "You were having a really bad dream and screaming in your sleep. Did you want to talk about it?"

Astrid studied him for a moment, remembering his true identity. "Hermes," she whispered. "No, I don't... but, thank you. Thank you for bringing me back."

Joey shrugged. "Sure. You're welcome."

Breaking eye contact, Astrid rested her head back into the seat and stared out the window. They were parked in the middle of nowhere in the middle of the night. "I think we should just get moving again," she mumbled to Cruz, barely looking at him. "You know what happens when we stay parked for too long. We get attacked."

Obeying, Cruz pulled back onto the road and carried on driving. They continued in silence, until Joey finally spoke again.

"So, anyone up for a round of questions? The silence in here is crippling."

"Questions?" Astrid asked him.

"Yeah... I mean, it's always a great icebreaker. We just continue to ask random questions to get to know each other... Don't worry Astrid... we won't ask about your nightmares."

Astrid stared over at Cruz, remembering their own game of questions after their first kiss. "Leave me out of it," she said.

"Me too," grumbled Cruz.

"Wow, it's a wonder how the two of you managed to fall in love in the first place... Where's Aphrodite when you need her?" Joey laughed. "Sorry, bad joke."

Joey was right. The silence in the car was crippling. Even Astrid couldn't understand why she was targeting her anger at Cruz. Maybe it had something to do with the sheer sense of vulnerability she felt when she was around him. But whatever it was, she needed to find a way to move forward.

Unfortunately, the only way to move forward from all that she had endured in the Underworld would take her needing to remember it all. She considered asking Hermes about her time there, maybe that game of questions would be a brilliant idea after all. "Okay, fine... I'll play," she announced. "My first question... What do you remember about me being in the Underworld, Joey? What did you see?"

She focused one hundred percent of her attention on him as she asked, scanning for tells. Joey buttoned his lip.

"What do you remember?" Cruz glanced over at them both in the rear-view mirror, briefly.

"I know what I remember, and I asked you first," Astrid replied, with the same unwavering tone. It was a verbal battle, neither one of them wanting to break their façade or reveal more information than necessary, until finally Joey lowered his guard and his tone.

"Okay... I remember that it wasn't fun for you... or for me having to see... or for Persephone either. But I do remember that I was glad to be able to stop it." Astrid nodded and wiped away a stray tear that had escaped from her left eye, as Joey looked down at his lap. The time that she had remembered was clearly not the only time that it had happened.

"He was a monster," Astrid said coldly. "Persephone is slowly feeding me my memories. But I don't know if I'm really ready to see them all."

Joey nodded, "Yeah, he is a monster."

"Astrid, I'm sorry," Cruz said. Cruz's apology hit Astrid hard. Why the hell was he apologizing again for? He had no need to. Sure, he had opened Pandora's Box and had caused the domino effect of all the events that had transpired, but how was he to know what the gods had in store? "Why are you sorry?" she asked.

"Because if it wasn't for me..."

"Just drop the apologies, alright Cruz! Just stop feeling sorry for yourself. Move on. Sure, you opened Pandora's Box, anybody else in your position would have done the exact same thing. If it wasn't you, it would've been somebody else. Somebody who wouldn't have given a damn about fixing the world. So, let's just stop Hades for once and for all, okay?"

"Alright." The glint of a smile formed at the corner of his mouth as he peered at Joey's reflection in the rear-view mirror. "Okay, Joe... I've got a question. What's the first thing you're looking forward to when the world goes back to normal? Well, whatever normal might be."

"I really don't know. I guess that all depends on if they allow me to stay with all of you... but if they do... I want to propose to Hannah. I want to make everything up to her."

Astrid acknowledged Cruz's look of surprise. "Wow, that's big."

"You're telling me. I've had so many partners in the past, this is all new to me. So, what about you two?"

In unison, Astrid and Cruz both choked on the air that they were breathing. Cruz looked to Astrid and then back to the road. "Marriage?" he asked weakly.

Joey laughed. "That's not what I was referring to, I meant your future plans... But while we're on that topic and the two of you can't exactly escape this moving vehicle. Where do the two of you see your relationship going?"

"You can't be serious," Astrid said, turning her head to the window. "I'm with Samuel."

Joey grinned sheepishly. "I get that. But I'm just thinking on what Tash said a while back. Cruz and

Samuel are only ever competing for your affections. Many tales in the past were about men fighting over a beautiful woman. Helen of Troy, the Karate Kid… men are suckers for a pretty face. If you love them both, why choose only one? They both get you and you get them. Do you know how many orgies I've walked in on because those involved were arguing over the same problem?"

Cruz choked on his own air again. "Wait, you walked in on them? Or did you participate? Because those are two entirely separate answers."

Joey's broad grin told them way more than Astrid was willing to hear.

"Excuse me?" Astrid scoffed. "Why the hell am I even a part of this conversation?" Doing his best not to burst into laughter, Cruz cleared his throat.

"The more you know about somebody. Huh, Astrid? But, no, Joey… Can we just drop the subject?

"You're both welcome," Joey laughed. "But at least I got rid of the damn angry tension."

There was a long awkward bout of silence, before Astrid and Cruz both burst into a loud fit of laughter and

Cruz choked out, "Damn Hermes! That was one way to drop the bomb."

With his broad grin still planted on his face, Joey looked to Astrid and then back to Cruz. "Sorry to offend you both, but think about it... There'd be a lot less fighting between you three... and we might actually work a little better as a team. Teamwork for the win, right?"

"You're sitting right next to a door, Joey," Cruz said, doing his best not to laugh. "You know how to use it, right?"

"Okay, okay," Joey replied, trying to maintain his own jokester composure. "I'm sorry to bring up this taboo subject. But love is love... and from the perspective of someone who has walked the earth centuries longer than either of you I just don't see what the problem is. You're demi-gods. You can do whatever you want. Why shun sexual empowerment because of what society once believed?"

Shaking his head in frustration, Cruz pulled the car to the side of the road. "This coming from a guy who slept with how many of his siblings?"

But carefree Joey continued to find the humor in the uncomfortable situation. "What's your take on the matter, Sutherland?" he asked. "Throughout time love triangles have been drawn out in stories to excite, thrill and break hearts. Nobody bats an eyelash for a man to have two women on his arms, yet it's a situation of inequality for a woman to have two men. She must choose one and break the other's heart. You have Cruz and soldier boy who would ultimately lay down their lives for you, but you must decide whose heart you're going to sacrifice for the sake of the other."

Astrid shook her head and turned to the window. "Simple, I'm with Samuel and Cruz respects that. Don't you, Cruz?"

Cruz stifled an uncommitted nod. "For the sake of our daughter, I'm going to say 'sure' and leave it at that."

Astrid turned to Cruz and then back to Joey who offered an award-winning smile. "Like I said. One of them must sacrifice their heart for you to choose the other. But at the same time, we all know that you love them both. Unfortunately, in this case, you'll end up with a broken heart too. Trust me, I've seen it more times than I'd like."

Astrid wanted to respond but couldn't think of the right thing to say. The truth was, that Joey was right. It would be simpler if she could pick both Samuel and Cruz. Unfortunately, that was not her individual decision to make, and she presumed that Cruz and Samuel would never agree to it either.

As the thought crossed her mind, she looked to Cruz who was devoting his attention to pulling the car back onto the road, until he noticed her watching him. "Ignore Joey," he said. "He was pretty obsessed when *Game of Thrones* came out... At least now I know why."

"Yeah, right," Joey said, pressing his back against his door and stretching his legs out onto the remainder of the back seat. "Ignore the guy who has only witnessed over a few millenniums filled with wars thanks to alpha male perspective points of views. Not to mention, my own father who spent so much time spreading his seed all over the place, while Hera remained the ever-faithful wife. Brooding in her own frustrations and hatred. I'm telling you, nothing good ever comes from a scorned, broken-hearted woman." And with those last words, Joey closed his eyes in a bid to get some sleep. Once the car was finally silent, Cruz whispered to Astrid, "Man, I thought he'd never shut up."

"Is he actually asleep?" Astrid asked.

"Not sure. I mean, he is part nymph. They sleep, but I still struggle to believe half the words that he spews from his mouth."

"Yeah, he really loves to weave those stories, doesn't he?" Astrid peered out her window, keeping her attention on the passing scenery outside the car as she attempted to process her thoughts.

But those thoughts were interrupted by Cruz finally speaking up again. "He was right about one thing, though."

Astrid turned her attention back to Cruz. "What do you mean?"

"Well, in the year that you were gone, despite a few minor arguments, Samuel and I... Well, we kind of got along. It's weird, but we actually became friends."

"Friends?"

"Yeah. We were able to put our competition for you on hold and focus on other important things. Like how to best take down a Minotaur. The guy willingly went with my opinion on that one and then he thanked me later."

"Wow."

"But there was more. It got to the point that he and I would choose to take the same car in a bid to not be the third wheels to the rest of the group. And we'd literally just talk for hours about everything."

On hearing Cruz's confession, Astrid couldn't help but see just why he had expressed a concern for her breaking Samuel's heart. The two were not only friends, but brothers in arms too.

"What does this have to do with Joey being right?" she was half expecting Cruz to tell her that she was the reason for their war, which she knew was undoubtedly true. But instead, he said the last thing she would have ever expected.

"Honestly, if you're right and it's not just some lustful side effect from the curse, but literal L-O-V-E love… well then, I wouldn't object to you choosing to be with us both."

Confused, Astrid stared at him, hard, believing it to be some weird joke at her expense. "You're not being serious, are you?"

He smiled. But that smile went away just as quickly as it had appeared. "It's quite literally the end of the world and while I don't ever want to kiss the guy, myself, I can think of worse things than having the woman I love, also in the arms of Sergeant Buzzkill." His voice adopted a deep and sincere tone that she recognized only when he was at his most vulnerable. "Astrid, I've tried letting you go. But I just can't."

Astrid was struck speechless. In the distance, she could see the sun making its arrival just above the horizon. They were entering the outskirts of a small town in the far distance. The scenery was familiar and probed her to ask the question to an answer she should've asked a while ago but found it the best choice to change the subject. "Where are we headed?"

"I'm not sure," Cruz said. "I just know that this is the way Zeus wants me to go. Maybe when we reach the next town, I'll question his motives."

At least the break in the next town would give her some time to converse with Persephone in private. While Joey's distracting conversation had succeeded in relieving her of the vividness of her dream, she still couldn't shake it from her core. They reached the town and were met by the devastation of what had once been a small peaceful town but now resembled nothing more than silent, cataclysmic ruin.

In need of privacy, Astrid walked over to the nearby park, where every tree, plant and grass lay dead. She knelt in a patch of dirt, placing her palms to the ground and focused, closing her eyes in the process. *'Why didn't you tell me earlier what he did to me?'* she asked Persephone within her mind.

'I didn't think you were ready. You're still not ready. But now we have no choice. After we bring back the powers of the gods, we need to send Hades to Tartarus.'

'I thought we were going to kill him. Athena gave me her spear.'

'Astrid, if you're to kill him, you only get one shot. He is much too strong, and far too clever, we won't be able to do it.'

Astrid could feel something within herself. Deep-seeded fear, but it wasn't her own fear. She was certain that it belonged to Persephone. Finally, she gave in to Persephone's choice. *'Well, how do we send Hades to Tartarus?'*

'We ask Cruz to reach out to Zeus. It's our only option.'

'But Zeus allowed for Hades to kidnap you in the first place, why would he even agree to this plan?' Persephone's response was saturated in desperation, Astrid had seen that same level in so many victims of abuse in the past. The goddess was clearly clinging at straws.

'Zeus must agree. For it was Hades' pithos that Zeus gave to Pandora. Clearly, Hades was the one responsible for trapping Zeus in it in the first place.'

That failsafe plan to send the god of the Underworld surely had its merit and while she promised to consider it, Astrid made her own request of the goddess. *'Persephone, I need you to show me all my memories. Show me everything that Hades has done to me.'*

'Astrid, while my spirit is inside of you, we share the same mind. For me to unlock all your memories, I will need to show

you all of mine too. There is just too much for one mind to handle at once.'

'I know. But I need to know. I can't have all my memories locked away until you decide to give them back. Please, I just need to know.'

'There is something else,' Persephone said, highly hesitant.

'Something else? What do you mean?'

She could feel Persephone's reluctance to answer, but after silently insisting that the goddess tell her everything, the goddess finally agreed. *'Astrid, the goddess, Pandora is a part of you. I'm not sure how it has been made possible, but you have the essence of her within your very soul. When I do this, there is a high chance that all of her memories will be unlocked to you too.'*

Before Astrid could dispute all that Persephone had just revealed, her mind was overwhelmed with a flood of memories. She saw them all. Each and every one, as they flashed through her mind at an alarming speed, including one memory in particular where Hades had declared that he would overthrow Zeus and make Astrid his bride goddess of the earth.

Her head ached in searing pain. She fell to her knees, clutching at her head and screaming out in unbearable agony. After she had seen each memory take its place within her mind, she spoke within her thoughts again. *'That was... that was unbelievable!'*

There were memories of her own life, of Persephone's and even of a life that she couldn't quite comprehend, which she assumed belonged to Pandora, herself.

'I warned you, Astrid. I had to use my power to ensure that your mind had the strength to tolerate them all,' Persephone said as Astrid felt the weight of exhaustion wash over her. Unable to handle the throbbing pressure to her head, Astrid fell asleep on the ground in the middle of the park.

***

Astrid awoke a few hours later to find Cruz kneeling over her. The moment her eyes had opened, she sat up and looked around at the beautiful garden that surrounded her. Joey was kneeling beside Cruz and they both seemed equally concerned for her wellbeing.

Astrid's eyes fell back to Cruz and instantly relayed Persephone's words out loud. "Hades needs to be sent to Tartarus for everything he's done." But Cruz simply studied her. "Astrid, I don't think that's possible. We don't have the power to do that."

"Well, it needs to be made possible. Tell Zeus that Hades is going to overthrow him. He needs to be ready." There was a sudden voice that boomed in the atmosphere all around them at Astrid's words.

"Is this true, Persephone?" It was undoubtedly the voice of Zeus.

Astrid got to her feet and felt the moment that Persephone took control of her entire body again. "Yes, father. It is. And I don't believe that killing him will be enough to ensure that he suffers the full extent of his wrongdoing."

"Acquire his bident and deliver it to me. The powers to restore the gods and the earth lie within that. Once you have done what is needed of you, I will send him to Tartarus myself. But then, you must go back to the Underworld, Persephone. You will be its new ruler, is that clear?"

"Yes, father." Persephone spoke obediently through Astrid's voice.

"No, father!" Joey shouted. "Persephone is doing everything in her power to fix your brother's wrongs. Why should she be forced to spend another eternity back down there?"

"Persephone can still return to the surface whenever she chooses, just as she will be able to do with the Underworld. This is a reward for her work. Not a punishment."

"Okay, that's fair. But can't we just bring down Hades once and for all? I feel that sending him to Tartarus will be a big mistake."

"I understand your resentment, Hermes. But it is how we've done things since the dawn of time. I assure you, he will not escape. Now, my son. I have some gifts for you, for all that you have done to guide my champion in his duty."

Joey, Cruz and Astrid looked to the ground to see a bundle of golden items in the grass nearby. A golden staff with two serpents intertwined, a golden helmet with two wings attached to the sides, and a pair of golden sandals. Zeus had brought all of Hermes' items there, together.

Excited, Joey picked them up, put them all on and then looked down at the sandals in distaste.

"I just wish I still found sandals fashionable." As he said the words, they magically turned into a pair of white sneakers, with golden wings imprinted on either side. His golden helmet turned into a black cap with a picture of the golden helmet on the front. "That's better!" He admired his staff, like a child with his favorite toy just as Zeus spoke again.

"Now, you must all travel south. And Cruz, I hope that I will have your decision, soon." Without a word, Cruz nodded, then led the group out of the beautiful garden and back to the car, ready to carry on with the trip.

***

Back in the car, Joey took over the driving with Astrid sitting alongside him. Cruz on the other hand, wanted to use that time to get some sleep in the back. But Astrid, however, had other plans. "Hey, Cruz? What is it that you need to do?" she asked, turning back to see him drifting off.

"Hmm?" came his murmured response as he opened his eyes to look at her.

"What was Zeus talking about? What does he want you to decide on?"

"Don't worry about it. Let me get some sleep." But his need to keep a secret just annoyed her.

"Seriously, Cruz? What are you hiding? Is this that offer you mentioned earlier?"

Clearly knowing, he wouldn't win that argument, Cruz sat up and studied her, though his tone remained calm. "While I won't pester you with your secrets, I'm just asking that you to leave me to mine."

"But if I tell you mine... You'll tell me yours?" she asked, hoping that would change his tune. She knew that he was highly curious about her secrets pertaining to her experience in the Underworld, but he would never force that information out of her.

Cruz stared at her with a changed expression. "Fine, if that's what you want to do. We'll trade secrets. What do you remember about the Underworld?"

To their surprise, Joey immediately came to Astrid's aid. "You don't need to tell him that, Astrid. Nothing's worth you needing to relive that experience."

"It's fine, Joey," Astrid replied. "If you must know, Cruz, Hades grew tired of Persephone and turned his eyes onto me... The descendant of Pandora. I was made to suffer what felt like an eternity down there as his new concubine."

As Cruz sat in sheer disbelief, Joey adopted sincere sympathy and placed his hand on her shoulder. "And that's why I don't think we should send him to Tartarus, despite what Persephone thinks. We need to stop him once and for all." While Astrid whole-heartedly agreed with Joey, she knew that Persephone was just biding her time to argue with the guy.

Picking up on the fact that there was more to Astrid's story, Cruz asked, "What aren't you telling me? What does Joey know that I don't?"

But Astrid shook her head. She had said enough. "No, Cruz. It's your turn."

After taking a deep breath, Cruz sighed out loud. "Zeus wants to be in human form again. His soul was locked in the pithos and while he doesn't know who did it he wants to personally hunt down those responsible."

"I'm sorry, but what did you just say?" Joey stammered.

"You didn't know that Zeus has a full-on revenge plan?"

"No, I knew that part. I meant the part about him wanting to be in human form again. Don't tell me you're going to say what I think you're going to say."

Of course, Zeus would want to use Cruz's body as a host. But Astrid needed to probe deeper. "Cruz? Just how much control would Zeus have? "

As if he had been expecting that question, Cruz bit down on his bottom lip. "He wants to take full control of my body. But unlike you, I'd be giving up my body entirely. My whole life because he wants to make more heirs."

"Son of a bitch!" Joey snapped. "Why didn't you tell us this sooner?"

"I'm sorry," Cruz replied. "He asked that I kept it a secret. That's why I was planning on leaving after we fixed everything, so you guys wouldn't have to see me as him. I don't even know why he picked me of all people. Buzzkill is far better suited to this than I am."

As Cruz slumped back in his seat, Astrid shook her head and considered his words. "Are you going to do it?" she finally asked. "Are you going to take Zeus up on his offer?"

"Do I really have a choice? He already held up his end of the bargain by bringing you back. This was my sacrifice." Astrid felt her mouth grow dry. Cruz had ultimately sacrificed his own freedom for Zeus to bring her back from the Underworld. Clearly, he was being literal when he told her that he loved her in a willing-to-give-up-his-soul kind of way. As if he could read her mind, Cruz hunched his shoulders and stared down into his lap, defeated.

"I'm sorry, Astrid. I never wanted to burden you with that. Can we just drop this conversation for now?"

Despite her need to persist, Astrid knew his expression far too well. She had no choice but to agree, instead, she decided to open up to him. "Cruz, you're right, there's more to what happened to me in the Underworld than I let on. I wasn't just his concubine. I became his bride. In fact, as a wedding gift, he gave me control over his creatures to assist with his plans to overthrow Zeus, he wanted me to become his queen on the earth."

A series of emotions flooded Cruz's face and then his dark eyes grew wide with shock. "Wait, you married him?"

"I had no choice. It's like these gods just love playing us like pawns on a chess board." Her metaphor was a deliberate tactic to lighten the mood, but Cruz did not see the humor. He shook his head in disbelief.

"So, you married the god of the Underworld? Astrid, those gods don't agree with divorce. That means you're tied to him!"

But Astrid already had something up her sleeve. "I know what it means, okay? It means that we can use my abilities against him and then after that, we'll find a way to get you out of this deal with Zeus. Because I will not allow you to become his puppet." On those words, Astrid saw something in Cruz's eyes that she had once thought disappeared. Hope.

CHAPTER FIFTEEN

Cruz, Joey, and Astrid had travelled for three days and as Astrid slept in the back seat of the car, her dreams, for the first time in a long time, were peaceful. That was until she heard Persephone's voice calling out to her. *'Astrid, we're going the wrong way... Wake up!'*

She opened her eyes in and instant and evaluated their surroundings only to find that Cruz had taken them to the devastating and silent ruins of San Francisco. She sat forward, alert. "What's going on? Did you even listen to Zeus? Hades isn't here, so why are we?"

"I told you she'd be mad," Cruz smirked to Joey.

"Yeah, you did," Joey replied. "So, now will you let us in on your plan?" Cruz pulled into a parking lot filled with smashed cars and turned off the engine. "Yeah, now that you're both awake, I can tell you. You see, we've been driving for days, without seeing a single person. Yet, we've driven past so many different creatures that I can barely count. The gods say that they want humans to walk alongside these creatures... but how can they when there are only the descendants of gods and heroes left? So, it had me wondering, where was the last place, outside of Vegas that we saw people?"

Astrid thought back to Arthur Jenkins and his family from the grocery store. "Jenkins and his family."

"Bingo! Right now, I just need that little glimmer of humankind. I need to know that the rest of humanity... that maybe some of them have survived... I want to check in on Arthur Jenkins and those scientists... they had a little community going, let's pray they still do."

"Alright," Astrid agreed. "I mean, it does set us back a little... but it's worth a shot."

After unfastening their seatbelts, they gathered their necessities then set off on foot, with Cruz leading the way. As they took in the sights, it was evident that San Francisco had certainly seen better days. The bodies that lined the streets had long-since decayed. Wooden planks from once-boarded up stores hung loosely from their nails. Then there was the occasional building which looked as if it had been crushed from an incredible force above. Luckily, there didn't seem to be any giants around now.

As they reached the street, of the laboratories, Astrid felt the rage build up inside of her. She remembered DR Reynolds clearly and while she understood his reasons, it still angered her more than she could stand. As Astrid brought her attention to her breathing in a bid to remain calm and collected, Joey placed his hand on her shoulder. "Are you alright?" he asked.

In front of them, Cruz turned to face them, mid-step. "You're thinking of Reynolds, aren't you?" Of course, he would know, judging by the expression on his face, his mind had gone to that memory too. But how could it not? This was the same street they had walked along. The same footpath that Reynolds had led them down. Back when the streets were filled with humans giving into the deadly sins. Astrid nodded.

"He was on my mind too. But we can't let our memories of him cloud our judgment. The rest of those scientists were good people. We'll be okay." Maybe it was the way Cruz had said it, but Astrid believed him.

It sounded like something she had once told a client in the past, to not judge an entire group for the actions of one man. Astrid offered Cruz the faintest of smiles, which he mirrored back before pressing the intercom button at the science facility that they had just approached. They heard a faintly high-pitched echo of the doorbell, coming from inside the building but there was no answer, so they waited... and waited... and waited. After a few more minutes, Cruz pushed it again, but still there was no answer. "Maybe we should just try Jenkins' shop?" he suggested.

They were about to leave when they heard a feminine voice coming from the speaker. "Hello? Is anybody out there?" Cruz raced back to the speaker and pushed the button.

"Hello? We're looking for survivors! Is everybody okay?"

"Yes. We're here. Who is this?" the woman on the other side of the intercom didn't sound nearly half as excited as Cruz did.

Astrid stepped toward the intercom and spoke into the speaker. "We were the ones who left to fix the curse."

On her words, the doors opened, and they were invited into the facility, where they found so many more people than there was the last time they had come. The science facility had been turned into a shelter for families who had survived the deadly sins curse. As well as for those who had been forced from their homes thanks to the centaurs, giants, and other creatures. There were over hundreds of families seeking shelter, food, and comfort. Cruz had found what he had been searching for. His last glimmer of hope for humankind.

***

Samuel and his men had been sailing for days now, battling through all kinds of weather conditions. The sun was currently set high in the sky, and they were traveling south along the coastline. Standing at the bow of the ship, Samuel breathed in the ocean breeze with a smile planted on his face. Growing up on a farm, he had never really been one for sailing, but being there in the middle of the action and the ocean, he couldn't imagine being happier.

He only wished that he could have Astrid standing at his side to enjoy it with him.

He, Tash, and Hannah had all been given navy blue uniforms to wear as well as cabins. His cabin, being the General's quarters had been the nicest of all. Their uniform belts had been upgraded with not only a gun holster but with also a sheath for their swords. Pressing his back into the golden railing, Samuel marveled at the majestic ship and its crew. As great as the feeling was, Samuel couldn't help but wonder just what the price might be for it all. The ship was supposed to have been lost to legend and they were sailing to the Lost City of Atlantis, of all places. How would they reach Atlantis? What would Samuel find when he got there? While he was certain that Poseidon would not lead him a stray, Samuel was certain that the sacrifices that should accompany such an adventure would have to be great. Before he could press on with his thoughts, he was joined by Tash and Hannah.

"I hope you know where you're leading us, General Buzzkill," Tash joked. "We'd hate to be going around in circles... especially when you're anything but a sailor."

"Honestly, Tash, I'm relying solely on this amulet."

The looks on their faces were priceless. "You're not serious?" Tash scoffed. "You and Cruz haven't swapped bodies, have you? Because that sounds just as crazy as something he would say."

"Crazy and genius are two sides of one coin," Hannah said with a smile. "We all thought he had lost his mind after what happened to Astrid… but now look, centaurs, demigods, giants, and nymphs. Somehow, science must go hand-in-hand with all this magic, though."

While Tash and Hannah continued their conversation, Samuel turned toward the ocean.

"You sound like you're on a mission of discovery," said Tash.

"Back in Vegas, Cruz and I were sitting on a few theories. Hermes may have deceived us all but he still gave us some details to work with. Unfortunately, it's just so hard to sort the truth from the bullshit."

At Hannah's use of a swearword, Tash gasped. "Hannah!"

"…Hey, did you girls see that?" Samuel interrupted, pointing out into the calm waves.

"No? What did you see?" Hannah asked.

"Let me guess, Moby Dick?" Tash laughed.

"I'm not sure," Samuel replied. "I just saw... something? It was larger than the rest of the waves and didn't seem natural."

Hannah and Tash followed his gaze but saw nothing.

"Maybe your eyes are playing tricks." Hannah suggested. "Being out at sea for too long can do that."

Before Samuel could consider her theory, there was another ripple and this time, they all saw it. Whatever it was, seemed to be a dark creature moving amongst the waves. Before it disappeared again, they caught a glimpse of its whale-like tail. "See? It is Moby Dick!" Tash declared.

Samuel shook his head, adamant. He had read enough adventure books to know exactly what the creature was. "No, it's not. Girls, get your weapons ready. Men! Prepare for an attack!"

As everybody heeded his orders, the large waves crashed against the ship. The cries of men in shock brought their attention to the beast that had just emerged starboard side.

Taking in the incredibly horrifying sight, Samuel was astounded that his hunch had been correct. The beast was a Cetus.

Roughly one-hundred feet high, loomed the large, black head of the beast with teeth like canines. It somewhat, resembled a black, reptilian dog crossed with a giant eel. There was a large fin that ran down the back of its long neck, which disappeared behind the edge of the ship and into the water. Without giving them a chance to hold on, their ship was lifted high out of the ocean, by the beast's massive tail.

"Hold onto something!" Samuel shouted, grabbing onto the railing as tightly as he could, with Tash and Hannah gripping it beside him. The fear in Samuel's gut was heavy, as the ship sailed through the air at lightning speed. It was nothing but a toy boat in the monster's giant bathtub. The vessel landed back onto the surface of the ocean, with a large and almighty splash, causing it to overflow with water.

Fortunately, they were still upright... for now. But Samuel and his crew were drenched in salt water and the deck was flooded. He heard the distant cries of someone calling out.

"Man overboard!" He groaned at the thought. Removing one hand from the railing to retrieve his firearm, Samuel turned his head to look for the beast. With clearly the same objective, his men began shooting at the sea monster. With his focus on the Cetus, Samuel watched as the bullets ricocheted off its body as if it were wearing an impenetrable shield.

"Sir, the bullets aren't working!" Tash called out.

"Where's Hannah?" Samuel demanded, looking around.

Tash's eyes grew wide, as she scanned the vicinity.

"I'm right here," Hannah said, emerging from the other side of the deck. Samuel noticed the beast's tail which was on the opposite side of the ship. Judging by its position, the beast was preparing to launch the ship into the air again.

"Everybody! Hold on tight!" Samuel cried.

"It's slippery," Tash's mumbled words were cloaked in fear. Despite her truth, Samuel tried to get a firm grip of the railing as they prepared for the ship's next launch. As the ship was thrown, Samuel's hands slipped from the bar, and he slid across the deck, knocking into a concrete wall behind him.

"What do we do, Sir?" Jenkins demanded as Samuel managed to clamber to his feet. "Conventional weapons aren't working, and we can't get close enough to sink our swords into its flesh." That was true. The only way to kill this thing would be to come into physical contact with the beast. It gave Samuel the idea he needed. He ran back to the edge where Tash was still hanging on for dear life and drew his sword. "Tash, if I don't get back... you're the new General! Is that clear?"

"What? Are you crazy?" she demanded.

Hugging her, he added, "Look after the others and tell Astrid, I love her." He attempted to release her, but she held on far too tight with obvious fear in her eyes.

"Don't... don't do this, Buzzkill. I can't lose you too." But ignorant to her plea, Samuel released her, climbed onto the ledge, and stepped over the railing, with his sword drawn. Praying to Poseidon himself, Samuel rubbed the amulet at his neck and then determined the best place to get a proper footing.

Suddenly, he saw the back of the Cetus emerge from the water, roughly five feet away. The huge beast was curled around their golden ship and its eyes were currently transfixed on the stern.

Now was Samuel's shot. He heard Tash trying to call him back, but Samuel refused to listen. He needed to jump. He needed to kill that thing. With one large leap, he bounded off the railing and practically flew through the air.

Surprisingly, Samuel made it. He landed on the slippery surface of the beast's body and clambered to find his footing. His heart pounded in his chest from fear and adrenaline. The Cetus was now very aware of his presence and did its best to shake him off. But, before Samuel could fall, he stabbed his sword between his feet and into the flesh of the creature, using his sword as an anchor to keep balance.

The Cetus let out a large roar that reminded Samuel of an injured whale. He felt the crashing of the waves come in over his head as the sea monster took a dive under the surface. Samuel held his breath as the water surrounded him. In that moment, he felt as if he was done for. But still, he refused to let go of the hilt of his sword.

Finally, relief came when he felt the sweet air surround him once more, as the creature's body writhed above the surface. Sucking in as much oxygen as he could, Samuel got to his feet, removed his sword from the thick flesh and started climbing up its back. He needed to make his way to the creature's head in order to bring it down. But it wasn't easy. His feet kept slipping. His clothes were soaked and heavy. But he refused to give up. He was almost at the head, he looked up at the beast, just as it had him in its sights.

It shook its head to shake him off. To keep his balance, Samuel sunk his blade just under its ear, holding on for dear life as he lost his footing again. His feet dangled in mid-air, as he felt his anchored blade begin to slip out.

Far down below, he could see that the ship was being ignored, despite his soldiers shooting the beast with their guns. He saw Tash pick up a shotgun, one that was sure to make an impact. She aimed the barrel for the monster's chest, called out something that sounded like it had something to do with sushi and then pulled the trigger.

The bullet hit the Cetus with such a force, that the beast's attention was no longer on Samuel.

It moved its neck toward the ship at the exact moment that Samuel's blade slipped out. He fell, but fortunately, he only fell onto the lower part of the monster's neck. As it launched its head towards the ship, Samuel used the timing to continue his run up to the top.

In seconds, he had made it. He stood at the very top of the monster's head, lifted his sword, just as the creature realized where he was and sunk his blade as far down as it would go. The immediate rush of blood and the fast collapse of the sea monster was all the proof Samuel needed in knowing that he had succeeded in killing the Cetus. Unfortunately, now the sea monster was sinking into the ocean fast. The monster's head sunk below the surface, and its body and tail began to wrap around it.

For Samuel to jump to the ship from where he was standing would be impossible, which meant that Samuel was sure to drown. He sucked in as much air as he could, right before he was inundated with the freezing cold water that came crashing in over his head along with the large thick tail of the beast.

Crushed between the overly heavily limbs of the beast, which were only made heavier by the ocean depths, Samuel was stuck and sinking fast. He tried to pull his sword from the monster, but it was no use. There was no escape. He watched as the Cetus pulled him down to the very depths of the ocean, right before he felt the large thud as the beast's body hit the deep bottom. And in those final moments, his mind went to Astrid and whether he would ever see her again.

***

Held back by Jenkins, Tash was inconsolable with grief. The guilt of having watched Samuel take the last kill and drown by doing so burdened her almost as much as witnessing her own family slaughter each other. She needed to do something. "He's gotta be alive. I need to save him," she cried out in a bid to shake Sergeant Jenkins away.

"No, you can't," Jenkins said. "With General Davids gone, you're the next chain of command."

"Well in that case, get your asses down there and look for him!" She looked to Hannah for assistance, as she managed to break free. "Tell them, Hannah. Please!"

Hannah went to speak, but unfortunately, for Tash it wasn't in her favor. "Samuel's been down there for twenty-three minutes now, Tash. No one can survive that long."

"No, you're wrong! You were wrong about Astrid, and you're wrong about him too. Buzzkill can't die! We need him. We need to save him!"

Tash looked around at Hannah and at the rest of the soldiers waiting for her level-headed orders. Something that she was in no way ready to give. "General Martinez. What are your orders?" Sergeant Jenkins asked, ready to move on. "We've lost twenty-four of our men, including General Davids."

"Twenty-four?" That news hit her hard. How the hell was she supposed to press on with that type of news? She looked around at the damaged ship and sighed in defeat. "Are you sure there aren't any survivors? Are you sure they're all dead?" Tash pleaded.

"Tash..." Hannah began softly as she led her away for privacy.

"He can't be dead," Tash interrupted. "What will we tell them? What do we tell Astrid and the others? What do I tell these men? Do we continue looking for Atlantis or what?" Hannah shrugged. She really didn't know, which forced Tash to punch her fist at the golden railing then writhe in pain.

"Why the hell would that asshole put me as General! I'm barely even trained!"

"You need to do something. They're all looking to you for answers."

Despite not wanting to hear those words, Tash turned back to the soldiers. "We wait," she commanded. "We need to look for survivors and we need to clean up this ship or we'll all drown." She knew that she sounded anything but professional, but honestly, she just didn't give a damn.

Fortunately, the men saluted her and the moment that they began to clean up the wreckage, Hannah commended her.

"That was a good start."

"Good," Tash said, handing both her shotgun and sword to Hannah. "Because I needed a distraction."

"A distraction? A distraction from what?" But before Hannah could receive an answer, Tash jumped over the railing and into the water. "Tash? What the hell are you doing?" Hannah cried out, but Tash had already ducked her head below the surface.

While Tash could barely see anything through the murky depths, she could, however, make out the tiny golden glow of something in the distance. Desperate and reckless, she swam towards it, going lower and lower. Whatever was making its way towards the surface was lit up like a Christmas Tree, acting as a beacon.

She trailed down towards it until she realized that she was losing air quickly. But the closer she got; she could see the silhouette of a person. It was Samuel! She was sure of it.

The light must've belonged to the amulet he wore around his neck. He had made it and he was swimming his way towards the surface. His legs and arms were kicking through the water with the sheer determination she knew him for, and he was still holding his sword. Tash felt her excitement wash over her, just as she felt the air from her lungs escaping. She tried to make her way back towards the surface, but it was harder than the descent had been. She struggled. Against the heaviness off the water. Against her minimal supply of oxygen. In an instant, she felt Samuel's arms wrap around her as he pulled her up with him on his way to the surface.

He had survived the battle with the sea monster and a torturous amount of time submerged under the water with no injuries whatsoever. Once they had made it above the surface, Tash let him experience the full roar of her anger. "How dare you!" she demanded through coughs and splutters. For emphasis, she punched him in the arm, hard. But he merely laughed it off. They turned back towards the ship where they saw Hannah's head peering over the railing at them.

"They're alive!" Hannah called out to the rest of the soldiers.

Within minutes, they had both been pulled back onto the ship and given blankets to warm them up. Once Hannah had checked over their vitals, Tash continued her tirade on Samuel.

"How the hell did you survive that? You should've died!"

"Well, look who's talking. I promoted you to General and the first thing you do is jump overboard." He laughed, while dodging her question. Tash punched him hard, again, this time forcing him to flinch, before pulling him into a tight hug.

"I refuse to accept the position, General. Besides, I couldn't lose any more of my family." As he smiled down at her, Sergeant Jenkins approached.

"General Davids, it's good to see that you're both okay. What are your orders?"

"We continue on our path," Samuel commanded. "See to the damages and then we'll set off immediately. Continue on to Atlantis!"

"Yes, sir!"

Once, Tash, Samuel, and Hannah were alone, Tash stared at the amulet around Samuel's neck. "That amulet really is magical, isn't it?"

"I guess it is."

CHAPTER SIXTEEN

After a brief rundown of how the curse had been broken, leaving out the incriminating part DR Reynolds had played, the scientists gave Astrid, Cruz and Joey a tour of the refuge that the San Francisco Laboratory had become. Fortunately, for Astrid and Cruz, when Dr Reynolds' name had been mentioned, Joey took the reign of the conversation.

"We heard a rumor that he joined up with the president. We did keep an eye out for him, though."

"I'm just glad the curse is over, and we can all think straight," DR Andrews replied. "But with the centaurs and giants invading the cities… well, the chaos has reached an all-new level. We've also heard of encounters involving vampires and werewolves."

"Vampires and werewolves?" Astrid asked, somewhat amused.

"I've done my research, Miss Sutherland. Those creatures all have one thing in common. They're tied in with Greek Mythology... just as the Seven Deadly Sins virus was... it's almost as if..."

"...as if Pandora's Box let in a whole new wave of destruction?" Cruz asked, entirely rhetorically.

"Precisely. I'm a man of science and even I can't explain the things I've seen. You'd imagine my surprise when the three of you arrived out of the blue. You stopped the seven deadly sins, surely you can fix whatever these side effects are too," the doctor said, focusing his attention entirely on Cruz, who was feeling undoubtedly uncomfortable.

"It's like an old video game," Cruz mumbled.

"I apologize, but we need answers, DR Cruz. You were the archaeologist who found the artefact and stopped the seven deadly sins virus. We all ignored the warnings you gave from the beginning, but now, you're our only hope. You must know something."

Hunching his shoulders in an effortless shrug, Cruz ran his hands through his hair with a long sigh. "I… I just wish I did." He looked pleadingly to Astrid and Joey before storming away without another word. Astrid and Joey exchanged glances knowing that neither of them could give up the full truth to the scientist or the refugees. That truth would lead to panic and in turn, would lead to further chaos.

It was that knowledge which provided Astrid with the empathy to forgive Joey for who he really was. Science and magic could never walk hand in hand in the practical world. They would always be at odds.

Astrid turned back to DR Andrews who had been left disappointed by Cruz's sudden departure. "Unfortunately, we're still pretty much in the dark," she lied. "But I promise you, we won't let humanity die out. In the end, we may have no choice but to live side by side with these creatures." To her surprise, the older doctor became bitter over the very concept.

"Are you crazy? No, don't answer that. Those creatures have been hunting us to extinction. They should be studied so we can determine how to fight back."

Had it been a few months earlier, Astrid might've agreed with the man, but over the time spent in the Vegas barrier, she had seen the future that she had just spoke of. Unfortunately, humanity would always fight back. It was in their blood.

In the distance, she could see Cruz pacing in an office, through the open door. "Excuse me for one minute," she said, leaving Joey to speak with the doctor.

She entered the office to find Cruz pacing with his hands interlocked behind his head, and his breathing low and deliberate. Something she had taught him to do time and time again. The office was cluttered, but he didn't seem to notice. There was a mild draft which told her that he was doing his best to keep his powers under control. Astrid closed the door so they could talk in private. "Cruz, I..."

"Please, don't. Just let me think for a minute." His tone was controlled, though he seemed to be struggling with that too. Astrid leaned against the door and waited for him to speak. Finally, after a crippling long bout of silence, he leaned against the desk and spoke up. "How the hell do we fix everything?"

"It's simple. We help the gods with their Hades problem and then they help us with helping humanity."

Her seemingly easy solution forced a hint of a smile to spread across his lips, but he wasn't convinced. "Funny, the most those *pendejos* want is to just use us. Humanity is screwed and we're... well, we're just along for the ride."

In agreement, Astrid leaned against the desk beside him. "Tell me about it. Like what does Hades have planned for me and what will happen if you do, or don't say no to Zeus?"

"It is a very scary thought, huh? We're supposed to be in this together, but they could end up driving us apart... I don't mean that in the way it sounds because I know you're with Buzzkill and all and... damn, I just keep messing this shit up, don't I?"

Feeling the weight of Cruz's frustrations, Astrid took hold of his hand in a bid to offer at least an ounce of her strength.

"I knew what you meant, Cruz. But yeah, we're in this together. We won't let those gods drive us apart. We're a beacon of hope to these people and that's what our daughter will represent."

The glimmer of a smile lit up into his cheek as he turned to face her. "You're saying we keep on fighting?"

"I'm saying we do what it takes to do our job. Speaking of, I want to thank you."

"Thank me? Thank me for what?"

"For not leaving my side when I died in those ruins. Hannah told me. She said that you even tried to fight off Joey."

"She's right, I did. And you don't need to thank me. I would never abandon you."

"I have to, Cruz. If it wasn't for you, I never would've come back. It was because of your offer that Zeus brought me back. And I promise, whatever it takes, that I'll make it up to you. You have my word."

At that point, they remembered that they were still holding hands, Cruz covered hers with his other. "Astrid, you don't need to make it up to me. I did it because staying by your side was the right thing to do. I never wanted you to pay for mistakes. It's because of me, that you were sent to the underworld. I still remember begging Zeus in my mind to bring you back. I told him I'd be willing to do anything he asked of me… anything."

"You did, and now he expects to take over your body as his reward. But I won't let that happen."

"You won't?"

"No, I'd go to the Underworld and back again to bring back your soul… after we take down Hades of course."

Cruz's smile crinkled into his eyes. "Of course. And I want to be right there with you when you take that spear and drive it into him after what he did to you and Persephone. Make him beg for mercy. That son of a bitch deserves it."

Astrid mirrored his expression with her own smile. "Sure, because taking down the god of the underworld is such an easy mission. In fact, Persephone thinks it's so hard that we should send him straight to Tartarus instead."

"We're demi-gods with a vendetta, so yeah, it'll be like a walk in the park."

With the energy in the room having been lifted, Astrid released his hands and turned her attention to the door. "Whatever we are, and whatever we become, we're still human. So, why don't we just get out there and talk to the masses. They need something to believe in, they need…"

"Hope. I think I've got it covered, so watch the maestro at work." With another smile in her direction, Cruz left the office with almost a skip in his step and Astrid following behind. Once they made it to the foyer, Cruz found a group of people to speak with, while Joey approached Astrid. "He's talking to crowds, now? Where were you when we were in college?"

Astrid smiled. "Gaining my degree in psychology."

"Huh. Paid off. So, what did you say to him?"

Astrid shifted her focus from Cruz and back to Joey, she was certain that he would've heard their conversation. "Can't your Hermes powers pick up godlike frequency communications from a mile away?"

"Only if it's an unlocked channel… Besides, I like to stay out of the private quarrels of star-crossed lovers. I've been burned before."

"I bet," Astrid chuckled. "This coming from the guy insisting Cruz, Buzzkill and I go polyamorous."

"Hey, don't knock it until you try it. Just pray you don't ever meet Eros, that son of a bitch is worse than his mother and will give you no choice in the matter. He's deadly with his arrows and just as vindictive."

Astrid was aware that Hermes and Aphrodite had quite an interesting past, which they never spoke about. In fact, Joey was uncomfortable around many of the women he had dated, mortal and immortal alike. For the god of luck, he certainly seemed unlucky when it came to love. But the mere mention of Eros surprised Astrid. Once again, another mythological figure that she was somewhat curious to meet. Before she could ask any further questions, Joey nodded in Cruz's direction. "Why don't we go and join him before he starts charging for autographs."

They approached Cruz, just as Astrid caught wind of a word that a tanned-skin woman, approximately in her mid-forties had used. "Vampires?" she repeated, just to be sure, tempted to ask if they sparkled but decided otherwise.

"Yes, they turned my husband into one of them and I've been on the run ever since," she said. "I know you're probably thinking that I'm insane or something. But I promise they're just as real as the centaurs that have been raiding the streets."

"Don't worry. I believe you," Cruz said boldly. "I promise we're doing everything we can. It won't be easy, but it's about having hope." His high level of confidence was a delight to see from a man who normally struggled in the spotlight. Every eye was on him, which included a few flirtatious smiles from some younger fans.

"Can I help?" A young man of African-American descent approached. He looked to be barely in his teens, though they recognized him at once. Arthur Jenkins' great-grandson.

"Hey man, is your grandfather around?" Cruz asked, offering him a 'high five'. After giving Cruz an excited 'high five', the boy's expression turned into a deep-set frown telling them just what it was, he was leaving unsaid. "Oh," Cruz mumbled.

"Jacob? Where are you... oh..." The voice of the boy's mother caught their attention as the woman saw just who her son was speaking with. "Pardon my intrusion. I thought he'd run off."

She was holding the hand of her daughter, who had also grown about two years older since the last time they had met. "That's okay," Cruz said, doing his best to remain optimistic. "He was just asking to join us on our adventure."

"I hope you told him absolutely not. Wait, I remember you. You all helped my grandfather a few years back, then you left to end the curse. By the looks of things, you did a remarkable job!"

Joey and Cruz both looked a little slapped by her words, so Astrid took the reign of the conversation. "These creatures may be entirely different to the deadly sin virus, but I assure you, they're our main concern. Do you mind if I ask about your grandfather? Your name was Alisha, wasn't it?"

"You remember me? Wow. Sorry, I wasn't expecting that. You must meet a lot of people," Alisha sighed. "My grandfather died trying to protect us. There was a herd of centaurs raiding the streets led by their king or something. We hid in one of the closets, but so many others weren't as lucky... My grandfather included."

"Do you mind if I ask the name of that centaur king?" Joey wondered.

"I don't care what his name was. He killed my grandfather!"

"If it gives you any relief," Astrid replied. "We battled some centaurs. We killed a king by the name of Alafan."

Alisha's eyes grew wide. "Oh my god! I'm so sorry I was so rude. How did you manage that? You must have been sent by God!" There were tears in her eyes as she pulled Astrid into a tight hug. After Alisha regained her composure, her children stared up at her.

"It's okay mommy. Don't cry," her daughter said.

Alisha wiped away a few tears, "I'm sorry. I just can't get a hold of myself. We've lost so many people. I just wish that my brother was still alive. He was a third-generation marine who got lost out at sea before all this. When my husband died, he was like a second father to my children."

Astrid placed her hand on Alisha's shoulder. "I'm sorry to hear that. If it helps, I can relate. My father was a General, he died so I could escape. I promise you, Alisha, we're doing everything in our power to set matters straight. We were able to end the Deadly Sins curse, and we'll stop at nothing to end the chaos that's going on now."

"Thank you!" Alisha replied.

"Can I go with them, mom?" her son asked.

"...and me?" her daughter added.

They laughed at the innocence of the children as Alisha wiped away her tears. "No, you two can leave the work to these people."

"To the heroes!" Jacob said equally excited and slightly disappointed.

"He's disappointed because he has dreams of being in the military, like the rest of the men in this family," Alisha explained.

"Maybe one day," Joey grinned.

"No! Please don't give him any ideas. When things go back to normal, I'd love to see him not cause me so much grief." The group picked up on Alisha's use of the words 'when' as opposed to 'if'. It was clear that this woman had faith that things would go back to normal.

Pleased that they had done what they had set out to do, Astrid knew that it was time to leave. "You guys, we should hit the road now why we still have daylight."

Excited, Cruz rubbed his hands together. "After you, boss. Let's go."

They said their goodbyes, loaded up the car with supplies and fuelled up the tank before leaving San Francisco. This time Astrid drove to ensure that there would be no further distractions.

***

Two days passed, and Astrid had taken on most of the driving, with Cruz sitting up alongside her and Joey lounging across the backseat. Over the course of those two days, there was a sense of optimism that the detour to San Francisco had provided. It had been three hours since their last stop, they were headed towards the border of Mexico and Cruz had fallen into a bout of silence.

"Are you alright?" Astrid asked.

"I'm actually feeling better than I have in a while."

"That's good, but you're quiet. What's on your mind?"

Cruz glanced back at Joey who was fast asleep, then sent a smile in Astrid's direction. "I haven't heard from

Zeus in a while. It's strange. When was the last time you spoke with Persephone?"

"I've been speaking on and off with her for the past hour. It'll be strange when she's no longer riding shotgun."

"It's just not like Zeus to be this silent, I mean, it's not like he's in my head or anything but still… it's just weird." As if on cue, Persephone sent an alarming thought to Astrid, telling her that Hades was nearby, just as they heard a loud, very low growl.

"Did you hear that, Astrid?" Joey asked, waking bolt upright.

"I did," she replied. "That growl. I know it far too well." Pulling the car to the side of the road, she turned off the engine.

"Why did you stop?" Cruz asked. "Whatever it is, we should be able to outdrive it."

"There's no outdriving this beast," Joey said as they heard the growl again, this time louder.

"You're Hermes! Can't you fly?" Astrid asked.

"Have you forgotten that my powers have been drained? I'm not fast enough. We'll need to face it."

"Maybe I can use my influence? He is a creature of the Underworld." Astrid suggested as they quickly collected their things.

"He's Hades guard dog," Joey replied. "I doubt you'd be getting him in the divorce!"

By this point, they had removed their seatbelts and gathered the essentials into backpacks. Cruz peered out his window, trying to get a glimpse of the beast, just as it growled again, shattering the front windscreen.

"Holy shit!" Cruz exclaimed as they stared out the cracked glass to see the very large, three-headed black dog. It was a Cerberus and all six of its eyes were on them. It barked loudly from all three mouths as it prepared to charge.

"Out of the car, now!" Astrid demanded.

"You don't have to tell me, twice!" Cruz said.

Instantly, they opened their doors, collected their weapons and only one backpack before they jumped out of the vehicle. Mere seconds had past as the creature collided with the car smashing it on impact against some large, jagged boulders nearby. The red convertible was beyond reparable.

"No!" Cruz cried out miserably, as he stood between Astrid and the beast. "That was such a beautiful car! Bad dog!"

"I think the car is the least of our worries," Astrid replied.

"Well, there goes my back up plan," Joey said. "I was going to play some Chicago... Figured some divine music normally works to tame the beast."

"And you picked Chicago, Joey?" Cruz asked, furrowing his brows. "I can name a few Broadway Musicals that received an amazing standing..."

"Focus, guys," Astrid interrupted. "Before we become dog food, remember?" They looked up at the Cerberus who was eyeing them all like play toys. The beast's snarling alone was intimidating to say the least. Astrid knew she needed to do something. "I'll see if I can use my influence."

Hesitant to allow her, but knowing they had no other choice, Cruz stepped out of her way. "Just give the word if you need back up."

Clutching Athena's spear in her right hand, Astrid eyed the Cerberus like one would their trained pet. This creature was not some ordinary creature. It was the guard dog for the underworld. *'Persephone? Any tips?'* she asked the goddess within her mind, while slowly inching closer. In turn, the Cerberus did not move, it just studied her curiously. *'I wish I did, Astrid. We both left the Underworld without permission. It could be dangerous. But remember, you're the one that Hades was allowing to rule the earth alongside him.'*

'So, it's a hit or miss?'

'Yes, I believe so. But beware, if the Cerberus is here, then Hades won't be too far away.'

'I was afraid you'd say that.' By this point, Astrid was standing merely a few feet away from the creature, which stood at least thirty feet tall. She stared directly into the eyes of the middle head. Drool dripped from its canines and onto the ground as it released another large growl. Astrid remembered the last time she had seen this creature back in the Underworld. It had acted as nothing more than a cute and playful puppy. While Hades had treated it as nothing more than a beast, Astrid had spent a little time petting it as if it were her own dog.

"Hey, buddy. Do you remember me?"

It studied her as if it did. Clearly, it knew that its job was to take her back to its master but still, the Cerberus seemed to soften its nature, as Astrid brought her hand to its fur. "That'a boy... It's okay." It lowered its middle head to nuzzle her arm, but then by a flare of its nostrils it was evident that it had changed its mind. Its head froze in an alert.

"Run, Astrid!" It was the fear in Cruz's tone that made her flinch. She went to look at him, just as Joey pulled her away from the Cerberus, holding her tight, ready to flee. When her eyes finally found Cruz, a frightening sight befell her.

Cruz was kneeling in the dirt, a scruff of his hair gripped in the very hand of the god of darkness himself. In his other hand, Hades held his pitchfork. His malice-filled eyes were focused on Astrid and Joey. "Hermes... We meet again," Hades cooed. "Unhand both my wives and I'll give you back the man your father sent you to watch over. If you refuse... Remember, that beast still obeys my every command. He will kill you and I will kill this pawn right here."

"Cruz!" Astrid stammered.

"Don't worry, *mi amor*... he's just bluffing. He is bluffing, right, Joey?"

Joey turned from Hades and then back to Cruz and neither tightened nor loosened his grip around Astrid's waist. Instead, he remained silent. "Well, even if he isn't joking," Cruz continued. "I can always say yes to Zeus."

"No!" Astrid and Joey yelled in unison.

"If you say 'yes', you'll no longer be you," Astrid continued.

For a moment, nobody dared to move until Hades again broke the silence. "Tick tock, Hermes. Tick tock!"

CHAPTER SEVENTEEN

The Cerberus let out a very low growl. The beast was waiting for an order from its master. Astrid could feel her heart pounding within her chest at the sight of Cruz being threatened by the god of darkness. As if the spear of Athena held the power to change the will of the god, Astrid's fingers wrapped around it tightly. With Joey's arm around her waist, he lowered his voice so that only she could hear. "We need to get you out of here."

"No, I can't let him kill Cruz," Astrid whispered back in the same tone. "He wants me and Persephone. Just let us go with him." But Joey's grip only held on tighter. He would not let her go, even for Cruz's sake. Astrid turned her demands back onto Hades, doing her best to not let the pain in Cruz's eyes derail her composure. "Let him go, Hades! Don't hurt him!"

"Still trying to make demands of me? You, foolish girl! Did you learn nothing?"

As if his words had a power over her, Astrid's mind drifted to a memory where he had exerted his dominance over her. She flinched to forget. "Just let him go and we can all walk away from this."

"I told you not to make demands of me. You and that whore, Persephone are nothing more than ungrateful witches. I treated you both like queens and this is how you repay me... Plotting my demise with the deceitful messenger boy and this... whelp!" As Hades barked his insults, his grip of Cruz's hair forced Cruz to loll about in the dirt and release a pain-filled groan.

But despite the pain in Cruz's eyes, Astrid recognized that look of concentration. Around them, the winds began to grow strong. The clouds began to darken. There was a clap of thunder and the rains began to pour. Cruz was releasing his anger all around them.

Joey tightened his grip around Astrid's waist, "We need to go," he repeated in a sterner tone. "You are too important to risk losing."

Confused, Astrid questioned him. "What do you mean too important? We can't abandon Cruz. He'll die." But Joey's face hardened. It was very unlike Joey. What other secrets was he hiding? How could she be far more important than Cruz? How could he even think of leaving his best friend at the mercy of this evil being? "Joey, if this is about Persephone…"

Joey shook his head. "No, this isn't about Persephone. This is about…" A loud crash of thunder broke out over Joey's sentence and Cruz called out over the sound of the thunderstorm that was taking place.

"Get her out of here, Joe! Now!" But Astrid was adamant. She pushed Joey away from her with such a force and ran towards Cruz and Hades, but Joey was too fast.

He caught her again, unwilling to let her anywhere near them. "Well, it looks as if that brother of mine gifted this pawn with some cheap party tricks," Hades mocked of Cruz, taking no notice of Astrid and Joey. "Zeus is still not brave enough to face me. After all this time being trapped in that box with all his pets you would think he would face me with open arms."

Hades turned his blue eyes onto Joey with a hard as stone expression, which Joey merely mirrored back to him. A smile formed at the corner of Hades mouth. "Oh, that's right, Zeus doesn't even have a physical form… and even he did, he'd be just as weak as his son who stands before me." Hades raised his bident in the air and the storm stopped. But then, the sky began to darken all the more, surprising even Cruz.

"How did you do it?" Joey demanded. "How did you consume our powers? Why aren't we strong enough to fight you?"

Hades laughed. "Like you don't know, Hermes. You really are deceitful, aren't you?" Hades turned his gaze onto Astrid. "How can you trust him? He's acting like he doesn't know." Hades menacing laugh chorused again. He turned back to Joey. "We both know that the box that Zeus gave to Pandora came from me. It would only make sense that I would lace my own curse inside. But then, it was never opened until a few years ago… Do you have any idea how long I had to wait until this imbecile opened that useless container? At least your deceitful ways had its uses, nephew."

Astrid turned back to Joey, who was riddled with shame. It had been his influence on Cruz which had led to the opening of Pandora's Box. But that manipulation had also cost Hermes and the other gods their powers. Astrid turned back to Hades.

"You once said that I wasn't meant to be in the Underworld... Why?"

"Because you were never meant to stay. I knew the gods would find some way to bring you back before I could take you as my own. You are much too important… much too powerful. That power is what I knew would make you the perfect queen… Now, we'll just be done with this pawn right here." Hades threw Cruz to the ground and aimed his pitchfork at his head.

"No!" Astrid and Joey both cried in unison. As adrenaline took a hold, Astrid escaped Joey's arms and ran to Cruz and Hades, positioning herself between them.

"Astrid, what are you doing?" Cruz stammered. "He'll kill you." But Astrid stared into the face of Hades.

"You will not hurt him. I won't let you. If you want me to go with you, I will. Just leave them alone!"

"You will come at your own volition?" Hades asked.

Astrid nodded. "Or else you will have to kill me, before I let you lay a hand on him!" Astrid turned back to Joey, who shook his head in anger at her, and then back at Cruz. "I'm going with him. Just please, promise me, you won't let Zeus take over your body... please, Cruz!"

"Astrid... no..." Cruz stammered, staring up at her, pleadingly. "If I let him take over my body, you'll be okay... everyone will be okay!"

"I can't let you do this. Think of our daughter, think of Hope... Please. Let me go with him!"

"Are you sure about this?" Cruz asked.

"Yes, I am. Let's say I love you in a willing-to-give-up-my-soul-for-you type way." She could see the flash of anger, but also that same broken-hearted sorrow that flashed through his eyes before he sighed in defeat.

"Okay. But Buzzkill will be so pissed and what do I tell Hope?"

"Tell them... Tell them I'm doing this for them." Astrid gave him a slight lingering smile that only reached up into her right cheek. A silent message to him alone that she would find a way to fix it all. But then, in the blink of an eye, she, Hades, and the Cerberus were gone.

***

Angry, Cruz sat on the ground with his face in his hands. He had barely moved in the hour since Astrid and Hades had disappeared. "Remind me again why we let her go?" Joey asked, sitting down beside him.

"Because it's Astrid."

"And what's that supposed to mean?"

Cruz glared at him, annoyed that he couldn't piece two and two together. "It means that I'm not like Buzzkill. I don't stop her from making her own decisions and I know she can do this. It's who she is."

In his fury, Joey kicked at the dirt, scuffing his sneakers just a little. "God, Cruz. Sometimes I wish you weren't so damn naïve! Every single minute that she is with Hades, she is in danger. Do you get that?"

"Of course, I get it!" Cruz snapped, getting to his feet. "But even you had to admit our decisions were slim. The guy is far more powerful than me. We only had two decisions. Either I had let Zeus take over my body and he hadn't been powerful enough, or we go with Astrid's plan for long enough to prepare ourselves for the final battle. And trust me, I know she has a plan."

From his position on the ground, Joey stared up at Cruz long and hard, then rolled his eyes as he got to his feet. "Why did she have to be so stupid? So reckless! Why didn't Persephone..."

"Hey, what's your deal with Persephone anyway? Ever since she's been back from the dead you've had a real... interest in Astrid. Wasn't Persephone your half-sister or something?" Joey grew silent, forcing Cruz to probe deeper. "What? What aren't you telling me?"

"Apollo and I were the reason that Persephone was taken away from the rest of the gods in the first place. But this... well, it's not about Persephone. It's about Pandora."

Cruz did a double take on what his best friend had just revealed. Sure, it would make sense that Hermes and Apollo would've been into Persephone. The Greek gods were riddled with incest... something about keeping it in the family. But the aspect of Joey's statement that had caught him by surprise was the part about Pandora. The fact that Joey knew more about Astrid's ancestry than he had been letting on, despite Cruz and Astrid's constant questions was infuriating. "Pandora?"

Joey nodded and got to pacing nervously. "I know you, Hannah, and Astrid have been pestering me these last few months for an explanation which I've refused to give… But this… This is difficult."

"But it's about Astrid? Correction, it's about the woman who quite literally just risked our asses so that Hades, or should I say, your uncle, wouldn't go all super villain on our asses! And it has to do with Pandora… Am I right?"

Joey sighed and then pursed his lips together. His stifled nod was enough to infuriate Cruz, whose anger came out with such a force, as he punched Joey hard, in the face, with a strength he didn't know he had.

The two stared at one another, both unwilling to back down on their demeanours. "You're a total dick, do you know that? God, Joe! How could I be so stupid to trust you again? Are you going to tell me what you're hiding? What it is that makes the love of my life such a hot commodity? Why was it specifically our daughter that broke the curse? And don't you dare tell me she's just the descendant of Pandora… That can't be it!"

Hermes got back to his feet and recomposed himself with such a Joey-like fashion. Cruz had always hated how Joey could remain so calm in the tensest of situations, opposed to his rambling mess of a persona. But for the first time, 'cool Joey' was nowhere to be found.

"Why don't you ask my father, Cruz? Oh wait, he doesn't know, either. Does he?"

"Are you kidding me? This isn't about Zeus! This is about…"

Joey raised his hand to silence him. His green eyes merely looked at Cruz as if he was seeing nothing more than an innocent child with very minimal understanding of the world around him. What frustrated him more was that he couldn't determine just what it was that Joey was hiding. Zeus had never even spoken of Pandora's lineage to him. "It's about Pandora, I know," Joey finally said. "It's also about Astrid… And of course, Zeus doesn't know… Because as you well know, this was a curse on the god who created the Pandora's curse himself."

"What's that got to do with…"

"…A whole lot more than you think." Joey looked around at their quiet environment, then brought his hand to Cruz's shoulder, who quickly tried to shrug him away.

"What are you doing?"

"I need you to trust me, Cruz. That's all I'm asking. I know I don't deserve it, but right now, I need it."

"I'm sorry. But I just can't."

"Well then, close your eyes and let me show you!"

"Close my…?" Before Cruz could finish his sentence, his entire mind was flooded with century's worth of memories. Thoughts, emotions, and experiences of the messenger god himself. Cruz saw the rise and fall of countless civilizations and the evolution of technology throughout time. It was a mental transaction that he doubted he could withstand, without the support of his best friend beside him. Cruz's mind ached for what felt like an eternity, but realistically, only lasted a few minutes. When he pulled away violently, his aching head brought him to the ground. "What the… What the hell was that? What did you just do to me?"

Joey crouched beside him. "I just shared some of my memories with you. Only a few, so nothing to make you feel too uncomfortable."

"Uncomfortable? That was torture!"

"You know what I mean. But now, do you see why I couldn't tell you?" Cruz immediately pinpointed the memories that had forced Joey into a deceptive standstill and sighed.

"I don't think grade A god liquor is going to work this time. Shit, this is all so damn fucked up!"

Joey nodded. "I told you so." Defeated, Cruz got to his feet and brushed himself off. His only optimism was in the fact that he had been right about Astrid's tie to Pandora. Unfortunately, the truth about Astrid meant that they were all headed for sheer cataclysmic destruction. Gods, creatures, and mortals alike.

***

Samuel and his men had been sailing on the Argo for a little over a week now and it had been days since his encounter with the Cetus. While it had all been smooth sailing, Samuel couldn't shake the feeling that something was amiss. As usual, he was standing at the bow, lost in thought when Tash and Hannah approached. "Do you think they found Hades?" Hannah asked. Samuel shook his head.

"I don't know. It's hard to tell when we haven't seen anyone or anything for days now."

Tash tapped him on the shoulder. "Don't worry, Buzzkill... she'll be fine. Astrid's a tough girl. Besides she has the god of luck and Cruz beside her."

Samuel gave a false smile. "While Astrid is always present on my mind, she isn't my current concern. I just have a strange feeling about something. These seas are too calm. Something feels off."

"Damn, and I was enjoying the peace," Tash complained.

"He's right," Hannah said, pointing out into the distance where a dark mist loomed. "Where did that fog come from?" There was a soft melodious humming that filled the atmosphere around them.

"You and your damn feelings, Buzzkill!" Tash said. "Can either of you hear that singing?"

Samuel nodded. "I knew something was up."

Suddenly, the ship made an abrupt turn and began sailing towards the fog. Tash and Samuel looked toward the captain's deck, unaware that Hannah was no longer with them. As if the melodious music had a will of its own, Samuel and Tash fought against their own temptation to resist the hypnotic effect that it had. "We're sailing into the fog!" Samuel exclaimed, pulling himself from his own enthrall. "We need to change direction!"

"Wait, where's Hannah?" Tash demanded. Samuel looked around, Hannah was gone, but he needed to act quickly. "Go find Hannah, I'll change the ship's direction!" Samuel barely hesitated as he made his way towards the Captain's deck, while the melodious humming grew louder and louder, in a bid to enslave the sailors.

Tash barely had a moment to think either. She ran around the edges of the ship with her fingers to her ears, searching and calling out for Hannah. The ship was headed straight towards the fog. But just as she saw the fog, Tash caught sight of some very large-jagged rocks amongst the waves... And swimming towards those rocks, was her friend.

Hannah had jumped into the ocean, enslaved to the music and was barely moments away from being crushed to death between the ship and the rocks. "Man overboard!" Tash exclaimed. "Somebody! Anybody! We have a man overboard!" But nobody was there to help. She would need to help Hannah, herself. But how?

***

Samuel bypassed multiple soldiers who had all been affected by the hypnotically beautiful humming. There was no doubt in his mind, that they were dealing with sirens.

While running through the ship, he noticed the glow of his amulet which had lit up like a beacon. He remembered the old legend, where Odysseus had used wax for his sailors' ears. But Samuel had come unprepared. He had overlooked the possibility of coming across sirens.

Finally, he was standing right outside the closed door to the cockpit. He opened it and found the captain transfixed on the fog, leading the ship right through it.

"Hey!" Samuel cried out, snapping his fingers. "You need to snap out of it!" But the ship captain didn't hear him. He was focused entirely on the beautiful music. From the corner of his eye, Samuel noticed the large rocks.

The ship was headed straight for them. He needed to take over the helm. With one swift move, he elbowed the captain in the face, knocking him out instantly. He took the helm and spun it to the right, changing the direction of the ship. As he steered, he could feel the presence of a dozen marines behind him. He heard a click and knew a weapon was being held on him. After ensuring the safer route was secured, Samuel turned around, praying that it would only be a matter of time until the hypnotic singing stopped.

Taking sight of the men and eyeing Sergeant Jenkins, who was holding the gun on him, General Samuel Davids prepared himself for a fight.

***

Tash struggled to swim through the fierce waves that were crashing all around her. The song of the sirens was nothing more than a deafeningly out of tune melody. But still, she remained unaffected without a clue as to why.

She could see Hannah struggling, which didn't stop the doctor from trying to reach the jagged rocks that would surely lead to her death. Despite the salt water that filled Tash's mouth, she continued to call out to her friend.

"Hannah… stop!" But there was a significant distance between them. It would be impossible for Hannah to hear her over the music. Suddenly, Hannah's head disappeared under the water, forcing Tash to pick up her pace as she swam against the current, just in time for Hannah's head to bob back up again.

Her face was bloody, but her eyes were still open. She seemed to still be alive for the moment. Tash neared the rocks as Hannah reached the outskirts of the rocky shoreline of the small bank. It had clearly been hidden in the mist from the ship's view.

To Tash's horror, Hannah's head disappeared back under the water again. She was drowning. "Hannah!" Tash cried, in stunned horror. "Don't die! Come back to me! Come back to me, please!"

From behind her, Tash could hear the whirring of the ship's engine as it sailed away from the fog.

"Oh, shit! Hannah, we need to go back. They're leaving without us!" Her tears were just as salty as the ocean all around. Hannah's head was still submerged under the surface of the water. The force of the waves weighed heavily on Tash's body, exhausting her and unfortunately, Tash knew that the worst had come to pass. Hannah had not made it back up and the ship was sailing away.

For a single moment, the soldier was hit by a crippling thought. Should she abandon all hope for Hannah in a bid to save herself? Or should she continue searching for her friend? She knew that she wasn't strong enough to escape the force of the current.

Tash looked back to the rocky shoreline where she caught sight of a woman with long grey hair sitting on a rock. The woman was dressed in black rags and looking down into the murky depths right where Hannah had disappeared. But surely that was impossible. They were stranded in the middle of the ocean. Nobody could survive out there, let alone a woman dressed in rags.

"You need to save her," Tash called out to the strange woman. "You need to save Hannah!" As if she had heard her cries, the woman looked up at Tash. Her face became distorted. It was not a woman at all. While she certainly looked somewhat humanoid, her face was horrific. Her eyes and mouth were nothing more than large eerily shaped holes in the face, where the features should have been. The creature opened her mouth wide and the melodious humming stopped. Instead, a piercing shriek filled the air, just as a large wave came crashing in over Tash's head. Unlike Samuel, she did not have a magical amulet to save her.

***

With the ship headed far from the fog, Samuel looked around at the soldiers that he had just taken down to keep them away from the helm. They were all bloodied, beaten and bruised, but otherwise okay.

He had handled himself very well. As the music stopped, the soldiers regained their minds. "I'm so sorry, General Davids. I don't know what came over me." Sergeant Jenkins' spell-broken apology was music to Samuel's ears.

"Don't mention it," he replied. "I'm just glad you're all okay." While Sergeant Jenkins attended to the captain's debriefing, Samuel searched for Tash and Hannah who had not yet arrived. Stricken with panic, he excused himself from the crew and ran through the ship, headed for the bow. He looked around to see that they were nowhere in sight. He ran to the stern, starboard side. Still no sign of them. He looked out towards the fog and was struck by a gut-wrenching thought. Maybe Hannah had swum towards the rocks. If that was the case, he had just sent Tash to her death in a bid to rescue her.

Samuel could feel the warmth of his amulet once more at his chest. He needed to find them, but thanks to the sirens and his amulet, it meant that only he would be able to travel through the fog safely, if at all. If Samuel was certain of anything it was that he would never leave his friends to die, no matter the cost. He hurried to inform the crew of his plans. They were hesitant at first, but then assisted him to a lifeboat and watched as he sailed back into the fog, entirely alone.

CHAPTER EIGHTEEN

Cruz and Joey sat in the middle of an old bar in a small, abandoned town. Centaurs had certainly destroyed all that had once made it 'human', but at least there was still enough liquor to keep them occupied. And fortunately, Joey had brought his flask of immortal-strength alcohol to add to their beverages. They had spent two days in the bar drowning in their sorrows and trying to drunkenly devise a plan. Cruz finished off his bourbon and refilled his glass with Joey's flask. "So, you're the immortal god here, what do we do?"

Joey stared at Cruz for a moment as if to be determining which part he was talking about. "That's the first thing you've said in the past three hours. Can you be a little more specific?"

Cruz stared down into his glass and pushed it away. "How do we get her back? How do we rescue her from Hades? What do you think he's doing? You don't think he's hurting her, do you?"

Joey stared down at his own empty glass and refilled it with the flask in Cruz's hand. He had seen enough of what Hades was capable of when he had ventured down in the Underworld.

His mind travelled back to the time that Astrid's body was laying in the hospital bed. Her pulse had returned, indicating that her soul could be used as a link to the Underworld. It had given him the chance to visit her through her dreams. But that link had consistently been interrupted.

He had seen Hades hurt Astrid multiple times. He had even witnessed their wedding. Cruz was fortunate that Joey had chosen not to divulge any of those memories to him.

"This isn't healthy for you," Joey finally said.

"And it wasn't right of you to hide her true identity from her. It wasn't right of anybody to hide it from her. Maybe if she had known, she might've had some knowledge to arm herself with. Maybe this is my fault. I never should've listened to you in the first place. I never should've opened that stupid thing."

Joey placed his hand on his friend's shoulder. There was no doubt about it, Cruz was drunk. Though drunk or not, Joey still agreed with him. He had been tasked to lead the descendant of Zeus to open the jar. Only Hermes and a small few had known that Zeus's soul was trapped in the pithos with his beasts. It had been a peaceful time without the controlling god in power. But now, they were all dealing with the consequences. Hermes included. Joey's thoughts were interrupted by the sight of Cruz wiping away a few drunken tears.

"I should've known she was special! I mean, just look at her. Not that we can, because we let her go off with Hades who will make her destroy the world."

Joey sighed and shook his head. "Whatever happens, you need to promise you won't breathe a word of this to anybody. Promise me!"

Cruz gave him a side-eyed stare. "Not even, Astrid?"

"Especially not Astrid. You need to promise."

"Fine, whatever." Cruz shook his head, in a bid to brush away the misery. "We should… we should get out of here. Despite her need to do this herself, we need to find a way to save her… Hopefully a way that will put all Buzzkill's techniques to shame."

"Do you have something in mind?" Joey asked, amused by his friend's false sense of confidence as they both got to their feet.

"I don't know. Maybe we could come riding in on a Pegasus. Or maybe even an oversized phoenix? We need to do something besides sitting around some shitty bar drinking bad alcohol."

Joey grinned. He had no idea how to stop Hades but at least his friend hadn't given up. Cruz picked up his still-full glass and drank it in one impressive mouthful, before slamming the empty container back down hard enough to shatter the glass. He wobbled a little on his feet, so Joey held out his hand to keep him steady. "Are you alright?" Joey asked. Cruz nodded, but leaned forward against the bar.

"I'm good. Just give me three moments and I'll be great… I'll be ready to save the day. Because I'm me!

Mario Cruz! The archaeologist, demigod... whatever the hell I am!" Joey smiled to himself as he watched his friend struggle to gain his composure. Whatever Cruz chose to do, he would always have Hermes by his side.

***

Feeling the warmth of Athena's spear in her right hand, Astrid followed Hades through the surprisingly busy streets of Athens, while keeping a steady eye on Hades' two-pronged pitchfork. Her plan was simple.

Distract him long enough so she could take his weapon. She was aware that it sounded foolish, but if she succeeded, she would have the upper hand. While they were still at odds in the decision of either killing or sending Hades to Tartarus, Persephone had explained to Astrid how she believed the bident should be used. But neither of them had ever actually used a weapon so powerful in their lives. The problem was, however, that Hades refused to put it down, even for a second. It was almost as if it was glued to his very hand. Astrid needed to bring up a conversation with the god, maybe getting him talking was the key to his distraction. "Hades, I need to know... If you expect me to be a queen, I imagine that I

431

should have some power. I'm nothing more than a descendant of Pandora... a mortal human to you."

Hades stopped and turned to her. His eyes studying her before he looked around at the people going about their usual business as if they weren't in the midst of an apocalypse. "I knew this question would come up sooner or later. You don't understand. Pandora was created by Hephaestus using both the elements of the earth and the oceans. She received her beauty from Aphrodite, her enticing charms from Athena, her love of music from Apollo and even your friend Hermes added to her creation, with the gift of persuasion. But he never told you that, did he?"

Astrid paused on that piece of information. Sure, she had heard the tale in the history books and from Cruz, but Hades was offering her a tell-all. She needed to know more.

"Joey? Really? He never mentioned it."

Hades noticed her surprise and went on. "Of course, that deceptive thief would leave out important details of Pandora's creation. But you would like to know how you fit into the grand scheme of things and why I chose you as my goddess of the earth. Well, the legends say that Pandora was the first mortal woman to walk on earth. That was a lie, just a fabricated tale by Hermes himself. Pandora was anything but mortal, a trick played on Zeus by the ones he trusted the most. Pandora was made from the earth and the oceans because she can control the earth and the oceans. Why do you think it is so simple for you to channel Persephone's powers? Or to have influence over my creatures. I guess you also wonder why so many men look at you the way they do... You have the beauty and the charm of both Aphrodite and Athena. You are the perfect embodiment of Pandora. Once we send Persephone back to the Underworld, I will teach you how to unlock your gifts. You will be able to control all the elements at will… and use them in the way that you were destined."

"I'm sorry, you just stumbled on your words." Astrid laughed. "You just got me a little mixed up with Pandora. It's like you actually think that I'm her or something."

Hades chuckled. Was he mocking her? She couldn't be sure. But then his tone changed to a more inquisitive one. "You really don't know... do you?"

"Know what?"

"You are Pandora. Your very body, your very soul... While Zeus was in that box, the other gods have been warring. Some knew that you were destined to reshape the earth and they feared what you would become. So, they got to you the day you were born, sucking your very life force from you. But Hekate had other plans. She ensured that you would live. Pandora's soul is blended into yours in a way that hasn't been done before."

Astrid was speechless. Cruz was right. She was nothing more than a trojan horse, a tool for war and destruction. A metaphorical pithos for carrying souls. " I don't believe you."

Hades stared at her. "You're merely lying to yourself. I'm quite surprised Hermes did not reveal this to you sooner."

He continued to lead her through the busy streets. While she was curious as to why there was so much peace in Athens, she was all the more bewildered and angrier that Joey had never been truly honest with her in the first place. Why had he lied to them for so long? She had trusted him when nobody else had. While she had prayed that he had a good reason to lie to them before, now, she wasn't so sure.

***

Tash awoke on the clear shorelines of a deserted island. The fog had drifted back out to sea and covered the large rocky bed in the distance, which seemed to have surrounded the island that she had found herself on. The rocky bed could be likened to a large impenetrable wall surrounding every ounce of the island from as far as she could see.

Tash's damp dark hair felt heavy over her face and shoulders. Her sun-burned body was covered in sand and the last thing she could remember was that she should have drowned. But there she was, on the rough sand of some deserted island.

She stood up, looked around while reaching for her sword and gun. But surprisingly, neither of which were attached to her. In the distance, she saw a group of women, dressed in something that reminded her of her old cosplay days. They looked like the old Amazon women of legend.

Two of the women had long dark hair, one with dark skin, the other tanned. The woman in the middle was blonde. The women were very beautiful, and certainly looked like they knew their way around a weapon or two. Drawing their swords, they made their way towards Tash, forcing her to back up with both hands raised.

"I don't mean any harm. I come in peace. Let me just find a boat and I'll be on my way... Do any of you have a phone by any chance?"

The blonde woman sheathed her sword. "What is your name, stranger?"

Tash eyed the other two, who still had their swords up ready, complying would be the safest strategy. "I'm Natasha Martinez. But my friends and my wife, just call me Tash. Is this the island that those sirens were on? Wait, none of you are sirens, are you? Did you see what happened to...?"

"...Silence!" the blonde woman yelled, making Tash instantly shut her mouth in fear.

"My sister here told me that she saved you. That something about you called to her. Why is that so?"

Tash stared at the beautiful dark-haired, tanned-skin woman that the blonde was referring to. Her eyes were a very dark shade of brown. They could've been related, but Tash was sure they had never met before. "I'm not sure," Tash said, shaking her head, confused. "I remember calling out to my friend Hannah... but..." Tash went silent as she remembered the last time that she had seen Hannah. "Is Hannah here? Is she safe?" But the women just stared at her in silence. "Look, I won't hold you up any longer!" Tash said, turning on her heels and running towards the ocean, in the direction of the fog. She needed to find Hannah.

"Stop!" The blonde woman beckoned of her.

"Please! My friends... They're out there... I need to find them." She said, looking back, practically begging.

The woman with the blonde hair and large crystal blue eyes stared over at the ocean and then back to Tash almost as if she wasn't accustomed to showing empathy but needed to, for the moment to go well. "I hate to disappoint you, but your friend, Hannah is dead. Her body was taken by the sirens. Inara had to pull you from their clutches before they devoured you... and if your friends even approach the siren wall, then they too will be killed."

Her words gave Tash whiplash. "Hannah is dead? But... She can't be dead. No, I won't believe it! But Buzzkill... He'll come and find me! Neither he nor I were affected by the sirens' music. I need to make sure he's okay."

"Men are strictly prohibited to venture onto this island. He will be cut down where he stands!"

But Tash was adamant. "No! You can't kill him. He's... He's my family!"

"We are your family, now." The woman who had been referred to as Inara earlier, spoke up.

"Inara, are you sure that's wise? She is a stranger." the blonde woman said.

"Yes... Natasha is one of us. I can feel it, can't you?" Inara's dark eyes pleaded with what was clearly the tribal leader.

All the more confused, Tash just stared. She thought that maybe they were planning to kidnap her to use as a human sacrifice. "No, I think you have me mistaken for somebody else. Look, just let me go and find Samuel and

I'll be on my way." Tash ran into the water until it was at waist level. But the waves kept stopping her.

"Natasha Martinez!" There was that commanding voice again, it willed her to turn back to the women with tears in her eyes. Deep down, Tash knew she stood no chance of swimming the oceans to find her friends, so she waited for the island queen to speak. "You will stay here, Natasha. You feel it within yourself that this is where you belong. You have been searching for a family that you felt you had long-since lost and have indeed found again. When you are ready, if you still choose, we will assist you in travelling back to your friends. Just let us explain who you truly are."

"But, what about Buzzkill?" When they didn't answer, Tash persisted. "Sorry, I mean, Samuel."

"If he means that much to you, we will decide what to do with him... if he makes it pass the siren wall, that is."

Tash stared at the women and then back at the crashing waves. She was quite literally stuck between a rock and a hard place. There was nothing more she could do. "Okay, well it seems I have no choice... but can I send for my wife? She'll be really upset if I..." Their cold stares gave her their answer. "Alright. Fine, point taken!" Tash stormed out of the water and back toward her captors with no clue what was to become of her.

***

Samuel paddled the small grey boat through the thick, dark fog with his amulet still glowing like a beacon. There was a huge thud as the boat hit something, but thanks to the mist, he couldn't be sure as to what it was. Assuming that it was nothing more than a rock, he was startled when he heard the large slap of water behind him. He felt the force of something tugging on the boat, turning it to the left and then pulling it in a new direction from underneath.

There was certainly something in the water with him. But what that something was and where it was taking him remained to be seen. As Samuel tried to determine what it was and how he could take it down, he brought up his paddles, sat them in the boat and pulled out his sword, praying that whatever was pulling him along, meant him no harm.

Curious, Samuel peered over the edge on the right but could only see the water lapping at the boat. He looked to the left, where something splashed above the surface. A long dark-blue tail with two fins at the end. It was clearly a very large fishtail. But that fishtail disappeared almost immediately.

Samuel counted minute by minute, the hours it took until the fog finally subsided, only to find that he had been brought to a rocky cave in the middle of the ocean, where his boat was pulled inside. The further he travelled into the cave, the darker his surroundings became and the darker his surroundings became, the brighter Samuel's amulet glowed. The black rocky walls of the cave were lined with what seemed to be crystals of every different color. A miner's dream. He was amazed at just how beautiful it all was. Just one crystal alone would be worth a fortune. But then the boat stopped. He had made it to the end of his trip, where a large white crystal stood in front of his boat, stopping him from venturing further.

On either side of the boat was a rocky bank. But he would still need to bring the boat to the edge before he could climb out. Catching his attention was a swirl and then a splash of water behind him.

Samuel turned to see the god of the sea standing there. But Poseidon wasn't wearing any clothes and his lower half was that of a large fish. Samuel laughed at himself. How had he not realized sooner? Poseidon had been following him the whole way, clearly testing him. "I must admit, I wasn't expecting that," Samuel said. "I was looking for Tash and Hannah."

"I do apologize, but this is where your current journey with them ends. Natasha Martinez has found her family."

Samuel's blood grew cold. "Found her family? What does that even mean? And what about Hannah? Where is she?"

Poseidon stared at him almost emotionless and then spoke with a tone with even less empathy. "Natasha Martinez is a child of the Amazons... and unfortunately, Hannah never survived the sirens. I will give you a few moments to process, but we need to continue onto Atlantis." Samuel stared into his lap in disbelief. He couldn't believe that Hannah had died, despite knowing that death never discriminated. He had been through the deaths of fellow soldiers, countless times before. Unfortunately for Samuel, he was still a General. He needed to push through the pain and press on with his mission. The thought of Tash having joined the Amazons in such a short amount of time, gave him faith that she would be okay. But then, as Samuel looked around and thought about his next step in his mission, he asked, "I'm guessing this cave is the front door to Atlantis, how has it been so easy for me to find? People have been searching for the lost city, forever. "

"The opening of the box made all this possible. The amulet around your neck is your key. If you had not been wearing it, what you see here would be nothing more than vast oceans. Now, are you ready, Samuel?"

Samuel nodded. Not only was he ready, but he was more excited than he had ever been in his entire life. For he was about to journey to the city of Atlantis.

CHAPTER NINETEEN

It had been almost a week and Tash had not only been shown around the island of the Amazon women but also given a place to stay. She had heard about the place in myths and comic books, but never in her life had she ever imagined that it was real.

The blonde queen, Caelene had done her best to answer all her questions yet had remained vague on the geographical aspects. The countries that the queen had mentioned, Tash knew were nothing more than ancient lands that had broken off over time. But of course, the queen had no knowledge of any of it.

The fashions, weaponry and everyday items used on the island reminded Natasha of ancient Greece, back when the gods had first roamed the earth. There were white temples with high ceilings held up by stone pillars, with marble white steps that reached on forever. Beautiful garden paradises and waterfalls summed up the island's exterior. And there was no modern-day technology, whatsoever.

The women bathed both naked and in their warrior attire in the crystal-clear lakes and busied themselves with their sword training and academic educations.

It was like something from a movie, but there were no cast, crew, or cameras. It was truly beautiful.

Tash only wished that she could bring Stacey there, knowing that her wife would love it. The entire place seemed so surreal. But then again, none of what she had encountered over the past few years had been logical. Centaurs, demigods, and even sea monsters. In the old world, all those things would have been nothing more than works of fiction.

What made matters more unbelievable was that these women were convinced that Tash was one of them. But Tash believed with every ounce of her being that they were mistaken. She didn't have an ounce of Greek ethnicity in her whatsoever. That was until Inara introduced her to the warrior known as Fada.

Fada was almost a splitting image of Tash only somewhat older, and she revealed a chilling tale of what she believed was the story behind Tash's lineage.

They were sitting on the concrete steps outside the palace, amongst the beauty and the serenity of the gardens where they could hear the rippling of the waterfall in front of them. Tash was holding a beautiful white flower in her hands as Fada began her story. According to the Amazon warrior, a long time ago she had left the island, venturing past the siren wall, where she had fallen in love with a sailor by the name of Amancio Martinez, from Spain. She had saved him from the sirens when the rest of his men had been killed.

When Fada had brought the man back to the tribe, Caelene had threatened to cut him down where he stood. Instead, Fada chose to leave with him, setting forth for Spain. Fada bore a son to the sailor and lived in happiness in his humble home. But, after a while, there were forces pulling them apart which disrupted their happiness and Fada knew that she could never return to the island with her son.

In the end, she was forced to abandon her family and return to the island for her safety. While Fada explained that there were forces at work, she never divulged just what they were. Tash knew that she could be a little naïve at times, though she still doubted that she was a descendant to that child, or that her lineage was in any way related to the Amazon women.

She was tempted to cough out the word 'bullshit' but resisted entirely. These women were far more skilled than she was with weapons, and she felt safer with them believing their stories. However, Tash still needed them to understand her skepticism. "So, I'm supposed to believe that I'm the descendant of the Amazon women of legend? I wish I could, but I don't. I'm sorry. For one thing, I'm not brave. I only joined the military because my survival depended on it. Plus, my family was killed. Besides, none of that explains why I'm immune to the sirens just off the island."

Fada stared at her. "That makes a lot more sense than you realize. You see, the sirens were not always that way. They were once nymphs. But a long time ago, they were cursed for allowing such a horrible act to befall such a beautiful young goddess. Demeter believed that they could have prevented the kidnapping of her child..."

"...Hades and Persephone?" Tash gasped.

"You know the story?"

"More than you know."

"Yes. Well, there was one nymph who was able to appeal to Demeter, after having been turned into a siren. That nymph had not yet succumbed to the siren's beastly nature. She was able to tell Demeter everything she had seen. She told Demeter that Zeus was an accomplice behind the capture of Persephone. Though, nobody believed her, and the nymph was made to look like a liar. But after a few months, Demeter grew to believe her and even attempted to turn her back... but, there were some... complications... this nymph became human and then she was hunted by the other gods. So, Demeter led her to the tribe of Amazons where she was protected. However, there were still traces of the siren within her. She and all her children that descended from her would all be immune to the song of the sirens."

"That nymph siren was you, wasn't it?"

Fada nodded. "Yes, Tash. It was. Persephone was my best friend and I saw her get taken. But then when I tried to appeal to Zeus, I overheard him speaking with Hades. He admitted his own fault and hoped it had gone unnoticed."

Tash gave a big grin, which confused the woman. "I have some news, that you are totally gonna want to hear." Tash revealed to Fada that the soul of Persephone had been brought back in the body of her friend, Astrid, and with that explanation, she revealed everything that she and her friends had experienced over the past few years.

***

Only a few days earlier, the buildings of Athens, had been restored to all their elegance and beauty with just a wave of Hades' pitchfork. To Astrid's modern-day knowledge of the world, seeing them stand as beautiful as they once did with the modern-day technology and electricity was truly remarkable.

It was getting late and Astrid and Hades had been walking through the streets for days without rest. She was exhausted, frustrated, and hungry and at the same time, she felt a flurry of emotions towards the god of darkness. While he had used and abused her in the Underworld, he was now showing that there was a love for beauty and peace within him too. Astrid also wondered if the reason he hadn't subjected her to any abuse in the past few days was because she had offered to go with him, or if that abuse was still yet to come.

The deserted streets were now bustling with not only people but also creatures of every sort, many of which Astrid remembered from the Underworld. In her mind, she tried to analyze Hades and come to an understanding of his many layers.

The other gods and even Hades himself had all led her to believe that he was planning on turning the world into nothing more than a wasteland. But those plans had clearly changed. *'Astrid, I know what you're thinking.'* Persephone spoke within her mind. *'You are trying to see if there is any good in Hades. Alas, you will only be disappointed. Do not forget that he tried to kill Cruz and he hurt you over and over down in the Underworld. Just imagine what he could do to Samuel if he were to know that he was your beloved.'*

Astrid grimaced at the thought of Hades hurting either Samuel or Cruz. Sadly, she knew that future would be inevitable if she didn't stop him. But it didn't stop her from trying to reason with Persephone. *'Yes, but he stopped himself from killing Cruz because I asked him too. He also told me the truth about who I am, even Joey kept that from me.'*

'But you know Hermes, personally. He would have his reasons to hide that information from you. He isn't as deceitful as Hades claims him to be.' Persephone's response caused Astrid to sigh out loud, which grasped Hades' attention. He stopped walking, forcing her to do the same.

"What troubles you, Pandora?"

"For your information, my name's Astrid. Even if you believe that I am Pandora reincarnated or whatever. But while we're talking... Why did you spare Cruz's life?"

Hades stared at her. His blue eyes that pierced through her, seemed somewhat calculating. He was very hard to read. "Because you asked me to."

"Yet, you forced me to marry you... you forced me to... well... you were horrible to me! What is your agenda?"

"I have no agenda. I am a god! I merely take what I want, as is my right. It has been your stories and myths that have merely painted me as an alternative to the devil of Christianity. You must realize that Zeus is far more... vindictive than I."

Astrid thought on this piece of information. There was some truth to what he was saying. "But you still wish to overthrow him. You've even taken all the gods powers to do so. You kidnapped Persephone, you forced me into marriage. I get that you're a god but those are all very narcissistic traits. How are you any better than he is?"

"Well, I guess that you have an eternity to find out."

"An eternity? Over my dead..." Astrid bit her lip as he gave her a stern look. She held the spear tighter in her hands and Hades once again transported her to an entirely separate location. They were now standing at the fully restored Acropolis overlooking the lights of the city, which had captivated Astrid's undivided attention.

"It's simply beautiful, isn't it?" Hades asked. "My brother forced me to live in the Underworld. Below all this beauty... And people call me evil."

"So, you're doing all this for revenge, then? Can't you just reason with him? A war with the gods can only lead to destruction. They believe that you want to wipe out all of humanity."

"Not all of humanity. I want to keep the ones who have a greater purpose..."

"...and the rest?"

"Will learn to fight for their own survival. It's about picking and choosing... creating the perfect world." Astrid felt her bitterness begging her to come out. The god was no better than Hitler. In fact, he was worse. She thought back to the innocent people in San Francisco and was glad that Cruz had chosen to see them. They were the people that Hades wanted to kill off. "But the people here in Greece?" Astrid asked. "There's so many of them... How are they not dead? Are they..."

"...all descendants of the gods? Yes, they are. They will all get their opportunity to worship their new god or death will befall them as well."

"You have got to be kidding me! So, what? Worship you or die? There is no alternative? This is why I was always a damn atheist!" Astrid went to storm away, but he gripped her by the hair, forcing her backwards.

"You will not address me in such a manner. I am your husband and your god! You will respect me!" He threw her to the ground. Astrid got to her feet angrily and felt her grasp around the spear tighten. Against Persephone's warning she instantly smacked it across Hades' head and spat "You're nothing but a piece of shit!"

Calmly, he stepped back, pointed his pitchfork at her and set off an invisible burst that flung her backward, forcing her to crack her head on a concrete step.

Immediately, Astrid got to her feet and ran at him again, bringing up her spear. But once again, his weapon was at the ready, releasing another force that sent her backwards. Astrid cursed and threw her spear at him, aiming for his head. But he simply raised his pitchfork in the direction of the incoming projectile.

The spear changed direction in mid-air and shot towards her instead, just missing her.

"Next time it won't miss!" Hades snapped. "It would be wise to be my ally, Astrid, not my enemy as I can easily replace you."

"It's funny," she scoffed. "You were so loyal to Persephone for such a long time... what changed your mind?"

"I needed company for both the earth and the underworld."

"I'm not buying it." Astrid stared hard at Hades and caught a glimpse of something that seemed almost human, and she knew exactly what it was. Her tone softened a little, and her eyebrows raised. "Huh! Persephone was in love with another man, wasn't she? She still is, isn't she?"

"Shut up, girl!"

Astrid was overcome with pity. She had just learned what made him tick. He was lacking in love. His own brother had subjected him to rule over the loneliest and emptiest place imaginable. His wife, sure, he had kidnapped her, did not love him and now he was only about to have his heart broken yet again when he learned that he could never win Astrid's heart either. "I'm sorry. I really shouldn't have said that," she apologized.

"I forgive you."

But Astrid continued with a plan in mind. She adopted a softer, slightly more seductive tone. "This side of you, Hades. It actually makes me feel... I don't know, some kind of empathy for you."

"I don't need your pity. I need your loyalty."

She smiled and ran her hand up his arm. "Trust needs to be earned. But the more you divulge... well, it makes me see that there is another side of you. One that I could learn to get used to. One that I could probably get to... love."

Hades stared at her, studying her manner. He stroked her cheek with his hand, starting from her ear and then bringing his fingers to her chin. Then he brought his fingers and thumb to the nape of her neck where he squeezed tightly, choking her. Astrid coughed and gasped for air.

"Do you really think I am so blind to your manipulation, girl? I've warned you not to mess with me. Let this be your final warning!"

Astrid tried to remove his hand from her throat, forgetting that he had the immortal strength of a god, but her efforts were only in vain. She was struggling to breathe. Dizziness was setting in. "Okay," she gasped. "I... I promise...please... let me go!" He held onto her throat for a few seconds longer and then threw her to the ground where she panted to get her breath back. "I'm... I'm sorry!"

she stammered, getting back to her feet in fear and frustration.

Her attempt to distract him to steal his pitchfork had failed and had almost cost Astrid, her life. Hades looked out to the city lights where he saw a flicker of lightning and two silhouettes flying through the night sky towards them. "It seems those two are just begging for a trip to the Underworld!" He said.

"Who?" Astrid asked, just as she realized who he was referring to. Hermes was flying very fast, carrying Cruz through the sky. But instead of allowing herself to be excited to see them, she was overcome with serious concern for their wellbeing.

She wanted them to be as far away from Hades as they could be. But at the same time, with Hades attention on Hermes and Cruz, it gave her the perfect opportunity to take the pitchfork. Astrid stepped towards him as fast as she could, then placed her hand on the metal bident and slipped it from his hands with ease.

With it, she stepped backward, pointing the prongs at him, threateningly. She was holding both Hades' bident and Athena's spear in her hands ready to attack with either. Hades turned to her, just as Hermes and Cruz landed on the ground beside them.

"Cruz, Joey! What's the plan?" she asked, showing them the bident. A fire ignited right where they were standing. Joey swore and attempted to flee, but it only followed him.

Cruz raised his hands and started mumbling, in a bid to conjure up a storm. The sudden heavy rain doused the flames a little, but the fire would not disappear. Hades was controlling the fire with his mind. "Now, hand me my bident, or you will all burn to death," he demanded.

"No, don't do it, Astrid!" Joey pleaded. The flames that were burning Cruz, grew higher. Judging by the pain in his face, he was struggling to focus on his storm. Joey lifted Cruz into the air, but the flames only burned higher, igniting their clothes. There was no escape from it. Astrid's temptation to hand over the pitchfork was high, but then they heard the voice of Zeus once more. "Brother, stop! Hermes, bring me the bident!"

"Do it, Joey," Cruz demanded. Joey looked to Cruz and then at Astrid, who barely noticed the fire at her own feet.

"I can't leave them, father!" Joey pleaded. "Not with Hades!"

"You must obey me, Hermes," Zeus's voice boomed back, giving him no choice.

"Do it, Joe!" Cruz demanded. "We'll be okay!"

Defeated, Joey sighed. "Okay, yes. I will, father." He hesitantly planted Cruz back onto the ground and took the pitchfork from Astrid. As Joey shot up into the air before Hades could stop him, the god of the underworld turned his anger back onto Cruz, who had gathered his bearings enough to douse the fires entirely with his rainfall. But Hades continued to rise up the flames.

It was a battle of flames verses the rains as the two used their abilities to control the elements around them. Unfortunately, Hades had the upper hand. He was focusing his abilities on burning Cruz alive.

"Stop it! Stop it!" Astrid demanded, to no avail. She ran to Cruz's side, oblivious to the fact that she was burning too. They were soaking thanks to the rain, but they were burning thanks to the flames.

Hades remained unaffected entirely. Astrid looked up into the sky where Hermes had disappeared. Where he was headed, only Joey knew. She would need to think up a way to save Cruz.

Then she remembered what Hades had told her earlier. The very thought that she had been trying to comprehend since he had revealed it to her. It had to be a lie, but if it wasn't, it would mean that she held influence over the oceans.

The ocean was made of water. She thought back to when Cruz had channeled her powers to create a rose with droplets of rain on its petals. They were quite literally surrounded by water.

Surely, it was worth a shot. She focused through the pain of the flames licking at her skin. Remembering everything she had learned through her training sessions, she grabbed for Cruz's hand and focused on whatever mental abilities she might contain. With the use of her anger, her fear for Cruz's life and every other emotion she could conjure up, she watched as the raindrops grew bigger and bigger. They started to form with other raindrops in the air. Cruz was thrown a little off guard as he watched the raindrops merging into pools of water just above the flames. "Wow, Astrid," he managed to stammer through gritted teeth. "Shh," she replied. "Just focus. Feel that warmth."

Cruz continued to create more raindrops, as Astrid manipulated them to form together until there was a swirling, floating river circling the two of them. She let that river fall, blanketing the flames beneath.

They continued to do this over and over, as Hades watched on in disbelief. The more flames he built up, the more magical rivers they created to blanket the fires. It was working! Within minutes the fire was nothing more than smoke from the extinguished flames.

Hades threw his hands up in disbelief. "Clever girl... But I still have one more trick up my sleeve!"

In the blink of an eye, he had teleported himself behind them, snatched Athena's spear from her and drove it right through Cruz's back. He pulled it out again, slowly as Cruz collapsed to the floor, a large wound in the middle of his back bleeding out fast. Zeus's voice echoed around them with pure warning.

"You will pay for your crimes, brother!" But as his last word was spoken, Hades disappeared, leaving Astrid in total disbelief of Cruz's current condition.

She tore the fabric of her shirt and pulled Cruz into her lap, comforting him. She pressed the fabric into his wound and held it there with her leg and used the front of his shirt to clot the exit wound at his stomach. "I told you it was a willing-to-give-up-my-soul-for-you type love," he chuckled, despite the tears in his eyes.

"Don't laugh. You'll bleed out. You just need to hang on until Joey gets back. He'll use his staff to heal you!"

"Damn girl, you're so stubborn. You know I don't have much time."

"Yes, you do... don't be stupid." A large sob had made its way into her throat. She choked it down and yelled out to Zeus. "Do something, Zeus! Heal him! He's your chosen one for god's sake! Do something! He suffered for you, so now help him!" But Zeus did not answer.

"I always said he was a vengeful *pendejo*. Didn't I?" Cruz joked again.

"Stop joking. I'm not going to let you die on me. Come on, hurry up, Joe! Where was he taking the bident again?"

"Shh, *mi amor*. There's nothing we can do... it's inevitable." Cruz brought his thumb to her cheek to wipe away her tears, smiling up at her. Staring down at him that way brought back the memory of the night that they had first met. She remembered knocking him out of the line of fire from those men in her building. She remembered the moment she had first laid eyes on him when he had been the only person to come to her rescue.

"I wanted a hero," she said. "You were my hero."

"What are you talking about?"

"That night we met. I was surprised that you came, and you said that I wanted a hero. It was the same thing tonight. You were my hero."

Cruz choked back on his own tears, as an involuntary laugh sprang forth. "You never needed a hero. You were mine. But you need to know the truth about who you are… what you're meant for. What all of this… is meant for."

Astrid froze for a moment. "Cruz, what are you…?"

"Joey will kill me for this, but I guess it doesn't matter now… He showed me the will of the gods. He showed me his memories about your creation… about the coming war. About our daughter and about… you… I'm not supposed to tell you but I…"

Despite her desperate desire to know, she brought her finger to his lips. "Shh. Don't tell me. Please, Cruz. Whatever it is. I don't need to know." Cruz pursed his lips together against her finger, as if to stop the secrets from spilling out.

"I love you, Cruz. Nothing will ever change that. Not even death can change that." His soft brown eyes smiled up at her through his tears.

"I love you too, *mi amor*." He covered her hand with his and released a soft kiss against her knuckles. His face screwed up as he remembered the pain he was feeling but he held on tight to her hand, bringing it to his chest so she could feel the soft beating of his heart. It was soft, faint and fading fast.

But she didn't need that gesture to know that he was dying. She could see it in his eyes. At that moment every other thought washed away. She was losing him and even if she had to return to the Underworld herself to bring him back, she would do it. She would stop at nothing to ensure that he stayed in her arms, in her life at least. They were destined to be together. No matter the cost, she would make it happen.

Astrid brought her face down and brushed her nose against his. "I'll bring you back," she whispered. Cruz brushed his hand lightly against her jawline. On impulse, they allowed their lips to meet. A soft passionate kiss. Not to say 'goodbye' but to say, 'until we meet again'. After a moment, Astrid felt Cruz's mouth relax as she pulled away, knowing that his soul was no longer in his body. Rocking him gently in her arms, she sobbed heart-broken tears.

CHAPTER TWENTY

Inara and Fada who had been appointed to keep watch over Tash, fitted her with some black and gold metal and brown leather attire, along with some weapons to match their own. Although Tash felt a large weight on her shoulders for not being home with Stacey, the thrill of being an Amazon warrior excited her more than she could have ever imagined. She only prayed that she wouldn't disappoint or do something to mess it all up. As Inara and Fada led her to an open paddock ready to train, Inara taunted Tash playfully. "You said you were a soldier. So come on, prove your worth. Prepare yourself!" Inara held up her sword and pointed it at Tash's chest.

Tash stood at the ready with her own sword drawn. She had always preferred to work with guns. Particularly big guns. She had even scoffed when Samuel had instructed them to begin training with such a primitive range of weaponry to begin with. "Just remember Inara, I've only been training with swords for..." Before Tash could finish her sentence, Inara swung her sword, and slashed it across Tash's left arm. "Ow! I wasn't ready!"

"Inara, go easy. She is your sister," Fada warned.

"She is not your daughter as I am, she is your granddaughter... or a descendant," Inara argued.

"While that is true, she is still a sister to us all...Tash, are you ready?"

Wiping the blood from her forearm, Tash nodded. She loosened her shoulders and twisted her neck in preparation. For a split second, she remembered an old movie filled with virtual reality fighting styles and then gestured for Inara to come at her with a very cocky grin, knowing that Inara had no clue what it was a reference to.

Inara thrusted her sword at Tash once more, as Tash countered it perfectly with her own move. In that moment, she thanked the gods that Samuel had been so stubborn and had taught her all he knew in relation to swordplay. But as good as Tash was with her defense,

Inara was still far better with her attacks. She sliced off a lock of Tash's dark hair, only stopping before her blade met the soldier's throat.

By the time the sun had set, Tash was exhausted and fed well at the large hall's dinner banquet. While Tash certainly missed Stacey, Buzzkill, Sutherland and the rest of the group. she truly felt as if she had found her place and knowing that she would eventually need to leave again actually made her feel teary. But, as it was Samuel's mission to go to Atlantis, she knew that it was her mission to go back to her wife and their friends.

***

The sun was rising back in Athens, where Astrid had fallen asleep clutching tightly to Cruz's cold body. She was somewhat delirious thanks to the mixture of shock and exhaustion that had sunk in. She reminisced back to the time when they had left San Francisco on her father's ship and had watched the sun go down together. "Look, Cruz, the sun is coming up. We never really get to take in that view anymore, do we?" Her tears sat present on her face as she pushed a lock of his hair behind his ear. "Do you remember the first sunrise we saw together? Or what about our…"

"I don't think he's going to reply." Joey's sudden voice startled her from behind. The moment she faced him, she felt her blood boil.

"Where the hell were you? You could have saved him!"

There were fresh tears in Joey's eyes as he knelt beside her. "I'm sorry. I wasn't fast enough. I wish I was… I wouldn't have…"

But Astrid's icy glare did not waver. She could tell he was hurting, but frankly, she just didn't care.

In her mind, Persephone told her not to be too hard on him. "Oh, shut up, Persephone!" she snapped out loud. "I don't need your voice in my head right now!" While Joey was taken aback by her anger, he remained quiet.

'Please, Astrid,' Persephone persisted. '*I understand the grief you are dealing with, but there is still so much to do.*'

Astrid's response was but a mere growl, directed at them both. "Right now, I don't want to listen to either one of you!"

She laid Cruz's head down onto the dirt as gently as she could, got to her feet and opposed Joey. "You both lied to me. Why didn't you tell me that I was Pandora? Why Joey? Why didn't you tell me that you had even added to my creation? And that I was doomed to be used as a pawn to destroy the earth? I had to find out through Hades! None of you could protect Cruz, not even Zeus!"

Joey stood at full height but stared shamefully at his feet. "Astrid, I'm… I'm sorry… I couldn't tell you… I was sworn to secrecy."

"You're so full of shit! Let me give you some advice about humans... we like the truth, Joey! Just look at how Hannah reacted when she found out that you lied to her! Why didn't you tell me that Pandora was a goddess? And that I… that my soul is some ridiculous science experiment!" Joey looked as if he was struggling to find the right words to use.

"You're not… you're not an experiment."

"No, I am a fucking goddess! No one told me! And if they had, maybe I could've prevented… I could've…" She was crying again and pointing at Cruz's lifeless body, struggling to finish her sentence.

"You don't know that you could have prevented his death," Joey said, placing his hand on her shoulder, only to anger her more.

Astrid shook him away with uncontrollable strength and her tears running down her face. "Don't touch me, Joe! Just because you and Persephone have some weird relationship going on... I am not Persephone! I am just her god-damn vessel! So, stay the hell away from me!"

Instead, Joey ignored her. Against her will, he forced her into a tight embrace as she gave into her overwhelming bout of fury and punched him hard in the chest. When that didn't work, she tried to push him away, but he refused to release her.

Instead, Joey stroked her hair from her face. "I'm sorry," he mumbled. "I wish I could have come back in time or done something... I'm sorry. He never should have died."

"No, he shouldn't have! But he's dead. Cruz is dead!"

Joey rested his cheek on top of her head, pulling her into an even tighter embrace, and giving into his own grief. His next three words were practically a whisper, but Astrid heard them ever so clearly. "So is Hannah."

Confused, Astrid shifted her head to face him. "What do you mean?"

Joey wiped at his eye with the palm of his hand but refused to release her. He cleared his throat and repeated his last statement. "So is Hannah. Zeus just told me. It's why I took so long."

"How can she be dead?"

Before he could relay the news, Joey cleared his throat and released her. "Poseidon sent Samuel on a mission to Atlantis. Tash and Hannah accompanied him. Hannah lost her life to a bunch of sirens. I don't understand how I didn't hear her soul calling out to me... I should have been able to hear her. This had to be Hekate's doing!"

"I'm so sorry. What about the others?"

"I don't know. There's been no word."

Heartbroken and guilty for the way she had treated Joey, Astrid wrapped her arms around him and buried her cheek into his chest.

She felt dizzy. Her legs were weak, and she could barely stand, but she needed to stay strong. "Oh god! We need to... We need to... I don't know... we need to do something. I'm so sorry." She felt as if she was about to fall but Joey kept her standing. She took a few deep breaths and caught a glimpse of Cruz's body still lying on the floor. It derailed her enough to close her eyes just to speak. "Did Zeus say what happened to Hades?"

"Yeah. Hades teleported somewhere. We just don't know where. But he has the rest of the gods after him. So don't worry. Without his bident, he doesn't stand a chance."

Astrid flinched at the thought of Hades still on the run. But that gave her an ounce of hope. "So, the Underworld has no current leader until we get Persephone back," she decided. "Maybe we can search for Cruz and Hannah's souls… and you… you can take us there!"

"It won't be that easy, Astrid. Hekate might have something to say on that matter."

"I don't care. If she took Cruz and Hannah's souls, then we will convince her to give them back."

Joey pursed his lips together and stepped back, releasing her in the process. "It won't be easy."

"Nothing worth having ever is. Please, tell me that we can at least try. If you can bring my soul back and Persephone's soul, we can do it, I know we can."

"It's not the same, Astrid. It was through your dreams that I was able to get to you. Just like Persephone, they will need a body to come through."

"But Persephone will be returning to the Underworld. If you and I both use our own bodies to bring them back it should work! If you don't help me, you know that I'll find another way to do it."

Joey shook his head. It was evident that he wanted desperately to help her but doing so would be a near impossible task. "If they're there, we'll only be able to bring one of them back. My body doesn't work as a vessel like yours does."

"Alright, we'll think of something when the time comes. So how do we do this?"

"We fly to the throne of Zeus."

"How the hell do we do that? Isn't that..." she pointed towards the clouds.

Joey laughed. "No, it's Mount Olympus, silly. Here, take my hand and hold on tight."

Astrid took one last look at Cruz's body. "Don't you think we should move him first?"

"No need. We're travelling to the Underworld and my powers have returned. We'll be back in no time." Astrid collected Athena's spear, then took Joey's outstretched hand. As he wrapped his arm around her waist and lifted them both up into the air, she was met with a heavy dizziness that took over her entire body.

***

Joey landed on Mytikas, the highest peak of Mt Olympus when the sun was at its highest, merely seconds after they had departed. With her eyes closed, and her cheek still pressed against Joey's chest, Astrid was afraid to look even though she could feel the ground beneath her feet.

"You can open your eyes now," he laughed, eyeing the view below his feet, and releasing his hold of her.

"No, I can't."

"Yes, you can. Just open your eyes. Who would've thought our fearless leaderette would be afraid of heights?"

"Shut up, Joey!" Astrid shook her head, refusing to open them, while Joey laughed whole-heartedly. After a moment, he placed his hand on her shoulder. "I promise, you can open your eyes now. I won't let anything happen to you. You can trust me."

His last sentence forced Astrid to do as he commanded. "I can trust you? Am I speaking to Joey or Hermes? Either way, you're still the guy who lied about my own creation."

Joey shrugged. "Alright, yeah I deserve that. But hey, whatever I've kept hidden, I've done it for the good of the mortals and that's a promise."

She gave him a side-eyed glance as she observed their surroundings and her footing, cautiously. "This doesn't look like a godly palace. Where is everybody? Where's Zeus? Where's the gateway to the Underworld?"

"You're not ready to see it… And even if you were, nobody's here. When the pithos was first sealed, everybody went their separate ways. They went into hiding… some amongst the mortals."

Astrid thought on this for a moment. "So, the gods have been walking amongst us all this time?"

"You thought I was the only one?"

Astrid remained silent. She didn't know what to believe. Nonetheless, she was giving him her undivided attention. "What are you seeing right now?" she asked.

"I'm seeing what it has truly become. A beautiful palace made from solid gold, fallen into centuries of ruin. His eyes rested on a specific spot in the distance. To Astrid, it looked as if he was staring directly into the clouds. "What's that?" she asked.

Joey stared back at Astrid, a fresh tear glistening in his green eyes. "That's my father's throne. It's empty... All the thrones around us are. This place... It brings back so many memories. It's not what it once was."

Astrid looked around at the mountains and gorges that stretched on forever around them. Joey certainly took on an entirely different persona standing in this place. She wondered if Cruz had ever seen this side of him. She brought her hand to his lower back. "We'll never be able to make the world what it once was. But we can certainly make it better," she told him.

"You don't understand, Astrid. Words and party tricks will never cut it. This is a war amongst the gods, and it is only going to get a whole lot worse." His stern expression was somewhat chilling. He was hiding a world of secrets, but Astrid doubted that she would ever manage to get the full truth from him. He surely had his reasons.

"Okay Joey. So, how do we get to the Underworld then?"

"You're going to hate me," he said with that damn cocky and instantaneous smile.

"Why?"

His smile completely broke through his visible sorrow. In one swift moment, he took her by the waist and flew up into the air. "No, no, no, no! Joey No!" she shrieked. They were hovering approximately a hundred feet above a wide-open gorge.

"We have to plummet into the Underworld," he said.

"I'm sorry. What did you just say?"

"Shut your eyes." Without further warning, Joey released her hand. Astrid screamed at the top of her lungs as they plummeted into the gorge. Astrid closed her eyes while Joey continued to laugh in amusement on their way down. But there was no sudden death or landing as she had been expecting.

While mid-drop, Joey grab for Astrid's hand again, catching her from above. She opened her eyes to the darkness of the Underworld surrounding them.

They had made it. To her surprise, she was hovering only mere inches from the ground. She stepped down in relief.

"Ha! You were so scared!" Joey laughed.

Astrid punched him hard in the arm. "That was a very horrible thing to do! How could you do that?"

"I'm sorry, but that force of falling is what opened the gateway."

Astrid studied him angrily, ready to choke him but knew he was telling the truth. "Fine, let's just go find the others! I'm assuming you know your way around here?"

"Hey, I was only ever the messenger or the mode of transportation. I never really spent too much time down here... But I know enough to get me through."

"Good. Because after that stunt, and the amount of pull that Persephone and I have around here, don't be surprised if I leave you in the hands of a monster." Astrid stormed on ahead, bypassing a very burnt out tree along the way.

"You wouldn't really do that, would you?" Joey asked, trailing behind. But a devilish smile was all he got from her in response.

They followed the path through the wastelands with no sun or stars, just a dull glowing mist that loomed over the horizons. There were no plants, just barren grey dirt and a few dead roots depicting that the Underworld once had plants.

After being exposed to the nature above the surface, Astrid knew that Persephone was aching to transform the Underworld for the better. It wasn't long until the skeletons of what had once been trees began to come to life. Plants and flowers shot up from the dirt and instantly began to color and blossom. Even the black murky swamps in the distance became clear pools of water. Despite the lack of sun, there was pure beauty all around them. "That's Persephone's doing, I gather?" Joey assumed, stopping mid-step.

"It sure is," Astrid said, marveling at the beauty. "Come on, we should keep going."

But Joey didn't move. "Actually, while we're on the subject of Persephone..."

Astrid stopped walking and turned to face him. "I know what this is about. I can feel her emotions, remember?"

"Yeah, about that..."

"Look, I get that you and she are, what? Half siblings or something, but she still holds out for you. She's still in love with you."

"And you feel that?"

Astrid considered the best way to answer his question without making things sound all the more awkward. Persephone loved Hermes. She had always known that, which put her in a really strange predicament with her friend. But the two needed closure and it would only be possible through her. Persephone had once told her that she and Hermes once had a relationship that went for centuries, despite her marriage to Hades.

But it had ended only a few years ago. Astrid knew for certain that that kind of love didn't just die. "Joey, I feel that they are her feelings, they're very different from my own of course. She really does love you and she continues to hold out for you."

Joey nodded, deep in thought. "Yeah, I know. Still, are you able to just bring her out for me? Please?"

Astrid hesitated and then gave in. "Sure, I can do that. But please just remember, that just because she inhabits my body, this body is still mine. Do you understand?"

"Yeah, of course."

Astrid felt her own control over her body subside as Persephone took the reign. "Hermes, it's so good to finally speak with you again. But why have you avoided conversing with me until now?"

***

Joey stared into the eyes of Astrid. It felt strange addressing the goddess that he had loved prior to the curse's unleash through her. Particularly, because Astrid was the woman both his friends loved.

Yet, he focused on the thick aura of Persephone and the subtle expression that she pulled, which looked somewhat foreign to Astrid. "Persephone? Wow, this is so weird. I guess I've been afraid because well… I've loved you for such a long time. Since the moment I first laid eyes on you. But I owe you the truth. After all this, you'll finally be free from Hades and while I can keep my promise about that. I can't keep my other promise."

Persephone's heart was clearly breaking but she kept her composure. "You were the one thing that kept my marriage with Hades bearable. I would count down the days until I could see you again. How can you tell me that this thing with the deceased mortal is far more important than what we had? When you stopped coming, and Hekate took over in your stead I knew the box was about to be opened. I knew it would change things, but surely it can't have changed what we had. How many other women have there been? You have always come back to me. It has always been us. We made the earth blossom. What makes this Hannah so special?"

"Persephone, please..."

"Don't you see? You cannot promise the mortal girl forever. You don't even know if you can bring her back from the dead. But I can promise you this, it doesn't matter what body I am in, I will always wait for you."

Without giving him a chance to respond, Persephone leaned up on her toes and planted a kiss on his mouth. Foolishly, Joey couldn't help but return the kiss. He pulled her into a tighter embrace, closed his eyes and gave in willingly. He had loved Persephone for centuries. She had been the one sure thing that had always made sense. Together, they had brought the seasons to the earth. But it was still a very foolish action on his part.

A very human act, which neither of them were. Joey loved Hannah, yet there he was, kissing Persephone in the body of his friend while he should've been locating Hannah's soul.

***

As the darkness from Persephone's control subsided, before she had even opened her eyes, Astrid felt the invasion of lips to her mouth and the smoothness of hands that she wasn't at all used to. To make matters worse, her tongue was dancing rhythmically with the highly skilled tongue of the messenger god. As realization sunk in, she opened her eyes and ripped herself away from him.

"What the hell, Joe! I warned you this was my body. Not Persephone's! Mine!" To act out her aggression, she slapped him over and over, until he brought his hands up to defend his face. "I'm sorry, Astrid. That was all Persephone's doing."

Hunching over, Astrid groaned. "I really wish I could believe that, but your tongue was in my mouth. Your hands were around my waist! Oh god, I think I'm... I think I'm about to be sick."

Joey cautiously, brought his hand to her back. "Are you alright?" But she tilted her head up and stared in wide-eyed horror. "No, of course I'm not alright! You just... you just kissed me. I think I need to scrub off my face. Maybe drink a shot of bleach?"

"If it helps, it wasn't all that great for me either. I don't get what Cruz and Buzzkill are always fighting over. I've kissed so many..."

Astrid shot him a piercing stare.

"I didn't mean it that... I mean, while you are a good kisser, in fact, you're actually quite irresistible... It's just..." Joey stammered, for the first time ever, not knowing what to say.

Filled with a combination of embarrassment, amusement and frustration, Astrid felt the need to help him... a little. "Let me guess, you meant to say that kissing me was like kissing your sister? Oh wait, you literally just did… through me, you idiot! Let's just go and find Cruz and Hannah. You know, your best friend and the woman you have claimed to love above all else?"

Without another word, Astrid stormed on ahead, leaving Joey in total disbelief at what had just happened. But before she could travel at least several feet in front of him, Joey called her back, with a hint of surprise in his tone.

"Wait, Astrid?" She stopped and turned back to face him only to see that Joey's smile had reached into his eyes and was being complimented by the light blush in his cheeks. "I think you should know that your aura changed seconds before you reacted to our kiss."

"Excuse me?" But she knew exactly what he was referring to. Still, Joey explained it out loud for her.

"For a moment you, Astrid, were really into our kiss. So, I mustn't be that bad."

Astrid pursed her lips together in pure frustration, at the embarrassment she felt for him being right. In that moment she was sure that if she didn't need him to help her take down Hades and bring back Cruz, she would certainly kill him. "That's not... That's not true, Joey."

Joey winked on approach. "Don't worry. You honestly have the kissing skills of a goddess. And at least now Buzzkill and I are even." As Joey raced on ahead, Astrid brought her hand to her mouth in embarrassment, swearing to herself that Hermes would die by her wielding the spear of Athena.

CHAPTER TWENTY-ONE

Astrid and Joey continued their journey along the dirt path as the wastelands around them persistently changed into a beautiful garden paradise, stretching on forever, with each step. They finally reached the bank of a vast and luminescent river, where a small rowboat sat, anchored to the dock. The river lit up the darkness around them with such intensity, that they had to shield their eyes to adjust. And even when they did, they couldn't see what loomed on the other side. Astrid peered down into the glowing ripples. It was impossible to see the bottom. "What's with the glowing river?" she asked.

"It's mixed with plasma and souls," Joey replied. "And not just the souls you would normally see down here, but the ones that have become so deranged after centuries of torment. They are nothing more than angry essences. You don't want to swim in it, or you'll be lost forever... or so the legend goes..."

"It's a pity I need you to get out of here because I was so tempted to push you in," Astrid said, noticing the boat. "So, where's the ferryman?"

Taking no notice of her teasing, Joey looked around. "I'm not sure. He's normally on the boat waiting for passengers. He shouldn't be too far."

"Do you think he followed the rest of them? The monsters and human souls, I mean. They all seem to have migrated to the surface."

"I don't see why he would. He's always been so devoted to his little boat. It's all he has left. Just hop in. I'll row us there."

With a shrug, Astrid climbed into the boat with Joey as he picked up the oars. Before he could sail them away, an emotionless older voice addressed them from behind.

"I do hope you were not intending on stealing my boat, Hermes. Once a thief, always a thief." They turned to see a tall figure dressed in a long black cloak, which shielded his face. "Where did he come from?" Astrid asked.

The cloaked figure held out his long, skinny and pale hand, instructing Joey to hand over the oar. His very appearance made Astrid wonder if he was even human at all. "Hi, Charon. So good to see you. I'm guessing you were on a lunch break?" Joey joked, "Or maybe spending your coins up in Vegas? I've heard that it's very exciting this time of era." The ferryman did not respond, instead, he climbed into the boat and once again, gestured for Joey to hand over the oars. "Fine, have it your way!" Joey handed over the oars and sat beside Astrid. But then Charon held out his hand again, but this time for Joey to hand over the fare for the trip.

"I shouldn't need to pay for Astrid. She isn't even dead," Joey whined. "Besides, we're only here to return Persephone's soul to the Underworld, because I'm not sure if you got the memo or not, but she's the new ruler, now."

Charon shook his head. "This is why I much prefer Hekate over you. She doesn't waste my time with mindless banter. Regardless, no souls, whether alive or dead, shall gain passage without paying the toll."

Joey shook his head but pulled out three gold coins regardless. "Here. I was hoping to save my money. Besides, Hekate? Really? That's stooping low. I thought we were friends!"

"Coming from the deceitful god of luck and money, that's rich!" Charon replied, paddling them away from the bank.

"Ha, ha! Very funny, you made a joke... and here I was thinking you would bore us to death, so we'd have no chance of ever returning to the surface."

Astrid couldn't help but laugh at their bickering. "You're really on a role, Joey. It's not even lunchtime and you've already made both me and the ferryman angry. I don't know how Cruz and Hannah..." Astrid stopped speaking as she realized just where her sentence was headed. For a moment she had forgotten that they were dead.

There was an awkward pause before Astrid addressed Charon. "You haven't seen a Hannah Jacobson and a Mario Cruz, have you?"

The ferryman tilted his head in her direction but then spoke slowly. "No, I haven't seen them."

"You do know who I'm talking about don't you?" she asked. "They would have arrived very recently in fact. Possibly, with Hekate?"

"Nobody has travelled this way in quite some time," Charon replied. "What Hekate has been doing with the souls is of no concern to me." While he seemed to be staring in her direction, his face was clouded in darkness so that she could not make out his features.

"You're kidding," Joey snapped. "But I was forced to let Hekate take over my role as soul escort. Why wouldn't she be leading them here? They're supposed to be here! Have you any idea as to how many people have died since the pithos has been opened? Haven't you seen any of them?" Charon shook his head and continued rowing. "Answer me, damn you!"

Charon turned back to Joey. "We all have our roles, Hermes. I know better than to intervene with the will of the gods. But to answer your question, every year the souls that Hekate has escorted have grown fewer. This woman beside you was the last soul Hekate escorted to the Underworld."

Astrid was struck by disbelief. Where had Hekate taken the souls? Furthermore, where were the souls of Hannah and Cruz? "So, if they aren't down here..." She began. "Then where are they?" Joey asked in unison. "I have my theories," Joey continued.

Judging by the look on his face, Astrid didn't need to hear what those theories were. The boat thudded and stopped. It had reached the other side of the bank. The darker side of the bank.

Astrid remembered this place far too well. It was the home of Hades. Everything around them, the ground, the walls and even the scenery was nothing but black rock. Augite. They climbed out of the boat and stepped onto the bank just as Persephone softly murmured that she could sense Hades' presence.

Astrid looked around her and held the spear ready, even though the god of the underworld wasn't anywhere to be seen. "What is it?" Joey asked.

"Hades is here!"

An uneasy nod was all that Joey could offer to display his reluctance, as Charon had already started sailing back in the opposite direction, leaving them alone. Astrid stared down at the luminescent ripples in the river and remembered a children's movie she had seen as a child, before looking back at Joey.

"So, Hades isn't as powerful without his bident, am I right?"

"Correct. Why do you ask?"

"Never mind," she smiled before calling out at the top of her lungs. "Hey, Hades! Come out here! I know you're there."

"What do you think you're doing?" Joey snapped. "We need to be careful!" Astrid glanced back down at her spear and remembered the crippling moment that Hades had used it to kill Cruz. She thought back to Athena's words of wisdom to answer Joey's question. "The real weapon is my mind. This spear is just a tool with the essence of Athena. I know exactly what I'm doing. I'm going to avenge Cruz!"

"Are you serious? What? No! You'll get yourself killed. If you die down here, there is no return for you. You have to know that. It isn't what Cruz or Samuel... or even your daughter would want."

But before Astrid could respond, they were met by a chillingly familiar voice which instantly elevated Astrid's anger, along with her fears. "How fitting the three of you would come after me," Hades said, emerging from the darkness.

Astrid battled through her own fears to approach Hades. He was nothing more than a monster and he would not get away with his actions. "You killed someone I love. I can't let you get away with that," she said, preparing her stance. Hades smirked at her, clearly humored by her foolish behavior and then at Joey. "Hermes, talk some sense into Pandora. You did gift her with persuasion after all, so, surely you can persuade her from risking her life out of sheer nonsense."

But Joey just readied his staff. "Not this time, uncle. Cruz was my friend and I'm giving her all the luck in the world to do what she needs to do. Besides, you don't have your pitchfork. I feel that you might be at a disadvantage, old friend."

Astrid smiled over at Joey as if to say, 'thank you' and then smirked back at Hades. "For all the torture you have put me through while I was down here, none of that pales to the pain you caused when you murdered Cruz. I was willing to give you a clean slate until I knew what you had planned for humanity. I hold in my hand the spear of Athena, the weapon that she lined with her own essence. The weapon that you used to kill Cruz. May that name haunt your very soul."

With every word she spoke, the anger surged through her. She was ready to end his life, despite Persephone begging to send him to Tartarus instead. "Just kill me, child," Hades sneered.

On an impulse, Astrid lunged for him with the spear in her hand. But he vanished right before her eyes. She turned, just as he reappeared from behind her... just as she had predicted. With one swing, she pulled back her arm driving the spear toward his abdomen, only for him to disappear once again.

Anger fueled through her veins. She held her breath as she tried to determine where he would reappear. Without warning, the ground below her feet caught alight with hot flames. Darting out the way, she caught a glimpse of Hades standing in the distance, on a rock, beside the river.

With every move she took in his direction, the flames spread beneath her feet, burning her every step.

He was toying with her. The god's foolish games reminded her of her training sessions with Samuel. Every word he had ever spoken to her. He was now missing. If she didn't survive this battle, she would never see him again. That was a definite possibility. She needed to stay alive.

Running through the flames was just another test. She needed to be quicker on her feet. So, she made it happen. With the death of Hades in her sights, she ran through the fire, faster than she ever had before… barely feeling the flame, until she had reached the god himself.

But, then the thought of Cruz derailed her. Seeing the spear move right through him, only to be ripped out again, so furiously, was enough to make her sick to her stomach. Seeing the look in his eyes, as he knew he was dying had both amazed and scared her. He had been so calm, while she had been a mess on the inside. But now, she needed to avenge him. As the action of Hades driving the spear into Cruz brought a tear to her eye, she used it to fuel her.

She drove her spear forward, until the tip had sunk directly into the space between his ribs. She stared down, to see that she had succeeded in doing so. But not in time to stop his hand from gripping at her throat and squeezing. He was choking her very quickly. Her strike on the god had certainly made an impact.

His blood, the color of tar spewed forth from his wound, but her life was running short too. She would surely die before he did.

"Astrid," Joey called out to her. She could see him in from her peripheral view holding up his staff. Using it to keep her alive, knowing full well that she was struggling to breathe.

'Come on, Astrid!' Persephone's voice spoke within her mind. *'You only need to drive the spear upwards. If you get his heart, you will kill him instantly.'*

'I don't stand a chance. He could drag us both into the river. I should've listened to you Persephone. I should've sent him to Tartarus.' Astrid thought back. *'Besides, I just can't kill him. I can't take his life. He only wanted to be loved. I can't fault him for that.'*

'Yes, you can. I didn't think you would have it in you, but you do. Hades is killing you. If he kills you, he kills me too and I can't let you throw your immortal life away. Take the spear and drive it up into his heart, please. Hermes can't hold out forever and he will not let you fall in. You need to trust him.'

Astrid's choking grew violent. Her body began to convulse. Dizziness had well and truly sunk in. But at the same time, Hades continued to bleed out. Tears ran down her face. *'No, I won't let you give up!'* Persephone continued. *'You can't give up! Think of Hope. Think of your daughter. Don't lose your hope for humanity. You can do this. If you don't, Hades will come for her… you know he will!'*

Those were the words needed to move mountains. With the last ounce of her strength, Astrid drove the spear in an upwards motion as she stared Hades directly in the eyes without hesitation. At first, she saw the pain in his eyes as he realized what she had done. He had anticipated for her to withdraw. But then, as his grip loosened at her throat, and her breath returned in a frenzy, she knew that she had done it. Astrid pulled the spear from the god's abdomen and hunched over forcing her oxygen levels to return to normal.

"I didn't think you would… you would deliver your vengeance," Hades muttered, as the liquid tar poured from his mouth. "That is merely your first act of destruction, Pandora. Savor it, because you will merely be the destruction of your earth… That is your fate. Unless I drag you down here with me."

Time slowed as Astrid continued to suck in air through her coughs. "What do you mean my fate? I won't be the earth's destruction. I'm preventing it!"

Hades groaned. His eyes turned to Hermes, before they returned to her. "It's innocent of you to believe such lies. But I will not let the earth be destroyed by you or anybody else."

Before Astrid could determine what Hades meant, he grabbed her by the arm, and pulled her into him at full force. Using the weight of them, he let gravity take hold ready to fall with purpose into the glowing river.

"No, what are you doing?" Astrid screamed. Her eyes fell to Joey to save her before Hades could succeed in dragging them both into the river of deranged spirits. "Joey, help!"

In the blink of an eye, Joey had reached her so fast she hadn't even seen him move. He grabbed for her hands just as Hades' body reached the surface of the river. The god of the underworld was already well and truly dead, so his grip on her bore no strength.

But she could still feel the heat of the river as Hades' soul disappeared from under her. Before her body could disappear in the same way, Joey ripped her up by her arms and pulled her back onto the bank.

They sat in silent disbelief for what felt like an eternity until Joey finally broke the silence. "Wow! So, Hades is actually gone... Now what?"

"I guess we go home and search for Hekate, maybe she can bring back the others." As she answered, she flicked her hair from the front of her face, drawing Joey's full attention. "What is it?" she asked.

Joey pointed to the lock that fell down the side of her face, which compared to the rest of her hair, had turned pale white. "When was the last time you colored your hair?" he asked.

While Joey had managed to rescue her, her body had still come in to contact with the river of deranged spirits. Astrid examined the lock with her fingers and gasped.

"What does that… what do you think it means?"

"I don't know. Nobody has ever touched the river and lived. Maybe Hekate might know."

Astrid agreed and the two prepared to venture back to Vegas until a thought crossed her mind. "You, deceitful bastard!" she snapped.

"What did I do, now?"

"Demeter's gift to Hope… she gifted Hope with rebirth so that if anyone she loves dies, they could be brought back. You knew that Cruz and Hannah wouldn't be down here, didn't you? But you still wanted us to come back to the Underworld, didn't you?" Joey pursed his lips together and nodded slowly. "Why? What the hell was your plan? Why would you make me come all the way down here for nothing?"

"Well it wasn't technically for nothing. Zeus knew Hades would be down here. He wanted to see if you were worthy to take on a god."

"That's why Zeus didn't bring him back. He let Cruz die for some stupid test, didn't he? Fuck! Let me guess, Athena was in on it too, wasn't she?" Joey nodded again.

"Argh! Those fucking gods!" Astrid threw the spear at a large nearby rock only for it to bounce onto the floor. "So, what? Cruz was really just another pawn?"

"Honestly, I really don't know anymore," Joey said drained of all optimism. "They only ever tell me half the plan. Because they don't trust me."

"Well, then what about Hannah?"

Joey shrugged his shoulders, clearly just as in the dark about that as she was.

"Well then, Joey... It's time for us to get our answers."

"Agreed. But shouldn't we release Persephone's soul first?"

"We should... but why don't we give her a chance to say goodbye to her mother first? Can you call back the ferryman? I'm tired of this place." As Joey turned back towards the bank just as exhausted as she was, Astrid placed her hand on his shoulder. "Oh, and Joey? If you ever kiss me or lie to me again... I swear I will shove this spear so far up your ass that you'll..." She finished her sentence leaving Joey a little more fearful of her than ever before, as they searched for a gateway out of the Underworld.

CHAPTER TWENTY-TWO

Astrid and Joey returned to the surface, and back to the place they had left Cruz's body overlooking the town below, only to find that it was no longer there.

Struck by stunned surprise, Joey surveyed the site while Astrid searched for tracks in the dirt which might explain his absence.

"Where is he?" she demanded. "He can't have just disappeared."

"My guess is as good as yours. We left him right here. I'm sure of it. We were barely ten surface minutes. Maybe someone followed us. Or maybe someone from the city removed him?"

"It doesn't make sense. There are no footprints. Why would somebody do this?"

When Joey couldn't give her an answer, Astrid yelled out to Zeus wherever he might've been hiding. "Zeus! Where the hell is he? Where's Cruz's body?" But the god would not respond. "Zeus? Answer me! Where is…?"

"Astrid, I don't think he's going to answer you. He's gone silent. I can't hear his voice at all."

"Silent? Why would he go silent? What do you think has happened?"

Joey shook his head. "I'm not sure. Maybe, the gods back in Vegas will have some answers. It's like every time we succeed somewhere, something else goes wrong."

"Or maybe things have gone right, this time and he and Hannah have already been revived and they're waiting for us to return to Las Vegas."

"You think that's possible?" Joey asked, slightly optimistic.

Astrid shrugged. "Right now, it's all I have to cling to. At least I can ask them why they lied about my identity while we're at it."

"I hope you're right. Okay, all aboard Hermes Express on our journey back to Las Vegas."

With the thought of Joey's awkward kiss still on her mind, Astrid was very reluctant to use him as a mode of transportation again. Knowing she had no choice in the matter, she shuffled uncomfortably as he wrapped his arms around her waist. "Alright, just be careful where you put your hands, okay?"

A jokester smile raised up in his face.

"You're worried about me? I'm a little more worried that Persephone might want to kiss me goodbye before we send her back to the Underworld. Now close your eyes, we're going up."

Deeply paranoid by the thought, Astrid pressed her head into Joey's chest, as he wrapped his arms around her. She felt the dizzying shift of gravity as he lifted her up into the air and took her back to Las Vegas.

***

Astrid and Joey arrived at Las Vegas by midday and the moment they entered the magical barrier, they went in search for the gods. Fortunately, Aphrodite, Demeter and Athena were all gathered at the church. With Joey following close behind, Astrid stormed in, disrupting the meeting that was being had.

"Why didn't any of you tell me about my identity?" she demanded. "I had to find out through Hades that I not only have Pandora's soul inside of me, but I am a goddam goddess! Tell me, is it true?"

Athena stopped speaking and stepped forward holding out her hand for the spear, which willingly Astrid handed over. Athena stared at the spear and then back at Astrid.

"Yes, it is true. Look inside yourself, you know that the powers of the oceans and the earth are within you."

"But this changes everything. It changes the myths… It changes history as we know it. It changes my entire life. Everything that I have ever believed in has been a total lie. How can I be Pandora? I am Astrid Hope Sutherland. None of this makes any sense! Pandora was supposed to be human and once again that was another lie!"

"Maybe I can be of some assistance?" The voice of a woman, somewhat wiser, whom Astrid was certain she had only met once before, entered through the doors at the back of the church. Every eye landed on the newcomer with great fascination.

Joey's eyes grew wide in bewilderment. The woman looked to be in her fifties but was dressed remarkably different to the rest of the gods. Her hair was straight, black, and long and she had piercing ocean-blue eyes. She wore black hunting boots and a long black and purple dress, lined with lace that flowed down past her boots and arms. The question of the woman's identity was instantly taken from her, when Persephone told her just who this woman was. *'Astrid, that's Hekate! She is not just a goddess, but a Titan. She holds all the answers which you seek.'*

Astrid's eyes opened wide. "Do I bow or something?" she whispered to Joey.

"Astrid Sutherland, if you'll accompany me, I will tell you all that you wish to know," Hekate said. "I will also free Persephone from your mind and bring her back to the underworld myself." Astrid nodded obediently and took hold of Hekate's outstretched hand, accompanying her out of the church and into the street.

She was not only nervous, but also excited that she was in the presence of a titan who was about to deliver the news that would change her entire life.

"I believe I need no introduction," Hekate said as she led Astrid down the road and away from the church.

"No, you don't need to introduce yourself. I'm just... I'm surprised you're here... in the open... I mean... You're a titan. This is... well, it's incredible!"

"Well, we are safe for the moment, and you need answers... answers that only I am at liberty to discuss."

"Yes, I do."

Hekate continued to speak in a soft, advisable tone. It was a tone that Astrid could've sworn she had heard a long time ago but couldn't quite place. "When your mother was pregnant, the prophecy came to light that the pithos was set to be opened. Cronus, the god of time, pinpointed the exact day that this would occur. The opening of Pandora's Box would set a series of events and change the course of the world in a way that some of the gods did not approve."

"Because it would unleash Zeus and all his creatures on the earth."

"You've been paying attention, child. Zeus's return while it has always been inevitable, means a world of control and a leash on the other gods. It means conformity and cruel punishments for those who do not agree to his will. Zeus has hurt so many, when all we seek is peace."

Astrid took note of the direction that they were headed. Her apartment was only a few blocks away. Within minutes she would be home with Hope and Stacey delivering the news of Cruz and Hannah, unless of course Hekate could find some way to bring them back. She waited for Hekate to continue.

"When the pithos was originally sealed with Zeus's soul along with all his creatures inside, it was Pandora who first ensured its secrecy. Centuries later, this burden became a risk to her family, so she sacrificed her physical form to keep it safe and to ensure that the balance would be maintained. This new legacy then fell to Hermes. He was tasked to guide the descendant of Zeus to the pithos, knowing that if he failed to carry out his task, the box would fall into the hands of another."

These words that Hekate was speaking sounded like nonsense. But at the same time, they made everything fall into place. It was no wonder she was destined to find Cruz. Pandora sacrificed her body to keep the pithos hidden. Joey, no, not Joey. Hermes had been tasked to lead Cruz to the pithos which had actually been calling out to her very soul. And for what? So, they could have a child to stop the deadly sins curse?

But now they had so much more to deal with. There were so many twists and turns in the story. Astrid needed to know more. She needed to know how this made she and Pandora linked biologically. She voiced her doubts and Hekate proceeded to answer them.

"Pandora's bloodline, your mother's bloodline, carried out throughout the ages, thanks to a little intervention from the gods, that is. I understand your father told you the story of your birth. That you were dying. The truth is, there were other forces at work. There were gods vowing to ensure you did not survive. But I would not let this occur, for your destiny is not yet complete. Hermes laid his hand upon your forehead, under my command, and gifted you the essence of Pandora to not only keep you alive, but to ensure that you would carry out your destiny. So, while you are still Astrid, you are also Pandora. A goddess amongst men who posed as a human woman."

Astrid could feel her entire body grow cold. Hermes had been there physically the very day that she had been born. Astrid's mother had gone insane believing in those nonsense stories. As if the titan could read Astrid's mind, she addressed this concern.

"Astrid, your mother was never truly sick. Hermes spoke through her. The medication she received through the facility dulled her mind so she could no longer communicate with the gods. Your bloodline is not the only one of value in this mortal world, but science has long since medicated what it does not understand." For the first time in a while, Astrid felt herself choke out a breath.

There was an overwhelming hurricane of emotions going on within her. Her logical reasoning trying to make sense of everything she had ever experienced and of everything that Hekate had just revealed to her.

"What you're saying Hekate… Well, it's something that's unbelievable for sure."

"I understand. Whether you believe it or not, you are no longer mortal like you once were. Returning from the dead, killing a god and then being tainted by the spirits themselves, you yourself are now immortal. Just like Hope and just like Mario Cruz."

The sheer mention of Cruz's name was too much for Astrid to take. "Do you know where Cruz is? If I'm supposed to be a god, can I bring him back? Or what about Hannah?"

Hekate offered a simple nod, but it was not lined with optimism. "While I cannot reach the descendant of Zeus, Hannah's soul has been transported for safe keeping. Neither you, nor I can bring them back."

Disappointment and grief forced Astrid's silence. It took all her strength to hold back her tears. Astrid was done with Hekate's bad news, but the titan, however, was not.

"It will only be a matter of time before the differences between the mortal humans and Zeus's creatures become difficult for them to handle. They will hunt each other down. There will be wars. You and your daughter will need to show them that there is another way. That there will always be another way."

Astrid stared down at the ground. That wasn't going to be easy. They would need their friends. They would need Cruz and Hannah. When Astrid raised her gaze, Hekate was no longer standing with her and by the silence in her mind, she was also free from Persephone's possession. For the first time in a long time, Astrid felt entirely alone. She turned back towards her apartment building.

It was time to head home. But before she could, Joey was standing by her side. The sorrow in his eyes told her more than his words ever could, though his lips were struggling to find the words. His news was that without Cruz or Hannah's bodies, Demeter would not be able to bring either one of them back. "Promise me we won't give up on them," Astrid said.

Joey stifled a nod. "Hannah's body was devoured by the sirens. Her soul is gone. Cruz is… well, he's gone too. But no, we won't give up on them. Ever." Astrid hid her inner doubt with a smile.

Once Samuel and Tash returned, they would continue with their search for Hannah and Cruz. They would never give up on their friends… Even if it killed them. "What do you say we head home?" she suggested.

For a brief moment, Joey tensed. But then with a sigh, he eased up and brought his arm around her shoulder. Instead of shrugging him away thanks to their kiss, she thought of what Hekate had told her about Hermes being present at her birth.

She considered the adventure and the losses that they had shared together from the very moment Cruz had saved them in that damn military prison cell. In spite of everything, Joey had become one of the most important people in her life. And not just this life, but also as Pandora. Astrid needed to address the matter.

"So, Joey. Rumour has it that you and I have been friends for countless centuries... That you actually witnessed both my births."

Joey stopped walking. "That's true, what's your point?"

Astrid shook her head. "No point. It's just, that Persephone unlocked the memories of Pandora within me and Hekate rectified that they were true. I just... I want to thank you. You kept my legacy as Pandora a secret and you've done everything in your power to keep me safe. I get that you lied... But still, I think you might just be my oldest and dearest friend." Joey went to say something but changed his mind at the last minute and simply nodded.

"You're welcome. I guess you and I are more alike than I thought. Bound by duty, but at the same time used by the gods to create chaos and destruction."

"Just like Cruz, huh?"

"Yeah, but in this case, we've been at it for much longer than he has."

They slowly made their way home, filled with a disarming level of hesitation in telling Hope and Stacey the heartbreaking news.

CHAPTER TWENTY-THREE

One month later

Samuel looked around. He was standing at the bottom of the ocean. No, not standing... he had a green tail made of scales. He was swimming just like the rest of the merfolk around him.

He was in the middle of Atlantis and had been protecting Poseidon and his son Triton from the rest of the merpeople, who had been compelled by a curse that had been unleashed thanks to Pandora's Box. Their instability had compelled them to destroy the walls of Atlantis and take down their own king.

Triton looked very similar in appearance to his father, Poseidon, only he had hair that wasn't quite as dark or as long. However, he looked somewhat similar age wise. His tail had been wounded during the battle.

Though, neither he nor Poseidon seemed phased in the slightest. But now it was as if the curse had been broken. They weren't sure why, but Samuel could only assume that Astrid and Cruz had succeeded in taking down Hades. The merfolk, whose eyes had once shown nothing but darkness, had since returned to the pure blue that they had once been.

Upon realizing what they had done, they regretted their actions instantly and sought to help Triton as fast as they could, pushing Samuel out of their paths and into the background.

But Samuel didn't mind. As he held his sword, face down in front of himself, he looked up at the beautiful underwater palace made entirely of solid gold. It would not take long to repair and even with the damage it was still as majestic as he had always dreamed it to be.

It was no wonder it had been kept a secret throughout time. Shaking himself from his admiration Samuel directed his attention back to the king and Poseidon as they made their way towards him.

"Samuel, son of Jason," King Triton began. "I don't believe we've been formally introduced. I am King Triton, son of Poseidon the rightful god and king of the seas."

"Yes, sir," Samuel spoke with much respect for the king.

Triton spoke on with great authority and assumption which greatly suited the king. "I understand that I have you to thank for my survival, but I wish that I could say the same for my wife. I must say, I do not know of a more fitting way to show my gratitude. But there may be one way, which I believe would be in both our best interest."

The king grew silent, as a beautiful dark-haired mermaid approached them. She was naked from the tail up, but her dark hair and the golden chains adorning her neck covered her breasts. Her tail was blue scaled.

The king placed his hand lovingly to the lower back of the mermaid with pride. "Let me introduce to you, my daughter… and your betrothed. Her name is Theresa and she is the heir to my throne. Which will make you the next in line to become the king of Atlantis."

Samuel felt his heart pounding deep within his chest. The rhythm was fierce and almost overpowering. His first thought was of Astrid. "I'm sorry your majesty, but I have to humbly decline..."

"Nonsense, Samuel! You will wed! I will not take 'no' for an answer. Take her as my gift to you." Triton was clearly not offering out of the kindness of his heart, but as an order to the obedient soldier.

***

It was a warm afternoon and Astrid, Stacey, Joey and Hope were sitting in their apartment watching DVDs of a paranormal TV show that had ended not long before the pithos had been opened.

"Are we like witches, mom?" Hope asked Astrid curiously, forcing Stacey to pause the program and wait for the explanation. Joey, who had been sitting in the armchair reading a book, looked up to watch the scene unfold. Astrid who had been sitting cross legged between Hope and Stacey on the couch, considered how best to answer that question.

"No, Hope. We're not. Sure, we have powerful abilities, but we are capable of far more than witches are."

Joey cleared his throat. "Think of it this way, witches channel their abilities through our names. You wouldn't believe how many times I've heard people calling out to me for safe passage and luck… I had to tune out a few times because I had other problems to contend with."

Hope nodded. But there was more on her mind.

"But witches can bring back the ones they love… yet we can't even bring back my father or Aunt Hannah… What's the point of having powers if we can't use them to do what we need to do? Why can't we use our gifts to locate their bodies? Why can't we…?"

"Hope, please!" Astrid's tone was blunt as she cut her daughter off. "We all miss them, but unfortunately, even our hands are tied."

There was a firm knock at the door, which they could all hear, but only Stacey went to answer it, leaving Astrid, Hope and Joey sitting in the living room in the thick, uncomfortable tension.

Joey had spent so much time searching for Hannah and Cruz's souls, but with no body to channel, it had been impossible. Joey got to his feet and sat beside Astrid in a bid to help her explain the situation.

"Hope, we have tried everything we can. As you have seen on that show you just watched, magic always comes with a price. Witches must pay a price… but even us gods do too. There must always be a balance. If we want the good, we must always expect a sacrifice in return. And we should never be selfish with our powers. That's just the way it is."

Astrid wished that she could hold the information that her daughter needed, but before she could add anything useful, Hope spoke up again.

"But the gods have always used their magic for selfish means. Look at Medusa, she was an act of revenge. So many of the creatures were… Why is it different for us?"

Astrid and Joey exchanged glances before Joey answered Hope's question. "Zeus's vengeful and chaotic ways were what led him to being cursed into the pithos in the first place. He hurt so many, that the gods decided to hurt him back. We need order, not chaos and so…"

"Hey, you guys…?" Stacey's tone of concern called over to them from the doorway, forcing all three of them to turn to her. Instantly, they got to their feet in sheer stunned horror toward the person who was standing beside her. "Look who's back!"

As if nothing had happened, Cruz watched them with an expression of surprise that mirrored their own. But his aura was a bright blue. Bluer than they had ever seen before.

"I don't... I don't understand," Astrid stammered, looking to Joey for the answers. Cautiously, Joey stepped towards the man with the shoulder length black hair and dark brown eyes.

"There's just no way," Joey stammered.

"Dad?" Hope gasped. Cruz looked directly to Astrid. His aura resembled pure power, even stronger than before, but his face displayed utter confusion.

"I don't know what happened to me, but somehow, I'm alive. I'm back." By the tone of his voice alone, it was evident that he was just as unaware as they were as to what was going on. Hesitant, Joey placed his hand on Cruz's shoulder and closed his eyes. The moment he did, an invisibly overwhelming force threw him across the room and into the bookshelf behind him. Joey scrambled to his feet in a panic to address the others.

"That's not Cruz, you guys... That's... That's Zeus!"

End

Author Bio

Driven on her quest for female-empowerment, Reign Atkins is an Australian writer with a passion for telling action, fantasy, comedy, and Sci-Fi stories to a worldwide audience. When not writing, Reign loves spending time with her family, playing video games, and binging on television, with a guilty pleasure for telenovelas.

www.ingramcontent.com/pod-product-compliance
Lightning Source LLC
Chambersburg PA
CBHW022359110726
47903CB00004B/1061